THE DAY THE RAINBOW DIED

Book One: The Early Days

James Bellis

Take a Peek Publishing—Conway, SC
Paperback ISBN: 979-8-9859469-5-6
eBook ISBN: 979-8-9859469-6-3
Title: *The Day the Rainbow Died: The Early Days*
Author: James Bellis
Digital distribution | 2026
Paperback | 2026

This is a work of fiction. The characters, names, incidents, places, and dialogue are products of the author's imagination, and are not to be construed as real.

DEDICATION

I would like to thank my fabulous daughter Isobeil for her belief and her skill at editing this novel.

Special thanks to Susan Benade, Anne Streaton and Margaret Sweetnam for their encouragement.

Although this is a work of fiction the period of time that it covers in the narrative highlights what was the situation around the world that we as white South Africans grew up in. The characters in the book are made up of composite people that passed through my life.

PROLOGUE

The dawning of the new millennium had brought the feeling of a new beginning, of an excitement never before felt in this young nation. A new start. A time to forget past bitterness. A time to embrace racial harmony; walk together into the future as brothers, equals in the eyes of all.

The start of a New Year, new century, and celebrations had begun in the east less than eight hours ago. On Islands of Tonga the local Tongan people will be among the first to usher in the new century. Celebrations will move west in an unstoppable march encompassing all in its wake; no one will escape the euphoric dawning of a new century.

As the gray light of a summer dawn begins to creep across the African continent to herald the start of the first day of this new century, one man sits surprisingly calm in his small 9 by 9 cell on the once infamous death row at Pollsmoor Prison. The one certainty he has is that the coming millennium will play no part in his life.

The sounds of a prison stirring brought unease to him and a knowledge that the last hope of a stay of execution has passed. His mind drifts back to the previous evening and the final visit of his lawyer and friend Desmond Rabinowitz and the inevitable news of a failed appeal to the president for clemency. Despite a growing public opinion on the way the original trial and appeal had seemed to ignore all evidence, and the passing of the shocking sentence, the appeal for clemency had been rejected out of hand.

He had read of the final moments of condemned men and how some accept their fate, or, of others making their peace with God in hope of forgiveness and absolution. The speed of events leading to this point and the unrealness of everything make it seem that this is happening to someone else and he is just a spectator watching from the sidelines.

He cannot remember what his final meal was but that he had slept soundly the previous night, they must have put something in the food.

The priest had tried to speak of the forgiveness and love of God and of his journey to an eternal life. He would be here this morning to pray for his soul and accompany him the final twelve steps.

The other cells on death row were not empty, but once moved to the execution cell no contact could be made with other inmates; he was totally isolated. The prison guards offered little or no conversation or solace. Those guards who avoided his eyes, both black and white were ashamed by the trial and the verdict, and those who weren't were openly aggressive and felt he deserved his fate. There were no fence sitters in this situation.

This would be the first execution performed since the re-instating of the death penalty and would make history. The bleeding hearts of those who opposed the death penalty were silently demonstrating outside the prison. Those who agreed and welcomed the re-instating of the death penalty were also present although more vociferous and walked in an endless circles with their placards saying 'No Reprieve' or 'All killers must Hang'. Wasn't it Andy Warhol who said everyone has fifteen minutes of fame? Well, his will last a little longer than that.

It was impossible to know the exact moment when the door would open and the short journey would begin. They had taken away his watch and he had no way of knowing the time.

The execution was scheduled for seven am. How much time did he have? He had made peace with God, or at least that was the impression he had given the priest, now it was time to make peace within himself.

He could sense a presence, probably the hangman preparing himself, and wondered if it would be soon. The cell seemed to crowd in on him, was this the first signs of panic? They said it would be swift and painless. Hell, how did they know, nobody had come back to confirm this. What would he feel the moment the trap door opened and he fell that short three feet before the thick rope took up its slack with the weight of his body? Was the effect of whatever they put in his food subsiding? The time must be near. He looked around his cell and tried to find some indication of the time. The gray walls and lowly dimmed light in the ceiling gave no indication.

He wondered about the other men and women who had passed through this cell on to the unknown. The cell had been repainted, not been in use for a good number years, no indication of any previous occupation. No names etched on the walls, no dates, no messages. Hell, what would one use for etching, everything sharp, blunt or otherwise had been taken from him. All he had were the prison shirt and pants, no belt and slip on shoes with no laces, as he might try to preempt the hangman. He had read that at the moment of death that your bowels released. Well, they tied your legs together when they hung you didn't they, was this to stop the shit running out the bottom of your pants or to prevent you kicking out and struggling?

Pull yourself together, he thought, these panicked thoughts are causing you to lose it. A feature of your life had always been calmness under pressure, but don't let everybody down by breaking up now. You have no control over the situation and no matter what you do; nothing will prevent your life ending. Accept it, if you cannot show courage now at least try to show calmness, don't let them see you break down. I wonder if those present will tell the outside world of my behavior in my final minutes. I have brought enough shame to friends and family already, no more! Christ, what is the time? How much longer? Should I be thinking of the four men who died because of my actions? The priest asked if I had any remorse, God would forgive me. My answer seemed to please him. I just wish I could convince myself of any remorse. No, they deserved to die.

The sound of a key being inserted to the lock of the cell door snapped him back to reality, this was it. The door silently swung open and the somber figure of Father Seamus Rogan appeared before him. Behind him stood what looked about half a dozen prison officials. The priest approached, bible clutched in his hands and placed a comforting hand on his shoulder.

'It is time my son,' said Father Rogan.

Jesus, he calls me my son, I must be fifteen to twenty years older than him.

Four of the prison warders circled around behind him, three black and one white. He felt his hands pulled behind his back and immediately secured. The two remaining officials turned as did Father Rogan, and the small procession moved quickly forward. They moved out of the door, turned sharp right and immediately right again. With a swiftness that came from a well-rehearsed routine, he was turned; his legs were pulled together and quickly bound. A white cotton bag was placed over his head and he felt the noose being pulled down to his neck. He sensed the people present moving away from him as he braced himself for that short sudden drop into oblivion.

'They say your life passes before your eyes just prior to the moment of death,' he thought.

The final sound he heard was one of a metallic click as the floor beneath his feet opened and sent him on that final journey. Death was instantaneous. The clock on the prison wall registered 07:00:14. A satisfactory job by all concerned.

The lifeless body was lowered and placed in a cheap coffin to be prepared for collection by family members. In the event of no one claiming the body it would be cremated and disposed of by the State.

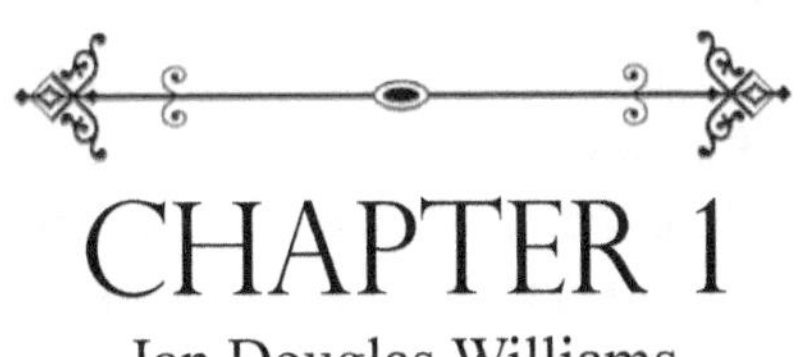

CHAPTER 1
Ian Douglas Williams

Ian Douglas Williams made his way into the world on April Fool's Day 1950, announcing his arrival with a bellow that brought pride and joy to his father who had waited so many years for this day. Ian Junior was the fourth child of Betty and Ian Williams and the first son after three daughters. Betty, through the pain and strain of the birth, silently offered a prayer of thanks to God that she had finally delivered a son for her husband, surely this was the last.

After bringing now fifteen-year old Angela, eleven-year old Miriam and ten-year old Celia into the world, she had given up hope of ever falling pregnant again. When informed of this pregnancy, Betty, being very religious, had prayed to both Lord Jesus and Mary that this one be a boy. Husband Ian had longed for a son to carry on the family name and in his perverse way, finally prove his manhood by siring a son. Thank God it was now over, it would be a strain on the family finances but at least she would not have to listen to her spouse's regular complaints of 'What this family needs is another male around all you females.'

Betty had taken maternity leave from her job as clerk in the Post Office three weeks earlier and was entitled to be paid in full for another six weeks. After this period, her job would remain open to her for a period of a further six months but with no pay. Although the birth had been painful and taken a lot out of her, Betty was convinced that she could be back at work before the six-week period was over thus not losing any income. She wondered if her estranged mother would ever know that she now had a grandson to add to her three granddaughters, none of whom she had ever acknowledged.

Just before midnight on March 31,1950, Betty woke her husband with the news that her labour. had started. Waking the maid to look after the girls, Ian bundled Betty into the car and started off on the half hour drive to Addington Hospital on the Durban beach front. They only just made it to the hospital. Betty was rushed to the delivery room where twenty minutes later, at one o'clock in the morning, she produced a healthy screaming baby boy. Ian, unable to watch the birth, was waiting just outside the delivery room, hearing a baby bellowing at the top of its lungs knew he had a son at last. He burst into the room and after briefly checking on Betty's condition, turned and took his son from the attending nurse.

Although Ian loved his daughters, he absolutely doted on his son and showing real originality, named him Ian Douglas. To avoid confusion in the Williams household baby Ian was known as Doog to all. From as early as he could walk and talk, Ian started teaching Doog all he could about the workings of a motor car. Ian would take Doog to work with him on Saturday mornings when it was quiet, and the garage only dealt with emergencies. Doog adored his father and loved these times together and listened intently to all his father told him.

By the time Doog started school at Bushlands Primary in the summer of 1956, he was fairly skilled in the ways of the combustion engine and had inherited his father's skill with anything mechanical. At this time Ian, disillusioned with the promises of a partnership in Brighton Beach Motors, decided to branch out on his own. He found a potential premises at the growing concern that was Crossways. Where Marine Drive and Beach Road intersected, a number of shops had sprung up. It was almost halfway between his home and Brighton Beach Motors, a perfect sight for Ian's new garage, Williams's Motors.

With a small loan from the bank, secured against his house, Ian bought a hydraulic jack, hired a black assistant and with all the tools he had gathered over the years, was ready for business. All of his regular customers, knowing his quality of workmanship, brought their business to him. Although it was a struggle at first, Ian found he was making enough money to quickly pay off the bank loan and turn a tidy profit.

By the time Doog was ten he was spending all his free time at his father's garage helping him wherever he could. He would pass his father the required spanner without Ian having to ask for it. He was allowed to 'service' cars on his own which meant draining and refilling the oil, changing the air and oil filters, the spark plugs and greasing all the relevant nipples. Confident in his son's ability, Ian left

Doog to complete these tasks on his own; they never had a single customer complaint. Doog had no doubts that when he was finished school, he would join his Dad and maybe they could call the business Williams and Son's Motors.

November 6 1962, just two weeks before the start of his final primary school exams, Doog's world came crumbling down. He was called out of his classroom by the headmaster and told he was to go home immediately, there had been an accident and his mother was waiting for him. Doog ran the three quarters of a mile home without stopping.

Doog was met at the front door by his red-eyed mother. With her arms around her son and between sobs, Betty told her son of the terrible accident that had befallen his father. The black assistant, she didn't even know his name even though he had worked for Ian for nearly ten years, had lowered the hydraulic jack while Ian was still under the vehicle. Unable to extricate himself in time, Ian had been trapped by the base of the jack. Hearing Ian's cries the black assistant had panicked and instead of raising the jack lowered it further. Ian's upper body had been crushed to a pulp and he had died almost instantly.

The assistant in his panic had fled the garage, fully aware that he would be blamed for his bosses' death. A customer arrived and getting no reply from the front office had walked into the workshop and upon finding Ian, had called the police. After a brief questioning the police were able to piece together what had happened. From Ian's records it was a fairly simple task to track down Lucas, Ian's assistant and bring him in for questioning.

A terrified Lucas, scared to admit what he had done even though it was an accident, contradicted each subsequent statement talking himself deeper and deeper into trouble. Instead of the whole incident being put down to what it was, an accident, Lucas talked himself into a charge of murder. The Sergeant had no time at all for *Kaffirs* and this one was as guilty as hell, justice would prevail, he was arrested on the spot and roughly bundled into the police van. Good man that Williams, *fucking Kaffir* he would get his just desserts.

The only assets Williams Motors had, were the jack and Ian's tools; the whole business was Ian himself. After selling the garage minus the tools to Ian's previous boss, Betty was left with very little money. After selling the business to Jacobus Steyn, Williams Motors was renamed to Steyn's Garage.

The three girls were all working and still living at home they would manage financially. Ian, who was normally a model student, did not do as well as expected in his final examinations, taking into consideration his state of mind due to his father's death the school passed him for High School.

The summer holidays of 1962 were terribly sad for Ian, (his mother had taken to calling him by his proper name as he was now the man of the house, a terrible burden for a twelve-year old boy). Unable to socialise with his school mates, Ian spent the entire holiday on his own, moping around the house, crying from time to time and cursing Lucas regularly for killing his father.

With almost indecent haste, Lucas was brought to trial and with the minimum of fuss found guilty of the murder of Ian Williams, and with no extenuating circumstances sentenced to be hung by the neck until dead. Ian followed the trial in the newspapers. The reporting of the trial was seriously biased against Lucas, typical case of a well looked after black employee turning on his white boss and murdering him in cold blood. This type of reporting and the verdict of the trial would leave a lasting impression on young Ian Williams. He would remain as convinced as the courts that his father had been needlessly murdered by Lucas.

CHAPTER 2
Angus Ross Stewart

Young Angus made his appearance in the early hours of June 10, 1950 at the Ixopo Hospital in rural Natal. He was the belated fifth child of Doctor Hamish Stewart and Matron Edith Stewart. His arrival coincided with the quietest time of the night shift at the small country hospital and as such, caused the least possible disturbance to Matron and the two nursing sisters on duty.

Angus had not been planned and the pregnancy had come as a surprise to both Doctor and Matron Stewart. As dedicated medical professionals, their careers had always taken precedence over their family and children. The last of the four children, daughter Emma, had been born eleven years ago and neither parent had considered the possibility of more children. Eldest son Bruce, sixteen, and his thirteen-year old brother, Patrick, were both boarders at Kearsney College near Pietermaritzburg and were only seen occasionally during school holidays. Fourteen-year old Elizabeth was a boarder at Collegiate Girls High School and usually spent her school holidays with her father's brother and his wife in Port Elizabeth. Eleven-year old Emma, who was in her final year of primary school at Collegiate, would join her elder sister as a boarder next year.

Edith, or Matron as she liked to be called, had considered herself at the age forty-two, well past child-bearing age. Despite her excellent medical skills, Matron paid little or no attention of her own physical well being. When her periods had become erratic, almost to the point of completely disappearing, she had just assumed that she had reached menopause.

One of the infrequent couplings between her and her husband had resulted in Edith becoming pregnant with Angus. Due to her being totally involved with her work and also her lack of personal care, it was fully six months before she realised that she was pregnant. Far past the time that abortion was an option, she resigned herself the fact that another child was on the way.

Angus' birth had been particularly swift and painless, and Matron was sure that she would be back on duty later the same day. The only attendees to the birth were the two nursing sisters who were on duty that night. Doctor Hamish Stewart had left earlier that afternoon to attend to a farmer who had broken both his legs. The accident had occurred when a tractor, driven by one of his black farm workers, had overturned on top of him, crushing his legs. It would be over a week before Hamish was even aware that he was a father again.

Edith, having no motherly instincts at all, had immediately on completing the birthing process, passed Angus over to the attending sisters and went to sleep. A luxury she would not allow any other new mother, she unhesitatingly granted herself. She needed a good night's rest if she wanted to be on duty later that day. Angus could be fed and cared for by the staff in the nursery, a routine that would continue until time for him to be sent home. Edith had her responsibilities at the hospital; child-care at her home was the duty of her Zulu maid, Patience. Like all the Stewart children, Angus would have more affinity with Patience than either of his parents.

Hamish, much to the disgust of the local white community, instituted a weekly clinic where he would travel to the surrounding black settlements, treating, where allowed, any reported aliments. On these days, any patients wishing attention at the hospital would just have to wait until the return of their good doctor. Although well respected as a doctor, Hamish was not well liked by the white community. He was seen as arrogant and aloof, and treated all patients as equals no matter of their station in life.

During these years, Hamish and Edith continued with their all-consuming duties at the hospital. Hamish had earned the trust and respect of all Ixopo's citizens both black and white. He had managed to successfully treat and operate on a number of blacks, who now took less and less of their ailments to the local Witch Doctor. Although most of the local population admired and respected their good doctor, there was a fair number of white Afrikaners who resented his treatment of blacks in the same hospital as he treated the whites.

Unable to treat his black patients at the same time as his white ones, Hamish spent more and more hours on the road, holding his local clinics in the black townships. All work at his 'private clinics' was not officially recognised by the hospital, no fees were ever charged, and any medicines given were those Hamish took from his supplies at the hospital. Often Hamish was offered payment in the form of goods, such as chickens or goats, which he took as not to offend the giver. These 'payments' were duly handed over to Thompson as they were of no use to Hamish. Thompson turned a blind eye to the use of hospital medications for a steady supply of fresh livestock.

By the end of March 1950 Edith realised she was pregnant again. She was devastated, the missed periods she had put down to oncoming menopause, she never once even considered the possibility of pregnancy. She had no idea when the child was due, she hardly remembered when her and Hamish had last had sex. Hamish, on being informed he was to become a father again after a lapse of eleven years, merely grunted and continued attending to his patient.

Edith continued to work, not letting her barely visible state of pregnancy hinder her in anyway. With little warning, Edith went into labour late in the evening of June 9th and four hours later, at two o'clock in the morning of June 10, 1950, gave birth to her fifth child, a boy whom they named Angus Ross Stewart. Young Angus was promptly handed over to the hospital nursery and Edith turned over and went to sleep, so as to be fresh and ready for duty later that day.

Angus, suffering the same fate as his four older siblings, was handed over to Patience's care, who once again had a child to care for. Edith, never one to display any motherly traits, got on with her life but it was Hamish who surprised everyone who, for some reason only known to himself, doted on the boy from the first day. He would spend his free time at home talking to Angus about Scotland and his time at Edinburgh Hospital, how he met his mother and their subsequent travels to Ixopo. Angus, far too young to understand anything, would smile at his father apparently engrossed with the tales.

As soon as he was old enough to walk, Hamish began taking his son with him to the hospital where the young lad would accompany him everywhere. The staff all loved Angus as he was angelic looking, with blond hair and huge round brown smiling eyes. Angus followed his father around like a doting puppy, always eager for any attention. Hamish would explain everything he did to his son, as though the boy was a medical student and Angus would smile at his father, as though he understood everything told to him.

It became a common sight at the hospital, the tall serious doctor on his rounds, accompanied by a little blond replica of himself running behind him in an attempt to keep up. The doctor would look at the patient's chart, discuss the symptoms, ask Angus for his opinion, answer for the boy and prescribe the treatment. Most of the patients were pleased to see Angus with the doctor, as they noticed a great improvement in his compassion and bedside manner when the boy was present.

With the older Stewart children finding excuses to spend fewer and fewer of their school holidays at home, Angus had the run of the household. He was popular with all and sundry, with the exception of his mother. Edith had, throughout her marriage and the previous four children, had the undivided attention of her husband. Her entire life revolved around her husband and the hospital and she had always enjoyed Hamish's undivided attention. Now, she had to fight for attention with her son and she began to unconsciously resent the little boy. Angus could never understand why he was fussed over by everyone but his mother, and after many attempts to win her over, he gave up and concentrated his love on his father.

By the time Angus started school at the age of five and a half in the January of 1956, he was well advanced in reading and writing; skills picked up from his father. Hamish had begun to take his son with him on his frequent trips to his rural clinics. Angus would help Hamish by carrying his medical bag, getting all the patients in an orderly queue and then passing his father the necessary equipment required for examination. The little boy, speaking perfect Zulu, a skill his father had never mastered, was the link between doctor and patient. Angus would question the patient in his or her own language and convey the symptoms to his father, who would treat the patient and pass on via Angus any instructions. Angus lived for these moments when he had his father all to himself and had only one desire; that was that one day he too would be a doctor. The future of the Stewart tradition was firmly in the hands of Angus.

A surprise birthday party had been arranged for Angus to celebrate his eighth birthday. All his school friends had been invited to attend, everything arranged by the ever-faithful Thompson and the Zulu maid, Patience. Angus, blissfully unaware of the impending party, had been looking forward to a trip with his father to one of the local clinics. His father was going to let him administer vaccinations for the first time.

Arriving home from school, excited by the prospect of an afternoon with his father, he was shocked to find nearly twenty of his friends eagerly waiting for him. A surprise party that would mean his father would have to leave without him. Hiding his disappointment as best he could, Angus joined in the festivities that had been laid on for him.

The last of his friends left the party shortly before five thirty and it was beginning to get dark when his mother arrived home from the hospital just after six o'clock. His father usually arrived home from the clinic sometime between seven and eight. Bitterly disappointed at not being able to help his father at the clinic, Angus settled down to his homework, which would take him until his father arrived home.

By ten o'clock that evening Hamish had not yet returned home, and Angus began to pester his mother about his whereabouts. Edith, although a little concerned, assumed that Hamish had been delayed by some patient problem and would be home as soon as he could. Angus was packed off to bed with the assurance that his father was fine and would be home soon. Edith retired to bed herself and as usual, promptly fell into a deep sleep.

At four o'clock in the morning Edith woke with a start and noticed that Hamish was still not home. Not wanting to panic, she dressed and walked over to the hospital where she found that Hamish had not been seen since the previous afternoon. Nervously, Edith picked up the telephone and called the local police station, where after a long delay, she was connected to the duty officer who informed her that there had been no reports of her husband. At Edith's pressing, the officer undertook to send someone out at first light to the area where her husband had visited.

Edith reluctantly took the officer's advice and returned home to wait for any news or to phone the police station in the event of Hamish's reappearance. By the time she got back to the house, Patience had arrived and was busy in the kitchen preparing breakfast for Angus and herself.

Angus, hearing the movement about the house, got out of bed and rushed into his father's bedroom, eager to find out how the trip had gone. Finding the bedroom empty, he dashed expectantly into the kitchen, only to be greeted by Patience and a worried looking Edith.

'Where's Dad?' demanded Angus. 'Has he left for the hospital already?'

'No,' said Edith, not quite knowing what to say, 'he hasn't come home from the clinic yet. I expect he had some complications and had to stay over. None of those areas have any phones. He'll probably be home any minute now.'

'Why are you looking so worried then? What has happened? I want to know.'

'Nothing has happened, the police will go out and see if they can find him. You have your breakfast and get ready for school. You can see your father when you get back from school.'

Reluctantly, Angus ate his breakfast, dressed and left for school.

Shortly before ten o'clock, during the history lesson, there was knock on the classroom door. Opening the door, the teacher was met by a worried looking headmaster. In muted tones the message was conveyed from headmaster to teacher.

'Angus, the headmaster wants you to go home immediately, your mother is waiting for you,' said the teacher, who looked very close to tears.

'What's the matter?' cried Angus, knowing something serious was afoot.

'Your mother will explain to you. Hurry now, she's waiting for you.'

Grabbing his school bag, Angus dashed out of the classroom and ran the short distance home. Rushing into the house he saw his mother looking ashen faced and two stern looking policemen, who appeared to be questioning her.

'What's wrong?' demanded Angus.

'Sit down, son,' said the taller of the two policemen, 'there has been an accident and we have some bad news for you.'

'It's my father, isn't it? Where is he? What's happened?'

'We found your father's body about an hour ago, he has been dead for a number of hours. We are investigating the matter,' said the policeman officiously.

Angus let out a wail and then screamed at the top of his voice. Edith, attempting to comfort her son, a thing she had never done before, picked him up in her arms and held him to her chest. Angus, kicking and shouting, would not be comforted and broke free from his mother's embrace.

'Leave me alone. It's my fault! I should have been with him instead of being at that stupid party,' wailed Angus, overcome with grief. He turned and ran straight into Patience's arms, the only mother he had really known.

Patience took a sobbing Angus to his bedroom, leaving the rest to continue their discussion. Edith, in a state of shock, could barely comprehend what had happened.

The police had found Hamish's body alongside the road, some three miles from where he had attended his clinic. The body, badly mutilated, had been stripped of all clothing and possessions. His ears had been cut off and eyes gouged out, apparently while still alive. His genitals had been removed and were nowhere to be found, his side was slashed open and his liver had been taken out. Experience of these type of crimes were usually associated with what was known as 'muti killings.'

Often, certain body parts of a victim were removed to be used in potions or medicines concocted for the use in curing of ailments. If the victim, as in Hamish's case, was a powerful presence, these organs were highly valued. What was different in this killing was that all valuables, like the car, the medical instruments, clothing and jewellery, were also missing. This did not seem like a straight-forward ritual killing.

The policeman, having completed proceedings, left Edith with her grief; she still had to identify the body for legal reasons. Angus, sitting numbly in his room, heard the policeman leave.

'Fucking Kaffirs, after all he did for them, to kill him like that. Shows you what happens when you treat the bastards like normal humans. If I had my way, I'd kill the fucking lot of them, ungrateful animals,' shouted Angus.

'I feel sorry for the woman and the kid. I wonder what will happen to them now. We'll find the bastards, as soon as we find the car. Hanging's too good for them,' said the attending policeman.

News of the killing travelled like wildfire through the town. Both the English and Afrikaans community were up in arms and were all for tracking down the killers and lynching them on the spot. Many of the Afrikaners in Ixopo had not approved of the way in which Hamish had fraternised with the blacks and treated them like equals, but all were in agreement that justice must be done. No killing of a white by a black must go unpunished.

Hamish's body, duly identified by a distraught Edith, was released to the hospital for a post-mortem to be performed. This was done by a visiting pathologist from Durban. The time of death was estimated at around ten o'clock the previous evening. Hamish had been tortured and was alive when his eyes were gouged out and his ears and genitals removed. He had eventually succumbed when his liver was removed. The murder was obviously made to look like a ritual killing, but the torture made it more like a revenge killing.

Edith found the best cure was to return to work in an attempt to get her mind off the tragedy. She found though, so many of the things around her would remind her of her beloved husband. She carried her grief with her for the rest of her life.

Two weeks after the funeral, Edith was informed that she and her son would have to vacate their house, as it was required for the new doctor and his family. A small two bedroomed cottage was found for them. Patience, who was paid for by the hospital was expected to remain and serve her new masters; this she refused point blank. She had been with the Stewart's for over sixteen years and was not staying on for the new doctor. As a mark of respect for Hamish's service, Thompson allowed Patience to continue to work for Edith at the hospital's expense.

Angus, devastated by the death of his father, took a long time to recover. He was even more determined to emulate his father as a doctor. When he was a doctor, he wouldn't work for and help those 'fucking Kaffirs' who killed his father. Those fateful words he had overheard from the policeman would stay with him for many years to come.

The trust fund left for the children's education would now no longer be supplemented by Hamish's additional earnings. Any moneys due to him would be paid out to Edith, which she would require for the days when she could no longer work. There would be enough money left for maybe one or two years of university for Angus, by the time he reached that age.

By the time Angus was nearing the end of his primary school days, it was obvious that there were no funds available to send him to one of the better private schools and he would have to complete his education in Ixopo. Fortunately for Edith, she received a letter in the October of 1962 from Hamish's sister, Heather.

Heather had married a doctor and he had opened a small practice in Scotland. Having made a comfortable amount of money, they had decided to immigrate to South Africa in 1950. Reading of Hamish's tragic death in the local newspaper, she had attempted to contact Edith but received no reply. Four years had gone by and now her husband had recently died, so she again attempted to make contact.

Edith vaguely remembered receiving the first letter but being still in a state of shock, had never replied to it. Composing a short but friendly reply, Edith told her sister-in-law that since Hamish's death, she had worked with little time for anything else. Her husband's killers had never been found or brought to justice. Her youngest son, Angus, was nearing the end of his primary school days and soon he would have to find another school as the local one would not afford him the best education.

It was this reply that led Heather to suggest to Edith that it may be in her son's best interest to come and live with her in Durban, where the schools were probably of a better standard. Heather, also being childless, warmed to the idea of helping bring up her brother's son. Edith, always ready to avoid emotional decisions, readily agreed to Heather's suggestion and so it was agreed that Angus would move to Durban for his High School education and live with his Aunt Heather.

December of 1962 saw Angus leave Ixopo for the last time, saying goodbye to a tearful Patience, who had been his mother for over twelve years. Edith, still grieving for her husband, was grateful that the responsibility of raising Angus was now no longer hers. Bags packed, Angus caught the train for Durban and a new life at Brighton Beach on the Bluff. He was determined as ever he would one day be a doctor just like his father.

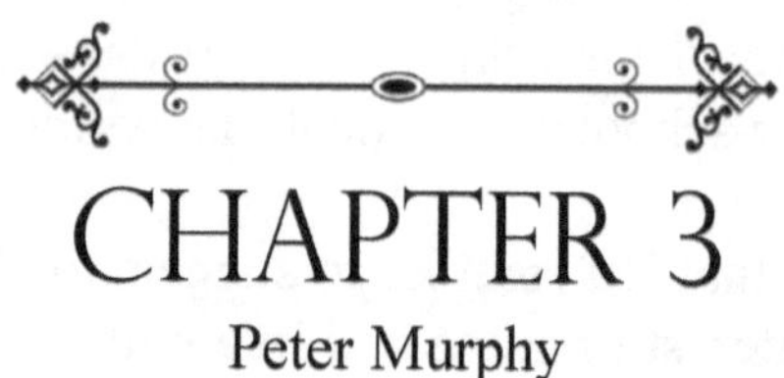

CHAPTER 3
Peter Murphy

Peter Anthony Murphy, born on January 1, 1950, the second son of reasonably well to do middle class parents, was blessed with a natural talent for any sporting activity involving a ball. His father was second generation South African, from English descent and his mother born in India of English parents. He was born into a stable Catholic family who lived in a moderate Durban suburb. Older brother George had arrived nearly three years ago, sister Mary was almost a year older than Peter and the two of them would remain the closest of all the children.

Peter would grow up with his older brother and sister in a modest home with few of the luxuries of many of their peers. Their father David was an honest lawyer, who found the vagaries and lack of ethics of private practice unsuited to his ideals and as such joined the local Durban Council in what would amount to a waste of his Legal training. Their mother Valerie was an incredible person who qualified as a physiotherapist but never had the opportunity to fully utilise her undoubted skills in this profession as her time was taken up almost entirely by her large family.

January 11,1949 Mary Anne Murphy was born. As far as Val was concerned her family was complete. She had always wanted a boy and a girl so that was it. She could probably start work again within the year and contribute financially to the family again. They weren't badly off for money but with her working again they could enjoy a few more luxuries.

Mary Anne was barely three months old when Val found out to her horror that she was pregnant once again. There went any chance of her helping with the family income for at least another year.

January 1, 1950, saw the arrival of Peter Anthony Murphy, the third and definitely the last of Val's children. While neither George nor Mary Anne had been much trouble as babies, Peter would prove to be a handful to his mother. He demanded attention from the start. Older brother George, now three, chose to ignore this intrusion into his quiet orderly life. Sister Mary Anne, not quite a year old and not yet walking, was blissfully unaware of the new arrival.

Peter slept in a cot in his parent's room as Val found herself spending many a night trying to get her youngest son to sleep or just in keeping him quiet. George and Mary Anne each slept in their own rooms, thankfully giving Val no problems at all. It was almost a year before she got a full night's sleep again. With two other children to keep her occupied during the day and Peter taking care of the nights, Val was in a perpetual state of near exhaustion.

Peter moved into the same room as his brother when he reached the age of six months. This didn't last even one night. George, now three and a half, took great exception to his younger brother waking him up. George got out of bed, walked over to Peter's cot, picked up an almost empty babies drinking bottle and hit his brother over the head with it. A stunned Peter stopped crying for an instant and then all hell broke loose.

Val rushed into the room to find George holding the bottle ready to clobber Peter again. She grabbed her eldest son to stop him hitting his brother again and took the bottle off him. Placing him back in his bed she picked Peter up out of his cot to comfort him. Once quieted she put him back in his cot and wheeled it into Mary Anne's room, where it would stay for the time being.

David decided that the best solution would be to add an additional room to the house. They achieved this with an addition to their existing bond, and Peter and George moved out of Mary Anne's room and into their own room. With the additional mortgage payments, money became even tighter. The Murphy children's clothing was one of hand me downs. George, as the oldest, got the clothes new, with his shirts, shorts, shoes and jerseys being passed down the line from Mary Anne to Peter. Very seldom was Mary Anne seen in a dress and apart from the long curly hair could easily have passed as a boy.

Mary Anne and Peter were the closest of the children. They played together at everything. Cricket matches were held in the backyard between the two, some titanic contests took place. Despite Peter's natural ability, Mary Anne more than held her own against her younger brother. It was during these contests that their will to win and determination to do well was developed.

When Mary Anne started school in January of 1955, Peter found himself without his best friend during the weekdays. he began to pester his mother to be allowed to go to school now. Val approached the headmaster at Fynnlands about Peter starting school a year early.

The Natal Provincial Administration rules on starting school were that the child had to be at least five years old and have their sixth birthday within that school year. Peter having been born on the 1st of January, missed starting by one day and as such would have to wait another year. The headmaster suggested that she enrol her son in an experimental scheme that he had started at Fynnlands. To ease children into starting school, an experimental 'pre-school' class had been started for the first time that year at Fynnlands.

The children one year away from starting normal school were given the opportunity to experience what school would be like but without the normal school rules and discipline. No uniforms were to be worn and there would be no involvement with the rest of the school's activities. The day would start at the same time as the rest of the junior school but would end one hour earlier.

Peter was immediately enrolled. He would finish his morning's school and wait the additional hour and return home with his brother George. The additional hour Peter spent at school each day found him at the sports fields. If there was a sports lesson underway, he would sit on the sidelines and stare longingly at the children. The sports master, Bob Crowley, who took all the Physical Education classes at the school noticed the little boy on the sidelines. After the second day Crowley called Peter over.

'Come here, son,' called Crowley, 'what's your name then?'

'Peter.'

'Well, Peter, what are you doing here, shouldn't you be at home?'

'I go to school with Miss Turner and I am waiting for my brother, we walk home together,' said Peter proudly.

'And who is your brother?'

'George Murphy, he's in standard one.'

'Oh yes, I know who he is,' said Crowley. *George Murphy, he is that ungainly boy who will try anything to get out of PE, thought the sports teacher.* 'How would you like to help me?'

'Thank you very much, sir,' replied Peter, leaving his suitcase and running over to the change rooms where Bob Crowley stood.

'Don't forget your suitcase, lad. Tell me, are you as good at games as your brother George?'

'Oh no, sir, I'm much better than him. Mary Anne and me beat him at everything,' said Peter modestly.

And, so it was that Bob Crowley allowed young Peter Murphy to help him with the final two PE lessons of the day. By the time Peter arrived each day, the second last lesson of the day had already started so his first duty was to tidy the sports equipment room. He would diligently sort and then pack away the equipment used from the previous lesson and then he would go out and watch the action from the sidelines.

On Thursdays the last lesson of the day was for the Grade One pupils, those children in their first year of junior school. It was on this day that Bob Crowley allowed Peter to join in the lesson. Although at least a year younger than all the other children, Peter more than held his own. In any bat/ball games he outshone all the other children; Bob realised he had found an extremely talented boy who was going to be a great sportsman one day.

It was on these Thursdays that George found himself having to wait for his little brother rather than the other way around. Other children had spoken to him about Peter, not yet at school and already sorting out all the Grade One kids. George, already barely tolerant of his brother, grew to resent him even more. Matters came to a head when George, in a huff at once again having to wait for Peter, left for home without him.

'George, where is your brother?' asked his mother nervously.

'I don't know,' said George sullenly.

'What do you mean you don't know? He is supposed to wait for you and the two of you to walk home together. Didn't you see him?' shouted Val, starting to panic.

'He's was probably still sucking up to Mr. Crowley. Anyway, he is supposed to wait for me, not me wait for him. It's not fair! He shouldn't even be at my school yet.'

On closer questioning, she found out what Peter was doing and the effect it had on her oldest son. It was obvious that George was extremely jealous of his younger brother's popularity and although she felt a little sorry for him, he would have to come to terms with it. Marching George back to school they found Peter sitting quietly in his usual place waiting for his brother, oblivious of the panic that had been caused. Val made it very clear to her two boys that they were never again to come home without each other, the responsibility for this was placed squarely on George's shoulders.

With this censure from his mother, George resented Peter even more. Why should he have to baby sit his brother? What about his friends? Peter was the favourite. George would grow up as a lonely child with very few friends, resenting the rest of his siblings. Peter, Mary Anne and in later years Richard, grew up very close to each other.

By the time Peter started school officially at Fynnlands in 1956, he was known by all and sundry. Although a conscientious student, Peter lived for his twice weekly PE lesson with Mr. Crowley. Adept with cricket bat and ball, or tennis racket he would try anything and invariably succeed at it. Other than PE, Peter was too young to partake in any of the organised school teams. Cricket, football and tennis teams started at the under nine level, three years away. Hockey was only played by the standard five boys and girls, a life-time away. Grade one and two pupils were limited to games of rounders and 'fun' non-competitive team games, like beanbag throwing and running races. In the summer terms all children would be allowed to do swimming, the one thing Peter found himself to be very average at.

Peter, unable to join in the team sports, took to hanging around the older children and playing ball boy whenever he could. The football season dawned without him having wangled himself into any of the cricket or tennis teams. A notice was placed on the school notice board that the first official practice and selection for the under nine football teams would take place after school. All boys who were interested were to report on Wednesday afternoon wearing white shorts, PE shirt and takkies (tennis shoes). Peter still had to wait and walk home with George and was upset that he would miss watching the football.

When George informed his brother that he was going to try out for the under-nines and he would just have to wait around until he was finished, Peter could hardly contain his surprise. George playing football, he must be joking. On the few occasions the boys had played football at home, Peter had run rings around George. Anyway, he was glad to just to be allowed to watch.

Two teams were to be entered in the under-nine primary schools league and as such, around twenty-five or so boys would be needed. The boys were divided up into goalkeepers, defenders and attackers. Most of the boys had never played football previously and they decided on their positions by what their friends chose. Those not making a choice themselves were placed by Bob Crowley. His method was if the boy was big, a defender; if not, an attacker. George found himself placed among the defenders. An equal number of each group were split up into two teams. Bob then picked two teams of eleven who would play each other. As the game progressed he would assess the boys and make the necessary changes; either positional or replacing the boy with one eagerly waiting on the touchline.

George, one of the original choices, managed to skilfully avoid any contact with the ball or an opponent for the first ten minutes and so remained on the field. Peter, quickly losing interest with the happenings on the field, had found a spare football and was running around kicking it with vigour. Although numerous changes had been made to the various teams, George was still on at the break.

Bob gathered the boys around him and attempted to explain what he wanted from them in the next half. He told them that even if they were replaced during the course of the game, it did not mean that they were not wanted. All boys were to stay to the end of the practice, whereupon he would select the boys that he felt would be wanted for the teams.

Bob had noticed Peter running up and down the sidelines during the first half and although three years younger and at least a head shorter than the other boys, he thought, 'Why not give this kid a run? If it doesn't work, I'll pull him off.'

'Peter, come over here,' called Bob, 'How would you like to have a bit of a game with these other boys?'

'Oh yes please, Sir,' said Peter excitedly.

'Ok then, you play for the side with the red sash,' said the master, giving Peter a red sash to put on, 'Play up front as a striker, but if it gets too tough I'll pull you off.'

Peter, almost beside himself with excitement putting on the sash, ran onto the field to take up his position. Whether by choice or coincidence, Peter found himself in direct opposition with his brother George. What happened in the next few minutes was embarrassing for the older boy. Every time Peter got the ball, he beat his older brother with ease. George, unable to stop his brother by fair means, attempted to use his height and weight advantage to push Peter to the ground. It made no difference as time and time again Peter ran past his older brother's clumsy attempts to stop him.

Bob mercifully brought George's humiliation to an end by replacing him with another boy, but not before George was crying tears of frustration. At this point he would have cheerfully murdered his younger brother. Peter, oblivious to his brother's agony, proceeded to do the same to his next opponent. Fearing that Peter would get himself hurt by showing up the bigger and older boys, Bob pulled him off.

Bob Crowley realised that he had unearthed a gem; the problem would be in getting the school authorities and Peter's parents to agree that he could play. The physical difference between a six and nine-year old was huge, but Peter had the ability to play at this level and Bob was determined to have him in his side.

Surprisingly, the school authorities had no objection to Bob letting six-year old Peter play football. Peter's mother was a more difficult proposition. She was concerned that Peter – being so much younger than the other boys – would get himself hurt. Bob assured her that physical contact at this level was minimal, but he would have his older brother George to look after him. This was a master stroke by the coach. Val was aware that George and Peter did not get on very well and thought that maybe playing together in the team would bring them closer to each other.

So it was that George and Peter formed part of the twenty-five boys who would play for the two Fynnlands under-nine teams. Peter and George were both picked for the 'B' team for the first game. Peter was the star of the side, but his older brother had an average game. The following week Peter was promoted to the 'A' side and George was selected as a reserve for the same team. This was the pattern for the rest of the season; Peter in the side and George a reserve, but never getting a game. Bob Crowley had kept his promise to Val that he would keep the two boys together, so George could 'look after' Peter.

The following year, Peter, now seven, still played for the under-nine 'A' side and George, now ten, retired less than gracefully from competitive football. Brotherly love on George's part had not been strengthened in the least. By the age of ten, Peter was playing regularly for the school first team. It made little difference that the majority of the boys he played with or against were two to three years older than him. He would play for the first team for three years – almost unheard of at junior school. If Fynnlands had been one of the more well-known schools Peter would surely have been picked for one of the provincial schoolboy teams.

In the summer seasons Peter played cricket with the same success as he had with the football. Whenever his football and cricket duties permitted, he played tennis for the school first team. By the time he reached standard five, he was captain of the cricket and football teams. During the football season, those not partaking had the opportunity to play hockey, the school fielding two boy's teams and one girl's. On the odd occasion that there was no football game, Peter was welcomed with open arms to the first hockey team.

It was no surprise that Peter was elected as head-boy in his final year at junior school thus emulating his older sister who had achieved the same honour at her school. George, who was now in high school at Marist Brothers College, resented his brother even more. It was obvious to Val that when Peter was to start high school, it would be better if it was at a different school to his brother's. It was with this in mind that she reluctantly enrolled Peter at Grosvenor Boy's High School and not at her preferred Marist Brothers College.

Peter Murphy left Fynnlands for the last time in early December 1962 as Head-boy, captain of the school first teams in football and cricket. He was, when available, a regular member of the school tennis and hockey teams. He was elected Victor Ladorum as the best all round sportsman and finished in the top ten of his class academically. His future looked bright.

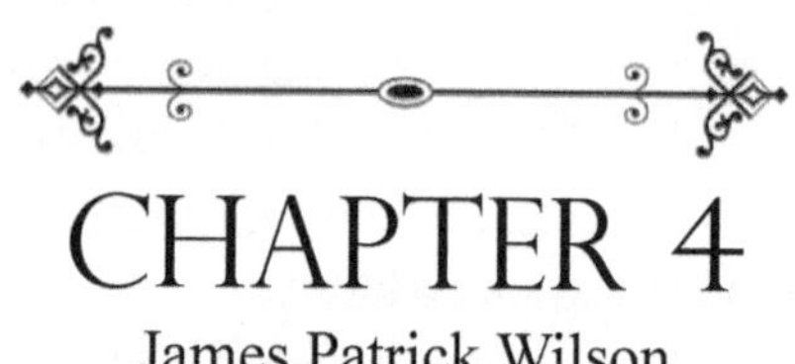

CHAPTER 4
James Patrick Wilson

James Patrick Wilson was born on the February 9, 1950 in Roodepoort, a small town west of Johannesburg, to an English mother Iris and first generation South African father Denis. Known as Jimmy from day one, he was a large baby, weighing in at 9 pounds 10 ounces, and his was a particularly difficult birth. Home was a modest house owned by the South African Railways for whom his Paternal Grandfather worked, and which much to the dismay of his mother, the family shared with the in-laws and her husband's older brother.

Times were difficult for this family as the incomes earned by Grandfather Arthur and Father Denis, who worked as the local station master and a flour miller respectively, barely covered their needs.

June 7, 1952 saw the birth of a baby girl. Denis wanted to name the baby Bridget after his mother, but Iris was adamant that her daughter was not going to be named after a woman who had made her life a misery. The argument raged for two days and eventually a compromise was reached. The baby would be named Maureen (after no one in particular) Bridget Wilson. Although slightly peeved, Bridget agreed that two Bridget Wilson's in one family would be slightly confusing and Maureen was a good old Irish name anyway.

Life for the Wilson's passed without much incident over the next two years. Denis had been passed over for promotion at the mill but seemed unconcerned as the new position would not have allowed him any overtime. Iris, however, would have preferred him being promoted as the position required no shift work and that would have meant him being home in the evenings every day as opposed to only every third week.

Fate took a hand in their lives when an old navy friend of Denis' paid them a visit. Archie Stewart had been aboard the same ship as Denis for the last two years of the war and subsequently immigrated to Southern Rhodesia where he had opened a small hardware shop in the Midlands town of Gwelo. He spoke glowingly of life in Southern Rhodesia, the great weather, good salaries and cheap housing. He knew the owner of the local flour mill, Midlands Milling, very well and was sure that they could use an experienced miller.

With the details from Archie and the promise that he would put in a good word, Denis wrote to Mr. Jan van der Molen of Midlands Milling applying for a job.

Two weeks later Denis received a reply from Midlands Milling offering him a job as a shift miller at a salary far in excess of what he was currently getting and with the promise of a fair annual bonus based on production output. The company would pay all relocation expenses and accommodate them at a local hotel for the period of one month while they found a suitable house. Denis was unsure of such a big step but with Iris pushing him, he finally agreed that it was a tempting offer and they should take the opportunity and leave for Gwelo as soon as possible.

The Wilson family settled into life in Gwelo as though born to it. Denis found them a single story house with a thatched roof and a large garden. The neighbors were a friendly bunch, all English speaking.

Jimmy had inherited his grandmother's intellect and started school shortly before his sixth birthday. He immediately impressed his teacher who predicted great things for him. Jimmy spent his first two years at Windsor Park Primary school where he excelled in all subjects and received glowing reports all of which were forwarded to Granny Bridget just to prove he didn't need the disciplined teaching of the Jesuit Brothers.

Maureen started school at Windsor Park in January 1958 and Jimmy moved on to Cecil John Rhodes Junior School. The two Wilson children were both model students, always on time, never in trouble, and in the top ten of their respective classes. Jimmy was average in most sports but an excellent swimmer and represented his school from an early age while his sister showed no interest in sports. Jimmy found himself in the same class as his father's boss's son, Jannie, with whom he became best friends. The ironic thing was that Jimmy was always held up to Jannie by his father as the perfect example of doing well in school.

Jimmy and Jannie became inseparable and spent most of their free time together on the van der Molen farm located a few miles outside

Gwelo on the Selukwe Road. Jimmy liked the easygoing opulence of the van der Molens and longed to have a similar way of life. Although the Wilson's had a reasonably comfortable lifestyle, they could never hope to emulate the van der Molens and Jimmy vowed that when he grew up he would be rich.

The van der Molens had a number of black servants, two houseboys, a chauffeur, a nanny for the three younger sisters, a full-time gardener and five farm workers who lived with their families on the property. This was the first time Jimmy experienced the master-servant relationship as Philemon was treated like one of the family by his parents. He was unused to being called 'Master' or 'Little Master' by anyone but soon became accustomed to it. Although the divide between blacks and whites in Southern Rhodesia was not as defined as in the South African Apartheid system, it was still the accepted way that they be segregated in all forms of social activities. All schools, housing, shops and cinemas etc. were racially segregated and as such Jimmy grew up with the master-servant attitude prevalent in all whites in Southern Africa.

The impending breakup of the Federation (Nyasaland, Northern and Southern Rhodesia) was the main topic of conversation in the early part of the nineteen sixties. Around this time Iris had saved up enough money for the family to take their first ever holiday. Denis suggested that they drive down to the Natal South Coast to Margate and pick up Bridget and her sister Maggie and take them along. Iris balked at the idea but realized four weeks with Bridget in Margate was much preferred to a lifetime of her in Gwelo.

May 1960 was spent with Bridget and Maggie in a holiday apartment in Margate. Iris found Bridget had mellowed and spent less and less time criticizing her. Fortunately for Iris, Bridget showed no inclination to live with them in Gwelo and no desire to visit them on any basis.

One disconcerting topic was the breakup of the Federation where Bridget continually worried aloud about what would happen to them once the blacks took over. There were also mutterings about what would happen to South Africa if Britain allowed it to become a self-governing republic. At least the NATS would be a white government and they would keep the blacks in their place. It was against this backdrop that Bridget surreptitiously planted the seeds of doubt in her son's mind about the future of life in Southern Rhodesia.

Iris and Denis took long walks along the Margate beaches late into the nights as a way to find a bit of privacy and discuss Bridget's concerns over the future. Iris was sure things would be fine once the Federation broke up but Denis wasn't convinced and said that maybe the time had come to look for a job 'down south,' surely it would be better to get out before things got too bad and they would then be unable to sell their house or get their money out.

With the holiday over, Bridget and Maggie were dropped off at the Sesfontein small holding with the promise to consider a return to South Africa if things got bad up north. On returning home to Gwelo the Wilson's found everything as they had left it, all peaceful, no trouble. With the children returning to school and Denis to work, Iris soon forgot all about returning to South Africa; as far as she was concerned Gwelo was her future.

Since returning from Margate, Iris had missed her period, and thinking maybe at nearly thirty-eight she was experiencing the early stages of menopause, she dismissed the idea that she might be pregnant. Once the morning sickness started, she knew that she was expecting again. Good God, after eight years she had no baby things left. She broke the news to Denis, not knowing what his reaction would be. He was delighted. Jimmy was horrified at the thought of a baby brother or sister nearly eleven years younger than him, Maureen on the other hand took the same stance as her dad.

Iris's pregnancy only served to increase Denis' desire to return to South Africa as the future was growing more and more uncertain with the breakup of the Federation and he began actively looking for a job outside of Rhodesia. The arrival of David Wilson on March 11, 1961 had still not brought any firm job offer and the family settled back into the quiet routine of life in Gwelo. David was a quiet and contented baby and presented no hardship on the Wilson household; he slept at night and only cried when hungry, Iris remarked that if she knew what a pleasure he was going to be she would have had him years ago.

Denis had joined the Police Reserve a number of years ago mainly for the social and sporting activities. One night a month he was required to stand a duty which mainly consisted of manning the telephone in the charge office at the local police station or accompanying a uniformed police officer on mobile patrol. In the early years, Denis had played football for the police team in the local first division, a requirement was you had to be an active police man or reservist. Now retired from active sports he found he still enjoyed the once a month camaraderie so continued with the Police Reserve.

Up until June 1962 Denis had never experienced anything more than the odd drunk or disturbance of the peace while on duty, but things were to change dramatically. More and more reports of blacks stoning cars on the main roads to Bulawayo and Que Que were being reported. No reports of any injuries were received and in all cases a couple of police vans would be dispatched to the scene and any blacks found would be forcibly arrested and dragged off to the local cells reserved for blacks. Proving culpability was almost impossible and usually they were released by the magistrate the following day.

When reports of robbery and assault by blacks upon whites started becoming more prevalent, Denis brought up the subject of a return to South Africa again. Iris was still not convinced and tried to discourage him. A compromise was reached, Denis would apply for jobs in South Africa and if successful they could then decide whether or not to accept. Iris hoped that the troubles would blow over and they could continue their life in Gwelo far away from Bridget; anything was preferable to a life made miserable by her mother-in-law.

Life continued as normal; Denis had received a couple of replies to his job applications but as none had seemed suitable, he had not yet accepted a position. All appeared to be returning to normal until one morning in early November 1962 Iris heard her next door neighbor Vera calling her. There was a telephone call from the Convent where Maureen attended school. As they had no telephone Iris had left Vera's number in case of emergencies. The school principal, Sister Mary Margaret was on the line. Maureen had been attacked by three black youths and they had stolen her bicycle and satchel while she was on the way to school. Ten-year old Maureen had put up a bit of a fight and for her troubles had a bloody nose and cut lip but was otherwise fine. Iris awoke Denis who was on night shift and related to him what had happened. He immediately dressed and the two of them drove into town to the convent.

Maureen – who up to this time had been very brave throughout her ordeal – on seeing her mother and father burst into tears. Running into her father's arms she buried her face in his chest and continued to sob uncontrollably. Maureen, who always knew when and for how long to cry, made the most of the situation. She was not crying for anything other than her father's attention. Thanking Sister Mary Margaret for her troubles they decided that they should take their shocked and grieving daughter home, excusing her from the day's schooling.

The trip home was spent in silence. Maureen was packed off to bed still sobbing. Iris and Denis sat down to discuss the morning's events.

'It's what I've been saying all along. This place will not be safe for much longer, we have to leave. I can't risk my family being hurt,' said Denis.

'I know I've been against leaving Gwelo, but I agree we should look to going back down South.'

'The one job offer from Durban wasn't too bad, not as much per month as here.'

'Maybe you should reply to them and see if the job is still open,' said Iris.

'I'll go into work early and phone them from there this afternoon.'

Denis contacted SASKO Flour Mills in Durban that afternoon and to his delight found that the position was still open and was his if he so desired. Verbally accepting the job, he arranged for the letter of appointment to be forwarded to him and he would report for duty the first working day of January 1963. Denis told his foreman of his decision and was taken through to the owner, Jan van der Molen, who reluctantly accepted his resignation. He would be allowed to leave on December 16.

Jimmy was devastated with the news that they were leaving Gwelo for Durban. Like any twelve-year old, his first thought was how could he leave his friends? He knew nobody in Durban. He had been the school swimming captain in his last year of junior school and was looking forward to high school where they had an excellent swimming program; his future was ruined, all because his silly sister had fallen off her bike and hurt herself.

The house was put up for sale, a common happening at this time, and sold rather quickly but at a price a little lower than what they had hoped for. The furniture was packed for storage only to be shipped off to Durban once a suitable house was found. Farewells were said to friends and Iris, Denis, Jimmy, Maureen, David and the family bulldog, Sally, packed themselves into the car, a 1960 Opel Kadet station wagon, and began the long, cramped journey back to South Africa.

They spent Christmas with Bridget and Maggie at Sesfontein. Directly after Christmas, Denis went on alone to Durban to search for a house and start his new job on time. Iris and the children were left alone on the small holding at Sesfontein. Bridget – much to Iris's delight – made it very clear that they shouldn't expect to see too much of her in Durban as the place was too damn hot and humid for her liking. She would only undertake short trips to visit them and see her grandchildren, especially David who she said was the spitting image of his father.

Denis found what he considered a suitable house for them on the Bluff in Durban. They could take occupation on January 25, on the basis of renting with an option to buy. Iris agreed that this was the best option as if they didn't like the place, they could always look for another in the three-month period. Denis would return and pick up Jimmy who would have to start school the week before they could move into the house. The rest of the family would come down a week later as the cost of extra people in the hotel was more than they wanted to spend.

Jimmy was registered at Grosvenor Boy's High School on the Bluff which would be within walking distance from their new home. Unaware that the schools in Natal usually started a week later than those in the Transvaal and Rhodesia, Jimmy found out that school only began in just over a week's time, he may as well have stayed in Sesfontein. On the same basis, Denis had scoured the area for a convent for Maureen to attend, the closest one being Saint Dominic's on the Berea. She would be able to catch a single bus to and from school that left from the local Catholic Church.

With everything in place, Denis and Jimmy returned to the Transvaal to fetch the rest of the family and after spending one final night at Sesfontein, returned to their new home in Durban sans Bridget. Settling into the new house over the weekend was a job for grown-ups so Jimmy and Maureen spent their first weekend on the Bluff exploring the neighborhood. The house was a ten-minute walk from the local beach and an even shorter one to the shopping center at Crossways.

Monday morning: the first day of High School in a new town, in a new country for twelve, going on thirteen-year old Jimmy Wilson.

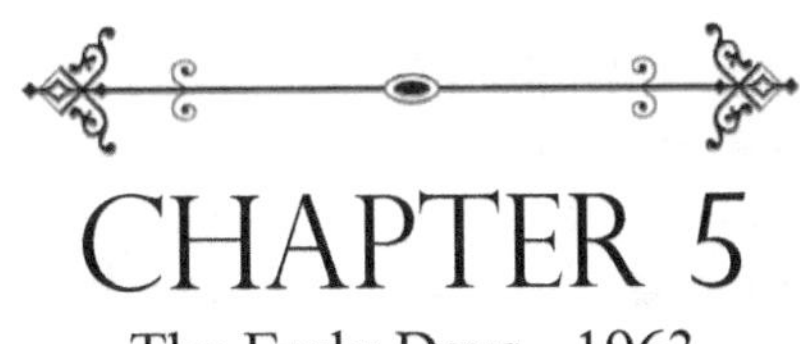

CHAPTER 5
The Early Days - 1963

Grosvenor Boy's High School, an English medium school, is located on the Durban's Bluff. The school is flanked on one side by houses belonging to the South African Railways, and on the other, by a vlei running parallel to the coastline and some two miles inland. Separated from what is now Grosvenor Girl's High School, at the end of 1962, the school opened for business for the first term of 1963.

The school year in South Africa runs from January through to December. The system was divided into kindergarten – grades 1 and 2; junior school standard 1 to 5 (grades 3 to 7); and high school standards 6 to 10 (grades 8 to 12)

To attend one of the better schools in the Durban area, one had to qualify by residency within a defined area, relative to the school in question. Failing this, the potential student either had to have excellent academic or sporting qualifications. A further option was to come from a wealthy family, where a donation to one of the school causes would ensure the student being accepted at the school. Grosvenor Boy's, being a new school in an unfashionable area, needed the only qualification of being a white male to attend. This resulted in students bussing in from various parts of Durban.

The one hundred and twenty-five standard six pupils that January 1963 came from varied backgrounds. The majority had graduated from the three primary schools on the Bluff, Fynnlands, Bushlands or Brighton Beach and were in the age group of twelve to thirteen. Several boys were from junior schools from other parts of Durban or had newly arrived from other parts of the country. There were also several boys, who for various reasons, had been rejected by other schools but found themselves accepted at Grosvenor Boy's High.

One of the requirements of the Natal Education Department was that no white child could leave school under the age of sixteen, and the minimum educational level in normal schools was a standard six leaving certificate. This resulted in the age spread of this standard six group, ranging from twelve to seventeen-year olds.

The difficulty facing teachers and administration staff, was how to place one hundred and twenty-five boys, of varied age and academic ability, into the six classes that they would be best suited to. Most of the boys could be placed based on their academic achievements at their junior schools of Fynnlands, Bushlands and Brighton Beach. Six classes, of approximately twenty pupils each, would be made up of the brighter students, starting with standard 6A and the less so through to standard 6F.

It was in these circumstances that Jimmy Wilson, Peter Murphy, Gus Stewart, and Ian Williams found themselves in standard 6C, with nineteen other boys, the oldest of whom were two seventeen year olds, hoping this was the year to finally get their school leaving certificates. Standard 6C was seen by the staff as the lower end of the advanced stream and based on their junior school results, most of the class were of a similar ability. Given the available information, the staff had grouped together twenty three boys of very average ability, who would be able to learn at the same pace.

There were, however, four notable exceptions, who through no fault of the staff, found themselves in this group. Jimmy, a tall, fair haired boy with piercing blue eyes and a ready smile, had arrived from Rhodesia with no knowledge of Afrikaans and as such, found himself fortunate to be in 6C and not even lower down.

Gus, of average height with fluffy blond hair and inquisitive brown eyes, had attended what amounted to a farm school in the Ixopo region, where he had shown excellent ability but was graded by the lack of perceived quality of his previous school.

Ian, tall, thin with jet black hair, had been graded by his final standard five school marks, with no consideration taken that his father had died just two weeks short of his final examinations. Due to this, his final examination results bore little resemblance to his true ability.

Peter, stocky with tight, almost peppercorn type dark blond curls and a permanent grin, had done particularly well in his junior school years and based on his report from Fynnlands, should have been placed in 6A. An administrative error, made by an overworked, undermanned office staffer, resulted in him being placed in 6C.

The first few weeks of the new school year were, to say the least, chaotic. The school was new, the teachers new and the hopelessly understaffed administration was new. The boys, across all the standards, had to be split up into the four sporting houses. King (named after the famous Dick King), with the colour yellow, acquired the sporting prowess of Jimmy, Gus, Peter and Ian.

This was achieved by their class teacher, Miss Smart, a pretty, young twenty-something music graduate, who all the boys had an immediate crush on, nominating each of the four rows of her class to a sporting house. No thought was given to age or sporting ability. As far as Miss Smart was concerned, sport was something that had to be done but she saw little or no point in sport of any kind.

Apart from her duties as class teacher to standard 6C, Miss Smart had the task of giving two music lessons per week to each of the standard six and seven classes individually, and one per week to those standard six and seven boys chosen for the school choir. The candidates for the choir would be selected in two sessions, one for the standard sixes and one for the standard sevens. All boys would attend, with no exceptions, as Miss Smart believed that all prepubescent young boys could sing.

It was during the choir trials that the friendship of the four boys really started. By no other reason than it just happened the boys found themselves seated behind one another in their home classroom. Other than music, art and science, the standard six boys remained in their classrooms and each subject teacher would come to their class. Music would take place in the school hall.

The standard six choir selection was allocated a full school day and one hundred and twenty odd boys trooped off to the school hall with mixed feelings. On the one hand, sitting about in the school hall was better that normal lessons, but on the other, the terror of having to sing notes to Miss Smart, in front of all your classmates, more than offset missing lessons.

The hall was in the very centre of the school, surrounded by the administration offices on one side and the science laboratories on the other. At the front of the hall was a raised stage where Miss Smart sat at the piano. The boys were seated on long benches facing the stage. The doors running along both sides of the hall were closed so as not to disturb the rest of the school; this would also improve the acoustics. Being January in Durban, the middle of summer, and no air conditioning, the heat and humidity soon became overbearing.

Miss Smart, oblivious to the growing discomfort of her potential choir, began by asking those boys who could sing to come forward and form a line at the bottom of the stage. A silence descended on the hall, each boy looking at another, but no movement towards the front.

'Come on boys, you will all have to have a chance. Let's have those of you who can sing,' said Miss Smart. 'If you don't come forward of your own accord, I'll select you myself.'

Miss Smart surveyed the sea of faces, all of whom were trying their best to avoid eye contact with her. Still, no movement.

'Ok, if that's the way it's going to be, I'll pick someone,' said Miss Smart, standing up and looking out over the gathering. A movement towards the back of the hall caught her eye.

'You there, boy, the one who is talking, stand up!' ordered Miss Smart. 'What is your name?'

'Wilson, Miss,' said a rapidly reddening Jimmy.

'Come here, boy, and the ones you were talking to.'

Jimmy, Gus, Peter and Ian walked slowly to the front of the hall, aware that the eyes of the entire standard six classes were focused on them. The whispering and sniggers followed them all the way to the bottom of the stage, where they stopped and looked up to the testy Miss Smart.

'All right, this is what we are going to do. You, Wilson, and then you, boy,' said Miss Smart pointing to Gus, 'will come up one at a time. I will play some notes on the piano and you will endeavour to sing the note in the same key. A "lah" will do. If I think you have a singing voice, you will stay on the stage, if not you will sit on the benches to my left, back in the hall. The rest of you boys will follow these four starting with the front row, one row a time.' Miss Smart walked back from the edge of the stage and sat down at the piano.

'Well, Wilson, what are you waiting for? Get up here and entertain us with your undoubted singing voice.'

Jimmy, acutely embarrassed, walked up the steps to the stage, tripped over the top step and stumbled across the stage to the giggles of the rest of the boys. 'In a rush all of a sudden, are we, Wilson?' said Miss Smart cruelly.

For Jimmy, already a nervous wreck, this was the final insult; he felt his throat drying up and his neck turning an even brighter shade of red.

'Stand there and face the hall so we can all hear your voice. I will play the note and you sing "lah".'

Miss Smart struck the first note and waited for Jimmy; his throat dry, Jimmy found he could utter no sound at all.

'Come on boy, sing!' ordered Miss Smart playing the note again.

Near to tears, Jimmy was able to utter what sounded like a dog's bark. There was a moment's silence and then a loud laugh from Miss Smart.

'Well, you're no singer, that's for sure. You can go and sit on the left. I am sure there will be other grunters with you shortly. Next!'

Jimmy walked rapidly off the stage, everyone's eyes on him. Without further misfortune, he managed to find his way to the far-left side of the hall, the first of the grunters.

Gus and Ian fared no better than Jimmy, and Peter, who had a good singing voice, deliberately sang off key so he could join his three classmates as the grunters. Jimmy, having suffered the greatest humiliation, felt his stomach rumbling with nervous tension. Not daring to ask Miss Smart's permission to visit the toilet, he had to put up with the discomfort.

As the two groups grew in size, Jimmy began to relax and recover his composure. Although feeling the embarrassment leaving him, he was still acutely aware of the growing wind cramps building up in his stomach. Realising that he would soon reach the point of no return, Jimmy decided on a rather drastic plan of action.

'Psst, Gus, check this out,' Jimmy whispered, placing his left hand through the front of his shirt and clasping it under his right armpit. With the eyes of his mates on him and making a great show of it, Jimmy pumped his right elbow up and down, making a not too loud farting sound. The boys around him giggled. Jimmy, now the centre of attraction with the grunters, pumped again, but this time broke the wind that had been building up in his stomach. At that same instant, there was a break in the music. The unmistakable sound of a loud fart resounded throughout the hall, followed by a short silence and then suppressed laughter.

Miss Smart stood up and looked across at the grunters where Jimmy sat with his hand still in his shirt. The entire hall was once again looking at him.

'You disgusting boy, making a sound like that, come here at once,' ordered Miss Smart, at this stage thinking Jimmy had made the sound artificially. This was just a schoolboy prank and secretly she found it quite amusing, but she had to show her authority and discipline the boy.

Jimmy slowly removed his hand, stood up and started his way towards Miss Smart at the front of the hall. Jimmy, now a bit of a hero with his mates, (anyone who could make that loud a noise with his armpit must be ok,) made his way swaggeringly towards the front. At the same time that he reached the stage, the smell hit.

Those young boys sitting in the immediate vicinity dramatically began clutching their throats and making gagging sounds.

Miss Smart, thinking the boys were making fun of her, shouted at them to stop misbehaving or they would be sent to the Headmaster's office. The smell quickly permeated throughout the stuffy closed hall, and soon the entire group of boys were gagging.

'My God, boy, you smell really terrible! Get those doors open so we can breathe again,' gasped Miss Smart.

A stampede towards both sets of doors ensued. Doors were flung open and boys, dramatically gagging, poured out into the school quadrangle. Miss Smart, rapidly losing control of her music class, tried in vain to get the boys back into the hall. The ruckus, caused by what started as a cover up for a fart, attracted the attention of the Headmaster, Mr. van Vuuren, a giant of a man, whose office was directly opposite the hall.

'Miss Smart, what in heaven's name is going on here?' bellowed van Vuuren.

'Sorry Headmaster, we have had a slight incident,' said Miss Smart, who went on to explain what had happened.

The Headmaster, barely able to suppress a smile, 'Wilson, you say, where is this boy? Send him to my office immediately. I will take care of this. The rest of you boys get back into the hall. Wilson, you wait outside of my office until I call for you,' said van Vuuren and turning on is heel, he headed off towards his office.

Jimmy stood nervously outside the Headmaster's office from where he could see through the still open doors of the hall. Trying to look anywhere but the hall, Jimmy spent the next twenty minutes in a state of near panic, awaiting his fate.

'Wilson, get yourself in here,' a loud voice boomed.

Jimmy, expecting the worst, opened the door and slowly entered the office.

'Do you have a wristwatch, boy?' demanded van Vuuren, not bothering to look up from the papers on he was working on.

'Yes, Sir,' stammered Jimmy, not knowing what to expect next.

'Take this timetable and that bell over there,' said van Vuuren pointing to a brass handheld bell, 'you will go up to the second floor and ring the bell at the times indicated. You will start at the south end and ring the bell continuously the length of both buildings. This will be used to indicate the change of lesson periods. You will tell your subject teachers of this chore and ensure that you are in place to start ringing the bell on time. This is your job for the duration of your stay at this school. Don't let me see you here again, dismissed.'

Taking the bell, a relieved Jimmy hurried out of the Headmaster's office, made his way up to the second floor and undertook his first ever ringing of the bell to indicate the end of mid-morning lessons and the start of the first break of the day.

Returning to his classroom to put the bell away, Jimmy waited for his pals. Ian, Gus and Peter were the first into the classroom and immediately grilled Jimmy.

'What happened, did you get the cane?' asked Gus.

'Jesus, you really stank the place out.' gasped Ian.

'Miss Smart was really pissed at you. I think she'll be gunning for you now,' said Peter.

'Shit, next to you the whaling station smells good.' remarked Gus.

Jimmy, from being an unknown twelve-year-old standard six boy that morning, was suddenly a celebrity. Everyone wanted to meet the kid whose fart was so bad that they had to clear the school hall. Peter, Ian and Gus bathed in the reflected glory. Jimmy was just grateful to have escaped without being caned. This was the start of a lifelong friendship and for the rest of their school days the four were always spoken of in the same breath.

Jimmy told his pals of his new duty and they immediately realised the potential of this new job. Jimmy had in his power, the ability to change lessons to suit himself. The lessons they disliked such as Afrikaans and Latin, could start a minute or two late and end a few minutes early. Lessons such as Art and Physical Training could be extended a few minutes. The power of the bell in the hands of a standard six pupil, this would have to be used carefully.

The choir selection over signalled the start of normal lessons for the standard six pupils. Being a new school with limited resources, the subject choice was rather limited. Examination subjects would be English, Afrikaans, Latin, History, Arithmetic, Geography, Science and Mathematics. Non examination subjects included Art, Music, Woodwork, Metalwork and Physical Training.

Ian, Gus and Peter had been brought up from junior school with Afrikaans, but Jimmy, having been schooled in Rhodesia, had absolutely no knowledge of this language and hence would have to suffer from this throughout his high school career. Due to a higher level of education, based on the United Kingdom curriculum, Jimmy did however have a higher level than the others in all the other subjects.

Jimmy's first run-in with Afrikaans came in his very first lesson. The Afrikaans teacher was a Mister Heunis, commonly called Kees behind his back, due to his perceived likeness to the cartoon character 'Kees the Bobbejaan' (baboon). Jimmy sat in the third desk at the extreme right of the classroom, alongside the windows that looked out over the sports fields. Jimmy, not having a clue about what was going on in the classroom, had let his attention wander and stared thoughtlessly out of the window. A short silence and then a loud guttural shout brought Jimmy back to his senses.

Kees, red faced with the veins in his neck almost popping, was staring at the boy to the right of Jimmy and shouting at the top of his voice.

'I'm glad it's not me he's shouting at,' thought Jimmy, *'but why are all the guys staring at me.'*

Kees continued to rant on and the rest of the boys continued to look at Jimmy, who in turn continued to look blankly at Kees.

'Wilson, he's talking to you,' whispered Dave Drew, the boy to Jimmy's right, who was supposedly the unfortunate that Kees was berating.

Kees, unable to contain himself any longer, strode down between the rows of desks and grabbed Jimmy by the tie and dragged him to his feet.

Jimmy, now terrified and confused, muttered, 'Sorry Sir, but I didn't know you were talking to me because you were looking at Drew.'

This was the last straw for Kees, still looking to the right of Jimmy and still holding him by the throat, struck him across the face with his open hand. *'Jy praat nie Engles in my klas nie. Uit!'* (You do not speak English in my class, out!), he shrieked, pushing Jimmy towards the classroom door.

Jimmy, confused, with a rapidly reddening hand imprint on his cheek, staggered towards the door; he would spend the rest of the lesson banished from the classroom. The twenty-five odd minutes remaining in the lesson dragged by slowly, with Jimmy trying to look as inconspicuous as possible, standing alone in the corridor, hoping that no one of authority would see him.

As the minutes dragged by, Jimmy realised with horror that the period was nearly up and he would have to go back into the classroom to fetch the bell and to ring it for the change of lesson. Remembering the Headmasters instruction, that he should always ring the bell on time, Jimmy took a deep breath, opened the door and entered.

Kees, still highly agitated, turned when he heard the door opening and seeing Jimmy standing in the doorway, went hysterical.

'Please Sir, I have to ring the bell,' pleaded Jimmy.

Kees reached Jimmy in two steps and screaming at him in Afrikaans, grabbed him by the shirt, tearing his pocket, hurled him out of the classroom and slammed the door after him. Jimmy, once again, found himself alone in the corridor.

The minutes dragged by, five minutes past the time for change of period. Standard 6C was the middle classroom on the second floor and was directly over the Headmaster's office with one floor between. At eight minutes past the time for changeover, Jimmy heard a door open on the ground floor. Peering over the balcony he saw the Headmaster stride into the quadrangle looking at his watch. Jimmy jumped back from the railing and pressed himself against the classroom wall, wishing that the wall would open and swallow him up.

Inevitably, the Headmaster appeared at the top of the stairs still looking at his watch.

'You boy! What are you doing standing there? You are nine minutes late, why haven't you rung the bell yet?' bellowed van Vuuren.

'Sir, I was sent out of the class by Mr. Heunis and he won't let me back in to get the bell.' stammered Jimmy.

'Don't be ridiculous boy, get back in there and do your duty.'

'Please, Sir.'

'In!' roared the Headmaster.

Jimmy, realising at this precise moment that Kees would be the lesser of two evils, turned and opened the classroom door. Kees, rising to once again handle this affront to his authority, was stopped in his tracks by the sight of the Headmaster in the doorway... Jimmy took this opportunity to grab the bell and dash out of the classroom. The last words he heard from the Headmaster were, 'Heunis, see me in my office during your next free period.'

Jimmy, his duty complete, returned to his classroom, the handprint on his cheek and the torn shirt pocket visible signs of his ordeal at the hands of Kees.

'Are you fucking crazy, winding up Kees like that?' said Gus. 'He'll have it in for you now, for sure.'

'I didn't know he was talking to me; I had no clue what he was on about, and anyway, he was looking at Drew.'

'He's squint, you dickhead, and that's what pissed him off even more than you talking English in his class. His wife used to teach us at Fynnlands, and we all knew that Kees hated anything English. You're fucked now,' said Peter.

By the time the break had come around, Jimmy's cheek had started turning blue and the hand imprint was still clearly visible. Unbeknownst to the class, Kees had been severely reprimanded by the Headmaster for striking a pupil. He was told that if he ever again struck any pupil, he would be suspended without pay and a charge of assault would be laid against him. Any physical disciplining of pupils would be done either by the Headmaster or Deputy-Headmaster and no one else. Bullying of pupils would not be tolerated. Jimmy had made, through no fault of his own, a bitter enemy who would at every opportunity, attempt to humiliate him and make his life a misery.

During the first few weeks of the new school year, it became abundantly clear to most of the standard 6C subject teachers, that four of their pupils were academically far above the rest of the class. The pace of learning had to be geared to the class average, with the result that Jimmy, Gus, Ian and Peter often found themselves bored.

The obvious solution would have been to promote the boys to a higher class 6B or 6A, but because the classes had been set and all were full, this was not done. Although the boys were held back by the pace of the class, they found the necessary stimulation in competing with each other. Jimmy had been informed, that as he had no previous Afrikaans, he would be granted a two-year exemption from having to pass the subject. Needless to say, this infuriated his nemesis, Kees, even further.

Away from school, the boys hung out together at every opportunity. Jimmy and Ian lived about two hundred yards from each other in the same street. Gus lived a short bicycle ride away near Anstey's beach. Peter lived in Lighthouse Road, about a mile away from the school and about the same distance from Ian's house.

The normal course of events was, first stop Peter's, where his mother, Val, always welcomed them with a glass of juice and a kind word. Jimmy, Gus and Ian all adored Peter's mother and never missed out on this stop. Depending on the season, it was cricket bats or soccer balls and next the stop was the park near Fynnlands School. Jimmy and Ian would make the short dash up the road to get changed, grab their gear and back to the park. Gus, who had a bit further to go and an aunt who always questioned his whereabouts, was always last to arrive back at the park.

Many a stirring match of 'Test Cricket' or two aside football was played out. Sides were always picked anew each time, except if a previous contest was unfinished. Success was virtually guaranteed if Peter was in your side. In cricket, he could bat forever and when his turn to field, would bowl you out with ease. With a football he was unstoppable; he could out-dribble the other three and could kick equally well with both feet. A more even contest would have been Peter versus the other three.

Feb 9, 1963
Joshua Nkomo arrested in Rhodesia under emergency regulations

Organised school sports started in the third week of school and being summer, the only choices were cricket and swimming. Being a new school, Grosvenor Boy's High had no swimming pool and had to use the pool facilities at Bushlands Junior. Cricket, on the other hand, was held on the school playing fields but on a matting wicket as opposed to grass.

Peter's cricketing talent was easily spotted, and he was immediately placed in the under thirteen A side where he was made captain, opening the batting and the bowling. Ian joined him in the A side and Jimmy and Gus made up the numbers in the B side. Jimmy and Ian were both selected for the school swimming team.

Life settled into a predictable routine; school eight to two Mondays to Fridays, school sport on Monday and Wednesday after school, a cricket match against some other emerging school on Saturday mornings, and the occasional swimming gala during the week. When not otherwise occupied, afternoons were spent at the park. Sundays, weather permitting, were often spent at Brighton Beach, a mile or so up the road from Gus's house. They were not allowed to swim at Anstey's Beach, as it wasn't protected by shark nets or lifeguards.

Brighton Beach consisted of a freshwater paddling pool, walled off from the beach and mostly frequented by mothers and very young children, and a sea water tidal swimming pool, that at high tide was often swamped by the incoming waves. There was a cafe, run by a Greek, serving cold drinks, ice creams, milk shakes, and a variety of hot dogs, ham burgers and toasted sandwiches. A funicular railway ran from just behind the cafe, up the hill to the top of Marine Drive, about three hundred feet up. The beach ran steeply down from the road to the water's edge and was at no time more than a hundred yards of sand. A lifesavers' duty hut was manned by the Dolphins Surf Lifesaving Club, who would test the currents daily and select and demarcate the swimming area with beacons.

Depending on the prevailing tides, the swimming area at Brighton Beach consisted of either an immediate plunge from the shore to a sand bank that extended sometimes thirty or forty yards into the sea. The currents and undertow were unpredictable, often rather dangerous and was generally not a good place to swim for inexperienced swimmers.

The Dolphins Lifesavers had a full-time job on their hands, rescuing swimmers in difficulty and as such, had little patience with those who disobeyed the rules of where to swim. Once past the crashing shore break, it was a reasonably easy swim out to the second break, about fifty yards offshore. The 'backies,' as they were known, was where most of the youth spent their time on surfboards, belly boards or just body surfing.

Body surfing was one of the few sporting activities where Jimmy, Gus and Ian excelled in ahead of Peter. As none of the boys had the luxury of a surfboard or belly board, body surfing was all they could do. When not in the surf, they would kick a football around on the beach or stare longingly at those lucky enough to own a surfboard. Peter, not used to playing second fiddle to anyone, would always be the first to suggest a game of beach football, where once again he would be the 'main man.'

June 1, 1963
Alabama Governor George Wallace vows to defy court order to open universities to Negroes.

As the first term at school drew to a close, the boys looked forward to the school holidays, three whole weeks of no school. The weather had turned cooler and less and less time was spent on the beach. Cricket gave way to soccer. Most of the white high schools in Natal played rugby and not soccer. Only Gus had any previous exposure to playing rugby from his 'farm school' days. All four decided that if they were to play soccer, they would have to join a club, the obvious choice being Fynnlands Sports Club, which was adjacent to the park. The club ran teams in the under 14, 16 & 19 age groups as well as three open teams.

Fynnlands Sports Club consisted of a single building that housed one set of change rooms, with showers, a hall seventy-five feet by thirty-five feet, a small kiosk and toilet facilities for both males and females. There was only one sports field that was used for cricket in summer and football in winter. The weak floodlights were used for evening training only, as they were not strong enough for match conditions.

The four boys were accepted with open arms at Fynnlands Sports Club; they were registered as members of the club and affiliated to the football section. Birth certificates were produced, and they were now available for the under 14 section for the next two years. Practice would be on Tuesdays and Thursdays from five to six in the evenings. Matches were only played on Saturday afternoons.

The coach of the under 14's was a genial man in his late forties who had never married, affectionately known to all as 'Pop' Churches. Pop's daytime job was teaching Science at Grosvenor Boy's, so he was well known to all of the boys.

The first training session saw twenty-eight boys, of which nineteen were in the group of already turned fourteen, and the remaining nine were twelve-and-thirteen year olds. It was obvious that, as there were only two teams, at least six boys a week were going to be disappointed. Eleven boys would be selected for each team. The two reserves would only play if someone dropped out before the game, as substitutes were not allowed. It broke Pop's heart each week when he announced the two teams and four young boys realised they wouldn't be playing a game that week. At least the two reserves had some hopes that someone would drop out.

Peter's talent at football was clearly obvious to Pop, who immediately put him in the 'A' side. Pop knew that once one of the bigger clubs saw this boy play, it would be impossible to hold on to him at Fynnlands. Ian also found himself in the 'A' side and while not as naturally talented as Peter, he made up for it in sheer determination. Jimmy and Gus made the 'B' side most weeks.

Pop Churches had an old Ford truck that he had converted into a van, which he used for transporting his boys to away games. Painted bright blue on the outside, the inside had been converted into padded bench seats. A small curtained window on each side provided ventilation and a ceiling light the illumination.

Two framed pictures adorned the walls. One of a young girl, photographed from the back, staring out to sea, it looked like she could have been naked but it was impossible to be sure. The other was very obviously naked and had been taken from the side, her breasts there for all to see. The poor girl was always the butt of many crude remarks. What the boys didn't know was the lady in question was the reason Pop was still a bachelor; she had died a few weeks before they were due to be married.

The first game of the season was away to a club called Ramblers, the games to be played at the Kingsmead football complex, located on the north side of Durban. Peter and Ian had made the 'A' side and Jimmy and Gus the 'B' side. The kit was piled onto the roof rack of the Ford and with three boys up front with Pop and twenty-one crammed in the back, they set off for the match.

Many of the boys had never played a competitive club football match before and the excitement was almost overwhelming. Fynnlands had never been much of a football power and were not expected to provide too much competition to Ramblers.

The 'B' side played the first game and were soundly beaten by the more skilful, and seemingly bigger and stronger, Ramblers boys. The 'A' team, watching from the side-lines, feared that their chances in the next game would not be much better. The only unconcerned person at the grounds seemed to be Peter.

Kingsmead football complex consisted of fourteen pitches, two abreast, stretching from just outside the main stadium for some eight hundred yards. Often scouts and coaches for the bigger clubs could be found watching these eagerly contested games. It was on just such an occasion that a coach for one of Durban's biggest clubs happened to be on the touchline for the game between the Fynnlands and Ramblers Under 14A teams.

The second game was a thrilling affair, with the Ramblers team winning by a score of four goals to three. The Fynnlands team were kept in the hunt by Peter's sheer brilliance, with him scoring all three of his side's goals. The rest of the side tried their best, but apart from

Ian's determination and ball winning skills, they were outclassed by a fitter and stronger Ramblers team.

The final whistle saw the Fynnlands team celebrate as though they had won the game, a four to three loss was the best result they had had against Ramblers in years. The only exception was Peter, who was visibly annoyed at being on the losing side. As the boys made their way back to the Ford, Pop's fears over Peter were realised.

The youth coach of Durban City, the most popular supported and glamorous professional club in the city, approached Peter who was slowly walking back with Ian.

'Good game, son. What's your name?' the question was directed at Peter.

'Thank you, sir. It's Murphy,' replied Peter.

'That was a pretty good game you had as well,' he said, indicating to Ian. 'Your ball winning skills help to set up a lot for your mate here. My name is Dan de Klerk, I coach the youngsters at City, I would like you two to come over and have a trial at the club.'

'That would be great,' enthused Peter.

'I thought the clubs were not allowed to approach other club's players directly,' said Ian.

'Here's my phone number. Get your parents to give me a ring and I'll fix up the trial,' said de Klerk, ignoring Ian's protests.

Peter and Ian made their way back to the rest of the team, to whom the exchange had not gone unnoticed.

'Who was that guy?' asked Jimmy.

'Only Dan de Klerk, City youth coach. He wants Ian and me to go for a trial,' said Peter, brandishing de Klerk's card.

Pop Churches, knowing the approach was illegal and that he should lodge an appeal, upon seeing the excitement on Peter's face, didn't have the heart to stop the boy from joining a bigger and better club. He hoped that Ian wouldn't be too disappointed if he didn't make it, as he had no doubts that Peter would.

The two boys had totally different reactions to the news they passed on to their respective families. Both Peter's parents agreed immediately and gave their permission, as long as it didn't interfere with his schoolwork and extra mural activities. Ian's mother refused at first, saying there was no chance of his being allowed to travel right across Durban twice a week for training, as there was no spare money for the bus fare.

Sunday morning the boys met at the park as usual. The topic of conversation was naturally yesterday's matches and Peter's and Ian's upcoming trial. Ian expressed his doubts over whether his mother would allow him to go, citing the bus fare as a problem.

'Don't worry, my Mom will take us through,' said Peter.

'Ok, I'll tell my Mom and maybe she'll agree.'

The trial for Peter and Ian was set up for the following Tuesday afternoon, as it was still school holidays. The two trialists, plus Jimmy and Gus, were transported across Durban to the City training grounds at Kingsmead Stadium. Val Murphy dropped the boys off after arranging to pick them up again later that afternoon at four thirty.

None of the boys had ever been into the Stadium before. The ground, owned by the City of Durban, was the home ground of the glamour club of the National Football League, the blue and white hooped Durban City. The stadium had originally been built to accommodate both football and cricket, although the latter had yet to be played at the ground.

Running down the length of the field, facing the ocean, was the main stand which seated around ten thousand spectators. At the north and south ends of the ground, behind each goal, rose two large concrete stands some thirty or so yards back from the goal line. The north stand was reserved for the black spectators and the south and main stands for whites only.

The non-white spectators were made up almost totally of Indians. At a big match as many as fifteen thousand out of thirty would be crammed into a quarter of the ground. This support was always present, even though no non-white players were allowed in any of the teams, from the juniors right through to the seniors.

The main match of the day would always be preceded by one or more curtain raisers, usually the reserve teams and before that, the youth teams. Anyone playing for the junior teams of Durban City, Durban United and Addington (the other Durban professional teams), was certain of a great deal of exposure to the fans. The best supported, with the biggest Indian following, was Durban City. Although the curtain raisers started up to two hours before the main game, the crowd was often in the thousands for the junior games.

With Jimmy and Gus finding seats in the main stand, an excited Peter and a nervous Ian went off to report to Dan de Klerk. De Klerk placed Peter and Ian in the same side. He had given instructions to a few of his players to give special attention to his two trialists, as he wanted to see how they would stand up to a bit of intimidation.

The first half of the trial saw both boys taking a lot of hard tackles and plenty of niggling. Ian showed absolutely no reaction to any of it and played his normal game. Peter, after a lot of initial reaction, realising he would get no sympathy, simply got on with his game. Ian completely tied up his opposite number and Peter gave his opposition a torrid time. De Klerk decided to stop the game and switch Peter and have him in direct opposition to Ian.

The remainder of the game saw Peter slightly more subdued, as Ian did a far better marking job on him than the previous boy. De Klerk realised that in Peter he had something special but also saw Ian's potential, whose calmness and composure marked him out as a player for the future.

The trial ended with De Klerk telling Peter and Ian that he would make up his mind in the next day or so and would then contact them with the decision. He thanked them for their time and effort.

'You guys are in. No doubt about it,' said Gus.

'You made that big central defender you played against in the first half, look really crap,' said Jimmy, 'I don't think you're too popular there.'

The conversation went back and forth about the way Peter had played. The other three, Ian included, agreed that Peter was a definite. Ian, said Peter, had played a lot better than his opposite number, and de Klerk would be crazy if he didn't offer him a place. Never one to hide his modesty, Peter had already started talking about 'when he plays for City'. Fynnlands under 14 was the furthest thing from his mind. Pop Churches had already resigned himself to losing two of his brightest prospects.

The following Tuesday afternoon, the telephone rang at the Williams household. De Klerk offered Ian a chance to join Durban City, the club would pay his registration and affiliation fees but he would have to get a signed clearance from Fynnlands Sports Club. Ian would have to attend training twice a week at Kingsmead and obviously travel to all matches. The club would supply the team jersey. Ian would have to buy the shorts and the socks himself. De Klerk looked forward to seeing him at practice on Thursday. Ian knew deep down that his mother didn't have the spare money for him to travel back and forth across Durban three times a week.

Twenty minutes later the telephone rang again.

'Hey, Ian, guess what? De Klerk phoned me and he wants me to join City. I wonder if he'll phone you.' shouted an excited Peter.

'Oh, he's already phoned me and asked me to join,' said Ian, in a disconsolate voice.

'He must have phoned you first as I've just put the phone down. You don't sound too happy about it.'

'I don't think my Mom will allow me to join, but I'll ask her when she gets home.'

'Get Gus and Jimmy and we'll meet at the park; I have to get Pop to sign a clearance anyway.'

'So, you're joining then?'

'Hell yes, see you at the park.'

It came as no surprise to Pop Churches that the first thing Peter asked for at practice that day, was for a clearance so he could join Durban City.

'What about you then, Ian? Surely, they want you as well?' asked Pop.

'Yes, they do but I'm not so sure that I want to join them,' replied Ian, hiding the fact that it was very likely his mother wouldn't allow him to join.

'For heaven's sake, why not? It's a great opportunity for both of you.'

'I'd rather stay here with my mates,' said Ian, glancing unfairly across at Peter.

'Well, I think Peter is doing the right thing. He'll get far better coaching at City than I could ever hope to give him. Dan de Klerk will make him a much better player at City. You should rethink.'

'I will,' said Ian sullenly.

After practice, Peter left training at Fynnlands for the final time and Ian rushed home to tell his mother about joining Durban City, still hopeful that she would allow him to.

'No, I afraid you can't. I have already had to fork out for your Fynnlands kit, and I don't have the money for another set. You know since your dad died last year, money has been very tight, I'm sorry but it would be impossible,' said Betty Williams firmly.

'But, Ma…'

'No buts, my boy, this discussion is over.'

Ian turned and ran out of the room. Just because some stupid black bastard had caused his father's death, he would have to suffer as well.

'I fucking hate blacks,' thought Ian as he ran out of the yard. Ian walked down to Jimmy's house, where he told him the news. Jimmy was secretly pleased that Ian would stay at Fynnlands, as he was good for the team.

Peter subsequently joined Durban City, where in the next few seasons he made a real hit with the fans. Being a little shorter and stockier than the other boys in the team, he acquired the nickname of 'Chubby,' given to him by the large Indian following. The name stuck with him through the rest of his life, even though he grew a lot taller and thinner from his fifteenth year onwards.

While Peter was undoubtedly the star at City, where he scored a load of goals, whenever his team played Fynnlands, he found himself played out of the game by Ian. In their first year of under fourteen football, both Peter and Ian found themselves selected for the Durban and District representative side. Ian, being the first ever player from Fynnlands given this honour.

The holidays over, it was back to school and rugby for the boys. Rugby was compulsory for all boys, unless excused for medical reasons. Van Vuuren had been a promising provincial level rugby player in his days at Stellenbosch University, until a badly broken leg put paid to his career. He was determined that his school would become a strong and respected rugby force, while he was headmaster. Traditionally, the English-speaking schools only started playing rugby from standard six, whereas the Afrikaans schools started as early as standard one. There were five years to catch up.

July 12, 1963
Security Police arrest ex African National Congress leader,
Walter Sisulu.

Gus, having played some rugby in Ixopo, was an obvious choice for the under thirteen 'A' side. Peter, or Chubby as everyone now called him, took to the game like a duck to water. With Gus playing as scrum half and Chubby in the glamour position of fly half, Grosvenor would have an unusually capable side. Ian found himself in the 'B' side and Jimmy in the 'C' side.

To his dismay, Jimmy found the coach of the 'C' team was his most hated enemy, Kees Heunis. Although Kees had never struck Jimmy again after that first time, the animosity was still there. If he couldn't touch him in class, he could quite legally work him over on the rugby training field. Jimmy hated rugby and tried his best to be dropped from the team but Kees continued to select him, giving him no way out.

Grosvenor's biggest and most hated rival at all school sports was Dirkie Uys Hoërskool, the local Afrikaans High School. Dirkie Uys was situated three miles from Grosvenor and overlooked Salisbury Island and the Durban harbour. The rivalry had started when Grosvenor High catered for both girls and boys, as did Dirkie Uys currently. The natural rivalry of the two high schools was increased by the social English versus Afrikaans differences.

The annual clash of the rugby sides was always marked down as something special. It became known by both schools as the Boer War for obvious reasons.

Attendance by all pupils was compulsory, without exception. The main rugby field hosted first the under 13A teams, followed by under 14A, under 15A, open seconds and then the first teams. The various other age group teams would play on the lesser fields. Traditionally, the Afrikaans schools dominated the age group games, whereas with the open teams, the English schools gave a far better account of themselves.

The first game of the morning on the main field at Grosvenor High that warm June afternoon, would be between the Under 13A sides. The match would be refereed by one of the Dirkie Uys masters and like all schoolboy games, there was to be a certain bias towards his own school. Grosvenor had never beaten Dirkie Uys at under 13 level in the eight-year history of games between these two schools.

Proof of age was often overlooked at many of the Afrikaans speaking schools and this group were no exception. Many of the much bigger Afrikaner boys looked way over the legal age for under 13 rugby, but as was the norm, no protests were made. Grosvenor, led by their captain and fly-half, Chubby Murphy, took to the field to face their much bigger and more experienced opponents.

Rugby at under 13 level comprised mainly of a lot of young boys chasing a rugby ball around, with not much tactics involved. The much bigger Dirkie Uys boys, with their huge size and weight advantage, dominated the scrums and line outs. The back lines of both sides, where size and strength count for less, were more even. Fierce tackling and sheer determination by the Grosvenor boys, kept the game scoreless at half time.

An early try by the Dirkie Uys team in the second half gave them a three point to nil lead, as the conversion was missed. A bad decision by the referee disallowed a try by the Grosvenor team and it looked like the game would end in a narrow victory to the visitors. A penalty, which even a biased referee couldn't fail to award, was given to the Grosvenor side just on the halfway line, too far away for a thirteen-year old to convert. Much to the amusement of the watching spectators, Chubby indicated to the referee he would try for the conversion. Making a small mound with sand, he perched the rugby ball in an upright position on top of it. Taking three steps back and then two to his left, he paused and looked up at the posts. What was he doing? Everyone knew that a conversion should be taken by stepping back in a direct line to the goalposts and kicking the ball with the toe of your boot. With derisive booing ringing in his ears, Chubby ran forward at an angle and with the instep of his right boot sent the ball sailing all of fifty yards straight through the goalposts. A stunned silence, then a huge cheer from the home supporters. Three all.

The remainder of the second half continued much as the first. With two minutes left and the game seemingly on its way to a valiant draw, Grosvenor were awarded a scrum some thirty-five yards out from their opponents try line. Chubby, giving Gus a sly signal, took up the unusual position of standing directly behind the scrum instead of to one side. Gus fed the ball into the scrum, ran around to the back of it, picked up the ball and flung it out to Chubby. Catching the ball, he took one step forward and drop kicked the ball over the goalposts, to give his side a six points to three lead.

The remaining minutes of the game were spent bravely defending their lead. The referee played an extra four minutes in vain, to try to allow his side to score. Eventually, even he had to blow the final whistle. A Grosvenor under 13 rugby side had beaten their fiercest rivals for the first time in their history. The team left the field as heroes, none more so than Chubby, who had translated his natural ability to kick a football to scoring points with a rugby ball.

Grosvenor lost all other matches, except for the third fifteen who managed a narrow win fifteen points to twelve. The first fifteen lost to their counterparts by a similar score-line. The under 13 A's were, however, the talking point of the day. Chubby was questioned at length about his 'round the corner' kicking style. No one had ever seen anything like it on a rugby field before.

On the following Monday morning at school assembly, the headmaster called the victorious Under 13 A rugby team to come forward, where he personally shook each boys' hand in turn. To resounding applause, the boys returned to their seats, Chubby, with the instruction to report to van Vuuren's office at the end of assembly.

Assembly over, the hall emptied with boys returning to their classrooms for the day's lessons. Chubby, on the other hand, reported to the headmaster's office. Knocking on the door, he waited.

'Come in,' shouted van Vuuren.

'Ah! It's you, Chubby,' said the headmaster, using Chubby's already well-known nick-name. 'Come over here, lad, I want to talk to you about that amazing display of yours on Saturday. I have never in all my years seen anyone kick a rugby ball in that way before. Tell me, why did you choose to kick like that?'

'I don't know, sir. I've always kicked a soccer ball that way and it seemed the best way to kick a rugby ball as well.'

Visibly blanching at the mention of soccer, van Vuuren replied, 'Well, what I would like you to do is report to Mr. Venter, the first team coach, after school and we'll see if you can pass this skill of yours onto some of the older boys. Well done again, it's a real feather in our cap to put one over on those Dirkie Uys boys.'

Chubby returned to his class and much to the annoyance of his mates, refused to say what had transpired in the Headmaster's office. All their questions were met with the answer, 'I'll tell you at break.'

Jimmy managed to get the bell rung a few minutes early and the boys eagerly trooped after Chubby and headed for the playground.

'Well, what happened?' asked Gus.

'He only wants me to teach the first team okes (guys) how to kick,' bragged Chubby, getting the complete wrong end of what van Vuuren meant.

'Talk shit!' said Jimmy.

'No, it's dinkum. I have to go after school today and see Venter, you okes can come along and see for yourselves,' said Chubby, with a self-satisfied grin on his face.

The lessons after the end of the break passed without too much fuss, other than Chubby hardly able to contain himself until the end of the school day. Word had got around that some little standard six snot nose was going to give the first, second and third teams kicking lessons. With the result, around a hundred boys of varying ages stayed after school and congregated on the grass banks behind the Physical Training room, where Mr. Venter spent his days. The members of the open rugby teams had been instructed to report for extra training after Saturday's performance.

'Right, boys,' said Venter to the forty-nine who made up the numbers of the first, second and third rugby teams. 'No doubt, most of you witnessed the under 13A rugby side put one over on Dirkie Uys on Saturday. At least they and the thirds won a game, the rest of you lost. The reason both the firsts and second's lost was your inability to convert the tries scored and penalties awarded. I want all of you who think you can kick a rugby ball over there (pointing to the main rugby field), the rest of you, so as not to feel left out, can do a few laps of the B-field.'

Naturally, none of the boys fancied running laps so the entire squad moved to the main field. Forty-nine potential match winning kickers. Venter, realising that this could take forever, decided to select his potential kickers without going through the entire forty-nine boys.

'Hold it, you lot. All the forwards, to the B-field. I want the three full backs and the three fly-halves to the main field and the rest of the backs can join your forward buddies and head for the B-field.'

All but the six selected boys, grudgingly trooped off for their laps. The remaining six, who ranged in age from sixteen to eighteen, made their way with Venter and thirteen-year old Chubby, to the main rugby field.

Taking the boys to about thirty yards directly in front of the goalposts, Venter stopped and said, 'Chubby, I want you to show this lot just how you take these kicks at goal.'

'Yes, sir,' replied Chubby, bending down and making a small mound of grass and sand and using his index finger, flattened the top. 'You place the ball in an upright position, pointing slightly in the direction of the goals.'

Making sure the ball was set to his requirements, he then stepped directly back three steps, pausing he then took two steps to his left and now addressed the ball at approximately forty-five degrees. Glancing up at the goalposts and taking a deep breath, he ran in towards the ball and striking it with the instep of his right foot, sent it sailing through the posts. A huge cheer went up from the watching boys and Chubby, never one to let an occasion slip by, turned and dramatically bowed.

'Chubby!' shouted Venter. 'This is not a bloody circus. You boys watching, any more disturbances from you and I chase the lot of you away. Ok, show us again.'

Chubby repeated the kick with exactly the same results. Venter moved the ball twenty yards to the right, the same results. Taking the ball to the far right touchline, he was sure Chubby would miss. Using the same routine, Chubby confidently struck the ball through the uprights. Ten kicks in a row from various distances and angles were dispatched with the same ease.

'Right, you've seen how it's done, your turn,' said Venter, throwing the ball to the closest of the six boys, who had been watching in fascination.

Under Chubby's instruction, the fly-half of the first fifteen placed the ball and stepped back. Running in and with a kicking style totally unfamiliar to him, scuffed the ball which flew end over end some fifteen yards, nowhere near the goal-posts. Angrily, he turned around and glared at Chubby.

'Try it again,' ordered Venter.

It took eight attempts before the ball reached its intended target. The next missed from slightly further out but the following one sailed through the posts, as did the next.

The rest of the boys all attempted this new kicking style, with varied success. Out of the six who tried, only the first fifteen fly-half and the full-back of the second fifteen had any reasonable success. After nearly an hour of kicking, Venter called the practice to a halt, instructing the boys to return for a further dose the following afternoon. He was determined that his rugby teams would not lose any more games because they were unable to convert kicks into points on the board. Chubby, who was now bored with the whole exercise, saw no reason to attend the next kicking practice and with the result, never bothered to turn up.

Venter and his senior rugby players dutifully waited for the appearance of their kicking coach and after an hour of idly sitting around, realised that Chubby was not coming. Venter was furious and undertook the kicking practice himself, but with limited success. He was determined that Chubby would be severely punished and would not play rugby for any of his teams until that punishment was served.

The following day Chubby was called into Venter's office and after a good bawling out, was informed that he would not be allowed to play rugby again that school term. Showing little concern, Chubby shrugged his shoulders and left the office.

The following Saturday, the Under 13A rugby team, minus Chubby, was soundly beaten by their Northlands High School equivalent. At assembly on the following Monday, a disappointed headmaster read out the weekend's result. He had not attended the weekend games and was unaware of the situation concerning Chubby. His comment, 'Better luck next time to Chubby and his boys,' was met by muffled laughter.

Later that day, when van Vuuren had his meeting with the sports master, he discovered that Chubby had been banned from rugby for the remainder of the term. On hearing the reasons for the banning, van Vuuren immediately overruled Venter and demanded Chubby's re-instatement. Despite Venter's protests about discipline, punctuality and rules, he was overruled and Chubby was re-instated. This was to be the pattern during Chubby's time at high school; he was untouchable as far as school sport went and knowing this, he made the most of it. Van Vuuren was vindicated, as far he was concerned, by the continued success of the Under 13A rugby team.

August 29, 1963
Martin Luther King gives his 'I have a dream speech.'

Most afternoons after school, when there was no football or rugby practice, the boys would meet at the Fynnlands Club and have a kick about amongst themselves. With just the four of them, it was becoming a bit monotonous and they decided that they needed to recruit a few more players.

Jimmy had noticed that each time they played, there were six or seven Indian and three black kids, who would sit on the side lines and watch them longingly. One afternoon, after the other three had left, he went over to the group and asked where they lived.

One of the Indian boys, Cyril Pillay, told him that they all lived on the Bluff down near Salisbury Island, which was a white area but as his mother ran a shop there, nobody seemed to bother them. The three black kids were children of his mother's shop assistant, who also lived on the premises. Jimmy asked the boys if they wanted to come around tomorrow and have a game with him and his mates. They readily agreed.

The following afternoon Jimmy, Gus and Peter arrived at the field to be greeted by Cyril Pillay and a mixed bag seven other Indian and black kids. Jimmy explained to Gus and Peter that he had fixed up some new opposition for them.

'Great, we'll wait for Ian and then we can take on the lot of them,' said Peter ready for a new challenge, 'It can be the blacks against the whites. Bet we stuff them out of sight, even with four against eight.'

'We'll have to play barefoot as none of them have boots,' suggested Jimmy. 'Hey, there's Ian now.'

'Who the fuck are this lot?' said Ian angrily. 'Don't think for one minute I'm playing soccer with a bunch of coolies and Kaffirs.'

'Don't be such a prick. It's only a game, get your boots off and come and help us beat these guys,' ordered Chubby.

'No chance. If I play, I'm playing in boots, tough shit if they haven't got any, it's not my problem.'

Ian, the only one wearing football boots, reluctantly joined his mates in what was to the first of many games between the two lots of boys. The white boys, bigger and physically stronger, were too much for the others, despite their numeric advantage. Apart from Ian, the game was played in good spirits, race and colour forgotten in the heat of competition.

During the following weeks, the contest became a regular feature, at first white against black and then when boredom set in, they mixed the teams, two white boys on each side and the rest made up of black kids. Ian, despite being more relaxed in mixed company, still refused to play barefoot like the rest of them. It seemed that he tackled the opposing black kids just that bit harder than was necessary.

Sept 15, 1963

Four Negro girls killed and twenty-three others injured when a bomb is exploded during a church service in Birmingham, Alabama.

By the time summer set in, football and rugby gave way to cricket and although it was often far too hot to play, the weekly game with Cyril and his mates continued. During this time, Jimmy and Cyril became good friends. Jimmy would often accompany Cyril back to his house near Salisbury Island, where Cyril's mother welcomed him as she would any other friend of her son's. Despite the numerous invitations, Cyril refused to go home to Jimmy's house. The friendship blossomed, despite Ian's objections to him spending so much time with the coolies.

Nov 22, 1963

US president John Kennedy shot by an assassin in Dallas Texas.

As the end of their first year of high school approached, the boys were forced, by their respective parents, in Gus's case his aunt, to cut back on their social and sporting activities, and concentrate on the year end examinations. All four of them had done well at school and were assured to be promoted to standard seven the following year. It was only a question of who would finish top of the class. Jimmy, the brightest of the four, was also the laziest at studies and it wasn't long before he sloped off to Fynnland's field looking for Cyril and a game of football.

Despite the lack of study time, when the final results came out it was Jimmy first, slightly ahead of Gus and Peter, with Ian trailing in sixth position. Gus, slightly annoyed, vowed to himself that this would be the last time he was beaten into second place by Jimmy.

Dec 3,1963
Nelson Mandela treason trial begins.

School over until late January 1964 gave the boys nearly seven weeks of holidays, as none of their families had any plans to leave Durban for the holidays. Weather permitting, it was off to Brighton beach every day

CHAPTER 6
The Early days - 1964

January of 1964 proved to be one of the hottest on record for Durban. Most days were spent on Brighton Beach.

Chubby would cycle over to Ian's house, they in turn would meet up with Jimmy and the three of them would make the one mile walk to Anstey's beach, where they would meet Gus. A short walk later, they would be at Brighton Beach.

The ultimate dream was to own a surfboard and join that handful lucky enough to have one and ride the waves in from the outer break (backies). In the meantime, their only option was body surfing. Not as glamorous but still a lot of fun.

As thirteen-and-fourteen-year olds, their interests had not yet turned to girls. Jimmy and Ian were the better swimmers, with Chubby the weakest of the four. Chubby did, however, own the only pair of flippers (swim fins). This proved somewhat of an equaliser and it was decided that Gus and Jimmy could share the flippers. Ian was out of luck as his feet were too big. A plan was needed as it was very difficult to 'catch' a wave from the backies without flippers.

Ian had heard the Butcher's shop at Crossways would buy crayfish (lobster) tails for fifty cents a time. So, it was decided that diving for crayfish was a priority. Jimmy and Chubby both had a set of goggles and snorkels. Garvies Beach was known to be a good spot for diving.

Totally clueless to the legal requirements needed for diving for crayfish, the four of them headed for Garvies. Arriving around ten in the morning, they found a group of older boys just finishing up.

'You guys catch any "bugs" (the cool slang name for crayfish)?' Chubby asked.

'We weren't diving for bugs, just spearfishing. If you want bugs the best spot is way over there,' said the boy pointing north, towards the whaling station. 'But you need to be here by six in the morning or after six at night, otherwise you have no chance.'

Disappointed, the boys gathered their gear and agreed to meet six o'clock the next day. Nothing else to do but to make the slightly longer trek back to Brighton.

Next morning at five thirty, Ian and Jimmy arrived at Garvies. Not another soul in sight. Jimmy decided to have a go at diving for bugs. Having no idea where to find them or what do if he found one, he headed into the rocky area just offshore.

By the time Chubby arrived, Jimmy had been at it for over forty minutes, with not so much as even a sighting of a crayfish. Chubby donned his goggles, put on his flippers and headed for the sea. Jimmy passed Chubby on his way out and called for Ian to take over.

By the time Ian took to the water, Gus arrived. So, Jimmy and Gus sat on the sand with Jimmy bemoaning the fact that this looked like a lost cause and maybe a new plan was needed. Hardly were the words out of his mouth, when Chubby appeared, heading for the shore.

'Hey, guys, I've got one.' Jesus, thought Jimmy, he's hardly been in the water two minutes and he's caught one, lucky bastard.

Chubby flip-flopped up the beach, with what looked like a rather large crayfish.

'Okay, so what do we do with it?' inquired Chubby.

'Dig a hole in the sand, fill it with water and put the bug in it, simple,' said Gus. This was done but it was very soon obvious that it was not a good idea.

While the three of them were contemplating what to do next, Ian came walking out with a crayfish of his own. It was obvious that a hole in the sand with a bit of water wasn't going to work.

'What we need is a sack that we can put the bugs in and tie up to one of the rocks in the water over there,' said Gus.

'Okay Gus, good idea, why don't you and Jimmy go up to Crossways and get us a couple of sacks? The way Ian and me are catching these things, we are going to need them.'

'Fuck you, Chubbs, why don't you go and give Gus and me a chance to catch a few?'

This went back and forth for a while until Gus volunteered.

By the time Gus got back with one canvas sack, the crayfish total was five; Ian had three and Chubby, two. The five crayfish were loaded in the sack and tied up to one of the nearby rocks.

'I got the sack from the butcher; he told me that you were only allowed two bugs per person, per day. He also said you need a fishing license and would get into trouble if caught without one.'

Totally ignoring the fishing license comment, Chubby announced that they needed three more for the day. Gus and Jimmy took to the sea and some twenty minutes later, Gus emerged with one large crayfish. Two more needed. Try as they might, two and a half hours later and no further catches, they decided to call it a day.

Six healthy, alive and kicking crayfishes rendered three rand from the Crossways Butcher. Cressy flippers were selling for one rand and ninety-five cents, so three pairs were going to set them back roughly six rand. Four sets of ankle straps to hold the flippers securely were also needed, at fifty cents per pair. A further eight more crayfish were required.

It took the boys six days to catch the final eight crayfish. Funds accumulated, it was off to Logan's Sports for three pairs of Cressy flippers and four sets of ankle straps.

The last days of the summer holidays were spent body surfing at Brighton beach. This was the one sport that Jimmy excelled at over the other three.

Monday, January 20, 1964, opening day of the new school year. The boys reported back to school, no longer the bottom of the totem pole. The first day back at school started with the entire intake seated in the school hall. Standard sixes in the first rows followed by each standard through to the Matrics.

After a rousing welcome speech by Van, each class teacher in turn stood up, introduced themselves and proceeded to call out each of their class by name. Once your name was called, you left the hall and proceeded to your home classroom, followed by your class teacher. The first class called were Standard 6A followed by 6B through to 6F.

Once the Standard sixes were done, it was then turn of the sevens. Needless to say, the four boys were eager to see who their class teachers were and which class they would end up in. Students were called up alphabetically.

Standard 7A (Ms. Whyte calling) M's were passed with no Murphy. 'S' was reached and Stewart was called. Gus, grinning, got up and said, 'See you soon, Jimmy' and left. W's reached and no Williams. Well, Jimmy thought, at least Gus and me will be together. W's passed and no Wilson. Ian and Chubby looked at a very surprised Jimmy. Must be a mistake, as Jimmy got better Standard six results than Gus.

Standard 7B's Mr Niven started his roll call, which ended up calling Jimmy and Chubby but not Ian, which was also a bit of a shock. Ian ended up in 7C with Kees Heunis as his class teacher. The first thing Jimmy did on his way to his new classroom was to pick up the bell; he wasn't going to let that slip out of his hands.

By the time the first break came around, all classes were filled, the new prefects appointed, and all roll calls completed. The four friends met up to discuss the new year's class arrangements.

'I don't understand why I got 7A and you didn't. It must be a mistake,' said Gus.

'Maybe Terry Niven wanted you in his class, as he is the standard seven Maths teacher and he knows what a genius you are at Maths,' joked Chubby.

'There are a lot of "maybes" here,' said Ian. 'Let's just get on with it and show them they have made a mistake.'

Jan 22, 1964
Kenneth Kaunda is sworn in as Northern Rhodesia's first premier.

School life settled into the normal routine. School sports turned to cricket and the newly introduced sport of hockey. Hockey was seen to be the less important of the two, so if you couldn't make the various cricket teams, you signed up for hockey.

Chubby and Gus made the Under 14A team, Jimmy and Ian the B team most weeks.

One of the first issues came about at practise. The cricket and hockey teams both shared the same field, so it became necessary to a bit of scheduling. Cricket, being the more important, would use the field first for 'game' practise. When finished, they would retreat to the cricket nets and the hockey boys would take over.

The cricket teams ran through from U13, U14, U15, and 1st and 2nd teams. Hockey, on the other hand, had only U15 and 1st team.

Chubby, ever keen on the 'match' environment and not so keen on waiting around for a turn in the nets, took to bringing his hockey stick and boots to cricket practice. No sooner had the cricketers retired to the nets, Chubby got bored. At the first opportunity, he donned his boots and sloped off to hockey practice.

The first time this happened, he wasn't missed in the nets and was welcomed with open arms to hockey practice. The hockey coach, Mr.

Madsen, was an ex provincial player and this was the main reason he was allowed to introduce hockey to the school.

It only took a few moments for Madsen to realise he had a real player on his hands and could see that Chubby could be the star of his U15 team. He was that much better than any other players and could conceivably play for the first team even at the age of fourteen. Chubby figured he had the best of both worlds, no time wasted practising, just games to be played.

It didn't take long for the cricket coaches to catch on to what was going on with Chubby. To resolve matters, Chubby was told if he didn't practice with the rest of the team, he wouldn't be selected for school matches. He needed to make a choice. Chubby said he would play hockey.

This did not go down well with the cricket coaches, as they just assumed that he would choose their sport as it was a higher priority with the school. Madsen was ecstatic, as he saw this as a victory for his 'minor' sport. Chubby, on the other hand, knew what he was doing. He figured if he played his cards right, he could play both. The only question would be when a cricket match and hockey match ended up clashing at the same time.

There were heated discussions between Madsen and the various cricket coaches. A consensus was agreed. Chubby would attend cricket practice in full, including the nets. Madsen agreed that he would allow Chubby to join hockey practice when the cricket coach released him after net practice. Some participation is better than none.

So, it came to pass. Chubby would play for the cricket U14A and for the 1st hockey team, as playing for the U15's would clash with the cricket. On the odd occasion of there being a clash, cricket would prevail.

Feb 25, 1964
Cassius Clay defeats Sonny Liston and becomes the new World Heavyweight boxing champion.

School life continued with the next milestone being the Easter holidays; two and a half weeks at the end of March.

With the weather cooling down, less and less time was spent on the beach. Thoughts turned to the new football season. Chubby would continue to play for Durban City and tried to encourage Ian to join him. Ian secretly wished he could, but finances prevented this and he remained loyal to Fynnlands Football club.

The previous season, all the boys played in the U14 leagues. Each season, the Durban and District Football Association changed the age groups. Last season it was U14, U16 and U18, the new season would be U13, U15 and U17. This worked well for some but in their case last season the boys were 13 playing U14 and this year 14 playing U15. Again, a year younger than most of the other players and teams.

The Fynnlands Club received the sad news that Pop Churches had decided that he was no longer able to coach the U13's and U15's. Again, playing with boys mostly a year older, Jimmy and Gus found it a bit more difficult getting a game each week. Ian was a shoo in for the A team but not so much for the other two and the B team.

The first game of the season for the B team set the pattern for the season. It was against Ramblers and it got off to bad start, with an own goal from Jimmy. The team never recovered and proceeded to lose 7-1; the single goal scored by Gus.

Willie Botha. The new U15 coach, known to all as Uncle Willie and hadn't actually watched the game as he was with the U15A team, read the boys the riot act at Tuesday evening practice. Much of the venom was directed at Jimmy, rather unfairly. Some of the team stood up for Jimmy but Uncle Willie was having none of it. As 'punishment,' Jimmy was made to do extra laps while the rest played a practise game.

A disillusioned Jimmy did the laps missing out on the practice, At the end of the session, the teams for Saturday's games were announced. Ian in the A team, Gus in the B team and Jimmy left out completely.

'This is a load of crap, Steffen gets a game and he is really fucking useless, and you are left out, not even named as a reserve,' said Gus.

'Seems that Willie has it in for you,' said in Ian in disgust.

'Maybe he is just trying to make point to wake us all up,' replied Jimmy. 'I'll just try harder and show him.'

Try as hard as he could, he made no inroads with Willie. The team lost the next two games, with Steffen an obvious handicap, but no change in the line-up. The only time he got a game was if there were not enough to fill the team with eleven players. Becoming more and more disillusioned, Jimmy decided to pack it in as long as Willie was coach.

April 20, 1964
Nelson Mandela admits to sabotage and conspiracy to overthrow the South African Government.

'I do not deny that I planned sabotage. We had either to accept inferiority or fight against it by violence.'

With results of both teams suffering and player motivation and confidence at an all-time low, a committee meeting was called. Several players (which included Ian and Gus) were called in to get to the bottom of the problems. Virtually every boy, independently interviewed, had the same thing to say. Willie was vindictive and would pick on individual players to blame if there was a loss. The players would be punished and as such, most were too scared to make a mistake for fear of being berated at practise. Football was no longer fun.

Willie was interviewed after the players. He was informed of the issues expressed by the players. Instead of accepting the input, he proceeded to give a foul mouth rant on the attitudes and efforts of his two teams, especially the B team. If the committee was going to take the words of a bunch of snot nosed kids over his, then they could shove the job up their arses. He was fired that night.

June 4,1964
Ian Smith warns he will Unilaterally declare Independence if relations with Britain worsen.

With a new coach in place, Jimmy returned to the club. The teams won more than they lost, Ian stayed in the A team and Jimmy and Gus played most weeks for the B team.

June 14, 1964
Mandela sentenced to life imprisonment for sabotage and plotting to overthrow the South African Government. He is flown from Pretoria to Cape Town and interred on Robben Island.

One of the highlights of the season was the game against Durban City U15. The game was scheduled as one of the curtain raisers to a Durban City versus Highland Park first teams. This game was scheduled for a

Sunday afternoon, which allowed Jimmy and Gus to attend. The early kick off meant that there was only a crowd of around two thousand which would, by main game time, be closer to thirty-five thousand. Nevertheless, it was a big deal for the four friends with a lot of trash talking between Chubby and his friends.

The game turned out to be one of the best seen by two U15 teams. Durban City won by three goals to two. Chubby was left goalless as he was totally marked out of the game by man of the match, Ian.

After the game, Ian was again approached by the Durban City coach to reconsider joining them. Ian again refused.

July 2, 1964
Lyndon Johnson, the United States president, signs sweeping Civil Rights Act.

On the rugby front, the headmaster and coaches decided that there was a need to promote Chubby to the U15 side rather than leave him in the U14's. It was thought of as a long-term plan towards him playing first team rugby. Hone his skills by playing against older stronger boys; make him work a bit harder.

Gus remained with the U14A, playing centre instead of scrum half and was appointed captain. Jimmy played for the U14B and Ian opted out of rugby and took up cross country running.

July 27, 1964
The National Guard is called in to quell race riots in Rochester, New York State after three successive nights of rioting.

With Chubby's bigger commitment to school rugby, it was becoming more and more difficult to cater for his twice a week trip into Durban for football practice. His mother was struggling to fit in the time driving to and from the Bluff to Durban. There were her other children to take care of. Rugby practice was also encroaching on football practice time, and school rugby had to take precedence. The only good solution was to give up Durban City.

Chubby approached coach Dan de Klerk with his problem. He would only be able to, at the most, attend one practice a week. De Klerk said that if, unless he was injured or ill, he didn't make practice, he would not be picked for the team.

Well, not to play was not in Chubby's plans. The only solution was to quit Durban City and go back to Fynnlands. To re-join Fynnlands would require a clearance form from Durban City signed by the coach, which Chubby requested.

De Klerk refused. This meant as far as the 1964 season was concerned for Chubby, it was either Durban City or no-one. He could appeal at the next annual general meeting which was in three months' time.

De Klerk figured Chubby would cave in and make a plan to continue with Durban City. All this did was ensure that he would never play for City again, under any circumstances. This was the beginning of the end of Chubby's football career. Football's loss would be rugby's gain.

Aug 3, 1964
150 people massacred by Lumpa church sect members.

With no football to distract him, Chubby threw himself into perfecting his rugby skills. Even playing with boys a year older than him, he stood out head and shoulders above the rest of them. This did result in him being a marked man against the opposition.

Aug 7, 1964
The US steps up action against Vietnam.

Aug 18, 1964
At a meeting in Switzerland, South Africa is banned from the Olympic games because of that government's apartheid policy.

The news of South Africa being banned from the Olympics came as no surprise but was met with apathy by the major sports bodies. Rugby and cricket were not affected so all was good in the South African government's eyes.

Aug 25, 1964
Kenneth Kaunda is sworn in as Zambia's (formally Northern Rhodesia) first prime minister.

The rugby season ended with the start of the spring school holidays. The U15A team had enjoyed their best season, only losing one game, but that was to the dreaded Dirkie Uys school. Chubby was voted player of the year for the U15's. The one sour note was that he was not picked for the Durban and District U15 side. Grosvenor Boy's High was still seen as a bit of a backwater school.

Sept 6, 1964
Ian Smith arrives in London for independence talks for Southern Rhodesia.

Spring school holidays. The water at the beach was still too cold to swim. Football season over, nothing to do. None of the boys had any money so even a trip into Durban was out of the question. A plan was needed to generate some money.

'I have a plan,' said Jimmy. 'Gus, your aunt is at work all day, right?'

'Yes, leaves for Durban at seven in the morning and only gets back at five thirtyish. Why?'

'She still has the new budgie in that flashy cage?'

'Yes, why?'

'Okay, here's the plan. We draw up some sheets with twenty numbers on each sheet and say, five sheets. That's one hundred numbers, right?'

'Yes, but what's the point?'

'Gus, you draw up the sheets as you have the best writing. Head it up "Charity Raffle," first prize, budgie and cage. We sell the tickets door to door for twenty cents each. If we sell them all, that's twenty rand.'

'Are you crazy? My aunt will shit herself when she sees the bird and cage are missing.'

'But this is the genius part. We carry the cage around while selling the tickets. When we do the draw, your aunt wins first prize. Piece of cake.'

'That's genius; let's get started,' enthused Chubby. Ian and Gus, not sure, agreed.

Armed with bird, cage and raffle 'tickets,' the boys set out to make their fortune. They had mixed results. Over three days they managed to sell twenty-eight tickets, garnering the sum of five rand and sixty cents.

There were some very tricky questions asked by several potential customers. The boys made sure that they never sold any tickets to people they knew as they didn't want any awkward comments getting back to their parents.

65

Deciding to quit when they were ahead, the raffle was 'drawn' and lo and behold Gus' aunt won first prize. She was never aware of raffle.

Thinking they were in the clear, the boys started to make plans on how to spend their ill-gotten gains. Many suggestions were put forward without any agreement reached. It was decided to split the proceeds four ways, one Rand and forty cents each. Plans were made for movies, Saturday morning, three days away.

Leaving Gus's place, Chubby headed home and Jimmy and Ian went back to Ian's house.

Ian was met at the front door by a very irate mother. One of the 'ticket holders,' who worked with Ian's mother, had mentioned the good deed Ian was doing in collecting money for charity. Jimmy tried to sneak away but failed.

'I don't know what you were thinking but what you did was totally illegal, and you could be arrested. I'm sure all four of you were involved so I will have to tell all of your parents.'

'You will all go around to everyone you sold a ticket to, return their money and apologise. And you, young man, (talking directly to Ian) are grounded until you go back to school.'

Ian's mother called Chubby's mother who took the same action on her son. Gus' aunt, when contacted, went ballistic threatening to send him back to his mother. There was no phone at Jimmy's house, so his mother got a personal visit and the same punishment was meted out.

The following day the task of handing back the money and apologising took place. Expecting to be crapped upon by every 'ticket' holder, in most instances the victim found it funny. Only two of the twenty-eight took back their money, leaving a profit of five rand twenty. The consensus was to keep that information to themselves.

Oct 22, 1964
Ian Smith sends an ultimatum to British Prime Minister Harold Wilson on the independence issue.

After ten days of solitary confinement at home, the boys returned to school for the final term of standard seven. Gus and Ian had spent their time studying for the year end exams that were coming up. Chubby spent his time practising cricket with his sister and older brother. Jimmy spent his time annoying his mother and sister so that he is told to go and play outside. He figured that 'outside' could mean anywhere outside and took off to the Fynnlands Football fields where, on most days, he spent his punishment playing soccer with Cyril and friends.

Oct 27, 1964
Wilson warns Smith that declaring UDI is tantamount to treason.

Although cricket and hockey were still played during the final term of the year, practice was cut to once per week, so as not to impact revision and study periods for the year end exams. Letters of the intention were sent to all parents so it was virtually impossible to escape study. A signed copy was to be returned. Jimmy signed his mother's name without her seeing the letter. His 'study time' was spent either at the soccer field or the beach.

Nov 13, 1964
Johnson overwhelmingly elected as President of the United States of America.

The start of the year end examinations. Only one exam per day, with normal lessons to complete the rest of the day. First off for the standard seven's was Jimmy's favourite, Afrikaans. When questioned by Gus, he said he reckoned he did enough to pass.

Nov 6, 1964
A referendum taken in Rhodesia comes out overwhelmingly in favour of UDI. (Unilateral Declaration of Independence)

One by one, each exam paper was handed out to be completed within the two-hour limit. After each exam the boys expressed their thoughts on how they did. It varied from 'A piece of cake' to 'Shit, I think I plugged that one.' Gus always positive and Ian mostly pessimistic.

Nov 17, 1964
UK imposes an arms embargo on South Africa.

Finally, all exams done it was now time to go through the motions of waiting on their results. Each subject teacher would mark all their student's papers, immaterial if they were in the A, B or C class.

First up was Afrikaans. Gus got an 'A,' Chubby and Ian 'C's' and Jimmy scraped through with a 'E.'

Maths results restored some of Jimmy's pride, like Gus, he also got an 'A,' but as Terry Niven announced to all and sundry, Jimmy's 'A' was 100%. Gus got a 95%.

When all the results were in, Gus came in first in the 7A class with an 'A' in all seven subjects. Jimmy came in first in 7B with four A's, two 'B's' and his one 'E'. He did receive an 'A' aggregate though. Chubby did okay but Ian was the shock because he took first place in 7C.

At the annual prize giving, Gus got the Student of the Year prize, the only one in the whole school to achieve an 'A' in all subjects. Jimmy got the prestigious Maths prize for the highest mark achieved in a single subject. Chubby's prize was Junior Sportsman of the Year.

Dec 10, 1964
Martin Luther King Jr. awarded the Nobel Peace Prize.

Friday, December 11, school broke up for the summer holidays. Seven whole weeks to be spent mostly on the beach or kicking around a football.

Dec 12, 1964
Kenya declares itself a Republic. Jomo Kenyatta elected President.

Monday December,14 the whole Wilson family was bundled into the family car, headed for Sesfontein. The plan was to spend a week on the smallholding to visit Grandmother Bridget and Aunt Maggie. Jimmy, despite his offer to stay at home and look after the house, was made join in the trip.

Although the trip was pretty boring for the kids, it would have a profound effect on the whole family. Everything was going smoothly until the day before the family was due to return. Denis, unbeknownst to Iris, who had planned this all along, made the fateful announcement to the whole family.

'Good news family, Granny Bridget is going to come and live with us in Durban. The Doctor thinks she needs the fresh air found at the coast to help her health.'

Iris was shocked by the announcement. How could he do this? He never said a word, we never discussed it. We have a three bedroomed house, where is she going to sleep? Two years of peace was about to be shattered.

Denis went on with, 'Granny will take Maureen's room and she will move into the front room with David. We'll put a bed in the dining room for Jimmy.'

What a pile of shit, thought Jimmy. If she didn't smoke eighty cigarettes a day and laid off the brandy, she wouldn't have health issues.

The family returned to Durban, fully loaded and cramped together. A normal driver would make the trip easily in six to seven hours. Denis with his conservative driving and Granny's need to stop every hour for a toilet break, extended the trip to eleven hours. By the time they arrived home the tension was obvious.

Once the car was unpacked and Granny ensconced in her new room, Iris took Denis aside. For over an hour behind their locked bedroom doors, one of the most heated arguments in Wilson family history occurred. The angry voices could be heard by the whole family. Granny seemed oblivious, Maureen and David were visibly upset and Jimmy seriously pissed off.

The outcome was Maureen moved in and took over David's bed, he would sleep with Mom and dad until another bed could be bought, Jimmy's bed was moved into the dining room. A most unsatisfactory arrangement.

Three days later David's new bed arrived, and he moved in with Maureen. Jimmy, in the meantime, had spent three very uncomfortable nights sleeping in the dining room with absolutely no privacy. There had to be a better solution. He suggested he move into the storeroom next to the garage as it had a sort of veranda. This was vetoed as it would cost too much to enclose the veranda.

The final solution came about when Jimmy asked if he could move into the 'Sewing Room.' This was a small room, about six by ten feet long, that was going to be used by Iris for sewing. If they moved out the sewing machine and small cupboard they could just about squeeze in Jimmy's bed. This would be Jimmy's life going forward.

It was not a great Christmas for the Wilson family that year of 1964. Not so for the Murphy family, some distant relative had passed away and left a substantial amount of money to David. David decided that part of the money would go towards building a swimming pool in the back yard of their house. The pool was completed on December 29.

Never one to flash the money, David's decision surprised the family. Christmas 1964 was well celebrated in the Murphy household. The centre of the universe had just been relocated to Casa Murphy, at least as far as Chubby, Ian, Gus and Jimmy were concerned.

CHAPTER 7
The Early days - 1965

On January 1, 1965 it was Peter Murphy's 15th birthday. To celebrate the occasion and launch the 'opening' of their new pool, David decided to throw a birthday bash for Chubby.

Due to the late decision to have a party, only twenty-five additional guests arrived. This was probably fortunate as the pool became the centre of the festivities. Most of the party goers were male friends of Chubby's, the lure of female company had not quite kicked in yet. 1965 would bring a big change to that situation.

The only girls present were Chubby's sister and two of her friends. Mary, being a year older and her two friends of a similar vintage, created two distinct groups at the party. Most of the boys fell into the 14 and 15 year old range, whereas Mary and her friends were aged 16. There is a huge gap in maturity and the physical development of a 14-year old boy and 16-year old girl.

Mary was Chubby's sister and most of the boys knew her or had at least seen her around. Dressed in a single piece swimsuit, she did not attract anywhere near the attention of her fiend, Fiona. Fiona had on a very small bikini and had the physical attributes to fill the top and bottom.

Fiona became the centre of attraction, with virtually every boy present making some effort to garner her attention, no matter how foolish. She lapped it up.

Mary soon became annoyed with what she considered the childish behaviour of her brother and his friends. She took Chubby one side and told her brother, 'Please get your friends to stop behaving like randy little boys!'

Chubby, ever condescending to his sister, turned around and walked over to the side of the pool and shouted out for all to hear, 'Hey, okes, Mary says to stop eye balling Fiona out and stop acting like randy little boys.'

Mary was horrified. Blushing profusely, she grabbed her other friend, Michelle, by the hand and headed inside to the sanctity of her bedroom. She expected Fiona to follow on, which she did, notwithstanding treating her audience to a slow and sexy exit.

With the girls' departure, the party in the pool resumed, back to boys 'things.' But the flame had been lit and a significant change of focus would happen in the year 1965.

Jan 8, 1965
Singer Adam Faith cancels his concert in Johannesburg, as he was not allowed to perform in front of a racially mixed audience.

January 18, 1965; the first day of the school year. As was the custom, the first morning was spent with class assignments. Being part of the Standard Eight intake, the boys were now seated right in the middle of the school hall and would have to sit through the whole process of assigning standard sixes and sevens.

By the time the Standard Eight assignments came around, it was almost time for the first break and Jimmy got up to retrieve the school bell thinking, like previous years, the 'eights' would be done after break.

'Where do you think you are going, boy?' boomed out the voice of one of the new teachers.

Thinking the new guy didn't know the way things worked on the first day, Jimmy explained. 'My job is to ring the bell for change of periods, Sir. I was just going to get the bell.'

The teacher, now slightly embarrassed, decided to assert his authority.

'We will complete the "eights" then you may retrieve the bell for the break.'

Jimmy sat down and waited for the process to continue, silently thinking *I wonder what Van is going to think about this*. He didn't have long to wait. 8A had only reached 'B' when Van descended on the school hall.

In a voice that could probably be heard at Bushland's Primary School ten miles away, 'Wilson, where are you? You are five minutes late, are you still on the beach or do you think you could grace us with your presence?'

Now Jimmy faced a dilemma. He could explain that the new teacher had forbidden him to leave the hall to ring the bell. This would probably result in the teacher getting all bent out of shape or he could suck it up.

'Sorry Sir, I slipped up, it won't happen again,' said Jimmy, making a hasty exit before anything else unpleasant took place.

The boys met up at their regular spot.

'Shit, you dodged a bullet there, Mr. Wilson, smooth move,' said Gus.

The consensus was you didn't want to piss off a teacher, especially as you didn't know what class or subject he was going to be assigned to.

Break over, everyone returned to the hall.

The assignments for 8A continued from where they left off. Gus was the first to be called when the 'S's' were reached, Chubby was bypassed and would end up in 8B. Jimmy was called when the 'W's' were reached. Ian was bypassed again and strangely would end up in 8C, which seemed wrong considering his Standard 7 results.

The big shocker was at the end of the 8A roll call when the class teacher was named; Mr. French, who would also be the Geography teacher. The same man who had called out Jimmy when he went to ring the bell. This could be a very bad move.

The first roll call for standard 8A, Mr. French decided to stamp his authority on the class. As was normal, the whole class of twenty-four had sorted themselves as far as seating was concerned. The back row and the window seats were prime targets.

'Right boys, you will seat yourselves in alphabetic sequence starting row by row from my left,' said Mr French.'

As only a bunch of boys can, this resulted in virtual chaos. No one wanted front row seats. A task that should have taken the best part of two minutes dragged on to over ten.

'What is wrong with you people? Four rows of six. How difficult is that? You are supposed to be the brightest of all the standard eights. God help those in 8F,' shouted French at the top of his voice.

Grabbing his roll call list, as maybe he should have done at the beginning, he personally rearranged the seating. Jimmy ended up with a window desk one row from the back. Gus, in the aisle next to him, one row ahead. Seated directly behind Jimmy was Robert van der Linde, a really good guy, but the owner of probably the worst stutter known to man.

Standard eight was the point where you made your subject choices. Up to this point, the subject choices were fixed for all. Grosvenor, being a bit of a backwater school, had limited choice. For the 'Advanced Stream' you had English, Afrikaans, History, Maths, Science, Geography or Latin, and then the choice of an additional voluntary subject – Applied Mathematics. Gus chose Latin and Applied Maths. Jimmy chose Geography, even though it meant having lessons with Mr. French.

Chubby, in 8B, chose the same set as Jimmy. Ian in 8C had an additional option not offered to the A & B classes –Technical Drawing in place of Geography.

At the first Maths class, Mr. Niven laid out the rules on how Applied Maths would work.

'Your exam marks are out of 300 for trigonometry and geometry. Anyone taking App Maths will write an exam for 100 marks. If you achieve a pass of forty percent or more, these marks will be added to your Maths marks as a bonus' explained Mr Niven. 'So, you Wilson, in theory, you could improve on your 100% of last year.'

'App Maths classes will be held three times per week, Monday, Wednesday and Thursday for one half hour at the end of the school day.'

Niven, perusing the App list, suddenly notice that Jimmy's name was missing.

'Wilson, why is your name not on this list? What the hell is wrong with you, boy? You have a great mathematical brain and you will attend, even if I have to chain you to your desk. I will not have my one student who is guaranteed an "A" in matric, screw this up for himself.'

Jimmy signed up for App Maths.

The school days up to the Easter holidays progressed with no major issues, except for Jimmy and Afrikaans.

The new Afrikaans teacher was a giant of a man called Coetzer. He was a bit of a lazy bastard who would nip out for a smoke halfway through lessons and was also suspected of taking a shot of alcohol at the same time.

His normal stunt, when he didn't feel like actual teaching, was to instruct the class to each read a page of the set workbook one after the other. This worked well until the sequence reached Robbie van der Linde. Robbie found it almost impossible to string two words together. So, the first time it got to him there was so much spluttering and stammering that Jimmy decided to read the page in his place. On finishing 'Robbie's' page, Jimmy sat back quite pleased with himself and expected the boy in front of him to continue, which he did.

Coetzer took exception to this and bellowed out in Afrikaans, 'Jy moet ook jou eie bladsy lees, seuntjie' (You have to read your own page as well, sonny)' And so it came to pass that Jimmy had two pages to read from then on.

Jan 25, 1965
Winston Churchill dies at the age of 90.

On the sporting front it was a quiet time. Chubby playing cricket for the U15A's and hockey for the 1st team. Gus played the odd game for the U15B cricket team. Ian and Jimmy did not take part in any school sports.

Weekends were spent at Brighton Beach, weather permitting, or at Chubby's house at their pool. There was a more than passing interest in Mary and her friends but other than acting like idiots around them, no progress was made.

Feb 1, 1965
Civil Rights leader Martin Luther King Jr. and 300 of his supporters are arrested in Selma, Alabama for parading without a permit.

February 9: Jimmy turned fifteen. Now at an official age to be able to get a part-time job.

Feb 21, 1965
Black Moslem leader, Malcom X, is shot dead.

April fool's day 1965; Ian joins the fifteen-year olds. Both he and Jimmy are keen to get a job selling programs at the Kingsmead Football stadium during the upcoming season. It would just be a question of getting Ian's mother to agree. The season would start around the middle of May. Games were usually played on Wednesday evenings or Sunday afternoons.

April 26, 1965
Rhodesian Government threatens to deport 500,000 African citizens if Britain imposes a trade embargo.

The Easter holidays came and went. The start of the second school term coincided with the start of the winter sports, namely rugby at school and football at Fynnlands. This year it would be U15 rugby and U16 soccer. Chubby's return to Fynnlands was looked forward to with great anticipation. Fynnlands U16A would be a team to be reckoned with in the Durban and District leagues.

The first setback happened on the first day of the new term. Chubby was called into the headmaster's office to be greeted by van Vuuren and the first team rugby coach.

'Chubby, as you know I rate you highly as a rugby player,' said van Vuuren. 'Mr. Venter and I have decided that we want you to move up from the U15's to play 1st team rugby. I know it's a bit of jump, but we think you are more than capable at that level. You play enough games and I assure you that full school colours will be forthcoming. You will be the only fifteen-year old to achieve this honour. What do you think about that?'

'Great, Sir. Thank you very much. I won't let you down.'

'With you in the team this year I think that we have the possibility of having a great season. It does mean a bit of sacrifice on your part, as it will mean attending extra practice after school. Well done, my boy, and good luck.'

Chubby left the headmaster's office elated and barely able to contain himself, he rushed off to find his mates to tell them the good news.

'Hey, guys, guess what? Van told me I am going to be playing first team rugby and will get full colours' boasted Chubby, jumping the gun somewhat with the comment about colours.

'You're shitting us,' said Jimmy.

'No, it's true I've just come from his office.'

What Chubby had failed to realise was this great news would also mean the end of his soccer career. The additional rugby practices would clash with Fynnlands soccer practice and the first team rugby matches would coincide with Saturday soccer matches.

Fynnlands had a strict policy of no train no play. Chubby's soccer career was effectively over at least for his school days.

The first Durban City game of the season at Kingsmead on a Sunday afternoon, kick off 3pm. Jimmy and Ian caught the bus from the Bluff to the city and then a connection to Kingsmead. The cost was 10 cents each. The bus service provided a special weekend 'Travel at Will' ticket allowing you to catch any number of buses for 10 cents between the hours of 8am to 6pm.

Jimmy and Ian joined several men and boys at the main gate, all looking for various jobs. The jobs ranged from supervisors down to program sellers.

Five supervisors, one at each set of gates, pay 10 rand. Five names were called out and five regulars stepped forward.

Next best were the turnstile ticket sellers. Ten for the European gates and eight for the non-European gates were needed. There were twelve regulars who stepped forward and were assigned gates. Six more were needed and ten of those looking for jobs put up their hands. The requirement was to be at least eighteen years old and preferably experienced, pay was five rand. Six seemed to be chosen at random.

Next up were the ticket tearers. Once a ticket was sold, the person would go through the turnstile and be confronted by a person who would tear the ticket in half. Twelve were needed, with pay being two rand. The age requirement was to be of at least sixteen years of age. Jimmy and Ian thought it best not to take a chance.

Last of all were the program sellers. You had to be at least fifteen and they would take as many as wanted a job. The payment was two cents per ten cent program sold. The boys had their names added to the list and were sent off the office where they would be given one hundred programs to sell. They were told if they needed more just to come back to the office, pay the eight rand for programs sold, keep their two rand and they would be issued with a further hundred programs.

Two hours to kick off, the gates were open for business. Jimmy and Ian being the 'new boys' were shunted off to the non-European gates by those more experienced boys. Jimmy thought *wait until next time and we will make sure we get to the front of the line and head for the European gates.*

The non-European crowd was about ninety-five percent Indian. What most never thought was that the crowd coming in through the 'Indian gates' were concentrated into one area. The 'White gates' were spread over four areas so the flow was more dispersed.

The program sellers were given a type of apron that could hold the programs and the money received. Strangely, they were given no change, the boys later found out the more experienced sellers brought their own change.

The spectators started off quite slowly and only a few programs were sold in the first hour. Change was a problem. There were a couple who walked on when there was no change available, but a few said, 'Keep the change.'

Half an hour before kick-off Jimmy was out of programs, so he rushed back to the office for a refill. Armed with his new load of programs, he passed Ian on the way back. He was stopped several times on the way back to the Indian gate to sell a program.

Making it back to the gate armed with plenty of programs and plenty of change, he sold out in less than ten minutes. Having to rush back and forth to the office was cutting into valuable selling time. On his third trip, he asked if he could have two hundred programs. He was told he could but would have to pay upfront for the extra hundred at a cost of eight rand. He filed the information away and took only the normal one hundred. He would be better prepared next time.

By kick-off time the flow of people had virtually stopped so the boys decided to head back to the office and cash in for the day. Being the first home game of the season, the attendance was bigger than normal.

The cashing up process was as follows – the ticket sellers were balanced up by the supervisors, who would pay the ticket sellers and the ticket tearers. The supervisors would extract their pay in the same process. All this was entered and balanced on a sheet and that was in turn handed in at the office. The program sellers would return any unsold programs and pay for those sold at eight cents each. Any money left over in their 'apron' was their commission.

Once Jimmy and Ian had cashed up their final sales and handed back their aprons, they found themselves with a pile of coins and no method of carrying them. Second lesson of the day: bring a vessel of some sort to carry home your earnings. A sweet lady in the office noticed their dilemma and gave each boy a canvas bank bag.

Rather than waste time counting their money, the boys decided to watch the game which was now starting the second half. Calculating that the game would be over by around 5pm giving plenty of time to make the bus to the Bluff before the 6pm deadline.

Third lesson of the day came at the end of the game. With the best part of twenty odd thousand leaving at the same time, there were huge queues for the busses. With the delays incurred, they arrived at the bus station two minutes after 6pm. The bus driver refused the 'travel at will ticket' and demanded full price of ten cents. Initially disappointed, Jimmy realised he had a pile of cash on his person and with a dramatic flourish extracted ten cents for his ticket. Ian followed suit.

Getting home just after 7pm, they went their separate ways. After counting their money Jimmy found he had cleared R12.15 and Ian R11.02. Jimmy, ever the optimist, calculated that at two Sunday's a month and two Wednesday's a month he would be making at least R48 every month and for a whole five-month season R240. The actual amount would be considerably less than that.

Monday, before school, Jimmy and Ian met up with Gus and Chubby to share their good news. Treats at the tuck shop would be on Jimmy and Ian. No arguments from Chubby and Gus as none of the boys were used to this kind of money.

May 28, 1965
Rhodesia declares a state of emergency in certain areas.

Their next venture in the program-selling business was not quite so productive. It was a Wednesday evening game with a 7.30pm kick off. No 'travel at will' tickets so bus fare was twenty cents to the ground and the same returning home. The crowd attendance was less than half the previous game. Both boys cleared less than R3. Not only was the pay disappointing but the bus trip got the boy's home after 11pm with school the next day. Ian was summarily banned by his mother from attending any more night games. Jimmy, on the other hand, convinced his mother to allow him to continue.

By the start of the July school holidays, Jimmy had accumulated just over R45 and Ian just over R20.

Jimmy's plan was to earn enough money to buy himself a surfboard. He reckoned he would need about R100 for a decent board. Ian had no plans other than he needed to compensate for not being able to work Wednesdays.

July 13, 1965
US president Johnson orders more troops to Vietnam.

Being the middle of winter, the beach and Chubby's pool were out of the equation. A new pastime would have to be found. Girls were now becoming of more interest to the group. Chubby's mother had found out that dancing lessons were being given at the Fynnland's Moth Hall on Tuesday evenings and insisted Chubby take part. She would pay the R1 per lesson. Amid the derisive banter, Chubby attended his first lesson.

The next day he met up with his three friends with a big grin on his face. They looked a bit surprised at his cheerful disposition as he was going to be mocked mercilessly.

'Hey, boys, before you start any crap, you've got to hear this. As you know, I went to the Smithers Dance Club last night for lessons. Jimmy, you can stop sniggering. I was the only guy there with six women. It was unreal, I think I'm well in with Jean Atkinson. She was all over me.'

Chubby went into all the gory details and when finished, had convinced the other three that this was the place to be. Jimmy volunteered to pay for Gus as he never had any money. Ian was a bit unsure, mainly because of his shyness around girls.

The following Tuesday evening, all four pitched up at Smithers Dance Club much to the delight of its owner, Janet Smithers. This week seven girls had turned up for lessons. One of them was Fiona, Mary's friend. Six of the girls were in the age group of 14 and 15, Fiona being the exception at 16.

The lessons included most ballroom type dances; the waltz, cha-cha, bossa nova and for a bit of fun, the new craze, the twist. It was a slow process but at least the boys got to get up close and personal with a member of the opposite sex.

Gus, being the best looking of the group, was in big demand. Ian, being terribly shy, had to be coerced onto the dance floor. Chubby was being Chubby, and Jimmy, never shy, did the rounds. Fiona took a shine to Gus, much to the disappointment of the other three.

The lesson ended and the typical teenage boy bravado commenced.

'Gee I can't make up my mind, Pam or Lorraine. Diane was also pretty hot,' said Jimmy.

'Yeah,' Chubby replied, 'I think Diane fancies me more than a bit. Did you see the tits on her? I think my ribs are bruised.'

Jimmy: hey Gus, what do you make of Fiona? She was all over you.

Gus: yes, she really was. I am into older women.

Chubby: what do you know about older women? Be careful or I'll tell my sister about you and her friend, then she will kick your arse.

The banter went back and forth with only Ian not contributing to the chat.

Jimmy: what's wrong, Williams, you nervous of women or what?

Ian: I was doing okay, just taking it easy, making them wait for it.

Chubby: what is 'it' then, Ian?

Tuesday evenings quickly became the highlight of the week. After each lesson, the girls started hanging out with the boys. There were always more girls than boys, which did present a bit of a problem. The girls, afraid of being left out if people started 'hooking up', made sure that nobody paired up.

The first sign of progress occurred when Fiona asked if Gus could walk her home as she was a bit nervous. Fiona lived about three hundred meters down Lighthouse Road, maybe a five-minute walk there and back for Gus. Gus agreed and amid cat calls and whistles, he left with Fiona.

By the time Gus returned some thirty-five minutes later, all the other girls had left. Some walking and some being picked up by their parents.

Jimmy noticed Gus standing slightly hunched over, looking a bit awkward.

'Hey, what's up with you, you look a bit pained? How did you shape with Fiona?'

'Nothing happened,' mumbled Gus.

'What do you mean? Shit, have you got a boner?' said Chubby, noticing a bulge in Gus' crotch. 'What the hell happened? Give details.'

'Well, we started walking towards Lighthouse Road and she grabbed me by the hand. So, we held hands all the way to her house and that was quite nice. When we got to her house, I walked her up to the door and turned to leave, that's when she grabbed me.'

'Then what? Come on, stop keeping us in suspense.'

'I wasn't sure what to do. She then leaned up, closed her eyes and kissed me. Next thing I knew she had her tongue in my mouth. She carried on doing this for quite some time, so I did the same. After a while she started rubbing herself up against me. That's when I got this boner,' he said pointing at the bulge in his pants.

'I didn't know what to, so I just kept kissing her. She kept grinding up against me. I was too scared to let go in case she saw what was happening to me.'

'She probably didn't have to see, she could feel it, you dumb shit. Then what did you do?' inquired Chubby.

'I eventually broke away and virtually ran down her pathway. What the fuck am I going to do with this?' he said pointing. 'It won't go away.'

'Well, the only cure for that is you are going to have a good old wank, it's the only way,' said Jimmy laughing. 'I'm off home, see you guys tomorrow.'

By the time school restarted, all four had had some success with one or more of the girls. Chubby had started 'going steady' with Diane. Gus was still being stalked by Fiona. Neither Gus nor Chubby ever had any money, so 'dates' were usually at the girl's houses. Not much chance of any hanky panky.

Jimmy and Ian, on the other hand, were always flush with cash. The modus operandi for them would be to arrange to meet two of the girls in Durban town and go to a movie. Always meet them inside the movie house to avoid paying for their tickets, the bus and the movie.

Ian had taken a fancy to Pam and she was normally his date. Jimmy gravitated between Lorraine, Jean and Paula. It didn't seem to bother the aforementioned girls that Jimmy wasn't interested in being serious about dating only one particular girl.

As alternatives to meeting the girls at the movies, Jimmy and Ian would go alone and hope to meet up with a pair of single girls. Jimmy, the instigator, would approach two girls sitting on their own and ask if Ian and he could join them. There was a surprisingly high rate of success in this approach.

This method was known colloquially as 'lumbering', who knows why? You would spend the duration of the movie kissing and trying to get 'lucky' by feeling up the girl's boobs, first on the outside and with any luck, nirvana, inside the bra. The boys had limited success in this venture. Jimmy had about three seconds inside a bra once before being rebuked, Ian never got beyond a quick feel outside the blouse.

Aug 10, 1965
Twelve-year-old Karin Muir breaks the world 110-yard
backstroke record in a time of 68.7 seconds.

Back at school for the third term, classes continued as normal. Half year results had Gus coming first in 8A, Jimmy a disappointing 15 out of 25; he seemed to be doing just enough to get by.

Chubby was still playing first team rugby but no longer at fly half. Being two or more years younger than virtually every other player on every team faced had taken its toll. Venter decided to move him first to the right wing, with limited success, before finally installing him as full back. Chubby's prodigious boot kept the score board ticking over with penalties, conversions and drop kicks fully justifying his selection. He was still the leading points scorer for the team.

Gus still played for the U15A team as captain and scrum half. Ian ran cross country and Jimmy avoided all sports as rugby no longer held any interest for him.

Aug 13, 1965
Troops move into the city of Los Angeles after three days of rioting by blacks.

Jimmy and Ian continued selling programs at the soccer matches, Ian only on alternate Sundays. Jimmy was nearing his goal of R100 for a surfboard, Ian was some R40 less well-off and decided he needed to find another or better job.

Ian noticed a job advert looking for a part-time motor mechanic at Brighton Beach Motors, which used to belong to his father until his untimely death. Taking the notice with him, he walked down to Crossways and into the garage office. The owner was a man name Steyn.

'What can I do for you, sonny?' asked Steyn.

'I am interested in the part time job you advertised,' said Ian, showing the newspaper cutting.

'I need a real mechanic, not some little kid. What do you know about fixing cars, what kind of experience do you have?

'My Dad used to own this garage, he taught me all about cars.'

'Your Dad was Ian Williams? What's your name?'

'Ian Williams, same as my Dad.'

'I'll tell you what. Come down here on Saturday morning at seven o'clock and you can help me book in cars and clean up in the garage. If you work out well, I will pay you R1 per hour, that's R5 for a Saturday morning. If you screw up, you are done. Okay?'

'Thank you, Sir, you won't be disappointed.' And so started Ian's career as a temporary motor mechanic.

It didn't take Steyn long to realise he had a gem on his hands. The third customer of the morning arrived while Steyn was busy with another customer who was taking up too much of his time with incessant questions.

83

Ian decided that rather than keep the new customer waiting, he would book him in on his own, which was a bit of a risk. Carefully asking all the right questions, he diagnosed the problem to be a damaged front wheel bearing. The customer requested an estimate, 'just a ballpark number', to get an idea of the cost.

Without hesitation, Ian got to work. He looked up the price of all the parts, checked the estimated labour charge, added it up and gave it to the customer with confirmation that it was just an estimate. His boss would have to confirm final totals. The customer said that estimate looks good and can Ian get a confirmation as he would like to schedule the repairs.

Ian retreated to the workshop where Steyn was just finishing up with his current customer. Ian explained what he had done but assured Steyn that the customer was aware that this was a 'ballpark' estimate and that he, Steyn, had to confirm.

Steyn took Ian aside out of hearing of anyone but the two of them.

'What the fuck are you trying to do? If this estimate is a load of shit, I am going to look stupid and you will be fired on the spot. You are only supposed to book cars in. Do you understand?'

'Yes Sir, sorry Sir,' stammered Ian, who then turned and headed back to the office.

'Sorry Sir,' apologised Steyn. 'My young lad here has only just started, and he should not be giving out any type of estimate, "ballpark" or otherwise. I will check your problem and redo the estimate. Give me five minutes.'

Steyn began his examination. Front wheel bearings damaged and need replacing. Well, at least Ian got that part right. Retreating to his office he looked up the spare part prices, all correct, none missing. He then looked up the labour cost, also correct. Total added up, also correct. After crapping all over Ian, this was a bit embarrassing.

Returning to the customer, Steyn announced, 'The quote was almost correct. My lad forgot we are offering a R10 discount this month on front wheel bearings. So, if all is okay, I can do the job on Wednesday.'

'That works for me. Looks like your appie knows his business. Good for him. See you Wednesday.'

Turning to Ian. 'It looks to me like you got lucky this time. You need to be careful. I had to give that guy a R10 discount to keep him happy.'

'Sorry Sir, I will in future.'

'By the way, how did you know what the problem was and what else can you do?'

'My Dad used to let me help when he was alive and owned this place. I did services, oil changes, etcetera. Did a few tune ups as well. I was much younger then, but I can do a lot more now.'

'Okay, I tell you what. You can do the same here but anything over R25 I will need to approve. It's my cock on the block if anything gets screwed up. Can you also work on Wednesday afternoons say from three to six? I will pay you R5 per hour, that's R25 per week.'

'Yes, Sir,' So ended Ian's program selling days and unfortunately many of his soccer matches. He was not always able to get away on Saturdays in time to travel for an away game. Being the player he was, the coach would always include him plus an extra reserve just in case Ian couldn't make it in time.

Jimmy continued selling programs at both Wednesday and Sunday matches but some weeks neither day had a match. He decided to try and get the same job at Hoy Park, the home of the less popular Durban United. He managed to secure a job at first attempt. The crowds were smaller and not that many Indians supported United. His first take amounted to R1.20 which was not worth the time and effort. Another plan had to be found.

A new girl had recently joined the dance lessons, Kerry, a friend of Jean's. She was a cute blond, a little shy initially. Once she came out of her shell, she garnered the interest of both Ian and Jimmy. As both boys had the same idea but neither gave the other a chance to get to 'know' Kerry better. The one positive that came out of this new friendship was the location of Kerry's house. It was equal distance from Jimmy and Ian's houses and just up the road from Crossways.

Ian started to 'drop in' to see Kerry on his way to and from work on Wednesday afternoons. Jimmy took notice of this and would conveniently arrive around the same times. The property was in a great location on Marine Drive, the house sunken slightly below street level. The great feature for the kids was the porch, which was off to the left side of the house, nice and semi-private.

Kerry's Dad was a bit of a grumpy fellow, not too crazy about all these kids (Gus, Jean and Chubby on occasion) invading his home, drinking his coffee. Her mother on the other hand was an absolute star; she enjoyed having the crowd at her home, and in her words, 'At least I know where my daughter is.'

Kerry's mother worked at the hardware store at Crossways; she worked mornings only, six days a week and Wednesday afternoons when her boss played golf. Initially she was okay with all the kids hanging out at her house but then decided it was not such a good idea leaving her daughter alone with a bunch of boys on Wednesday afternoons. She had a choice to ban them Wednesdays or find someone to take over her job that afternoon. She decided to ban them and asked Kerry to pass on the bad news.

A highly embarrassed Kerry told the boys the whole story. It was Jimmy who saw a great opportunity in this situation. He approached Mrs. Vermeulen and asked if it would be possible for him to help out on Wednesdays, with a view to maybe taking over her job so she could have that afternoon off. She said she would check with her boss and let him know.

The next day Mrs. Vermeulen told Jimmy her boss was not too sure, but for him to come into the shop tomorrow afternoon and she would go with him.

The next day straight after school, Jimmy and Kerry's Mom took the short walk down to Crossways. She introduced Jimmy to the owner, Jack, a twenty-something, laid back character, who had inherited the shop when his father died. Jack never had a great interest in a hardware shop but with very little effort made a good living.

Jack and Jimmy hit it off straight away. A decision was made for Jimmy to come in the next day, Friday, and get familiar with the store and what his job would be. If it worked out ok, he could start on Saturday morning with Mrs. Vermeulen. If she gave the ok, he could take her place on Wednesday afternoons. The pay would be R5 from 2.30pm to 5.30pm when the store closed. He would have to wait until 6pm when Jack would return from his golf.

It took only two Saturdays and two Wednesdays for Mrs. Vermeulen to proclaim Jimmy ready to take over her Wednesday spot. She also suggested that if it was okay with Jack, could Jimmy take over her Saturday job as well? Jack, only too happy to have someone around to do the actual work, agreed immediately. He offered Jimmy the job, hours 8am to 1pm and as Saturday was way busier than Wednesday afternoons, Jimmy would be paid R10. Jack could sit in his office at the back of the store and be on call if needed; this suited him down to the ground. A bonus was that Jimmy would also be cheaper than Mrs. Vermeulen.

The other good part was the hardware shop was directly opposite Ian's garage. They would walk to and from work together, leaving neither alone with Kerry. The funny thing was that Kerry, although loving the attention, didn't really fancy either of them; she had her eyes on Gus. Kerry knew she couldn't compete with Fiona and her abundant assets but that didn't stop her longing.

As Jimmy and Ian were accumulating money at an astounding rate, they both decided to open savings accounts at the local Standard Bank. Jimmy's first deposit was R118; Ian topped that by depositing R132.

Jimmy had reached his goal for buying a surfboard but as summer was a ways off still, he would continue to save. Ian was a bit secretive about his plans. He told no one that he was saving up for a motorcycle. He had his eyes on a Honda 50cc but couldn't ride one until he was 16.

Oct 29, 1965
Harold Wilson, the British Prime Minister, flies to Rhodesia in an attempt to stave off UDI.

Jimmy cut off his Wednesday program selling job as there wasn't enough time to get to Kingsmead before the game started. Anyway, his recent earnings on Wednesday hardly ever reached the R5 he was making at the store. Also, his mother had been grumbling about his monthly test scores at school. She hinted he should be spending more time studying, Granny Bridget, for once, agreed with Iris.

Oct 30, 1965
US planes bomb a friendly village in Vietnam by mistake, killing 48 and injuring 55.

Rugby season over, it was time for the sports awards. The U13 and U14 teams had had mixed results but the U15A under Gus' captaincy, had an excellent season only losing twice. Unfortunately, one of the losses was against the dreaded enemy, Dirkie Uys. Gus received the U15 player of the year award.

The first team had a very good season, losing only three matches. All three matches were against schools that normally would not consider playing Grosvenor. Durban High School, Maritzburg College and Glenwood, three schools playing against Grosvenor for the first time. Apart from the game against Glenwood, all the games were close.

The highlight of the season was the thrashing handed out to Dirkie Uys first team. Grosvenor winning by a record score between the two schools. A great number of accusations were levelled at the referee, a Grosvenor teacher, by the Dirkie Uys masters over the awarding of penalties.

There may have been a couple of dubious calls by the ref handing out penalties in favour of Grosvenor. But the real reason was that Chubby's kicking was unbelievable.

He kicked nine penalties (27 points), three drop goals (9 points) and converted all ten tries scored (20 points). Two of the ten tries Chubby scored himself (6 points), giving him a total 62 points out of the 86 scored by Grosvenor to the 10 scored by Dirkie Uys.

Rugby colours were handed out to all first team players who had not yet been awarded colours. Chubby became the first fifteen-year old to be awarded full colours for any achievement in the history of the school. Gus, Jimmy and Ian bathed in reflected glory; their mate was a hero.

Nov 11, 1965
White Rhodesia breaks with Britain by declaring UDI.

The start of the year end examinations. Gus had been studying hard and was confident in all subjects. Jimmy had barely studied but didn't seem too bothered. Chubby and Ian were both a bit nervous.

Nov 16, 1965
Economic sanctions drawn up to bring Rhodesia to heel.

All exams over, the boys were just waiting for the results.

Gus got seven As as expected and placed first in 8A. Jimmy, much too every one's surprise placed, seventh in class. He got two A's (Maths and Geography), three B's (English, History, Science), one C (Chemistry) and his regular F for Afrikaans. Overall a B aggregate.

Gus got the standard eight prize and Jimmy the Maths prize. Chubby and Ian both passed with acceptable scores.

Time for the summer holidays, six weeks of no school; which would it be, the beach or the pool? Meeting up with girls, at least that was the plan. Reality was that Ian now worked full time at Steyn's garage. Steyn knew he was onto a good thing, paying low wages to an unqualified mechanic who could do a better job than any other mechanic he had. Wages in cash, no tax or unemployment benefits. Still charging the customer full mechanic's rates; a nice little extra profit.

Jimmy also had the opportunity for more hours at the hardware store, working all afternoons and Saturday mornings. It suited Jack, who could do as little as possible knowing things would move along smoothly.

Jimmy would join Gus and Chubby most mornings at the beach or at Chubby's swimming pool before heading off to work.

The money was rolling in for Ian and Jimmy. Jimmy's plan was to buy his surfboard in January, telling Jack he wouldn't be able work every afternoon but would still do Wednesdays and Saturdays. Ian, on the other hand, not only loved his job but also wanted to save as much as he could, so he continued working throughout the school holidays.

Dec 27, 1965
Petrol rationing introduced in Rhodesia after Wilson staunches oil flow supply.

A rather significant event occurred in the Wilson household on December 30. Denis had managed to get a day off and decided to take Iris out for a meal. A very unusual occurrence. He told his mother about his plan and asked her to look after Maureen and David. For some reason, Bridget took exception to the request; she had had a couple of drinks and was a bit bolshie.

'I don't see why I should stay at home looking after your children, Jimmy should do that, he is old enough. If you cared for me at all, you should have invited me with you and not be taking advantage of me,' she said, looking directly at Iris.

For once in his life, Denis stood up to his Mother.

'Taking advantage of you! You have been imposing yourself on us and picking on Iris from the day you met her. You look down on her and belittle her at every opportunity. I want you out of my house.'

'Out of your house. Where do you think I can go?'

'To Maggie, I will call her tomorrow and make arrangements.'

'When I left her last time, she told me that I would not be welcomed back. So, what are you going to do? Throw me, your Mother, out on the street?'

Denis didn't answer and turned to Iris and said, 'Okay dear, that's the end of dinner plans for tonight. Come with me.' They retreated to the bedroom.

'What are you going to do? You need to stand up to her.'

'I am going to call on the Salvation Army. Their Berea branch takes in old people who have nowhere else to go. If they can't take her in, then I will find some old age home for her. I have had enough of her nonsense.'

The following morning, Denis drove around to the Salvation Army headquarters to see the officer in charge. After a short discussion, the Officer in charge said yes, they would take Bridget in but Denis would have to make a monthly donation. Denis explained that there was not much money available, but Bridget would be able to pay her way as she got a decent monthly pension from the Railways. On this basis, Bridget was accepted. Denis arranged to drop her off later that day.

Denis returned home to break the news. Iris was ecstatic, Bridget not so much. Gathering up her belongings and packing them into two suitcases, he loaded up the car. Bridget, thinking he was just making a point at first, refused to move. When she finally realised he was serious, she tried playing the sympathy card.

'I am sorry for last night. I wasn't feeling well and maybe I shouldn't have reacted the way I did. Sorry, Iris, it was wrong of me, it won't happen again.'

'You are right, it won't happen again! Because you are leaving and will not be welcome in this house again,' shouted Denis.

'I am your Mother. After all I have done for you, this is the way you treat me? Your Father will be turning in his grave.'

Ignoring her protests, Denis took her by the hand and led her to the car. Making sure everything was in the car, he took off for the Berea, much to Iris's relief. Unbeknownst to Iris at the time, it would be the last time she would see Bridget alive.

In the ensuing months, Denis would visit his mother at least twice a month, but Iris would not accompany him. Despite Bridget's pleading at every visit, Denis remained strong.

The good news was Maureen was moved back into her room and Jimmy back to his. Although he had to share with four-year old David, it was better than the 'sewing room.'

CHAPTER 8
The Early days - 1966

January 1, Chubby's 16th birthday. A party was arranged but this time the invites were better planned. Chubby was still dating Diane and Ian invited Pam. Fiona, knowing the party was on, coerced Gus into inviting her; this would cause a bit of tension with Chubby's sister, Mary.

Jimmy, with no fixed girlfriend, invited Kerry; much to his surprise she agreed. He wasn't sure if this was an actual date or if she was just coming along as one of the 'crowd'. He decided to play it cool and see where it took him.

A hot summer's day and swimming cozzies were the order of the day. Diane and Pam were well developed for soon to be fifteen years old. Kerry, just turned fifteen, was somewhat less developed but still filled a bikini satisfactorily. The star of the show was again Fiona, with her sensational figure, well developed breasts and the tiniest bikini, totally overshadowed the other three girls.

Diane and Pam kept a close hold on their men. Kerry just played it cool, not showing how intimidated she was by Fiona. Mary joined the party and kept an eye on her friend, Fiona, ready to intervene if things got out of hand. Jimmy, noticing how good Mary looked, regretted inviting Kerry as he knew there was no promise of romance there. He thought maybe it was a good thing Kerry was there; after all Mary was Chubby's sister. Mary had given no indication of being interested in any of Chubby's friends.

Fiona flitted between making a fuss of Gus, much to Kerry's despair, and flirting with Jimmy. Gus had come to realise that Kerry had a 'thing' for him but had not had the opportunity to do anything about it. It seemed that Chubby's party was not going to be that opportunity.

When Fiona and Mary got out of the pool, Gus swam over to Jimmy.

'Hey, any chance you could get a bit friendly with Fiona? I would really like to get to know Kerry better, I think she likes me. I really fancy her. Fiona is a bit too much for me. She is very sexy and does put out a bit, mostly tits but I have had my hand in her panties,' whispered Gus, trying to up sell Fiona.

Jimmy was a bit torn as he really liked Kerry but had never made any moves on her. She obviously fancied Gus, so he agreed to distract Fiona. Gus thanked Jimmy and swam over to Kerry and was soon deep in conversation with her. Kerry was grinning from ear to ear, Gus was looking around nervously. Ian, Chubby and their partners looked on, not a hundred percent sure what was going on, but knew there was something.

The fun started with the return of Fiona and Mary. Jimmy positioned himself to intercept Fiona, when she spotted Gus and Kerry. Fiona, being very self-centred, didn't notice Gus and Kerry together when she jumped into the pool. Jimmy dove under the water and grabbed Fiona around the waist and ducked her under the water. This started some playful wrestling between the two. Gus took the opportunity to take Kerry by the hand, jump out of the pool and head to the front porch.

With Fiona having fun with Jimmy, she appeared not to notice that Gus was missing. To add to the confusion, Jimmy grabbed Mary and pulled her into the pool to join the rumpus. Chubby and Ian, catching on to what was happening, joined in with their partners. It took some time for Fiona to realise Gus was missing.

'Anyone seen Gus?' inquired Fiona.

'I think Kerry wasn't feeling well and Gus offered to take her home. He said he would be back shortly,' offered Jimmy, hoping that Gus had done a runner.

Not missing a beat, Fiona turned to Jimmy and said, 'Well, if he's not back by the time the party is over, you will have to walk me home.'

Jimmy was stuck between a rock and a hard place. He felt he had been making some progress with Mary, who was giving him some encouragement. Mary was his best friend's sister and Fiona was his other best friend's girlfriend. In his opinion, he was screwed either way.

As the party was breaking up, Fiona told Jimmy she was just going to take off her wet cozzie and change; she would only be a few minutes and then he could walk her home.

Mary, who was a year ahead of Jimmy in school and a very good student, surprised Jimmy by asking, 'I've heard you are great at Maths and I wonder if you could help me out with some guidance? Maybe just a couple of afternoons, before we have to go back to school? I would really appreciate it.'

'Sure, when do you want to do it?'

'Can we try Monday afternoon, the day after tomorrow?'

'Okay, see you about two o'clock.'

By the time Fiona emerged Jimmy had changed and was ready to walk her home. Home was all of half a kilometre down Lighthouse Road, a distance she could quite safely walk on her own. Taking Jimmy by the hand, she waved goodbye to the rest of the group and flounced off down the road. Less than five minutes later they arrived at her house. Great, Jimmy thought, I can get back to the party and see what Mary is up to.

'Jimmy, my folks are out. Can you wait until I get inside and check if everything is okay? One cannot be too careful,' pouted Fiona.

Jimmy nodded, this should only take a second. Fiona unlocked the door and then stepped back indicating Jimmy should go in first to check for any danger. Really? he thought. What possible danger could there be? As soon as Jimmy stepped in, Fiona followed closing the door behind her.

'I've been checking you out all afternoon,' said Fiona. 'Come over here.'

Now, this is the point that Jimmy should have made a quick exit.

'What about Gus?' asked Jimmy, being concerned about his best friend.

'Gus is very immature, and we are just friends, nothing serious. I need a more mature man, someone like you.' Fiona moved closer to Jimmy and put her arms around his neck.

Jimmy, being a fifteen-year old male, acted absolutely in character, all moral thoughts went out of the window. Fiona leaned in and with an open mouth kissed Jimmy who responded in kind. When Fiona had changed out of her bikini she had not bothered to put on any underwear; no bra or panties.

Jimmy, initially unaware of this, just concentrated on kissing her and wrestling with her tongue. As the kissing became more intense, his hand began to roam. His standard move was to try and cop a feel of a girl's breasts on the outside of the blouse, which he did and got no push back. Still unaware that she had no bra on, he continued to massage Fiona's breast.

Suddenly, Fiona pushed Jimmy's hand away. Thinking he had blown his chances, he stepped back waiting for the expected reprimand. To his utter shock, Fiona ripped off her blouse, exposing two beautiful naked breasts. She stepped back into Jimmy, pressed her crotch into Jimmy's rapidly hardening penis and relocked lips.

Jimmy continued to massage Fiona's right breast and placed his right hand in the middle of her back. Fiona then pulled her crotch slightly away from Jimmy but remained kissing. Taking Jimmy's right hand, she moved back slightly and placed his hand under the waistband of her skirt. Jimmy was in uncharted territory here and just left his hand where she placed it.

Fiona, sensing no movement, took the initiative and moved Jimmy's hand down through her pubic hairs and placed it directly over her vagina.

'I want you to finger me,' she said, spreading her legs.

Jimmy, still not sure what to do, moved his fingers to cup her vagina. Feeling it very wet and spongy he started to explore and more with luck than knowledge, he managed to insert a finger into Fiona. She moaned, pulled back slightly and dropped her skirt to the floor; she was now completely naked.

Jimmy, still completely dressed and in possession of the biggest boner of his young life, just continued pounding away with his fingers, not sure what to do next. Fiona solved that problem for him. She reached in, undid his waistband button, unzipping his shorts, releasing his erect penis. Jimmy, with his penis pressed tight up to Fiona's stomach, continued with his fingering.

A few minutes later he felt Fiona shuddering; unaware that she was experiencing an orgasm, he just continued fingering her. He was scared to pull away from her as he wasn't sure what would happen next. Fiona, again, solved his dilemma.

Backing off, she took hold of his cock and said, 'Okay, now it's your turn.'

Pushing him back into a sitting position on the couch, she knelt down in front of him. Taking his cock in her right hand, she began to masturbate him, starting slowly and building up speed. In no time at all, Jimmy felt himself coming, shuddering and with a feeling that exceeded anything he had experienced before, his semen shot out all over Fiona's hand and much of her arm.

Jimmy, embarrassed at the mess he had caused, looked over at Fiona who just grinned at him. Releasing his rapidly shrinking cock, she stood up and told Jimmy she was going to clean up and maybe he should as well. She pointed to the guest bathroom, and still naked, turned and headed for her bedroom.

Jimmy stood, pulled up his pants and walked over to the bathroom. He spent a few minutes cleaning up the mess he had caused and as he was nervous to return and face Fiona, he sat fully dressed on the toilet to contemplate. What had just happened? She was Gus' girlfriend, was he also doing this with her? I cannot tell him what happened.

'Hey, Jimmy, what's keeping you? Come on out, it's time for you to leave. My folks will be home soon.'

Plucking up courage, Jimmy opened the door and returned to the lounge. There he found Fiona, still naked. One look and Jimmy felt his penis starting to get hard all over again; she really had a stunning body. Desperate to get out of the house he headed for the front door, Fiona beat him to it.

One hand around the back of his neck and the other grabbing hold of his totally erect cock, she proceeded to stick her tongue halfway down his throat.

Breaking away, she said, 'Next time bring some condoms and maybe I'll let you go all the way. Now, go before I wank you off again.' She stepped back, opened the door and with a seductive grin pushed Jimmy out. 'See you soon.'

Jimmy, still with a serious erection needed no second invitation to leave. Two questions in his mind. First, will this erection go down and quickly? Secondly, was there going to be a next time? He would have to speak to Gus. He decided to go home rather than back to the party.

Monday morning, Ian pitched up at Jimmy's house. Desperate for details Ian quizzed him.

'What happened to you? You never came back to the party. Chub's sister seemed a bit pissed off with you. Come on, details.'

'You cannot tell Gus until I talk to him. You will never believe what happened,' said Jimmy and he proceeded to supply Ian with all the gory details.

'Fuck, are you going to see her again? Maybe she'll let you screw her. Shit, where can we get condoms? Man, do you think Gus will be pissed off? Maybe he has already screwed her.' babbled Ian, barely able to believe his ears.

'She scares me a bit. I will wait and see what Gus says when I tell him. God, I hope he is not pissed. What did Mary say?'

'I don't think Gus will be pissed off. He said she never stopped phoning him, I think he will be happy as he can now make a move on Kerry.'

'Great, what about Mary?'

'I think she wasn't happy about you leaving with her friend. She said she will warn you about her when you see her on Monday. That's today, my old mate. Good luck with that.'

'Oh shit, I forgot about that.'

What a start to the new year. No female attachments and now two who are supposed to be best friends. Thank God we don't have a phone. I'm going to have to duck and dive. Maybe I can just pretend I forgot about the Maths and just not pitch up today. Man, its Chubby's sister, maybe she really does only want Maths help. I have to go. With all these thoughts rushing through his head, he decided to do the right thing.

Promptly at two o'clock, Jimmy pitched up at the Murphy household. Chubby met him at the front door but before he could be interrogated, Mary appeared.

'Ah Jimmy, thanks for coming. I have my books ready, let's get started,' said Mary, taking Jimmy by the hand and leading him off to her bedroom.

Seeing all her books laid out on the desk next to the bed, Jimmy breathed a sigh of relief. Mary, getting down to business, directed Jimmy to one of the chairs next to her desk.

.Opening her standard nine trigonometry book, she proceeded to explain to Jimmy that she had gotten only a C for her year-end exams and hoped he could give her get a better understanding of Maths. Jimmy, only starting standard nine, had not had any exposure to this level of Maths.

'I have only done standard eight level maths and I am not sure if I can help you, but I will try.' Maybe she would see that, and he could duck out.

'I am sure you will pick it up and give me some pointers as to where I went wrong. Should we start?'

'Okay.'

'Did you manage to get Fiona home okay? She can be a bit overwhelming at times.'

Here it comes, thought Jimmy. 'I just walked her to her place, dropped her off and went home. I thought the party would be over, so I went directly home. Right, where do you want to start?'

Mary, realising no further details of the walk home would be forthcoming, opened her book and explained just where she was having problems. The two of them spent the next two hours going over Mary's issues in dealing with Mathematical problems.

Jimmy enjoyed Mary's close proximity and more than enjoyed going over, in great detail, how to simplify Mathematics. At the end of the two hours, Mary had, in that short time, already found a better understanding of how to solve problems much easier than she had previously. Her original plan was just to spend some time alone with Jimmy, but she realised that he was also a great teacher; double bonus.

Mary, desperate to keep this going, suggested they do it again on Wednesday.

'Unfortunately, I am going into Durban to order my new surfboard. I have been saving like crazy but now I have enough. If it's okay with you, we can do it next Monday,' offered Jimmy, hoping that unlike the guys, girls didn't share their 'sexual experiences'.

'Oh, that's great. I hope to see you surfing the waves. Come around here anytime for a swim. Don't wait for that brother of mine to invite you. Thanks for coming, you have been a great help,' said Mary, giving Jimmy a peck on the cheek.

I sure hope Fiona keeps her mouth shut as I quite like Mary, thought Jimmy. I must be careful not to cock this one up, too many friends involved. Jimmy managed to make an exit without being accosted by Chubby.

The next day, the four friends met up at Brighton beach, Jimmy and Ian the last to arrive. Jimmy was extremely nervous about having to tell Gus. He needn't have worried.

'Hey Jimmy, thanks for distracting Fiona so as I could get away with Kerry. You are a real mate. I am really stoked with Kerry; we get on so well. Fiona was too overwhelming for me. She was always phoning me and ordering me around. Kerry is just really cool.'

'That's okay, anything for a friend. I am sure that you would do the same for me. Good luck with Kerry, she's a great chick, a really nice Mom too.' Glad that's all out in the open, we can move on, thought Jimmy.

'Surf's up, let's hit the waves,' shouted Jimmy.

'Not so fast, we need details and we have to compare notes on how you did, compared to Gus,' said Chubby.

'Gentlemen don't kiss and tell,' offered Jimmy. 'Anyway, I am sure I didn't do anything that Gus didn't do.'

'Fuck that, supply details,' said Chubby and Gus in tandem.

This left Jimmy in a bit of a conundrum. If he left out all the details and Fiona told Mary, he was sure Chubby would find out and tell Gus. Best plan was to lay out all the details, which he did. Ian already had all the details, but Gus and Chubby listened with mouths agape.

At the end of the story, Chubby turned to Gus and said, 'Gee Gus, did you get that far with her as well?'

'Fuck no. We did some serious kissing; I felt her tits on the outside but nothing more. To tell the truth, she scared the crap out of me. Anyway, we were only together alone a few times. Shit, if only I'd known.'

'Are you okay with what happened between me and her?' asked Jimmy.

'Hell yes, she's all yours,' replied Gus.

'Thanks, but she scares me a bit too. I may have to do a bit of ducking and diving, but she is tempting.'

'Hey, what's going on with you and my sister? You know her and Fiona are going to talk,' said Chubby.

'Nothing I am helping her with Maths. I really like her, she is nice and we get on fine but that is all,' replied Jimmy. Changing the subject, 'Don't forget we are going into Durban tomorrow to organise my surfboard.'

'What a guy. First to almost fuck a girl and now getting a surfboard. What a legend,' mocked Chubby. 'Let's hit the surf.'

The following day, the four friends caught the bus into Durban. Ian had taken the day off work, eager to be part of 'the surfboard selection'. On arrival, the boys took the short walk down West Street to Max Whetland's Surf Shop. Whetland, one of South Africa's pioneer surfers, had a thriving business making and selling surf boards, belly boards and various other surfing paraphernalia.

Four teenagers, chattering noisily, entered the shop. The staff's immediate reaction was one of suspicion. Shoplifting was a huge problem and generally happened when a group of kids entered together. The staff figured keeping a close eye on this group was necessary.

Jimmy and team headed straight for the twenty-odd surfboards stacked against the one wall. Loudly evaluating each board in turn and going into great detail, attracted one of the staff, who strolled over.

'What are you kids looking for here? You need to tone down the noise as you are starting to annoy the other customers,' said the heavily tanned, bleach blond sales assistant. 'You are obviously not buying, so what do you want? I have my eyes on you lot.'

'Do you work on sales commission?' Jimmy asked.

'Yes. what's it to you?'

'Oh nothing, just interested, I might want a job like this one day and it's good to know about commission.'

'Ok kiddies, either buy something or get out the shop, and don't try to steal anything.'

Jimmy looked the guy up and down, turned around and walked up to the sales counter. Recognising Max Whetland, he said, 'I want to buy a surfboard, but I don't see one I like so I will need it to be built. Can you help me?'

'Sure, I'll get my assistant to help you,' said Max, pointing to the guy who had just accosted the boys.'

'Sorry, not from that arsehole, it will either have to be you or someone else.'

'Why is that?'

'Let him explain.'

Max called over surfer dude, took him aside and a protracted discussion took part. Jimmy couldn't hear what they were saying but it was obvious surfer dude was getting crapped on. Conversation over, Max returned.

'Hey, gotta apologise, you are right; he can be a bit of an arsehole. Right, let's see what I can do for you.'

Max spent the next hour questioning Jimmy on what his needs were and giving back ideas on what his board should be like. A tailored Whetland design was going to cost a bit more than Jimmy had planned. Max thought the design would be a bit out of this kid's budget, but he was repairing the damage caused by surfer dude. The kid would probably buy one off the shelf, if he was buying at all.

After discussion with his mates, Jimmy settled on the shape and design Max had drawn up for him. Nine foot six inches long, weighing thirty pounds; a Whetland designed surfboard.

'Ok Sir, what's the cost and how long will it take to build?'

Confident little bugger, Max thought. 'Let me see. I can get this done in about ten days, say two weeks from when you pay me. I'll give you a special price of R120.' Thinking that would be the end of the conversation, Max stepped back to wait the response.

'Ok Sir. I'll just have to get to the Bank. I will be back in about ten minutes.'

'I'll make up the order as soon as you get back,' said a very surprised Max. He wasn't sure whether the kid had the money, or if it was just an exit strategy.

Armed with his Standard Bank savings book, Jimmy headed for the bank. He was back in just over fifteen minutes, armed with the required R120. Max promised his board would be ready by around the 18th. Jimmy gave him Ian's phone number; Max would call when the board was ready.

As they were leaving, Max called them back. 'I have a storage unit just off Addington beach if you want to do some surfing while waiting for your board. You can use a couple of the boards I have there. It's just opposite Gremmie's Corner, tell Pete I sent you. Good luck, here's some wax to get you started.'

With the rest of the day ahead of them, they headed for Max's storage. Finding Pete, Jimmy and Gus arranged to return the next day. Ian had work and Chubby was meeting up with Diane.

Every day, bar Saturdays, Jimmy and Gus pitched up and Pete provided them with a surfboard each, with the strict instruction to return by five o'clock. Ironically, Gus picked up surfing quicker than Jimmy. Jimmy figured once he had his own board, he would show Gus a thing or two.

Jan 13, 1966
Three visiting Labour M.P.'s expelled from Rhodesia.

Max called Ian's house and left a message that Jimmy's board would be ready for pickup on 19th. School was due to start on Monday 17th so Jimmy called Max up and asked if he could pick it up on Saturday 22nd, Max agreed.

The start of standard nine; second last year of high school. Also, the year all four would have to register for identification cards, which would then place their details on file for National Service. Chubby, already sixteen, had registered, Jimmy, Ian and Gus would follow once they turned sixteen.

First day of school and class assignments. Gus and Jimmy assigned to 9A, with Terry Niven as class teacher. Chubby was in 9B. Ian 9C as he was taking a non-academic subject, Technical Drawing. Finally, a different Afrikaans teacher, Mrs. Meiring. Jimmy hoped this would provide an upturn in his Afrikaans proficiency.

One immediate benefit was that Mrs. Meiring, due to some childhood sickness, had no sense of smell. For every benefit like being able to secretly eat anything during her lessons, there was the apparent negative of being able to drop a silent fart and stink out the classroom.

Saturday morning 9am Jimmy, Gus and Chubby pitched up at Whetland Surf Shop to take delivery of Jimmy's new surfboard. It was a thing of beauty.

'Where is your home surf spot?' asked Max.

'Well, I live on the Bluff, so I suppose Brighton,' replied Jimmy.

'So, you have transport to get the board home?'

'Shit,' said Jimmy. In the excitement, no one had given any thought on just how to get the board home.

'I tell you what, son. Take the board down to my storage. Tell Pete I said not to let anyone touch your board or I'll have his nuts. Leave it there as long as you like or until you get it home. Enjoy it, any problems you come and see me. Good luck.'

The boys took turns carrying the board the three quarters of a mile down to Gremmies corner, all the time trying to look cool. They arrived at Addington and Jimmy went through the ritual of waxing up his board. Each had a turn. Eventually Jimmy proclaimed it was ready for its first wave.

There was quite a strong onshore easterly wind blowing. This made the surf very choppy with an indiscernible even wave break. Undeterred, Jimmy paddled out to just beyond the break-line, sat up and surveyed the scene. The first thing he noticed was that he was the only youngster out there, the half a dozen or so other surfers were all a whole lot older. He sat for a while, supposedly waiting for the right wave, but in reality, he was watching the other surfers to see how good or bad they were. Best not to make a fool of yourself, he thought.

He eventually plucked up the courage and paddled into a small three-foot wave. He got up okay and retained his balance. Not trying anything fancy, he rode the wave until it petered out and he fell off. Standing in the water waiting for him was Gus.

'Okay, my turn china.' called Gus.

Jimmy pushed the board towards him, and Gus hopped aboard and paddled out. Gus had barely reached the break line when he spotted a neat five-footer. He turned, paddled and was up on his feet. Pulling a few cutbacks and walk up to the nose, Gus showed off his skill. Gus finished the ride and Jimmy called Chubby over for his turn.

Chubby managed to get out okay but had some difficulty picking up a wave. For the best part of ten minutes he struggled before catching a small wave. He tried to stand up but fell off immediately. The board bobbed its way into shore to be snapped up by Jimmy who passed Chubby on his way in.

Jimmy, feeling a bit more confident after Chubby's effort, caught a decent ride in and passed the board to Gus. Gus caught his wave in and looked for Chubby. He found him on the shore kicking a football around with a bunch of other youngsters. Not managing to master riding a surfboard, he gravitated towards what he was best at.

Gus and Jimmy swapped rides until around 4pm when it was time to get the board to Pete for storage. Packing up their stuff they headed off. Pete was expecting them. He showed them where the board would be stored and inquired when they would be back next.

'Oh tomorrow, right guys?' said Jimmy.

'I can't make it; Diane is coming over.'

'Neither can I; my aunt says I have to study in the morning and I'm seeing Kerry in the afternoon. Maybe Ian will come with you.'

'That's okay, I get the message. I'm starving, who's up for Bunny Chow? I'm paying. Then we'll head home.'

The boys headed over to Point Road Café and ordered one of Durban's finest Bunny Chows. It consisted of half a loaf of bread. The soft inside is scooped out and the loaf filled with mutton curry. The scoop is then squashed up and plugged back into the top of the loaf, all for twenty-five cents.

The Bunny was devoured quickly and they made a hasty retreat for the bus home to the Bluff.

With school restarting, beach time was severely curtailed. Weekdays were out of the question. Jimmy and Ian both worked Saturday mornings and by the time they were finished it was too late to head for Durban. Chubby and Ian both played cricket Saturday mornings. Both had steady girlfriends, who had no interest in going through to Durban, not that either boy had any spare cash.

Jimmy had not told his parents about his surfboard purchase and as they never asked questions, he thought why bother. The only problem was that he was going to have to ask his father to pick up his board and bring it home.

The problem was eventually solved. A fellow surfer, one Benny Holmes who lived right off Anstey's Beach, had dinged his board and had been sent into Max's shop to be repaired. Jimmy heard that Benny's dad was taking him into Durban to pick up his board. Knowing Benny quite well, Jimmy asked if he could hitch a ride back with his board. So, it came to pass. Jimmy arranged to leave his board at Benny's house, adding to the collection already stored there.

Mar 15, 1966
The Royal Air Force is granted a base on Madagascar to patrol the African coast for Rhodesian sanctions busters.

Unbeknownst to the other three, Ian had saved up enough to purchase his Honda 50cc motorcycle and had already paid a deposit. Before he could pick it up, he would have to provide proof that he was at least sixteen years old and had the permission of a parent. Ian, always able to talk his mother around, broke the news on the Wednesday. His birthday was on Friday, April 1 and he hoped he could take delivery on the Saturday. He would have to register for National Service sometime on or shortly after his birthday. After initial resistance to the idea, his mother agreed to accompany him to the Honda dealer on Saturday. Ian picked up his sparkling new red Honda with the strict instructions it could only be used on and around the Bluff.

Mar 31, 1966
Verwoerd's National Party retains power in South Africa after a white's only election.

Two and a half weeks of Easter school holidays. The weather was still warm enough for the beach. Apart from Ian, who was working every day, the other three spent the windy days at Chubby's pool and the windless days at Brighton Beach.

One positive as far as Jimmy was concerned, was Fiona's arrival at the beach, accompanied by Mary. Fiona had had no method of contacting Jimmy, so she decided to persuade Mary to accompany her to the beach with the plan of tracking Jimmy down. Mary, who still harboured desires for Jimmy, had reluctantly agreed.

The two girls arrived much to the boys' surprise and concern. Chubby didn't want his sister hanging around and Jimmy didn't want Fiona for company. The minute he laid eyes on Fiona, Jimmy grabbed his board and headed for the surf.

Fiona, making a production of it, stripped down to her tiny bikini. She really had a magnificent body and drew many approving looks. Realising Jimmy had headed out to the surf to avoid her, she decided to check out the rest of the talent. Spotting a group of lifesavers of the Dolphin Surf Life Savers Club lounging around their clubhouse, she decided a walk in that direction was called for.

The Dolphin lifesavers were well known for their ability to attract female company, Fiona was no exception. As she neared the clubhouse she was motioned over. Being out of earshot, it was impossible to make out what was said to her, but it was obvious that that was the last they would see of her for a while. The normal plan with the lifesavers was to take a person on a 'tour' of the club house. Fiona disappeared inside with one of the guys. Fifteen minutes later he emerged and one of his buddies got up and went into the clubhouse.

It was obvious what was going on. Mary was horrified and wanted to intervene, but Chubby stopped her. Jimmy spotted what was happening and caught the next wave in. On reaching the beach, he called Gus over to look after his board and he headed over to the clubhouse where he was stopped by the group of lifesavers.

'Fuck off, sonny, this is none of your business,' he was told.

'Sure. I just thought I would warn you she is only fourteen and pulls this stunt all the time. A couple of you will fuck her and then she will call rape. Her Dad is a criminal lawyer so you have been warned. Your best bet is to kick her out of there before the shit hits the fan.'

The guy who was the first to take Fiona on a 'tour', leapt up and ran into the clubhouse. He emerged less than a minute later dragging Fiona with him.

'Don't let me see you around here again, you silly girl, you are banned from this beach.'

Fiona, fortunately with her bikini intact, ran crying back to where Mary was sitting. Gathering their things, they got ready to leave. Mary glanced over to Jimmy and mouthed a thank you to him; she was even more infatuated with Jimmy for his show of gallantry in rescuing

Fiona. Mary was sure that that was the last Jimmy would see of Fiona, maybe there was hope for her yet.

Apr 4, 1966
**A Greek tanker laden with oil believed to be bound for Rhodesia
is intercepted by the Royal Navy off Mozambique.**

The start of the second school term meant it was rugby season. Heading towards winter also meant that the new National Football League season was starting. Jimmy was keen to get back to a job at Kingsmead. Ian wasn't interested as he was making enough money and anyway, now that he had transport, his mother would only allow him to ride his motorcycle on the Bluff.

May 13, 1966
**3000 students demonstrate in Johannesburg over the banning of
student leader, Ian Robertson.**

With the rugby season underway, Chubby found himself picked as fly-half for the first team with Gus starting out as scrum-half for the second fifteen. Ian returned to Fynnlands to play for the Under 17 team. Jimmy, having given up football, was more concerned in getting a ticket seller's job at Kingsmead.

June 1' Gus' sixteenth birthday. Gus, always one to stick to the rules, decided to go to the Department of Home Affairs to register for his Identity Document. Ian and Jimmy, who hadn't registered yet, decided to join him. Their first step into eventual National Service.

Jun 7, 1966
**James Meredith, the first black to brave the colour bar at the
University of Mississippi in 1962 was shot in the back and legs
just after he entered into Mississippi on a civil rights march. All
he was carrying was a bible.**

The first home game of the season was on Sunday June 9. Jimmy arrived early at the main gate where he found several other people also lining up for jobs. A few of them were known to him but most were newcomers.

The 'roll call' started with the gate supervisors. All who were allocated were regulars. The call for ticket sellers was next. Jimmy

105

placed himself front and centre. The prime jobs were on the main gates and the European south gates, R10 per game. The regulars got these jobs, Jimmy was lucky to get a position on the north gates which were predominately Indian at R8 per game.

Jimmy's first stint selling tickets went well; he balanced his cash to the tickets sold. Fifty cents per adult and twenty-five for a child. Indians; being Indians; would always try and get an adult in for a child's price, but usually they took it in good faith. Jimmy found that he enjoyed the banter. Further on in the season he had the opportunity to get one of the 'white' gates but chose to stay on the 'Indian' gates.

One of the drawbacks of working at Kingsmead was if you wanted to guarantee your job; you needed to turn up for every game. This meant if there was a midweek game; you had to show up. A new Durban team; Addington FC; had started playing their home games at Kingsmead and the same ground staff was expected to man the jobs. This meant every Sunday and maybe one or two week-night games.

With his job at Kingsmead and his job at the hardware store, Jimmy's bank balance was growing. The issue was that his schoolwork was suffering. The monthly test results showed that, other than Maths and Geography, he was just doing enough to get by. The monthly test cards were handed to the students and required to be returned with a parent's signature. Neither of Jimmy's parents ever inquired about his schoolwork and so were blissfully unaware of the situation. Jimmy just took to signing the monthly report card himself; no one was any the wiser.

Jun 30, 1966
US bombs hit Hanoi for the first time.

School breaks up for the three-week July holidays. It was too cold for surfing without a wetsuit and the same problem with Chubby's pool. With Ian working most days and Gus forced by his aunt to study more, it was left to Chubby and Jimmy to hang out together.

Jimmy, flush with money, had taken Mary out to movies a couple of times. He liked Mary but was nervous of trying his luck too much, as she was one of his best friends' sister. Mary, on the other hand, was a very insecure girl and didn't have the confidence to force a move in their friendship. She did enjoy going out with Jimmy but really wanted more than what went on between them.

Gus' relationship with Kerry had begun cooling off. Kerry, frustrated that Gus had to spend so much time studying, only saw him on weekends. During the school holidays she thought she would see him every day. When this did not happen, she went to a party with her friend, Jenny. At the party she met a guy from Westville named Dave Fagan.

At the party, she spent the entire evening dancing with Dave. This was, under normal circumstances, no big deal, but to Jenny's surprise Kerry and Dave kept disappearing. On the trip home all Kerry could talk about was Dave, Dave, Dave. When asked what about Gus? all she would say was that Dave was everything Gus wasn't.

The next day, Sunday, Gus and Jimmy arrived at the Vermeulen home to see Kerry, totally unaware of what was going to happen. Jimmy walked up and knocked on the door, which was answered by Ingrid, Kerry's older sister.

'I am glad you are here. Maybe you can talk some sense into my sister,' said Ingrid. 'I am sick and tired of hearing all about Dave! She's an idiot.'

'Who's Dave?' asked Jimmy.

'Best to let her explain, Kerry. your friends are here!'

Kerry appeared, looking nonplussed. 'Jimmy, I need to talk to Gus alone.'

'Okay, I came to see your Mom anyway. I need to check about working Wednesdays.'

Jimmy went to chat to Mrs. Vermeulen and left Kerry alone with Gus. A few minutes later, Gus appeared in the kitchen.

'Hi Mrs. Vermeulen, Jimmy and I have to leave. Bye,' said Gus.

Gus and Jimmy left, saying goodbye to Ingrid and her mother. Stopping at the end of the driveway, Gus turned to Jimmy and related his talk with Kerry.

'Well, that's all over between us. I don't know who this Dave guy is, but if she falls madly in love with him after one party, he can have her. I think it just proves how immature and silly she is. I doubt I will be visiting this house again. I am off home. See you around.'

Wow, Jimmy thought, this might get awkward. Jimmy, Gus, Chubby and Ian would often stop off at the Vermeulen home for coffee and a chat. Could the three of them still do that without pissing Gus off? At our age, true love is measured in weeks or days not months and years. As much as I fancy Kerry, I think I will just stay friend's and not get all romantic. The same applies to Mary. Friendship seems to last longer than true love.

Wednesday July 13 would turn out to be a significant day in Jimmy Wilson's life. Working at Kingsmead that evening, Jimmy was designated to the last gate open. He had balanced up his cash and tickets but had to remain open for any latecomers. About five minutes after kick-off, a breathless young Indian boy arrived at his gate.

'Please Sir, I have been attacked and robbed of all my money. I am scared, can I come in?' he pleaded.

Jimmy, looking at the boy of about the same age as himself, noticed the torn shirt, a bloody nose and a cut above his eye. He heard all sorts of stories from Indians but sensed this one was true.

'How can I help you?'

'Just let me in and maybe they will have left by the end of the game. I live in Chatsworth and can hitch-hike home after the game.'

Gee, he has been beaten and robbed but still wants to see the game. He must be a true fan; he doesn't seem like a chancer, thought Jimmy.

'I tell you what. Go in for free and here's fifty cents for bus fare. You can pay me back next time you are here, okay? My name is Jimmy, what's yours?'

'Thank you, thank you Sir, my name is Raj Moodley. I will pay you back on Sunday.'

With that Raj disappeared up the steps and headed for the grandstand. That's probably the last I'll see of him Jimmy thought, but what's fifty cents after all.

The following Sunday, Raj appeared with his father, mother, three brothers and two cousins all in tow.

'This is my Dad; he has come to thank you and pay for my Wednesday's ticket and the bus fare you lent me,' said Raj.

'Raj told me what you did for him, we are very grateful. Our whole family is here to say thank you and pay back what Raj owes you.'

'It's no problem. Raj seemed like a genuine guy and he is a City fan, no need to pay me back. Why don't you all go in? This one's on me,' said Jimmy, taking the brake off the turnstile and ushering through eight 'Moodleys'. 'Hey Raj, you can come through my gate anytime. Up the City!'

Mister Moodley was the last through the turnstile, he leaned over and shook Jimmy's hand and passed him a business card. It was from House of Lords Clothing, R.J. Moodley owner.

'Jimmy, any time you need clothes, you just come and see me. I'll give you the best deal in town.'

Jimmy pocketed the card. Raj never paid for another match as long as Jimmy was on the gate. A casual friendship developed.

One thing he noticed during this episode was that no-one seemed to care that a whole bunch of people had entered the stadium without a ticket. The ticket tearer figured Jimmy had some deal going on and the supervisor, if he even noticed, didn't seem to care. Once through the turnstile, you didn't need a ticket. In many cases the ticket holder was in such a rush that they didn't bother to wait for their half of the ticket to be returned to them by the ticket tearer. As long as they got their ticket and got through the turnstile, they couldn't care what happened to the ticket.

During a lull in the incoming crowds, Jimmy motioned his ticket tearer, Mickey, over.

'What do you do with the torn ticket stubs?'

'I just chuck them in the bin.'

'Both pieces if they don't wait for their half?'

'Yes, for sure.'

'I tell you what, if you end up with an untorn "adult" ticket, see if you can get it back to me without being noticed. I have a plan; maybe we can make a few bucks on the side.'

It didn't take long for Mickey to smuggle two adult tickets back to Jimmy. Jimmy sorted the untorn tickets into his 'live' ticket book and shortly thereafter resold them. Easy R1 in the pocket. Throughout the course of the game they repeated the process several times, turning a profit of R4 each.

After cashing up they got together to split up the proceeds. Mickey mentioned to Jimmy that many times the Indians would just say, 'Keep it' when he went to tear their ticket. He reckoned that they knew that there was a plan to be made. Whenever they worked together, Jimmy and Mickey, careful not to get too greedy, would make anything up to R10 each.

July 30, 1966
England beat West Germany by four goals to two after extra time to win the World Cup at Wembley in London.

Back at school, life continued along a regular pattern. Ian worked most days after school, Gus studied and Chubby played or practised rugby.

Jimmy found himself spending more and more time at the Vermeulen's house. He still worked Saturdays but had given up on Wednesday afternoons. The only major change was Jimmy's performance or lack of it at school. Kerry was still love-struck on Dave, even though she hadn't had any contact with him since the party.

Sept 6, 1966

Seven minutes after taking his seat in the House of Assembly, the South African Prime minister, Doctor Hendrik Verwoerd, the father of apartheid, was assassinated by Demetrio Tsafendaas. The assassin, of Greek and Portuguese parentage, stabbed Verwoed four times in the chest.

Verwoerd's assassination brought the whole apartheid issue into more focus. The boys were aware of the policy but in the main were not directly touched by it so had never paid much attention to it. The fact that there was no television, and the newspapers were somewhat censored, hid what the rest of the world thought of South Africa and its policies. Out of the group, only Gus had an opinion and voiced his objections to the others. By his reckoning, the rest of the world would start boycotting South African goods very soon and then move on to sports boycotts.

Sept 13, 1966

Balthazar Johannes Vorster is sworn in as the new South African Prime minister.

Vorster's appointment would have a direct influence on the whole group's future. The world's universal hatred of the man would have direct consequences on Jimmy, Gus and in particular Chubby's futures.

As the final term of the year started, thoughts turned towards the 'matric dance'. It was the job of the standard nine pupils to plan and organise the matric dance. When the organising committee was formed, both Jimmy and Gus were missing in action. Ian wasn't asked but Chubby was coerced into joining. He promptly appointed himself in charge and spent the entire process delegating.

The next major decision was who to take as a partner. Chubby had a steady girlfriend. Gus, Jimmy and Ian were single. It was also around this

110

time that the boys had started going to the regular 'sessions' held at the Fynnlands Sports Club and the Alex. Kerry was only allowed to attend the dances if Jimmy escorted her to and from the event. This proved a bit of an issue with Gus, but as Jimmy spent so much time at the Vermeulen house, he felt obliged to agree with Kerry's mother's request.

The normal process was that Jimmy would have the first dance with Kerry and then head off to try his luck with some unsuspecting young girl. As the band called the last dance, Jimmy would locate Kerry and have that dance with her. Most times that last dance was a slow one and it always felt a bit strange getting that intimately close to her.

After the session, Jimmy would walk Kerry home and stop for coffee. Ian would often join them which would preclude any further activities of a romantic nature. Kerry still jabbered on about Dave so Jimmy figured it would be a waste of effort to make a move on her.

As the matric dance neared, Jimmy eventually plucked up the courage to ask Kerry if she would accompany him to the dance.

'Why did you leave it so late to ask? Ian has already asked, and I said yes.' she replied.

'Ian? Are you kidding me?

'Yes, Ian; at least he asked. I didn't think you were ever going to ask. Anyway, I am only going with him as a friend.'

'Okay then, I'll ask Mary, we always have a good time together.'

'Who is Gus going with?'

'I don't know. Why would you care?'

'I don't care, I was just asking.'

'Okay then, I am off. See you on Friday,' said Jimmy. Ian? That was a bit of a sneaky move. Oh well, he can deal with invisible Dave, at least Mary and I will have some fun. He asked her the next day and she agreed. The dance was scheduled for Saturday November 19.

The start of the year end examinations coincided with the matriculants finishing up and leaving for study time. This also meant that temporary prefects were required for the remainder of the school year. Chubby, Gus and, surprising to everyone, Jimmy were selected. Exams written and completed by November 14 it meant lessons were over for the year with nothing much going on until prize-giving on the 17th. School would break up on December 2.

The exam results showed Gus to have seven A's and first in class. Jimmy had one A for Maths, one B for Geography and rest a mixture of C's, D's and an F for Afrikaans.

Chubby and Ian both passed comfortably. Prize-giving saw Gus get the prize for best in Standard, Jimmy the Maths prize (and an admonishment from Van for his very average overall results), Chubby, the sportsman of the year and a reward of school colours.

The matric dance music was supplied by a local Bluff band called the Stilettos, who also performed at many of the sessions. The tables were setup for groups of six which meant one of the couples would have to sit apart. Gus and his date Jenny (Kerry's friend) offered to move, which took any tension out of the evening.

Jimmy had organised a bottle of vodka, which he hid in the bushes near the toilet area. They would take it in turns to duck out and have a nip, hoping not to be caught. Dancing with Mary for the first time and fortified with a good couple of nips of vodka, Jimmy relaxed and enjoyed himself.

As the evening wore on, the music slowed, and lights dimmed; couples locked at the hips shuffled around the dance floor. Chubby and Diane, Gus and Jenny were among the couples kissing. Ian was being held at arm's length by Kerry, nothing much going on there.

Jimmy, now rather mellowed, forgot himself for a second and leaned in to kiss Mary. Surprised at first, Mary pulled back, then realising what was going to happen she moved, opened her mouth slightly and kissed Jimmy for the first time. The kiss lasted the entire length of the song and was repeated enthusiastically for the rest of the evening.

Kerry, seeing what going on with Jimmy and Gus, decided to join in the fun. After keeping Ian at a distance for the whole evening, she moved in closer, put her arms around his neck and moved in to kiss him. Ian, shocked at first, quickly responded. He later told the boys that Kerry was an exceptional kisser and he thinks he should start dating her.

At the end of the dance, Gus got a lift back to Jenny's house with her father. Chubby and Jimmy got a ride with Chubby's mother, who dropped Diane off first and then Jimmy. Much to Mary's dismay there was no goodnight kiss. Ian and Kerry got a lift back to the Vermeulen house from where he would take the short walk home. When he went kiss her goodnight, she brushed him off with no explanation.

With the exams and dance over, Jimmy decided, that as far as he was concerned, the holidays started now. He took off the last two weeks of the official school year and went surfing. He saw very little of Mary as she was writing her matric finals and had no time for anything or anyone.

With the school year officially over, Jimmy and Gus decided it was time to find a summer holiday job. They headed into Durban to Greenacres Department Store. Finding their way to the personnel department, both boys were offered jobs; Jimmy in the Hardware Department due to his experience at Crossways and Gus lucked out with a job in the Music Department.

Dec 2, 1966
Harold Wilson and Ian Smith open talks about ending Rhodesia's UDI, aboard HMS Tiger in the Mediterranean.

Work hours were Monday to Friday, 8am to 5pm, and Saturday 8am to 12pm. The pay was good, and an added bonus was a staff discount on any purchases. Staff had to enter and leave via a secure point to avoid any thievery.

As usual, Jimmy found a way to beat the system. He had a visit from one of his school friends, Richard Crowe, who was looking to buy a Christmas present for his mother. Richard picked out a set of flower-pots and Jimmy asked if he wanted them wrapped. Richard replied in the affirmative. Jimmy suggested that Richard continue his shopping for the rest of his 'gifts' and return to collect the flower-pots when he was finished.

The pots would be left with a note 'To be collected'. Jimmy collected the exact amount, walked over to the till and rang up a zero amount. Pocketing the money, he walked back to Richard and informed him that he needed to collect his parcel before the store closed at 5pm. Richard left and returned just before closing time, retrieved his parcel and left. The two of them met up as soon as Jimmy and Gus finished work. Jimmy returned Richard's money, less a R1 'service fee'.

The 'to be collected scheme' was used several times throughout the season. With Gus buying into the process and being in a more popular department for gifts, he made quite a bit more than Jimmy. Not being too greedy, both boys made some extra cash that season.

Dec 22, 1966
Rhodesia leaves the Commonwealth.

Christmas Eve: their final day of work and payday. The shop closed at 12pm, pay was handed out in cash shortly thereafter. Both boys, flush with money, headed back to the Bluff.

Jimmy's parents and siblings were leaving for Sesfontein on Boxing Day to visit Aunt Maggie and would only be back on January 2. Jimmy begged off the trip stating he had promised Jack he would work at Crossways. So, the family left and Jimmy was home alone. He was left with the instruction that if he needed any help, he was to call on Mr. Wiggett, a neighbour who lived diagonally across the road. Mr. Wiggett was a Railway Policeman and Denis figured he would keep a close eye on Jimmy.

It was Ian who suggested a New Year's Eve party; a nice intimate group of six males and six females. The four of them, along with Ashton Martin and Richard Crowe. The girls, Diane, Jenny, Kerry, Mary, Elizabeth Fisher (Ashton's girlfriend). Kerry suggested inviting Janet Promnitz as the extra girl, and that was where everything got out of hand.

Most parties on the Bluff always started out small and by invitation only. What tended to happen was word got out and uninvited guests arrived. The boys had all been party to a number of these. so were determined to keep it a secret, nice and intimate. Unfortunately, Janet happened to mention the party to several of her friends, who told a number of their friends and with that, the mob rolled up.

Jimmy had organised booze for the six of them and when the crowds started arriving, he decided the best solution was to get drunk. Details of the party would only come to light the next day.

Jimmy woke up in just a pair of underpants; Mary had undressed him and put him to bed; he couldn't remember anything after midnight. Gus was asleep in David's bed. There was some unknown person asleep on the floor between the beds.

Dragging himself out of bed, he went to survey the damage. Nothing appeared to be broken or missing. There were empty beer, wine and booze bottles all over the place. He looked out the back door to find Peter Kendall asleep in the dog's kennel. It was eleven thirty on a steaming hot Durban morning, so he decided to hop over the neighbour's wall and have a swim to clear his head. Fortunately, the neighbours were away.

Reaching the pool, he found Peter Kendall's older brother, Dave, passed out on a lilo, floating in the pool. He was only wearing a pair of socks and was sunburnt from head to toe. Jimmy, in his wisdom, decided it would be fun to dive bomb Dave, which he did, causing Dave to fall into the water. This revived a shocked Dave, who had no idea where he was.

'Jesus, Kendall, how pissed were you last night? How the fuck did you end up here and where are your clothes?'

'Fuck me. I am in agony. Headache and sunburn. I have no idea what the fuck happened. Where are my clothes?'

'No idea, china. Here, take my towel and let's get back to my place. Your brother is in the dog's kennel, literally. Maybe he can shed some light. I have no fucking clue what happened last night.'

Dave and Jimmy returned to find Mary and Kerry busy tidying up. Gus was awake, as was Peter Kendall, both complaining of a severe headache. The story of the party unfolded as told by Mary, with additional input from Kerry.

Jimmy had got drunk and passed out, Mary put him to bed. Gus had made a move on Janet with minimum luck and joined Ian (who had been rejected by Kerry) in trying to out drink each other. Diane, sensing the brewing disaster, had dragged Chubby off home before midnight. The body that was asleep between the beds was unknown but had been a bit of a pest. He was wearing a new silk shirt, which Ian decided would be useful to clean his motorcycle with, which he proceeded to do.

Peter Kendall had also struck out with Kerry because he was drunk, so he took off and fell asleep in the dog's kennel. Dave took up the challenge with Kerry, and according to sources (Mary), made some significant progress. Having had a bit too much to drink, and in an attempt to 'speed' things up with Kerry, took off all his clothes. Reading all the signs wrong, all he got for his efforts was a smart slap from Kerry. The funny part was that even though he was seriously sunburnt, the hand imprint from the slap was still clearly visible.

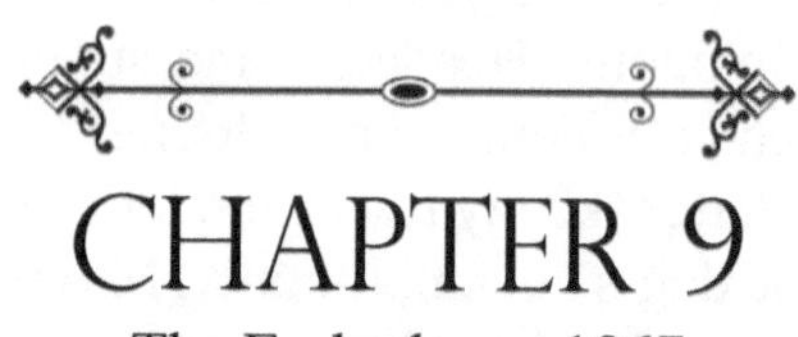

CHAPTER 9
The Early days - 1967

New Year's Day 1967: No damage at the Wilson household other than raging hangovers. It was Chubby's seventeenth birthday and the start of their last year of high school. Jimmy's family arrived home on the afternoon of January 2 and had barely gotten out of the car when Mr. Wiggett arrived. Jimmy watched his father and Wiggett in deep animated conversation. Denis glaring repeatedly at Jimmy, shaking his head. Conversation over, Wiggett left and Denis confronted his son.

'Mr. Wiggett has just told me about your so-called party. What the hell were you thinking? Whatever has been damaged, you will pay for.'

'There was no damage and it was just a few friends celebrating New Year. I don't know what Wiggett told you, but it was quiet affair. You know how he overreacts. I am sorry if I have upset you. How is Aunty Maggie doing?'

'Maggie is getting really old and looks her age, but otherwise she is well. Your Grandmother is not doing so well. We are going to visit her next Sunday and that includes you.'

With two weeks of the summer holidays left and nothing else to do, the boys relocated to the beach. Ian still worked a couple of days whenever Steyn was overloaded, but once school started, his Mother had given strict instructions that he would have to give up his job.

As surfing was growing in popularity, conditions at Brighton Beach were becoming crowded. The lifesavers were continually harassing the surfers to move further and further away from the swimming area. Due to the rocky conditions either side of the main swimming area, it meant that if you wiped out that there a good chance of your board ending up on the rocks and getting dinged.

Anstey's Beach, about a mile up the road near Marine Drive, had good surf, a lot less rocks but wasn't protected by shark nets like

Brighton was. Benny Holmes lived about one hundred meters from Anstey's and was where Jimmy and several others stored their boards. A group of the younger surfers got together and as a group decided to relocate to Ansteys. It would be closer to where they stored their boards so they'd no longer need to carry them the one mile down to Brighton.

Their theory was the lack of shark nets would not be a problem, because the whaling station five miles further up the shore provided plenty of food for the sharks, so there would be no need for them to venture further south looking for food. So it was that Anstey's became the new surfing centre on the bluff.

The four friends, Kerry, Diane, Mary and Jenny spent every possible day at the beach. Mary, having passed her matric finals, was busy sorting out accommodation in Durban with a view to enrolling at Natal Teachers Training College. Jimmy and Mary had been dating regularly and were making good progress. Mary was concerned that living away from home would limit her spending time with her boyfriend and hoped he would stay true to her. The lure of the young holiday makers visiting the caravan park adjacent to the beach would prove difficult to turn down, so Mary was correctly concerned.

January 16. Start of the final school year.

As normal, the entire school congregated in the school hall, standard sixes in the front and by row to the matrics at the back. First order of business was to appoint the prefects, deputy and head boy. The previous year's temporary prefects were called up alphabetically to be presented with their prefect badges. The M's & S's were reached and passed, with no call for Gus & Chubby. The W's were passed with no call for Jimmy; surely, he wasn't one of the two top positions.

Van puffed out his chest, 'Deputy Head boy: Peter Murphy. Come up here Chubby well done.'

Everyone held their breath, surely not. 'Head Boy 1967, Angus Stewart, well done son, most deserved, come on up here.' Jimmy was the only temporary prefect not to get called, the first time that had ever happened. That's what happens when you bunk the last two weeks of the school year.

Class assignments: Gus and Jimmy in 10A, Chubby in 10B and Ian in 10C. Situation normal.

The next big surprise arrived in the mail. Each of the boys received their notifications to report for their medicals for national service. The date was Saturday January 28, 1967, at 8am at the Durban Drill Hall. Non-attendance would require a doctor's certificate.

Seven hundred and twenty-nine sixteen, seventeen and eighteen-year old white males reported for their medical. Lanes were setup alphabetically and the boys were directed to their relevant lane. You would think that this would be a simple process, but it took nearly an hour to get them organised.

Being M's, S's and W's, the boys were in for a long day. Boredom set in. Ian and Jimmy found some small stones on the parade ground and started throwing them at Ian and Chubby. National Servicemen patrolling the lanes soon put a stop to that. As each lane moved through the process, they were allowed to leave.

By 1pm the M lane started moving. The remaining 'troops' were by now thirsty and hungry. Typical Army; no thought of feeding anyone other than themselves, they only provided a water bowser, which by this time held only warm water. Sensing this, the organisers decided to speed up the process.

1.30pm: Gus and Peter emerged, medical complete in double quick time. They were immediately dispatched by Ian and Jimmy to go and find food. Before they arrived back, lane W was called.

The process went something like this:

Walk up to the entrance and present your registration document. You were handed you medical document to be carried through for presentation and completion at each 'station'. Each relevant station had to be signed off.

First station: height and weight. Before Jimmy could get to the scale he was registered as six foot four and one hundred and twenty pounds: as opposed to five eleven and one sixty.

Second station: eyesight check. 'Read the chart.'

'The one on the wall over there?'

'Yes, 20/20, move on.'

Next up: urine test. You were handed a small metal cup to urinate in. Down the centre of the line was a huge forty-four-gallon drum cut in half, to take any overflow. It was a complete cock up. When you had completed the task, you held the cup towards the medical officer who dipped a test strip into it and checked for who knows what. Ian and Jimmy passed whatever the test was for and started to move on. Suddenly, there was a bit of a commotion behind them. Three boys in a row tested positive for diabetes. They were taken aside and had their medical forms marked 'unfit for duty'. It turned out that one of the boys was diabetic and the two behind him were unable to urinate due to dehydration, so he filled their cups as well. You'd think someone would have put two and two together, but no. Two lucky bastards got off not having to do national service.

Last post was injections: two injections, no explanation given. By the time Ian and Jimmy reached this station, the medics had done over six hundred injections between them. Tired and irritated, very little care was given to the process. The kid in front of them had a needle snap off in his arm which caused him to faint. During the commotion, Ian and Jimmy took a gap, bypassed the medics and handed in their forms as though they had had their injections.

Medical complete, they emerged to be greeted by Gus and Chubby armed with two Bunny Chows and cokes.

Three weeks later the official call up papers arrived. Jimmy and Chubby: Army January 1968 intake assigned to Natal Mounted Rifles. Ian: Army January 1968 intake assigned to Durban Light Infantry. Gus: Army October 1968 intake assigned to Natal Mounted Rifles. Gus immediately appealed that he was going to University and requested either the January or April intake of 1968. Four months later he received approved request for January 1968 intake assigned to Natal Mounted Rifles.

As the summer of 1967 continued, very little changed in the way of life on Durban's Bluff.

Jimmy spent every spare moment surfing at Anstey's, Saturday mornings working at the Crossways Hardware store and whenever allowed, could be found at the Vermeulen house, visiting with Kerry. A strong platonic bond had developed between them. The invisible Dave was still omnipresent, discouraging Jimmy from making any further effort.

Ian was forced by his mother to give up his job at Steyn's, except for Saturday mornings, in order to study.

Gus' aunt ensured he spent all his time studying.

Chubby and Diane spent most of their spare time together. Virtually every month there was a panic on waiting for confirmation of arrival of Diane's period.

Both Gus and Chubby's positions at school also took up a considerable amount of their time.

By the time the Easter holidays rolled around, the weather was turning away from summer and the sea was getting colder. Jimmy debated whether to buy a wet suit and decided that with the army coming up, it would be a waste of money.

The surfer group at Anstey's had grown in number since the move away from Brighton. The constant worry of sharks was always around and was brought to a head one Sunday morning. One of the surfers, Keith Steffen, was sitting alone on his board at the back break when he spotted a huge shark swimming around near him. Keith estimated its size to be about two feet longer than his board, approximately twelve to thirteen feet long.

Keith quickly got his legs out of the water, knelt up on his board and caught the next wave in towards shore, desperate not to wipe out. Once the wave petered out, he paddled on and rode the shore break into the beach. Nobody in their right mind rode the Anstey's shore break and survived, but Keith did that morning.

The watching group on the beach, seeing some surfing skills not normally associated with Keith, raucously cheered him on, unaware of the circumstances. Keith dragged his board safely up the beach and staggered over to the cheering crowd. Shaking, he recounted what had happened. Surfing over for the day.

The direct result of this incident led a group of mothers, led by Mrs. McMullan, to approach the Durban City Council to install shark nets at Anstey's Beach. They got approval for the nets to be installed by December 1967. Surfing Anstey's until then would be a risk that only a few would chance. Jimmy, not being one of them, declared surfing over until the spring.

On April 15 Granny Bridget died suddenly. Only Denis and Maureen attended her cremation service. Iris could not bring herself to attend and Jimmy volunteered to stay with his mother to 'console her', David was deemed too young to attend.

Apr 30, 1967
Muhammad Ali is stripped of his world heavyweight title for refusing to enter the US army on religious grounds. 'I ain't got no quarrel with them Viet Congs,' was his comment.

Day to day school life continued through the second semester.

Chubby was appointed Captain of the first rugby fifteen and Gus Vice-Captain. Chubby at fly-half and Gus at scrum-half. The two stars of Grosvenor Boy's High School.

Gus continued to shine academically, Jimmy on the other hand seemed to have lost interest in all his subjects, even Maths. This was of great concern to his teachers, who knew he was capable of so much more. The matter came to a head when he came twenty-second out of twenty-two in the monthly tests. He was summoned to the headmaster's office.

'Wilson, what has got into you, boy? It seems like you have gone off track ever since the end of last year. That whole thing of missing the last few weeks of school and now these pathetic test scores. What exactly is your problem?' demanded Van.

'Sir, I can't seem to concentrate since my Grandmother died. We were very close, and her death has affected me quite a lot,' Jimmy lied, hoping for sympathy and to avoid a dressing down. 'I am slowly getting over it and I'm sure I will turn things around.'

'My sympathies for your loss but you need to get over it. By the way, Mr. Niven took me a bet in 1964 that he guaranteed you would get "A" for maths in matric. You don't want to disappoint him, do you?'

'No, Sir.'

'I had better see a marked improvement in next month's test scores or we will be having this conversation again. You may go now.'

'Yes Sir, thank you, Sir,' said Jimmy, making a hasty retreat.

May 8, 1967
Muhammad Ali is indicted for his refusal to enter the US Army.

Jimmy, never one to take the monthly tests too seriously, as they had no bearing on any year end marks, decided to make an effort during the month of May. This resulted in him moving up from twenty second to fifteenth which included an 'A' in Maths and Geography. He saw this as a way to get off Van's shit list and it worked.

The National Football League season started up again. Jimmy decided to continue selling tickets and make as much money as possible. His friendship with Raj almost cost him his job when an overzealous supervisor decided to check on Raj's ticket stub. Fortunately, the ticket tearer saw what was developing and ran over to Raj and handed him a ticket stub, apologising for forgetting to hand it to him. Due to this incident, Jimmy decided to shut down the operation until he could figure out the supervisor.

Over the next few games, it became obvious that the supervisors had been instructed to be more diligent in their duties. It was no longer worth the risk. Based on the amount of time spent travelling to and from the games and their frequency, Jimmy decided it was not worth the financial reward and with this, he decided to put an end to his ticket selling career.

June 5, 1967 to June 10, 1967.
The Six-Day war between Israel and Egypt.

With more time on his hands, Jimmy spent most afternoons at the Vermeulen household. No longer having to travel into Durban on Wednesday afternoons, he volunteered to work at Crossways Hardware to help out Mrs. Vermeulen. With that and his Saturday morning job kept him in pocket money.

With school broken up for the July school holidays, Chubby, Ian and Jimmy decided to reignite the pickup football games at Fynnlands Football field. As before, Ian refused to play without boots and always seemed to go in a bit harder than required.

With Ian's mother allowing him to work at Steyn's three days a week and Gus having to spend all free time studying, Jimmy and Chubby spent more time together. Mary was also on school break and with Jimmy spending more and more time at the Murphy residence, their 'romance' was rekindled.

The two couples went on their first double date, Saturday night movies in Durban. Mary, now eighteen, was legally allowed to purchase alcohol. The Playhouse movie theatre had a lounge attached to it. Attracting the attention of an Indian waiter, Mary ordered a round of drinks, Lion Ale's for the boys, gin and tonics for the girls.

Mellowed by three rounds of drinks, the two couples took their seats in the back row of the upstairs gallery. Mary, not used to alcohol, was more affectionate than usual and her inhibitions were somewhat lowered. Jimmy, sensing what was happening, decided to try his luck for the first time with Mary.

During one prolonged kissing session, Jimmy moved his hand up and cupped Mary's left breast on the outside of her dress. Getting no resistance, he left his hand in place and gently massaged her. Mary seemed happy to leave his hand where it was, so Jimmy decided to go for the next step.

Moving his hand up, he caressed the bottom of her neck and then quickly slipped his hand into her bra. Mary, caught by surprise initially, left his hand cupped around her breast, her nipple hard and erect. Realisation set in and Mary grabbed Jimmy's wrist and forcibly removed his hand from inside her bra and relocated it the outside of her dress. Jimmy got the message, but he had already crossed a line for the first time.

For the rest of the July holidays, the romance between Mary and Jimmy simmered, moving nearer and nearer to going to the next step. It was Mary's restraint that prevented that next step. It was a bit of relief when school reopened as Mary felt she was getting very close to capitulating.

July 27, 1967
Race riots sweep through the American city of Detroit. The riot began on July 24 when police were called to a party to welcome home a black soldier returning from Vietnam.

Back at school for the third semester, all efforts would be concentrated on completing the matric syllabus and getting in the right frame of mind for the year end finals.

The rugby season was drawing to a close and the first team remained unbeaten. This was in the main due to Chubby's form. He had been immense with the result that he was becoming a marked man by opposing teams. In most games the opposition had the instruction to get to him as soon as possible. With this tactic in place, Chubby saw less opportunity to run the ball and score tries, but with this he drew penalty after penalty. With the score for a penalty being the same as that for a try, Chubby's unerring boot kept the scoreboard ticking over.

With Grosvenor still playing only second level high schools, Chubby's skills would go virtually unnoticed by those who selected the provincial teams. With only two games to go, he would have one last chance to get noticed by the selectors. Glenwood, celebrating their fiftieth year of existence, had condescended to play a couple of second level schools, Grosvenor being one of them.

One of Glenwood's other claims to fame was that their school marching band were multiple award winners. The drum major leader of the band was also the captain of the rugby team and as such, a key component of them retaining their band trophy.

The game was played on a Wednesday afternoon at Grosvenor, which was a bit of a slight, as normally 'big' games were held on

Saturdays. Grosvenor recognised that they were being taken lightly, as not being important enough to warrant a Saturday fixture. If they needed any motivation, this was it.

The game started off at a great pace. From the Grosvenor kick off, Glenwood secured the ball and without a Grosvenor player touching the ball, scored under the posts 5-0. The way Glenwood barely celebrated irked Chubby; they were too sure of themselves, but they hadn't seen him play before.

Before restarting the match with a kick-off, Chubby motioned Gus and Dave Kendall over for a briefing.

'Ok, I know we normally kick-off long but I want kick-off up to the ten-yard line. Dave, you secure the ball; they won't be expecting it. Gus, you let me have it quickly. Let's show these arseholes we are no walk over.'

Chubby, making all the same signals, motioned to his players to go for the long ball. Glenwood lined up deep on their twenty-five yard line, ready to recover the kick. Instead, Chubby tapped the ball forward the required ten yards. Dave recovered the ball, swung it back to Gus, who in turn fed Chubby. Catching the ball, Chubby took two steps forward and drop kicked the ball through the Glenwood posts, 5-3.

The Grosvenor fans, made up of the entire school, went crazy. Chubby just glared at the Glenwood captain, who still had that smirk on his face. Chubby decided to 'wipe that look' off his face. He called big Johnny Squires and Dave over.

'Hey guys, I want you, Johnny, to take the kick-off and turn your back towards them. Dave, you give him support. I expect their captain to lead the charge, but if not, then the first one of theirs to arrive. Dave, as soon as Johnny is tackled, flatten the one who made the tackle. Make him feel some pain.'

Right on cue, Johnny caught the ball, turned and braced himself. The first tackler was in fact the Glenwood captain. Dave went in with intent; he caught his man at the same time as he caught Johnny. The result was both Dave and Johnny ended up on top of their man. Dave got up and accidentality stepped on the opponent's hand and Johnny on his ankle. Chubby hacked the loose ball into touch. The Glenwood team and their supports cried foul and the referee awarded a penalty to Glenwood which they converted to make the score 8-3. A message had been sent.

By half time Glenwood had scored two more tries with one converted, giving them 16 points. Grosvenor had not scored any tries, but Chubby had kicked four penalties and a drop goal to make the score 16-15.

Van gave the boys a rousing half time team talk. Walking out after the interval, Grosvenor were inspired by their headmaster.

The second half was a tense but exciting forty minutes. A Chubby penalty made the score 16-18, Grosvenor leading for the first time. Glenwood immediately regained the lead with a penalty of their own: 19-18. They then went further ahead with an unconverted try: 22-18. This was followed by a converted try: 27-18. The game looked over.

Chubby, never one to give up, called his players into a huddle.

'We are unbeaten this season. You want to give that up to these fuckers with the whole school watching? Look at them smirking. I, for one, want to wipe that look off their fucking faces, are you with me?' To a man, they responded positively and ran to take up their positions for kick off.

With less than ten minutes to go and ten points behind it looked like the game was beyond them. Gus and Chubby had other ideas. A long touch line kick put Grosvenor just five yards out from the try line. The ball was thrown in by Glenwood but not straight which awarded Grosvenor an easily kickable penalty. The ball was thrown to Chubby, Everyone, including Glenwood, assumed he would kick for posts. Chubby bent down as if to place the ball. Instead he tapped it forward, picked it up and passed to Gus who scuttled over for a try. The crowd went nuts. Chubby converted: 27-23.

With just about a minute to go, Chubby went on a run. He beat three Glenwood forwards and headed for the try line. Glenwood forced him wide out towards the right touchline. Sensing someone arriving at speed on his outside, Chubby flicked the ball towards him. The flying winger went over in the corner: 27-26.

With conversion to come and the clock fully run down, this would be the last action of the game. The Glenwood boys gathered around under the posts, pretty sure that the kick was impossible with strong wind and a bad angle; game over and survival by a point.

Chubby went through his ritual, apparently oblivious to the occasion. A small mound of sand, flatten the top, place the ball upright angled slightly to the left of the poles. Three steps back, two to the left, check the wind and with the entire school holding their breath, strode forward and with the inside of his right boot sent the ball sailing between the poles: 27-28.

No time to restart the game the referee blew the whistle. Grosvenor had beaten a level one school at first time of asking. The crowd invaded the pitch and mobbed the players. Chubby fought off spectators left and right and made his way to the Glenwood captain to shake his hand.

'Great game; you guys deserve the win even if it spoils our record. Where did you learn to kick like that? I'm glad we don't play you every week. Well, thanks for the game. I'll see you at the Natal Schools trials in a couple of weeks. I hope I'm on your side there.'

'Thanks for playing us, it was a great game. Good luck at the National Band Competition, sorry about that first tackle. I don't know what that was about.'

The team gathered in the locker room to celebrate their stunning victory. Van, holding back tears, gave an emotional speech about how proud he was and that this was the finest group of young men he had ever had the privilege of knowing. Just one more game to go, win it and they would go down in school history.

The final game of the season was against the old foe; Dirkie Uys, with the game referred to as the Boer War. After the victory against Glenwood, Dirkie Uys never had a hope and were slaughtered 45-10.

Sept 12, 1967
Governor Reagan of California urges an escalation of the war effort in Vietnam in order to bring the conflict to a swift end.

The short spring break was over, and attention turned to the busy final semester of their school life.

First up: the matric trials, which were set to be a simulation of their final exams. Concentrated into two hectic weeks, it would give an indication of where they were and what additional work was needed to ensure a pass for matriculation. Once the daily exams were over for the day, they were free to leave.

With the results in, to nobodies surprise, Gus achieved first place with seven A's. To everyone's surprise other than his own, Jimmy achieved third place with six A's and his regular F for Afrikaans. Chubby passed with a high C aggregate and Ian passed with a low C aggregate.

At prize giving, Gus was named as Dux of the school. Jimmy got the Maths and Geography prizes. Chubby was named Rugby, Cricket and Hockey player of the year plus Sportsman of the year. The big disappointment was that he never got the call for the Natal School trials.

In his head boy speech, Gus extolled the achievements of the Rugby team and their historic year, the leadership and unbelievable skill of their Captain. He thanked the teaching staff and pointed to the great results achieved in the trials. All the normal rah-rah stuff about the future and taking it with both hands. He congratulated Robin Baker, the boy who came second and had a special comment for the third placed boy, ending his speech with: 'Special thanks go to James Wilson, who, if he wasn't so bad at Afrikaans, this trophy would likely have been his. Thanks mate, I appreciate it!'

Oct 16, 1967
Singer Joan Baez is arrested in California at an anti-Vietnam War protest.

Other than the final Matric Examinations, high school was over. One last and very anticipated event was the Matric Dance. The standard nines outdid themselves; they had organised one of Durban's top bands, 'The Flames', and decorated the school hall in an 'Op-Art' theme.

Gus, by tradition, had arranged to be partnered with the head girl of Grosvenor Girls. Jimmy had asked Mary; Chubby was with his regular girlfriend, Diane and Ian, not having learnt his lesson, invited Kerry. Gus had to sit at the main table and the other three couples secured a table near the back of the hall.

As the evening wore on, the music slowed and many couples appeared to be joined at the hip. Lights were dimmed and romances blossomed. Chubby and Diane disappeared every now and again. Jimmy and Mary were making up for lost time, though not quite as animated as they usually were. Kerry, who had been holding Ian at arm's length, seeing the others getting amorous, finally pulled Ian towards her so as not to miss out on the fun. Ian obliged, and knowing it was a one off, made the most of it.

After the dance, Chubby's mother picked up her daughter and son plus their partners and drove them back to the Murphy home. Kerry's

127

father retrieved his daughter and Ian and drove them home, dropping Ian off on the way. No complaint from Kerry pretty much indicated her intentions.

Chubby and Diane retreated to his bedroom, leaving Jimmy alone with Mary. Jimmy, thinking he was in, got a very quick wakeup call. Mary, staring directly into Jimmy's eyes, dropped the bombshell.

'Jimmy, I've been thinking seriously about our relationship. I really do like you a lot but with me being away at college and you going off to the Army in a few months, we won't be seeing very much of each other and maybe it's best if we break it off. Well, what do you think about it?'

'Wow, this comes as a bit of a surprise. I thought we were getting on well together?'

'We are but I don't want to drag it out and keep you hanging. When I finish college next year, I have an opportunity to go overseas on a working holiday. I might be away for up to two years. The longer we keep going out, the harder it will be next year. I think it's for the best, don't you?'

'I suppose you are right. Come over here, let's have one last session to remember how good we are together,' said Jimmy, thinking he had one last chance to go for broke.

'I don't think that's a good idea; we should make a clean break but stay friends. It's better this way so I want you to leave now please; before I change my mind.'

'Okay then; cheers; I'll see you around,' said Jimmy and off he went, without so much as a glance over his shoulder. The next time he would see Mary would be at Durban station on his way to the Army.

Oct 21, 1967
Anti-war demonstration at the Pentagon turns violent. 250 people arrested.

With Ian and Gus confined to their respective homes studying and not wanting to bump into Mary at the Murphy household, Jimmy was at a bit of a loose end. The shark nets at Anstey's were not yet installed, so surfing was out of the question. With nothing else to keep his attention, Jimmy decided for the first time to do some studying.

Pretty comfortable with all his subjects except Afrikaans, Jimmy looked around to see if he could get some extra lessons. On the corner of Doble Road, directly opposite to Ian's house, there was an Afrikaans family; the wife was an ex teacher at Dirkie Uys. She had recently given birth and was on maternity leave, so Jimmy made an approach for some lessons.

They agreed on a price for three one-hour lessons per week for the next two weeks. She was rather astonished at his level of understanding, especially for a matriculant, and had her doubts that she could get him up to standard in just two weeks. When Jimmy said he just needed to get a passing mark, she figured he must be a little bit thick, but she would try.

Study time over, it was now all or nothing: the first exams started on Monday 13 November. The tests would be held in the school hall with seating prearranged alphabetically. Each exam lasted three hours and once started, no one could leave the hall until the time was up. The exams were spread out over three weeks, with the final exam being applied mathematics (for Gus and Jimmy) on December 1.

Ian and Chubby, having written their final exam a few days earlier, arranged to meet Gus and Jimmy at Brighton Beach Café directly after their final exam. Both Gus and Jimmy had broken school protocol and not worn their school uniform on the final day. The moderator for the exam had been Terry Niven, probably the most laid-back teacher at the school. He was unperturbed at this flaunting of the rules, as he knew that his two favourite pupils were guaranteed A's and he would win his five-year old bet with Van Vuuren. He wished them good luck and sent them on their way.

Gus and Jimmy rushed off to Brighton Beach, meeting up with Chubby and Ian, who had left his motorcycle at home. Greeting them, Jimmy and Gus suggested celebrating with a few beers. They climbed aboard the funicular that ran from the beach up to Marine Drive and the Harcourt Hotel and the Men's Bar.

Legally, none of the boys were old enough to be served drinks. They had previously been served alcohol at the hotel but had taken the drinks out to the terrace. With some trepidation, Chubby walked up to the bar and ordered four Lion Ales, worried he would be refused. He needn't have worried as his fame preceded him. Bert, the barman, greeted him loudly and stated the first round was on him, 'For the Bluffs greatest ever Rugby player.'

With cheers ringing in his ears, Chubby returned to the table with four Lion Ales in hand. The boys proceeded to get stuck into the beers.

They were joined by several school friends and an epic party ensued. By the time eleven o'clock closing time rolled around, only Ian was still standing and in any state to get his mates home. Chubby and Gus had beer and vomit mix down the front of their shirts and Jimmy was asleep on the floor in the corner.

Ian, rallying the troops, got them to their feet and suggested coffee would be a good idea. So, the four of them headed for the Vermeulen home two miles down the road. Oblivious of the time, they arrived at twenty minutes past midnight after staggering the two miles from the Harcourt.

Finding the house in darkness did not deter them one bit. Chubby staggered up to the front door and knocked loudly, claiming 'Wake up, we've come for coffee!'

First the lounge lights came on, then the porch lights. The front door swung open and a very angry Mr. Vermeulen appeared.

'What is the meaning of this, are you all mad? You are all drunk, clear off before I call the police!'

'Sir, we have just come for coffee and to see your beautiful daughter, so can you please call her?' slurred Chubby.

An apoplectic Mr. Vermeulen turned back in towards the house and yelled, 'Kerry, come here immediately, and get rid of these drunken friends of yours! What the hell are they thinking?'

He turned and slammed the door. Seconds later, Kerry appeared wearing her dressing gown. She took one look at the boys and burst out laughing. She ushered them to the couch and chairs on the right of the veranda. Settling them down, she went to make coffee. Five minutes later she returned with five cups of coffee, only to find all four of them passed out and snoring. Shaking her head, she went back into the kitchen, poured the coffee down the drain and went back to bed.

Gus was the first to awake at around 5am. Confused as to his whereabouts, it took him a few minutes to realise where he was. Having no recollection of the previous night's happenings, he was smart enough to know that something bad had occurred if they were all asleep at the Vermeulens.

Ian, Jimmy and Chubby surfaced in stages. In the ten minutes it took to get them awake and focused, Gus managed to convince them to get the hell out of the place before the Vermeulens woke and found them. All of them, unaware of what had occurred earlier, agreed and left post haste.

'How the hell did we end up sleeping on their porch? Jesus, if old man Vermeulen had found out we were here, we would be in deep shit,' said Chubby. 'I have to get home; my folks are going to crap all over me if they find out. Hopefully they haven't missed me yet. I'll see you guys later; come around for a swim.'

Ian, Gus and Jimmy arrived home and managed to sneak in without disturbing anyone.

Chubby arrived home to find his mother and father wide awake and really angry. His no-show had caused some consternation and his mother had taken to calling Ian's mother and Gus' aunt, neither had seen nor heard from Chubby. In a panic, she called the local police station and hospital with the same results.

Seeing the condition Chubby was in, it was obvious what had happened. Relief overcame anger for Mrs. Murphy; her husband still looking rather stern, secretly chuckled.

'Okay, son, I realise you and your friends were blowing off some steam as your school days are over, but you should have called home. Your mother and I were worried.'

'So sorry, Mom and Dad, it won't happen again. I have to go and lie down as I have a very bad headache.'

'Take a shower first; you are a mess and smell bad,' said Mrs Murphy.

Back at Doble Road, Jimmy's alarm clock went off, it was time to get up for work. With his head exploding, he dragged himself to the bathroom for a shower hoping it would help; it didn't. Feeling very fragile, he dressed and headed off to work. Jack noticed immediately that Jimmy was seriously hungover and went to make him coffee.

'Tie one on there, mate? You look like shit. Drink this coffee; it might help.'

'Shit, Jack, I don't know what happened last night. We were celebrating the end of school so went for a couple of beers at the Harcourt. Me and my mates woke up on the Vermeulen veranda at five o'clock this morning. I have no idea how we got there or even why we were there. Thank God, we left before anyone knew we were there.'

The shop had been open for about an hour when Kerry appeared, which was unusual as she had never paid a visit before.

'How are you feeling? That must have been some party.'

'What do you mean, "How am I feeling". What party are you talking about?'

'Don't you remember pitching up at our house with your three mates and waking us up, demanding coffee?'

'Oh shit, I don't remember a thing. What happened? Did your folks see us?'

'Oh yes, they did. My Dad nearly had a fit, but he'll get over it,' replied Kerry and she went over the whole incident in great detail. On completion, she leaned over and giggling gave Jimmy a kiss on the cheek and flounced out the door.

When the store closed at one o'clock, Jimmy realised he would have to go and apologise to the Vermeulens for his behaviour. He would pick Ian up on the way and the two of them could apologise on behalf of all of them. He agreed that he would work the next three Saturday's but didn't want to do Wednesday afternoons. He was going to spend every possible waking hour surfing. The new shark nets were being installed in a few days' time.

Walking across the road to Steyn's garage, he found an equally frail-looking Ian. Ian admitted that going to the Vermeulens may have been his idea and not a clever one at that. He had no recollection of arriving at their house though. Jimmy suggested the two of them go and apologise for their behaviour. Ian offered Jimmy a lift on his motorcycle; although it was illegal, it was just a short ride. No one would know.

Ian and Jimmy walked up the front door and knocked, hoping that Misses and not Mister would answer the door. Ingrid answered; shaking her head she turned and called out to Kerry that her friends were here to see her. Before Kerry could answer, her father appeared, striding angrily towards the front door, followed by his wife.

'Just what do you idiots think you were doing here last night? I have a good mind to call your parents and tell them just how inebriated you were. What do you have to say for yourselves?'

Before either boy could answer, Mrs. Vermeulen pulled her husband aside. 'Come on, dear, they were just letting off a bit of steam having finished high school. Let them be; you can see that they are sorry.'

Reluctantly, he turned and walked back into the house muttering about the youth of today. Mrs Vermeulen smiled and winked at the two sorry looking boys and went to join her husband. Kerry, almost wetting herself with laughter, joined her friends.

'Oh my God, you four were so drunk last night. By the way, where are the other two?'

'I don't know; probably at home with serious hangovers. We were here; so I thought it best to apologise and get it over with. Sorry about last night. I don't know what we, namely Ian, were thinking, but we were seriously vrot. How about that cup of coffee now, the one you didn't bring us last night?'

'What? I made coffee and brought it out. only to find you buggers all passed out, and then when we all got up. you were gone. I am not making coffee now; my Dad will probably have a heart attack if I did. I have never seen him so cross. Get those other two reprobates and come back this evening if you want. He should be calmed down by then. There's a party at the MOTH Hall, if you are interested.'

Jimmy said he was interested; Ian was unsure but would contact Gus and Chubby. Once they got to Ian's house, he phoned Gus and Chubby, who both confirmed they would go to the party but would go there directly and not via the Vermeulens. Ian agreed to join them, leaving Jimmy to collect Kerry.

Just after 7pm, Jimmy collected Kerry and they made the short walk to the MOTH Hall. On arriving, Jimmy paid the fifty cents per person for both Kerry and himself. Spotting Ian, Gus, Chubby and Diane, they walked over.

'Hey Jimbo, guess what? You should be in for some fun tonight. Mary is here with good old Fiona. I reckon you should do a runner while you can. The two of them look as thick as thieves, and I don't think you can handle both of them.'

'Jesus, that's all I need. You do know Mary dumped me? I thought her and Fiona had stopped being friends. I hope Fiona doesn't want to make a comeback with me, she scares the crap out of me.'

'Don't worry, you big baby, I'll look after you,' said Kerry coyly, taking Jimmy by the hand. 'The band has started up, let's go and have a dance.'

Making quite a production of it as they were the first couple to hit the dance floor, Kerry got up close and personal. It was not a slow dance, but Kerry put her arms around Jimmy's neck and pulled him close. Jimmy thought, 'What the fuck, why not?' and put his arms around her waist. Anyone watching would have thought, 'There was a couple deeply in love.'

By the time the song ended, there were quite a few couples on the floor. Jimmy, holding Kerry firmly by the hand, looked over to where Mary and Fiona were sitting. Two of the locals sauntered over, presumably to ask for a dance, only to receive a polite refusal; how embarrassing.

The band started the second song; a good old rock and roll number. A few seconds into it, Fiona walked over, looked Kerry in the eyes and said, 'Mind if I cut in?'

What came out of Kerry's mouth shocked Jimmy. 'Yes, I do so. So, fuck off. We are going steady so leave him alone.'

Fiona and Jimmy both looked at Kerry in disbelief. Fiona, not knowing what to say and highly embarrassed, turned and walked back to where Mary was still sitting. Jimmy, not sure what to do next, just stared at Kerry, who was master of the situation, pulled him towards her and proceeded to kiss him passionately. Never one to fight a good thing, he responded. She really was a magnificent kisser. That set the trend for the night; the only time they sat down was during band breaks.

At the first break, Kerry grabbed Diane and the two of them headed for the ladies, leaving Jimmy to face his three buddies.

'What the fuck's going on with you and Kerry?' inquired Ian.

'Fucked if I know but she bailed me out with Fiona. Man, she's a fantastic kisser, who knew?'

'Gus and I both know, and I think Chubby has had a nibble there, but he won't admit it. I wonder what happened to the "Invisible Dave"? He's bound to turn up when you get back to her place. I reckon she's a bit of a cock teaser.'

'Never, I have never touched her. Diane would cut my cock off if she thought I had. So, stop shit-stirring,' demanded Chubby. 'What's up with you, Wilson? Are you working your way through all the females: Fiona, my sister and now Kerry? Touch Diane and you are a dead man.'

'Well, I'm going to make the most of it. If she finds Invisible Dave when we get back to her place, too bad for me, but I'm still going for it.'

As the night wore on, Kerry and Jimmy spent the entire time dancing and a good part of it kissing. Fiona had hooked up with some lucky, or depending how you looked at it, unfortunate bloke, leaving Mary alone. Mary, not wanting or having much luck, joined her brother, Diane, Ian and Gus. Mary's presence was a problem for Jimmy so when the music stopped, he and Kerry headed outside for some 'fresh air'.

By the time the band played the last song, Mary had left with Chubby and Diane. Thankfully Fiona was nowhere to be seen. Jimmy and Kerry joined up with Gus and Ian for the walk back to her house for coffee, or so they thought.

'Hey guys, I'm feeling a bit tired, so I won't invite you back for coffee. Jimmy, can you still walk me home? I think I'll turn in straight away.'

Ian and Gus turned to Jimmy, giving him the knowing look. Invisible Dave was about to make an appearance. Bad luck mate. Jimmy just shrugged his shoulders said goodbye to his mates and with Kerry in tow, headed off towards Marine Drive. Kerry walked up to Jimmy and took him by the hand, a most unusual occurrence. Well, maybe Invisible Dave is off tonight.

Getting back to the Vermeulens, Jimmy found that Invisible Dave really was off tonight. Kerry guided him to the veranda couch. She was wearing a short and very loose fitting 'tent' dress. Every time she lifted her arms, she exposed her white panties. Lying on her back with her head in his lap, she pulled Jimmy down towards her. Her dress rode up high on her thighs giving Jimmy an eyeful of her underwear.

They began kissing passionately and Jimmy's hands began to wander. He began to caress her breast on the outside of her dress; its design allowed no access to reach into her bra. Kerry gave no indication that he should stop. With her head firmly in his crotch, he began to feel the start of an erection, which she was surely aware of as well.

The kissing became more intense, tongues thrusting in and out, fighting for breath. Kerry suddenly pushed Jimmy's hand away from her breast, he was momentarily surprised, she had seemed as keen as he was. She reached up under her dress, which was now around her waist, and unclipped her bra freeing her breasts. Taking Jimmy's hand, she moved it up under her dress until he cupped her right breast. Her nipples were fully erect, as was Jimmy's penis.

Not sure how far this was going, Jimmy just kept on kissing and caressing, not wanting it to end. Kerry, still with her lips locked onto Jimmy's, removed her right hand under her head and placed it firmly on his hard penis and began rubbing it. Jimmy, scared he might come, started concentrating on anything but what Kerry was doing. After a few minutes, Kerry removed her hand and reached up and grabbing him by the wrist, pulled his hand away from her breast.

Thinking that was it, he breathed a sigh of relief; it had been a close thing. To his absolute surprise, Kerry guided his hand down to her panties and opened her legs slightly. Jimmy looked down at her, she smiled and mouthed 'yes.' He slipped his hand under her panties, feeling her neatly trimmed blond pubic hair. She groaned as he slipped a finger into her soaking wet vagina. His only other experience was with Fiona, so he proceeded to do the same.

With his finger going quickly in and out Kerry returned her hand to his penis, still safely ensconced in his underpants. Kerry, now completely overcome by lust, suddenly stood up and pulled down her panties. Kicking them to one side she straddled Jimmy, facing him and began grinding herself against the bulge in his pants, continuing to kiss him. Passing the point of no return, she reached down and began feverishly trying to undo his belt. Jimmy moved her hands away and started to help her unbuckle his belt. This is it, he thought. I am going to have sex for the first time with the one girl I really care about.

Before he could get his belt undone both noticed a set of car headlights turn into the driveway. Kerry leapt off Jimmy and frantically searched for her panties. Not finding them, she pulled her dress down as far as it would go and plonked herself down at the opposite end of the couch. Jimmy grabbed one of the cushions and placed it firmly in his lap. A few moments later, Ingrid and her boyfriend Dan reached the veranda.

'Hey, what are you two up to?' asked Ingrid.

'Jimmy walked me home from the session. We were going to have coffee but decided not to. We were just chatting; he was just about to leave.'

'That's right. Cheers, I'll see you tomorrow then.'

'Don't leave because of us; we are going to sit inside. By the way, sister mine, your bra is sticking out the side of your sleeve and if I'm not mistaken, that bit of white cloth on the window sill is either a hankie or your knickers,' said Ingrid, grinning as she turned and went indoors.

Kerry, embarrassed beyond belief, leapt up to retrieve her panties and quickly put them on, giving Jimmy one last look at her vagina. Jimmy's erection had disappeared the minute he saw the car headlights. The passion over for the night, he stood up and went to kiss Kerry good night. She brushed him off and ran into the house, slamming the door behind her.

Well, so much for that, he thought. It's going feel strange when I see her tomorrow. Should I even mention it or wait for her? With those thoughts rolling around in his head, he walked home and went to bed.

The next morning, Jimmy got up early and headed for Anstey's on his own for an early surf. Collecting his board, he found he was the only one there; he had the waves all to himself. About half an hour later other surfers started arriving and the conditions started to get a bit crowded, so he headed for the shore. He stacked his board, rolled out his towel and laid down on his stomach in the warm sunshine.

Sometime later, he was rudely awakened by a sharp kick in the ribs. Standing next to him were his three mates, grinning.

'Wake up, you bastard, how long have you been down here?' asked Chubby.

'Since about six thirty. What's up?'

'Jesus, you and Kerry were going at it last night, at the session. Did "Invisible Dave" make an appearance when you got back to her place? Mary thought you were putting on a show for her. You weren't just upsetting my big sister, were you?'

'No, I just asked Kerry to help avoid Fiona. She did a good job at that. And yes, Invisible Dave did show up the minute I got her home. You know Kerry.'

Just after lunch time, Kerry, Diane and Jenny rocked up. Jimmy pretended not to notice and remained sitting staring out at the surf. Gus had borrowed his board so there was no escape, he would play it by ear and act as though nothing had happened the previous night. Diane headed for Chubby and Kerry and Jenny walked over to Jimmy.

Kerry leaned over behind Jimmy and put her arms around his neck. Nibbling on his ear, she asked, 'Don't I get a kiss hello then?'

Jimmy turned to respond, and Kerry immediately almost devoured him with a tonsil-cleaning kiss. Confused Jimmy responded only breaking off the taunts of: Get a room; Come up for air sometime; money or the box, take the money.

Kerry plonked herself down next to Jimmy, took his arm and placed it around her shoulders. Chubby and Ian looked on open-mouthed, what was going on here? Gus returned a few minutes later and following Ian and Chubby's gesticulations looked over to see Kerry nestled snugly against Jimmy. So, no repercussions from last night's activities and probably no need to bring up the subject with Kerry.

The minute the three girls decided to go for a swim in the paddling pool, the three boys descended on their friend.

'Okay, Wilson, what the fuck's going on? You said Invisible Dave appeared as soon as you got to her place,' demanded Chubby.

'Yes, he did.'

'Then why is she hanging onto you like her life depended on it? Come, arsehole, we want the details.'

'There's nothing to tell, maybe she just likes me. You never know when Dave will make an appearance. So, I'll just take it as it comes. You do know she is the best kisser ever.'

All three boys nodded in agreement; yes she is.

'What are you nodding for, Fats, how do you know? Any crap from you and maybe I have a word with Miss Diane.'

'No, I am just agreeing with Gus and Ian. Jesus, Diane would kill me.'

For the rest of the day, Kerry never left his side for more than a few minutes. At the end of the afternoon, she helped Jimmy carry his board back to Benny's house and they walked hand in hand back to her place. Not a word was spoken about last night. He dropped her off, had a quick kiss and arranged to meet her after supper.

Jimmy arrived directly after supper and the two of them settled down on the couch. As the family were still up and about, the two of them just sat around chatting and holding hands. Ingrid and Dan took off and an hour later Mr. and Mrs. headed for bed.

Almost immediately, they locked lips. Kerry was dressed in jeans and a buttoned-up blouse, Jimmy, in his regulation black PT shorts and T-shirt. Jimmy moved his hand towards her breast and feeling no rejection, unbuttoned some of her blouse. He slipped his hand into her shirt and found she was not wearing a bra. Although she had smallish breasts, she had amazing rock-hard nipples. He leaned in and took one in his mouth, sucking it gently and rolling it around with his tongue.

This had an immediate effect on Kerry; she groaned with pleasure and reached down to feel Jimmy's already hard cock. She slipped her hand inside his shorts and for the first time held his actual penis in her hand. Jimmy took this to be a sign to get inside her pants. He leant down and started undoing her belt.

She released his cock and pushed him away. 'Stop, we can't do this, we will get caught. As much as I want you to do it, we cannot do this here.'

'Where can we go then? God, my balls are going to explode.'

'I don't know but definitely not here. When we do this, it will be the first time for me, I want it to be special, not just in the bush or the beach somewhere.'

'I want my first time to be with you, as well.'

'You haven't done this before? What about Fiona? I thought you two definitely screwed.'

'No, we didn't. She said I had to bring condoms if I wanted to screw her. Luckily, I never had any. That girl scares the crap out of me. Thank you again for saving me at the session. Do you think I should get some condoms for us?'

'No, let's wait and see. I am so glad you never had sex with Fiona. How far did you go?'

'Just some kissing and I felt her tits,' lied Jimmy. No sense in ruining the moment.

Fortunately, Kerry started her period the next day and that put paid, at least in the interim, to any heavy petting. The pattern was set for the next three weeks, all the action was to be above the waist. Jimmy spent a good deal of time masturbating to ease the pain in his testicles, especially after a visit to his girlfriend. They spent virtually every waking minute together, at the beach, the movies and just hanging at her house.

With the four boys being the first of their crowd to be leaving for the Army, Mrs. Vermeulen thought it a good idea to have a going away party at their house. It was arranged for December 23. Several friends were invited, and even Kerry's father approved, so much so that he invited Jimmy to share a couple of his home brewed beers with him. The beer was barely palatable, but Jimmy said how good they were and thanked him for the party. The old man got all emotional and said how proud he was of his daughter's boyfriend going off to defend the country's borders. He was pleased that Jimmy treated his youngest daughter with respect and kindness, and he would be welcome in this house any time. Wow, thought Jimmy, that's a change in attitude, must be the beer.

The party went very well, and everyone seemed to enjoy themselves. A lot of slow music and slow dancing and a lot of couples hooking up. The couch on the veranda was well attended, as were parts of the backyard. As the party was winding down and people were leaving, Kerry asked Jimmy if he would stay on and help clean up; he agreed.

The parents were fast asleep in bed, Ingrid was staying over at a 'friends' place, Kerry took this to mean Dan's house. They had been going out for over four years and Kerry reckoned if they weren't doing it now, then they never would.

When everything was tidy and packed away, Kerry excused herself and disappeared to her bedroom. She emerged a few minutes later clad in her dressing gown.

She motioned to Jimmy. 'Come with me, I have a present for you. But be quiet. I don't want to wake my folks.'

Jimmy followed her to bedroom. She closed the door behind them and indicated he should sit on the bed. He sat down wondering what present she had for him, hoping it was something small, as he hadn't got anything for her. She stood directly in front of him, undid her belt and dropped her gown to the floor. She was stark naked. Jimmy's mouth dropped open. Taking him by the hand, she pulled him to his feet and pulled his shirt over his head. She undid his belt, unbuttoned his jeans and lowered them to the floor. Next, off came the underpants. They were both naked.

She pulled him in close and whispered in his ear, 'I know you don't have any condoms, so you can't fuck me, but we are going to do the next best thing.' She took his hand and placed it between her legs. 'Finger me slowly so that I can come.'

Jimmy inserted a finger into her soaking wet vagina and started a slow rhythmic in and out motion. Kerry took a firm grip on his cock and held it tightly against her stomach. All the while they were kissing passionately. After what seemed like forever, Kerry started her orgasm. She shuddered, gasped and finally collapsed in a heap on the floor. She had never felt anything like that before; it was amazing. Jimmy smiled down at her, still with a huge erection.

Kerry knelt and looked up at him. She pushed him onto the bed and said, 'That was your present to me, now let me give you yours.'

Here we go, he thought, shades of Fiona. The difference was his girlfriend was going to toss him off, next best thing to actual sex. Kerry knelt between his parted legs, gave him a sly smile, leaned in took his cock in her hand but instead of stroking it placed it in her mouth. Jimmy nearly passed out. He wasn't sure what to do, so he just lay there. For someone performing this act for the first time, she showed a skill beyond her years. Moving her head and hand in unison, it took her no time at all to bring him to a mind-blowing climax. Despite an initial gag, Kerry took his full load and swallowed it all.

She continued licking the tip of his cock and made him shudder again. She looked up at him and said, 'Merry Christmas, my darling. How was that?'

Jimmy was barely able to speak, 'Oh my God, I thought I was going to die. Where did you learn to do that?'

'I read about it in a book and some of the girls at school have done it. I thought it might be a bit messy, but it was okay. I quite liked doing it. You better go now though, before I try it again. I'll see tomorrow.'

'Okay. Thank you again; you are amazing. I think I'm in love. God, I'm going to miss you. See you tomorrow.'

Kerry gave him a soulful look as she kissed him good night.

Shortly after lunch the next day, he took the short walk over to Marine Drive, eager to see his amazing girlfriend. Knocking on the door, he was met by an angry looking Ingrid.

'What happened between you and my sister last night? She's been crying her eyes out all day. She's now on the phone to some old boyfriend, Dave someone or the other. She said she doesn't want to see you. I think you better leave.'

Jimmy was flabbergasted. What could have happened between last night and now? Shit, was it because I came in her mouth? But it can't be, she said she liked it. Invisible Dave, what the fuck was that about? Shrugging his shoulders, he turned and left. The next time he would see her would be at Durban Station when he left for the Army.

Unbeknownst to him, Kerry was only pretending to call Dave. The real reason she was in tears was that Jimmy was leaving for the next nine months. She didn't think either of them would wait for each other. Rather than suffer the hurt, she decided to break it off. She knew mentioning Dave's name would put Jimmy off completely. This one act changed both of their lives forever.

Gus, in the meantime, decided to make the arduous journey to Ixopo to see his mother. Arriving at the station, he took the long walk up to the hospital. He had been told by his Aunt that his mother spent every waking minute at the hospital.

He presented himself to reception and asked to see the matron. She asked who was calling. Gus replied, 'I am her son.'

The nurse picked up the phone and relayed the information to the matron. Gus could hear her blunt reply, 'Which one?'

'Tell her it's Angus, her youngest son.'

The nurse relayed the message and Gus could hear his mother's reply, 'Tell him I'm am very busy right now and I can spare him some time when my shift ends at six o'clock.'

Gus checked his watch; a five and half hour wait to see his mother for the first time in five years. All the unanswered letters and unreturned phone calls, what was the point in him being here? He shrugged his shoulders, turned around and headed back to the station to catch the next train back to Durban.

Christmas and the New Year passed with the boys in a bit of a funk. Matric results and the Army were looming heavily on their minds. Ian, Gus and Jimmy, with no female attachments spent most days at the beach; Chubby joined them when he could tear himself away from Diane.

Ian and Chubby both had their hair trimmed short ready for the Army. Neither Jimmy nor Gus had had a haircut for the best part of three months and had no plans to, as the Army were sure to oblige in a few days' time.

Prior to leaving for the Army, the boys made a pact. They would, whenever possible, get together on January 1 each year. Every ten years they would ensure a reunion.

CHAPTER 10
Army Days

Durban station was crowded with mothers, fathers, brothers, sisters, friends and girlfriends gathered to see their loved ones depart on a journey to manhood. At least that's what their fathers had told them it would be. The boys knew better, it was nine months, or two hundred and seventy-two days until their return.

The train would be leaving Durban station on its journey to Bloemfontein's Tempe army base. The bulk of the passengers were already at the station, many more would be picked up at Pietermaritzburg, Escort and Mooi River, until the full complement of around three hundred young men was reached. These young men would range in age from seventeen to twenty-one, all white, all conscripts, most leaving home for the first time.

The final matriculation results had been received that very afternoon. Gus got seven straight A's, Peter and Ian both with comfortable passes and Jimmy hadn't even bothered to open his; he just stashed it at the bottom of his kitbag to be opened later. Of all their parents, only Chubby's mother and older sister, Mary, had made it to the station to see the boys off. Ian's mother, being too upset, Jimmy's father working afternoon shift and Gus's aunt, seeing her responsibility to her sister-in-law's son as now at an end, had other commitments.

Along with David Drew, the four of them were the first intake of their matriculation class to leave for the army. Gus, Chubby and Jimmy had been drafted into the tank regiment of Natal Mounted Rifles, while Ian had the honour of joining Durban Light Infantry. The infantry would outnumber the armour at Tempe by a ratio of three to one, the two camps enclosed within the same base.

The fact that the train was clearly segregated by armour and infantry meant nothing to the boys, and they secured a compartment in the infantry section. Their orders had been clear: bring one set of civilian clothes, toiletries and any sporting gear you wished. Gus, Ian and Jimmy had each packed their football boots as their sole sporting equipment. Chubby, on the other hand, had included his football boots, a hockey stick, cricket boots, pads and wicket keeper's gloves. All the gear stashed away and under the careful watch of Dave Drew, the four of them retired to the station bar for a farewell drink.

Chubby, officially the only one old enough to buy alcohol at eighteen years and two days old, did the honours. Lion Ale's with rum chasers rapidly disappeared down four youthful throats followed by three more rounds in quick succession. Fortified, they staggered out of the bar, now ready to say their final farewells to the waiting entourage.

Chubby's regular girlfriend, Diane Dale, clung tearfully to Mary who tried vainly to console her. Jimmy and Gus, with no fixed girlfriends, kissed any and all who crossed their paths, while Ian, ever shy in female company, hung around the fringes eager to be on his way.

A tall Afrikaans speaking military policeman tried in vain to assemble over two hundred young men together in order to take a roll call. Sensing he was doomed to failure, he decided to 'save face' and exert his authority and set some sort of example. Glancing around, he spotted Jimmy and Gus doing the rounds with a bunch of tearful girls and decided these two would make a perfect example.

'*Julle twee, kom hier onmiddellik,*' (you two, come here immediately), he screamed at the top of his voice. Rising to his full height of about six foot six inches, he pointed his swagger stick in Jimmy and Gus' direction.

Jimmy, in the process of kissing Mary farewell for the umpteenth time, ignored the command. Gus, on the other hand, burst out laughing. It was unclear which irritated the big MP the most. He strode over, grabbed Gus by the scruff of the neck and turning, stuck Jimmy a solid blow across the head with his swagger stick. Jimmy fell to the ground, more from shock than anything else, pulling Mary with him.

Far from having a quieting effect, the action had a reverse effect. Chubby's mother and sister, horrified by what they had seen, tore into the bewildered MP, berating him for his actions. All those in the immediate vicinity started booing and clapping. The MP dropped Gus, turned around and strode off with the ominous parting words, '*Ek sal julle twee sien*' (I will see you two).

The train, scheduled to leave Durban at 5.30 p.m., eventually left at almost eight o'clock. With the final civilian removed from the train, it pulled out of Durban station on its four hundred odd mile journey to Bloemfontein. Any normal trip between these two cities should take less than twenty-four hours, but this being a troop train with a low priority; it would take closer to twice that.

The scene at Durban station was repeated all the way through the Natal Midlands, the only difference being that those young men boarding the train had not only to contend with tearful friends and relatives, but a growing number of leering spectators leaning out of the train windows. Each hug and kiss was greeted with a mixture of catcalls, indecent suggestions and cheers.

Midway through the first day the train reached its final pickup point of Ladysmith. Waiting at the station was not only the next complement of boys but a detachment of Infantry troops stationed at Ladysmith.

The normal routine of army training in the South African Defence Force was that, the first three months would be spent in a camp like Tempe, where the troops would undergo basic and specialist training. During the first six weeks, intense drilling and fitness exercises would take place.

These new soldiers fell under the common derogatory name of '*Roof,*' or scab. At the end of those first three months, unless selected as an instructor or for officer training, you would be posted to your permanent camp. For the infantry soldier, Ladysmith was one of the permanent camps you were likely to be posted to.

The group of infantrymen gathered at Ladysmith station were all doing their final six months and were there to rev up the new troops. Comments like 'We're waiting for you,' 'Tempe is a holiday camp compared to here,' 'Are you missing your Mommies already?' 'Don't worry, we'll take care of your girlfriends in Durban when we go on pass.' Insults were traded back and forth but with less enthusiasm from the boys on the train, better not to be too cocky in case you are remembered.

The rest of the journey, apart from the odd scuffle, was relatively uneventful. The train crossed the Drakensberg Mountains, leaving Natal behind and entering the Orange Free State, where the standing joke from the Natal boys was, 'There's no oranges, nothing's free and it's in a hell of a state.'

Jan 3, 1968
**Professor Chris Barnard performs the world's first heart
transplant at Groote Schuur Hospital in Cape Town. The
recipient is a 53-year old grocer, Louis Washkansky, and the
donor is Denise Darvall, a 25-year old bank clerk. Her kidneys
were transplanted into a coloured boy at another hospital.**

It was dark when the train pulled into Bloemfontein Station at nine fifteen, some fifty hours after leaving Durban. The scene was one of absolute chaos. Hordes of men in military uniform, some regular army but mostly conscripts, descended on the platform, shouting out orders, mostly in Afrikaans, attempting to form up the boys in some type of order. Eventually, deciding that the only way to get these boys off the train would be to herd them off to the waiting Bedford trucks and do a roll call later.

Jimmy, Gus, Ian and Chubby were piled into the back of a waiting Bedford, along with about forty other boys all clinging to their bags. The journey to Tempe Army base took nearly half an hour and by the time they arrived, it was clear that Jimmy, Gus and Chubby were on the wrong Bedford, they were the only Armour troops with a bunch of Infantry. Although the Tempe base was for both Armour and Infantry, the two disciplines had their own, clearly demarcated areas. The only time the two crossed was during mealtimes as they shared a common Mess. Any other time was seen as a breach of lines and usually a fight started, often becoming very violent. This rivalry was encouraged by the members of the Permanent Force.

The trucks were unloaded at what was the Infantry parade ground and the boys formed up in lines of three. A sergeant major stood facing them with megaphone in hand. In Afrikaans, he informed the waiting troops that he would call out their regiment name and would indicate where they should form up. As each regiment was called, the assembled group in front of the sergeant major grew smaller. Ian went off to join the rest of the Durban Light Infantry and eventually there were only three boys left.

Shouting at the top of his voice in Afrikaans, the sergeant major approached the boys, 'Are you fucking deaf or stupid? What regiment are you from?'

'Natal Mounted Rifles, sir,' replied Jimmy, in English.

'Fucking Armour, what the fuck are you doing here?'

'We got mixed up with the Infantry boys, sir,' said Jimmy, now wishing he had shut up and not said anything.

'You see that area there?' screamed the sergeant major, pointing to an area about half a mile away, 'That's where you should be, now fuck off and don't let me catch you anywhere near the Infantry lines again.'

Jimmy and Gus picked up their bags, turned and ran off in the direction indicated. Chubby, struggling with all his sporting equipment, followed in their wake, pleading for some help with his gear. His pleas fell on deaf ears as Jimmy and Gus headed for the safety of the Armour lines.

By the time the three arrived at the Armour parade ground, they had already been marked down as missing. Jimmy, the least proficient in Afrikaans, coerced by the other two, was sent to find someone to report to. Gus and Chubby sat down on their luggage to catch their breath and wait for Jimmy to return. They didn't have long to wait, from the far corner of the parade ground came Jimmy at the double. He was followed by a corporal who was shouting out commands, alternating between, 'mark time' and 'at the double'. Jimmy was halted in front of an astonished and bemused Gus and Chubby.

'Fall in behind him, you useless specimens!' roared the corporal.

The three of them were double time marched off the parade ground towards a line of bungalows. At the first bungalow they were halted.

'Murphy, fall out. You are in bungalow "D."' Chubby had in his absence been mustered as a driver.

'You two, forward march.'

Gus and Jimmy were marched back across the parade ground towards a second line of bungalows. They were halted in front of the second last bungalow.

'You two fuckheads are mustered as gunners. I am the corporal in charge of gunnery, and I will make sure you two shit off. I don't like fucking beach boys. Take your stuff into this bungalow. Fall out.' Neither Jimmy nor Gus needed any translation from Afrikaans to know that Corporal Cloete was going to be a real problem in their lives.

The bungalows at Tempe were around fifty feet in length and twenty wide. There was a door at each end and windows along each side. The floor was smooth concrete and highly polished. Each room contained twenty-four beds, twelve along each side, separated by a cupboard or '*Kas.*'

Jimmy and Gus opened the door and entered their new home. Twenty-two pairs of eyes locked onto them. There were two spare

beds but not next to each other. Jimmy walked up to the closest empty
bed and put his bags down.

'Hey mate,' he said turning to the boy next to him, 'how about you
take that bed over there and let my buddy have this one.'

'*Nee, ek was eerste hier* (No, I was here first),' the boy replied in
Afrikaans.

'Fuck, it's only a bed. They're all the same. Here, I'll help you
move,' said Jimmy, taking no notice of the boy's protestations. 'Ok
Gus all sorted.'

Now with adjacent beds, Jimmy and Gus surveyed the new surroundings. The other twenty-two stared at the two newcomers. Neither Jimmy nor Gus had had a haircut in the last three months, and
both had hair over their ears and down to their collars, not that common for 1968 in South Africa.

'Where are you okes from?' inquired Jimmy, trying to strike up a
conversation in what was an almost silent room.

From the replies it turned out that apart from Jimmy and Gus, there
was only one other English-speaking boy in the room, Malcolm Good-
ing, from Northlands Boy's High in Durban.

'Jesus, twenty-one fucking Dutchmen, this is going to be fun,'
whispered Gus,' Let's go and find Chubby and see how he is doing.'

'The corporal said we were not to leave the bungalow,' said one of
the boys as he saw Jimmy and Gus start to leave.

'Don't panic, just going for a piss,' said Gus over his shoulder as
they went through the door.

Retracing their steps across the parade ground, they found
Chubby's bungalow, opened the door and entered.

'Hey fat man, how's it going?' shouted Gus.

'Fuck, what are you guys doing here?' said Chubby. 'They said we
had to stay in our bungalows.'

'Well, it was a choice of visiting you, or to go looking for Ian, and
I'm fucked if I want to go back over to the Infantry lines. How was
that sergeant-major? I nearly crapped myself when we were the last
three left over there.' babbled Jimmy, completely ignoring Chubby's
concerned remarks.

'What sort have you guys got? We are totally outnumbered by
Dutchmen,' asked Gus.

'About half and half here,' replied Chubby.

'Hey, where are you okes from? asked a voice from behind Chubby.

'Durban and you?' replied Jimmy.

'No, you stupid pricks. Are you Drivers?'

'No, we are Gunners, our bungalows are just across the parade ground.'

'Best you fuck off back there then, this is a Drivers bungalow, we don't want any pussy type Gunners here.'

Knowing they were seriously outnumbered and not wanting to get into an argument, Jimmy and Gus turned to leave.

'Cheers Chubs. Not only do we have to put up with shit from the Infantry and the Dutchmen, but from each different mustering. Jesus, this is going to be fun,' said Jimmy, in a voice loud enough to be heard by all in the room.

Jimmy and Gus returned to their bungalow, where their absence had gone unnoticed by any person of authority. As they entered the room, a rather large fellow stepped forward to confront the two of them. It was obvious that during their short absence much discussion had gone on about the two of them. The officially appointed Theodorus Nel now stood between them and their beds. He addressed them in Afrikaans.

'You okes had better follow the rules. If you step out of line, we will all shit off together. The corporal said not to leave the bungalow, so why do you not obey?'

'Who died and made you chief? We went to visit our mate and it's got fuck all to do with you. You fucking Dutchmen are all the same too, "*Kop toe*" (take everything too seriously). Get out of my fucking way, I am tired and have been fucked about more than enough for one day,' said Jimmy, pushing his way past Nel and flopping down on his bed, Gus doing the same.

Nel started to object but seeing most of the rest of the bungalow turning away, decided that discretion was the better part of valor.

'Are you crazy? There are twenty-odd of them and two of us,' whispered Gus.

'I knew they would back down. Anyway, it's best to establish the rules right up front otherwise we'll take endless shit from these Rockspiders. Now at least they know who's in charge,' replied Jimmy, turning over and falling asleep almost immediately.

Long before the first grey light of dawn would struggle across the Free State, the bungalow door was flung open, and the lights turned on.

'Up, you fucking disgusting creatures! This is not a holiday camp,' roared the voice of one Corporal Cloete, as he entered the room, taking two quick steps, overturned the first bed, its sleeping occupant unable to extricate himself before landing face first on the hard floor.

The effect on the bungalow was instantaneous. Apart from the poor unfortunate who was trapped on the floor with his bed on top of him, the other twenty-three inmates were immediately out of bed and standing at attention.

'When an N.C.O. or officer enters this bungalow, the first person to see him will shout *"Aandag"* (Attention), and the rest of you pussies will drop what you are doing and stand at attention next to the foot of your bed. Do I make myself clear?'

There was a muted halfhearted mumbling of assent. 'I can't fucking hear you! I said do I make myself clear?' roared Cloete.

'Yes, Corporal,' replied the entire bungalow this time with far more vigor.

'You have half an hour to shit, shave and shampoo. I want this bungalow sparkling when I get back. We will have an inspection and if this bungalow does not sparkle, you will all run to the fence and back,' said Cloete, and turning on his heel left the room.

'Fuck me, it's four-thirty; is he mad or what?' muttered Gus.

'Hey, it could be worse, you could have got the bed closest to the door and ended up like that poor prick,' said Jimmy, pointing to the unfortunate who was still trying to extricate himself from his bed. 'I bet he sleeps lightly from now on.'

Two ablution blocks, one of which was located directly opposite the boy's bungalow, were to serve nearly one hundred and fifty boys. Immaterial of whether you needed to or not, it was compulsory to shave every day. To their horror, Gus and Jimmy noticed a large number of boys who didn't bother with a shower or brush their teeth.

By the time they had finished with their shower, shave and cleaning of their teeth, they were the last two in the ablution block.

'Jesus, I hope those okes who didn't bother with the shower just forgot in the general panic. If not, we are in for some really smelly situations,' commented Gus as they made their way back to the bungalow.

The bungalow was a hive of activity, people rushing around trying to tidy up the room to be ready for inspection. Beds were being aligned, cupboards being straightened, two boys were pulling what looked like an old blanket up and down the floor, and two others sat on the blanket to give it some purchase.

'Hey, you two get moving; we have inspection in ten minutes and Corporal Cloete said this bungalow must sparkle,' ordered Nel.

'What the fuck is there to inspect? We have nothing to polish the floor with, no blankets or sheets just sleeping bags, and no kit to put in our *Trommels* (large metal footlocker). Just what is it you want us do?' replied Jimmy irritably.

A reply was interrupted by a shout of 'Attention.' All activity ceased as twenty-four troopers snapped to attention where they stood.

'Put on your overalls and form-up outside the bungalow in five minutes,' ordered Cloete, who then turned and left the bungalow without so much as a cursory glance around.

Donning their single piece khaki tank overalls, which differed to the two-piece Infantry version, all twenty-four members of bungalow 8 were formed up in rows of three with four minutes to spare. A similar scene was taking place in front of all the other bungalows. On both sides of bungalow 8 were the other two gunnery bungalows. Bungalows four, five and six were allocated to the crew commanders. Bungalow three belonged to the cooks and clerks, with one and two being for the instructors. It was from this direction that Cloete appeared in the company of a Permanent Force sergeant, a short fat man with an English name of Brown. Brown was in his early thirties and had progressed as far as he was likely to in the army. He had a mean sadistic streak in him and couldn't string two English words together. With much shouting and threatening, the three gunnery squads were formed up as one. The day's activity was laid out for them, first roll call, followed by breakfast, haircuts and then kit issue.

Roll call taken, the squad was brought to attention, left turned and double marched to the mess hall. The mess hall was situated at the bottom end of the Armour bungalows and stretched across the bottom area of the Infantry lines. This was the only time the two disciplines would meet in a non-aggressive situation. Being from the bungalows furthest from the mess, Gunnery was at the very end of the queue.

At the entrance to the Mess, each soldier picked up a flat stainless steel *'varkpan'* (pig pan), a plastic cup, knife, fork and spoon. The *varkpan* had indentations on it to hold the cup and various food types. First stop was a huge urn where a cook stood with the tap running; each person had to pass his cup under the tap, careful not to burn himself, and fill his cup with what turned out to be coffee. Next, two slices of bread, stuck together with butter and jam were plonked on the tray.

A huge ladle of lumpy porridge joined the bread and coffee; milk was added at the next stop. The remaining indentation was quickly filled by a greasy egg, a piece of sausage and some sour tasting gravy.

The Mess was a mass of humanity, long metal tables seating twenty, stretched in rows. The Mess could seat nearly a thousand at one time. Gus and Jimmy looked in vain for a sight of Chubby or Ian and eventually found a seat at a table near the exit. Neither Gus nor Jimmy was able to eat the lumpy porridge and it was only the fact that they were starving that they managed the egg and sausage. Breakfast over, they returned their eating implements to the washing area and returned to their bungalow. Unbelievably, the main topic of conversation in the bungalow was about the *'lekker'* (great) breakfast.

They had hardly sat down when the shout of 'fall out and form up' was heard. The entire Armour group was marched up to the parade ground and addressed by the Regimental Sergeant Major. In Afrikaans, he informed them that they were to have haircuts and be issued with kit. They would not be allowed to be drilled unless they had army boots and a helmet, so the sooner they got these tasks done, the sooner they could enjoy the thrill of marching. Laughing at his own joke, he handed over to Sergeant Brown.

Jimmy had, in the meantime, spotted Chubby and was trying vainly to communicate to him with sign language. Brown spotted the movement in the squad and strode over. His first sight was of Gus and his long blond hair.

'Hey, you, "Fluffy", you are first in line for haircuts,' the sergeant shouted, pointing at Gus. Jimmy, standing directly behind Gus, chuckled. 'And you "Goldilocks", you're next.'

The entire body of soldiers, with Gus and Jimmy at their head, were marched off to the barbers, who were located next to the Mess. There were just six barbers to cut the hair of nearly two hundred and fifty soldiers. Unbeknownst to him, Brown had actually done Gus and Jimmy a favor by selecting them for the first haircuts. With less than a dozen strokes of the electric clippers, a haircut was complete. Gus and Jimmy, with around a quarter of an inch of hair on their heads, emerged to the cheers of the waiting line. They were allowed to return to the bungalow and wait for the rest of the haircuts to be completed.

As the others returned in dribs and drabs, it became obvious that being first and second in line was a blessing in disguise. The electric clippers being used had heated up as time went on. Boys were returning with burn marks on their necks and complaints that, as the clippers heated up, so they jammed, and hair was pulled out in chunks. The one thing the haircuts had achieved was to reduce all of them to the same look, the removal of individuality. By the time hair cutting was over, it was lunch time, kit issue would begin directly thereafter.

Lunch was no better than breakfast, the coffee replaced by sweet tea, the two chunks of bread remained and were joined on the *varkpan* by cabbage, boiled white, a stringy meat stew and a piece of bread pudding covered by lumpy custard. With the pushing and shoving and the cook's nasty disposition, the whole mess mixed itself into one. Hunger won the day and both Jimmy and Gus ate almost all their meal; Jimmy refusing to eat anything covered in custard.

In the searing January heat that covered the Free State, two hundred and fifty-three potential soldiers were formed up alphabetically and the issuing of kit began. Two large hangars, side by side, contained the Quarter Master's stores. As each name was called and marked off, the boy would enter the first hangar where he was immediately give a large black canvas kit bag, following this, in what seemed an endless procession, various items of army kit were thrust at him. Little concern was given to the size and fit of all items, except the two pair of army boots. Can't have the troopies getting blisters that prevented them from drilling.

Kit issue over, they returned to their bungalows, where the rest of the day and evening was spent swapping kit with some other unfortunate, until you found some semblance of a fit. All items of kit were to be marked with name and army serial number. It was during this time, shortly after supper, that the bungalow burst open and in rushed a breathless Chubby.

'Hey okes, how's it going?' greeted Chubby, to no one in particular.

'Hey Chubs, what are you doing here? How come those poofters in your bungalow let you out?' said Jimmy.

'Ah, don't give me shit, you know what it's like. I see you've got a right crew here. Anyway, I've come with great news. Get your soccer boots; we're off to play baseball in town. Second night in camp and we're out.'

'What do you mean, baseball? What the fuck do we know about baseball?' asked Gus.

'What's to know? It's like rounders, how hard can that be? The Sergeant Major here is a big baseball freak and with the changeover of intakes, he hasn't had a chance to get his team organized and he has a game in town tonight. I overheard some guy asking for baseball players, so I told him I played and had two mates in gunnery who also played, but we had no kit. He said no problem, as long as we could play ball, they had plenty of kit. So here we are, off to town,' said Chubby.

Chubby hustled a protesting Gus and Jimmy out of the bungalow, who turned at the door and informed the rest of the bungalow that they would be back after 10.30 and they were to inform Cloete at roll call that the Sergeant Major had requested that they turn out for baseball.

Chubby, full of confidence, had told the captain of the baseball team that he played catcher; must be something like a wicket keeper in cricket, he told Gus and Jimmy. Fortunately for the other two, thirteen boys in total had turned up and needing only nine at one time, they retired to the small grandstand to watch Chubby make a complete fool of himself, or so they thought.

Chubby, quick to grasp the intricacies of the game, and given his natural ability for any type of bat/ball game, more than held his own. Missing nothing behind the batter, he managed to bat three times, getting a base hit each time and scoring one run.

Although Chubby shone, the team lost narrowly to their opponents. Despite this the Sergeant Major was sufficiently impressed with his new catcher, with his obvious will to win, to personally congratulate him. Chubby was informed that practice was Monday nights and Wednesday afternoon sports parade. 'Just tell your N.C.O. to excuse you from other duties at this time, any problem you just tell me.'

The following morning, the drudgery of basic training began: woken at four thirty in the morning, ablutions, roll call, inspection, breakfast, march until tea time, march until lunch, march until supper and if you were really unfortunate, you pulled guard duty for the night. Most evenings were spent cleaning kit and making the bungalow ready for morning inspection. This continued Monday to Friday until lunch time on Saturday. The only relief being Wednesday afternoon sports parade.

Sports parade at Bloemfontein's Tempe base during summers comprised of either cricket, baseball or cross country running. So, if one wanted to avoid three hours of running around an army base, you quickly joined one of the other disciplines. Jimmy, Gus and Chubby made their way posthaste to the cricket field, with around sixty other boys. Chubby, never one to miss an opportunity, donned his pads and wicket keeper's gloves and stationed himself behind the stumps in the middle of the three bowling nets. By the time the officer in charge of cricket arrived, Chubby was well in control of activity at the nets.

At the same time this was going on, the baseball sergeant major was frantically looking for his star catcher. He dispatched two runners, one to the athletic field and the other to the cricket ground, with the explicit instruction to return with Chubby. With the arrival of the runner, a heated discussion took place between the major and the messenger. Although officially outranking the sergeant major, no officer wanted to get on the wrong side of the 'man who ran the camp.'

Leaving Chubby in charge of practice, the major left for the baseball field to attempt to resolve the matter of who should have Chubby in their team. Twenty minutes later, a red faced major returned, summoned Chubby and instructed him go to the baseball field. The result of all of this was that Chubby would practice with baseball on Mondays and alternate Wednesdays, and with cricket on Tuesdays and alternating Wednesdays. As cricket matches were held on Saturdays and baseball usually on Wednesday evenings, this arrangement suited everybody, particularly Chubby as this ensured he would seldom, if ever, stand guard duty. It also ensured that every effort would be made to keep Chubby at Tempe for the duration of his army training.

On the morning of the fourth Sunday, Jimmy, Gus and Chubby were lying around the Gunnery bungalow. Jimmy was tidying out his *trommel,* when he noticed his still unopened matriculation results. Casually picking up the envelope, watched by his two friends, he tossed it onto his bed. Gus, unable to wait, grabbed the envelope and opened it.

'Fuck, six As and an F. Still an A average; pity about the Afrikaans though,' chirped Gus, knowing that Jimmy's average was probably as high as his was with seven As.

'Let's have a look,' said Jimmy, taking the letter from Gus. 'Hey, it says here I can do a re-write of Afrikaans in March, maybe I can get a few days off the army. Dave Drew is getting off five days to re-write maths and science. Hey, I'm off to see Major van Zyl to organize some leave.'

Jimmy leapt off the bed and armed with his matriculation results, headed for the door. Twenty minutes later, a grinning Jimmy reappeared.

'So, did you get some study leave?' asked Gus.

'Sure did, only three weeks.'

'Three weeks to re-write one subject; how the fuck did you manage that?' exclaimed Chubby.

'Well, you know what these Dutchmen are like. I showed him my results; six A's and the F for Afrikaans and told him with tears in my eyes that I felt I had let down my parents, my country and myself. As Afrikaans is the main language of the country, I have to re-write in an effort to improve myself. I figured I'd get off three or four days; when he signed my pass and I saw it was three weeks, I nearly crapped in my pants.'

'Let's see that pass,; shit, you leave the day we finish basic training, you lucky bastard,' said Gus.

Jan 31, 1968
The island of Mauritius becomes independent of Britain after days of race riots.

At the end of six weeks of basic training, the various disciplines spent less time on the parade ground and more time learning the finer points of their mustering. It was also at this time that one could choose to specialize. For Ian, who had seen very little of his mates during basic training, it was a time of decisions. For a reason he could never really explain, he volunteered to join the parachute regiment. The 'Parabats' as they were known, had a stringent physical and mental entrance examination, only the fittest and toughest were accepted. Acceptance alone didn't guarantee their survival and the eventual awarding of the prestigious purple beret and 'wings'. For Ian, it would mean three days of intense mental and physical stress, and then a further six weeks of training that would make basic training seem like a picnic.

On the day Jimmy left for his study leave, Ian was accepted into the 'Parabats'.

Mar 4, 1968
The Rhodesian Appeals Court overturns the Queen's reprieve of three blacks sentenced to death.

Mar 16, 1968
President Johnson sends an additional 50,000 troops to Vietnam.

For the next three weeks, Jimmy spent his days at the beach and his nights getting better acquainted with Karen Booth. Without having opened a book, Jimmy reported to Durban Boy's High School to re-write Afrikaans. The following afternoon, bidding Karen a fond fare-well, Jimmy caught the train for Bloemfontein. Unlike the troop train, this one arrived the following morning and hitching a ride, Jimmy got to camp in time for lunch.

Still attired in his 'stepping out' clothes, Jimmy stood out like a sore thumb and was easily spotted by Gus and Chubby.

'Hey, look who is back,' shouted Chubby, slapping Jimmy on the back.

Lunch was taken up with questions about Durban, Karen, Chubby's girlfriend Diane and the beach. Ian, they had heard, qualified for the Parabats but they hadn't seen him as they were in an adjacent camp and had no contact. Gus had failed to be selected for the officer's course because of color blindness, but Chubby had been selected for the in-structor's course, which would keep him at Tempe. Jimmy, in his ab-sence, along with Gus, had been posted to Zeerust on the Western Transvaal border, just about as far away from Durban as you could get.

The following two weeks were spent brushing up on gunnery and driving skills and waiting for the end of the first period of their army training. Soon no longer to be known as *'Roofs'* but the equally un-pleasant name of *'blougat'* (blue bum), so called because they are con-tinually getting their arses kicked by the *'ou manne'* (old men, those in their final three months of army life).

At the passing out parade held to mark the end of the quarter, the entire Armour Squadron was marched back and forth in front of the assembled dignitaries and then treated to a rousing speech from the camp commandant. Those not remaining as candidate officers or in-structors, would be posted to one of three camps. The most fortunate would go the School of Armour, located just behind the Parabats camp. The second group would be posted to Walvis Bay in South West Africa, where they would protect the South African-owned port, lo-cated on the edge of the Namib desert. Apart from the heat and the smell of the fish processing factories, it was not too unpleasant.

The third group would be posted to Zeerust, where according to the camp commandant, they would be the first line of defense, protecting the country's western border against the communist sponsored infil-trators that threatened the safety of our fatherland. It was with these patriotic words ringing in their ears that Jimmy and Gus bade Chubby farewell and left Tempe for Zeerust.

ZEERUST – Gus and Jimmy

The train trip from Bloemfontein to Zeerust would be via Johannesburg, where there was a five hour stopover. A permanent force corporal from Zeerust accompanied the contingent on their journey. Corporal van Staaden was assigned to the Zeerust base as a clerk and looked the part, short and bespectacled. The rank of two stripe corporal given to van Staaden, who was officially a private, were known as kit-bag stripes, as it was common practice that no PF should be outranked by any citizen force soldier.

Despite instructions from van Staaden that no one should leave the station at Johannesburg, both Jimmy and Gus, along with Alan Kozinsky, who lived in Johannesburg, left for a look around the city. Although officially not allowed to drink whilst in army uniform, the three managed to visit half a dozen pubs in the vicinity. Arriving back at the station, just in time for the train's departure and well under the influence, they figured they would sleep off the effects and be fresh and strong for their arrival at Zeerust.

At exactly 3.20 am. Jimmy was awoken, lifted by the scruff of the neck and the seat of his trousers and thrown out of the train window and onto the station platform; welcome to Zeerust. Shaking the effects of sleep and alcohol from his system, he staggered to his feet ready to take on his assailant. At the same moment, Gus landed at his feet and was followed shortly thereafter by Kozinsky. Looking up into the train compartment, Jimmy saw two of the biggest guys he had ever seen. Blond, six foot eight Bert Brits and equally as tall, dark haired Dup du Plessis, both corporals and part of the welcoming committee.

Amid screaming threats, this latest contingent of *'Blougats'* were loaded onto the waiting Bedford trucks for the short trip to the Military base located on the outskirts of the tiny Western Transvaal town of Zeerust. The camp was relatively new and still partly under construction. The base is located some five miles west of Zeerust, on the main road to Gaborone, the capital of Botswana. The north and western sides of the camp are boarded by slate-bearing hills. This was to be home for Jimmy, Gus and some sixty other *'Blougats'* for the next six months.

The Permanent Force contingent at Zeerust comprised of Commandant De la Rae, two majors, one of whom was the chief medical officer, Major Clara De la Rae, the Commandant's wife, a lieutenant, a sergeant major, three staff sergeants, two corporals, one a cook and the other a clerk.

Although Commandant De la Rae was commanding officer, the camp was run by Sergeant Major Halliday, known to one and all as 'Sammy' (derived from the Afrikaans, Sam-majoer).

The camp was made up of three different regiments of Armour; Natal Mounted Rifles (N.M.R.), consisting of mainly Durban boys, Umvoti Mounted Rifles (U.M.R.), made up of boys from the rural and farming communities of Natal and Zululand. The third contingent were from the Afrikaans Regiment Molopo (R.M.), drawn from no particular area of the country but all were typically Afrikaans.

The average age of this new intake was eighteen and a half, and nearly all were Matriculants. Although the content of the camp was almost two thirds English, the commands and instruction were given in Afrikaans. The only black faces to be found within the camp were those of two cleaners who helped in the kitchen and the gardener who tended the rugby field.

The '*oumanne*' at Zeerust were from the previous year's October intake and unlike their *'blougats,'* their average age was closer to twenty. For some reason, the previous year, the South African Defense Force decided to attempt to break up the traditions of the English regiments by posting an older, more mixed bag to both N.M.R. and U.M.R. This resulted in both the regiments being manned by an older and more diverse group, most of whom had been out of the school environment for at least two years.

The tradition at Zeerust, encouraged by the PF's who turned a blind eye to it, was that the '*ou manne*' would subject the *'blougats'* to physical and mental abuse in an attempt to keep them in a state of fear and subjugation, which would make discipline much easier to maintain. This was perpetuated at each intake as the incoming one would pay for the ways of the outgoing one.

The rules were in fact very simple; you obeyed all the corporals and '*ou manne*' without question, you ran from point to point when outside of a building, you were assigned to a corporal or an '*ou manne*' for whom you would do chores for, and any gift or food parcel you received from home was taken from you. Any breech of these rules was met with instant punishment. It was under these conditions that Jimmy and Gus arrived at Zeerust and would spend three frustrating months of abuse.

Apr 4, 1968
Doctor Martin Luther King Jr. is gunned down in Memphis, Tennessee.

Jimmy had the misfortune to be 'claimed' by Corporal Johnny Kranidiotis, known to his peers as 'Granny' and to the blougats as 'that fucking Greek Granny' from East London. He was a mean, short man who had been subjected to a fair amount of abuse in his *'blougat'* days and was determined to avenge himself. Gus was more fortunate; Lance-corporal Sandy Arbuckle, from Johannesburg, was his assignment. Whereas Granny had a mean streak, Arbuckle was a slob; Jimmy had the physical abuse, but Gus had the onerous task of cleaning Arbuckle's kit.

The living quarters consisted of eight bungalows in two rows of four, running along the southern side of the camp. There were fourteen beds, seven to a side, separated by a row of high cupboards running down the middle of the room, effectively splitting the room into two sections. The seven or eight *'blougats'* per bungalow were responsible for cleaning the windows, polishing the floors and ensuring everyone's kit was up to scratch for inspection.

Jimmy and Gus's beds were flanked by Granny's and Arbuckle's on the one side, but it was the occupant to the left of Jimmy who was to give him the most trouble. Its occupant was one Private Klaus Kuter from Wolmaransstad, who spoke no English and whose teeth had never seen toothpaste.

Being one *'blougat'* short, Kuter had no one assigned to him; unable to hide his frustration he decided to take it out on the one nearest to him, namely Jimmy. Unable to refuse any order from him, Jimmy found himself loaded with twice the amount of washing and ironing. Not being particularly fond of anything or anyone Afrikaans, Jimmy did this work grudgingly, which did not go unnoticed by Kuter, who used every opportunity to goad Jimmy more.

A derogatory term used by many Afrikaners to describe those of English origin is *'Soutpiel'*, the literal translation is 'salt cock'. This term is derived from the fact that the English cannot make up their

160

minds where or who they are, so they have one leg in England and the other in South Africa with their penis's hanging in the Atlantic Ocean, hence the term. Kuter took great delight in calling Jimmy this at every opportunity, cackling away as though he had invented the phrase himself. Jimmy, from his side, wasn't in the slightest bit bothered by what this ignorant Dutchman called him, it was after all just a name.

Apr 11, 1968
President Johnson signs the Civil Rights Bill, making it illegal to refuse housing on grounds of race.

The camp at Zeerust was situated about 5 miles outside the town on the road to the capital of Botswana, Gaborone. The camp was set back about 500 yards from the main road. The fenced off perimeter of the camp was approximately two-and-three quarter miles.

There were two different type of physical training (PT). Three times a week, Monday, Wednesday and Friday mornings, the entire camp, including all permanent forces members. reported to the parade ground at 7am for one hour of intense PT. The only exception was the camp nurse, the Commandant's wife.

The sessions were run by Sammy. He took great joy in the process. Every person on that parade ground was subjected to exactly the same exercises, no exceptions. He took great delight in calling out the PF's by name if he saw any slacking. The Commandant came in for much of Sammy's abuse, which often contained derogatory references in his inability to service his wife, if unable to complete the exercises with the rest of the troops.

The *blougats* dreaded Tuesdays and Thursdays. You formed up on the rugby field in overalls and boots at 6.30am. This version of PT was only for the conscripts, no PF's, only Sammy ensuring everyone was present. Each person picked up two large bricks (*baksteen*) and on command ran the 500 yards toward the main gate. At the main gate you made a left turn. Some fifty yards, out of sight of any PF's, you were handed your corporal's or *ouman*'s two *baksteen* to carry as well.

You made one two-and-a-half mile lap of the camp, marking time just before the main gate to make sure that all the corporals and *oumanne* were together. Continuing along the perimeter, you would reach the other gate approximately halfway around, almost directly opposite the main gate. At this point, you handed back your additional *baksteen* to its original owner. When done, you ran the 500 yards back to the rugby field and the waiting Sammy. You had to make sure that all *blougats* brought up the rear.

Other than soldiering, the only other activities at Zeerust were sports and being the end of summer there were only two; rugby and cross county running. Zeerust fielded two rugby teams, the first team played in the Western Transvaal first division and the second fifteen one league lower. Although the opposition were in all cases much larger, stronger and older than the army boys, superior fitness evened things up somewhat. Another factor was that rugby provided the only outlet for aggression open to many of the '*blougats*'. It was in this environment that Jimmy flourished on the rugby field. Never having been much of a rugby player before, Jimmy found a source to channel his frustration and through sheer aggression ended up being selected for the first fifteen rugby team.

It was this selection that was to lead to a confrontation with Kuter. Kuter was one of the unfortunates who had to spend sport's day running around the outside of the two-and-three-quarter mile boundary that surrounded the camp. Jimmy, returning from rugby practice, found Kuter rummaging through his locker.

'Are you looking for something of mine?' inquired Jimmy sarcastically.

'I need clean socks and you haven't washed mine, so I'll take a pair of yours,' replied Kuter, taking a pair of Jimmy's clean socks.

'No, you won't. I'll go and wash yours now.'

'Fuck you, Soutpiel, give me twenty push-ups now.'

Jimmy walked up to Kuter, grabbed his socks, returned them to his locker and started the push-ups. Kuter, not wanting to push the sock issue, as he had not expected to be caught stealing the socks, sat back on his bed to watch Jimmy. At the end of twenty push-ups, Jimmy stood up.

'Who told you to stop? Give me another twenty.'

Jimmy gave Kuter a look of pure hatred, which did not go unnoticed, and got down to start the next twenty push-ups. Another twenty followed, Kuter was enjoying himself.

'Enough,' shouted Kuter, 'start bunny-hops.'

Bunny-hops consisted of squatting on your haunches and hopping up and down ensuring both feet left the ground. The effect this had was to tighten the upper thigh muscles and cause cramps of the calf; two or three minutes of this was about all one could take before the cramps started. Cramping, Jimmy attempted to rise to relieve the strain, Kuter raising the heel of his army boot, brought it down on Jimmy's upper thigh, knocking him to the ground.

'You will do this until you cry, Soutpiel,' sneered Kuter, 'so cry for me and you can stop.'

Fuck you, thought Jimmy, I'll die before I cry for this arsehole. Seeing the look of determination on Jimmy's face and knowing that others would be returning to the bungalow soon, Kuter decided to force the issue and picking up his rifle by the barrel, he brought the wooden butt of it down on Jimmy's upper right thigh and then immediately on the left. Jimmy fell to the floor, holding his aching legs. Looking up he saw Kuter's stupid green-toothed grin and he snapped. Leaping up, he swung a right fist at Kuter's mouth, catching him totally by surprise. Blood spurted everywhere and Kuter fell back onto his bed; at that instant the bungalow door open and Granny walked in.

'What the fuck is going on here? Blougat, did you hit Kuter?' screamed Kranidiotis. 'You'll shit for this, that I promise you. Get down to the showers I'll see you there in a few minutes.'

Jimmy turned and walked past the returning occupants, knowing he was now in serious trouble. Anyone ordered to the showers was there for only one reason, he would be physically punished for what had happened. The shower block was the further most point away from any Permanent Force interruptions. Kranidiotis and four other corporals arrived with the still bleeding Kuter, all others were chased from the shower block, it would be Jimmy and his five tormentors.

'Ok you shit, you want to fight, pick on one of us, someone of your own size,' shouted Granny. 'Come, who do you want?'

'Christ,' thought Jimmy, 'none of these fuckers is anywhere near my size.'

Apart from Granny, the other options were Kuter, who was in fact quite a bit bigger than Jimmy, Bert Brits and Dup du Plessis, both at six foot eight, Keith Wilson and Frog Ferguson, at twenty and twenty one respectively and much older and more physically developed. Jimmy knew he was in trouble and the best he could do was take what was coming and make no attempt to defend himself, lest it be construed as aggression.

Unable to goad Jimmy into fighting, they decided to make an example of him that would leave all '*blougats*' in no doubt about what would happen if they attacked any of the '*oumanne*.' For the next two and a half hours, Jimmy was subjected to endless push-ups, bunny-hops, star jumps and sit-ups. When he fell to the floor in exhaustion, he was doused with a bucket of water and made to continue. Eventually bored with the whole thing, they left him lying on the wet floor. Kuter, last to leave and making sure no one was looking, kicked Jimmy once in the ribs and then with all his weight behind him, jumped down on his ankle.

Gus and Kozinsky were sent to fetch Jimmy. Seeing him lying on the floor, they rushed over to pick him up.

'What the fuck did you hit Kuter for?' asked Gus, 'You must have known you'd shit for it. Are you ok?'

'No, I'm totally fucked, but I'll be ok. I hope I don't get some fucking disease from that Kuter pricks mouth, I should have hit him in the nose,' replied Jimmy, trying hard to be casual despite the pain he was in.

Jimmy was helped back to the bungalow and placed on his bed. Kuter and Granny avoided looking at him, realising that maybe they had gone too far. Jimmy ignored Granny and looked across at Kuter; he would make this ignorant Dutchman pay somehow.

The following morning, still in great pain, Jimmy formed up with the rest of the camp on the parade ground. The daily orders were given out and Sammy told the members of the two rugby sides to report for extra training that afternoon, as they had an important grudge match against Mafeking Police on Saturday. Jimmy made it painfully through to lunch time, the story of what had happened had spread throughout the camp and the results of what he did were plainly visible to everyone.

After lunch, Jimmy and Gus donned their rugby kit and at a slow trot, headed for the rugby field.

'How the hell are you going to train in your condition?' inquired Gus.

'I'm stuffed if I know, maybe Sammy won't notice. Hopefully we just run and don't play a practice match. If I catch another one in the ribs, I'll shit myself.'

Jimmy's hopes were immediately dashed. 'Alright, I want the first team backs and the second team forwards on the right and the first team forwards and second team backs on the left. We will play a full eighty-minute game,' ordered Sammy.

It only took the first scrum to find Jimmy out. Unable to push with any weight from his side, when the scrum wheeled around and collapsed, the culprit was obvious.

'Wilson, what the hell are you up to boy?' roared Sammy, 'You are pushing like a girl. Scrum again.'

The second scrum had the same result as the first, Jimmy reeled away holding his ribs.

'Come here, Wilson. What the hell is wrong with you?'

'I slipped in the shower and hurt my ribs sir,' said Jimmy, limping up to the tiny Sergeant Major.

'Hurt your ankle as well, did you?' inquired Sammy. 'And the hand cut when you fell. What happened? I want the truth.'

'I slipped in the shower. sir.'

Sammy had been around a long time and could read the signs of what probably happened, and under any other circumstances couldn't have cared less how or why Jimmy had been beaten up, but this affected his rugby team.

'Don't lie to me, sonny, who did this? You tell me now or you'll really be in trouble,' demanded Sammy.

'I slipped in the shower, sir.'

'Well, you better be fit by Saturday or I will personally make sure that you sit in the guard house until you tell me who the culprits are. Now, get to the side of the field.'

With one of the reserves replacing him, Jimmy took up his position on the lower row of the grandstand and spent the next eighty minutes mulling over how the hell was he going to be ok to play on Saturday. There was no way he could tell Sammy about what happened.

Apr 21, 1968
'As I look ahead, I am filled with foreboding. Like the Roman, I see the River Tiber flowing with much blood.'
—quoted Enoch Powell, the Tory Shadow Minister of Defence.

These comments triggered off fierce controversy over race relations in Britain.

'Britain must be mad, literally mad, to allow 50,000 dependents of immigrants into the country each year.'
—74% of Britons support Powell on immigration.

Jimmy was left pretty much alone for the remainder of the week and his bruises and sprains healed to some extent. The short trip to

165

Mafeking was made in two Bedford trucks, most of the *oumanne* kept their eyes on Jimmy, wondering whether he was able to play or whether he would have to tell Sammy who it was that caused his injuries. Jimmy, in his wisdom, had a plan figured out. He would commit some really bad foul and get himself sent off as early as possible.

The first match was between the respective second teams and not surprisingly was won by the bigger and stronger Police team. Zeerust military had never beaten any Mafeking Police side in the five years that they had played each other. By the time the first teams took the field, Jimmy had formulated a plan. At the first line out he would break ranks early and flatten the first person that he could find who was wearing a purple jersey.

Less than two minutes into the game he had his chance. Totally ignoring the ball, he broke around the back of the line out and launched himself two footed at the unfortunate Mafeking fly-half. Catching him at the same time as he caught the ball, Jimmy crashed into the midriff of the opposing fly-half, bringing him heavily to the ground. Jimmy was immediately surrounded by angry Mafeking players. Amid the confusion, the referee pulled Jimmy to one side and told him in no uncertain manner that anymore of that kind of play and he would be off.

The unfortunate fly-half, Mafeking's star player, was loaded onto the stretcher and carried off to take no further part in the game. As no substitutes were allowed, Zeerust enjoyed a one-man advantage for the rest of the match. Jimmy spent the next seventy-five minutes running away from the huge pack of Police players, determined to extract revenge for their injured teammate. It was with this disruption that Zeerust managed to beat their Police opponents for the first time.

Sammy was ecstatic, his rugby team had achieved the impossible, beaten the mighty Mafeking Police. He also realized that if he didn't get Jimmy off the field and out of the way at the end of the match, there was likely to be trouble. At the final whistle, Sammy rushed onto the field to congratulate his players. When he reached Jimmy, Sammy told him to get to the parking lot and wait by his jeep, they would be leaving as soon as possible. Jimmy needed no second invitation; Gus was instructed to collect Jimmy's belongings from the change rooms and bring them back to camp.

Sammy and Jimmy left within minutes of the final whistle and returned to camp together. Sammy, unable to contain himself over the victory, replayed the game blow by blow to Jimmy on the return trip. From that day on Sammy had a new favorite, Jimmy became untouchable and never again had to suffer at the hands of any *ouman* or corporal. He had given Sammy the one thing he wanted more than anything, a victory over Mafeking Police, and although his part in the victory was dubious, Jimmy was not going to argue the point.

Back in Zeerust, life continued much as before. Both Jimmy and Gus continued with their duties, learning the finer art of gunnery and radio communications. Jimmy no longer suffered physical damage at the hands of the corporals and *oumanne* but still had the regular *blougat* duties of cleaning, etc. Due to his reputation after the Mafeking game, Jimmy became a marked target of opposing rugby teams and Sammy felt it best that he was no longer selected for the first team, as there was a strong possibility of him being badly hurt.

The end of the semester drew near, and one last task had to be completed before the corporals and *oumanne* departed.. The dreaded fitness test.

In all other Army camps around the country a similar process was taking place; the only subtle difference was the standard army fitness test of a nine mile run in full kit, a two hundred yard run carrying an equally-sized comrade across your shoulders, a fifty yard swim, all in full army gear and ending off with a two mile run in PT kit, was done over two days; at Zeerust it was done all before lunch.

The one thing that Jimmy, and to a lesser extent Gus, had suffered most was a lack of sleep. If not standing guard, the process was to clean the bungalow, do your *blougat* chores and be in bed at exactly 10.30pm. The second in command of that day's guard would wake you at 3.20am. The significance of this time is that it is the exact time the train arrives at Zeerust from Johannesburg.

With the departure of the outgoing semester, the new corporals were announced. Gus and Jimmy were among the corporals. Gus, by effort and accomplishments, and Jimmy by virtue of one rugby game.

There was one final twist to the end of the semester. The outgoing mob left after lunch by Bedford truck to the station. There were a few who had their own vehicles and they were only allowed to leave at the same time as the departing train – 3pm. That left a few nervous individuals, who were now outnumbered by the 'new' corporals and *oumanne*. Worried that some revenge may be taken, they were segregated to the canteen until time to leave.

Jimmy took the first opportunity to hit the sack and catch up on well needed sleep.

He hadn't been asleep for more than an hour when Gus shook him awake.

'Wake up, you lazy bastard. You'll never guess who is back in camp.'

'Fuck off, leave me alone.'

'It's your mate, Kuter. He was leaving with Spies and their car broke down a couple of miles from camp.'

Jimmy was instantly awake.

'Where is he?'

'In the guard house, it looks like he is shitting himself.'

Without a word, Jimmy leapt up and headed for the guard house.

He found Kuter huddled up in the corner, trying very hard to be invisible. Spies was standing up right next to him, not quite protecting him but sort of showing solidarity. They were now civilians and should be treated as such.

Jimmy walked over to Kuter and pushed Spies out of the way.

'Stand up, you miserable cunt, it's payback time.'

Kuter (in Afrikaans) 'You can't touch me. I am a Civvie. Anyway, I was just joking around with you.'

Jimmy grabbed Kuter by the collar and slammed him up against the wall. When extremely angry, Jimmy's eyes turned ice blue, and Kuter could see that there was a pile of shit coming down on his head.

'Right, give me twenty push-ups.'

Kuter looked disbelievingly but dropped and started his push-ups. Twenty completed Jimmy gave him twenty bunny hops. Kuter was starting to struggle. Halfway through the bunny hops, he stood up suffering from thigh cramps.

'What the fuck are you stopping for? Get back down there. I will tell you when you are done.'

'*Ek kannie meer doen nie.*' (I can't do any more), panted Kuter. '*Ek wil nie meer doen nie.*' (I will not do any more).

'Okay then, let's go down to the showers and settle this. I am going to fuck you up, you miserable piece of shit.'

Jimmy grabbed Kuter by the scruff of his neck and started to drag him towards the guard room door. As he opened the door he turned and looked at Kuter, who was now in a deep state of agitation.

'You can't do this to me, I am a Civvie. I am sorry for what I did; please don't fuck me up,' blubbered Kuter and promptly burst into tears.

'I can do this to you, but I won't. You are twenty years old and are crying like a little girl. If you want to give it then you should learn to take it. So, fuck off you piece of shit, if I ever see you in Civvie street I will fuck you up. I am going back to bed!'

Jimmy turned and left the building, vowing that he was not going to treat the incoming blougats the way that he was treated.

Later it was found that someone had tampered with Spies' car.

The new blougats arrived at Zeerust station at 3.20am and Jimmy was not one of the welcoming committee, much to chagrin of the other corporals. He was still asleep when he was awakened by the arrival of the new blougats being herded into the canteen for briefing and roll call.

Sometime later the arrival of ten brand new *blougats*. Jimmy was now awake and out of bed, ready to line them up.

'Right. This is an English bungalow. Any of you lot Dutchmen?' bellowed Jimmy.

One terrified looking *blougat* stepped forward. 'Ja Corporal.'

'Okay, fuck off to the next bungalow, they are all Dutchmen and send me one Soutpiel.'

Two minutes later a new terrified *blougat* arrived.

'Ten blogats, ten corporals and oumanne. Perfect. Who do you want Gus?'

'I'll take matey over there.' Pointing to a guy about the same height and build as himself. 'What's your name, *blougat*?'

'Thompson, corporal.'

'Right, Thompson, your bed is over there.'

'I'll take this one, what's your name?' asked Jimmy.

'Sandburg, Corporal.'

'Okay *blougat,* you are over there.'

So, there it was; Thompson, surfer dude and Sandberg tall and strong. Two *blougats* rescued from three months of arse kicking. It was not to say that they weren't disciplined and put through the rigours' of a typical Zeerust *blougat* but they were never subjected to petty violence by either Gus or Jimmy.

During their final three months in Zeerust, things went quietly except for two significant incidents both effecting Jimmy.

The first was his parents and younger brother David emigrated to England, leaving sister Maureen behind in Durban to finish her school year. She was living with family friends and would leave for England in December. After showing Sammy the letter, he was given a long weekend pass to say goodbye.

The second incident was a bit more dramatic and occurred on one of the few times Jimmy stood as guard commander. Standing as guard commander at the magazine was a bit of a cushy number, as it was a bit away from the camp, but standing beat was a little scary. It was dark and the 'beat' ran along the northernmost edge of the camp, between that fence and the fence guarding the magazine.

During July and August 1968 they had been doing exercises to combat the oncoming '*Rooi Gevaar*' (Red danger). These were heavily-armed black terrorists expected to infiltrate from Botswana. As a result, there was always a bit of tension standing guard at the magazine, armed only with an R1 rifle and six live rounds.

On this particular night, Johnny Miller was standing the ten to twelve o'clock watch. Johnny was a bit simple with a very nervous disposition and under normal conditions was not someone you would want walking about with a loaded rifle.

At approximately eleven thirty, two shots rang out waking a half-asleep Jimmy.

Grabbing his loaded pistol, he ran out of the guard room bumping into the guard walking the lower beat.

'What the fuck is going on, *blougat*?' he barked.

'It's Miller, Corporal. He has fired two shots. Is it the terrorists?'

'Who the hell knows. Stay here and keep alert and remember to challenge anyone with the password. You get the wrong answer, shoot first,' said Jimmy, heading for the upper beat.

Reaching the point of the upper beat furthest from the camp, Jimmy found Johnny Miller shaking, his rifle on the floor and him crouched tight against the fence. He wouldn't be much use in an attack, thought Jimmy.

'Okay Miller, what's going on here, what happened?'

'I heard people moving and challenged them with the password and got no reply, so I let off two shots. I heard a crying sound. I think I shot someone,' he blabbered.

Hearing no further sounds, Jimmy turned on his flash light and moved forward to investigate, Miller following closely behind.

About twenty-five meters into the bush, they found the victim. There, lying with its legs in the air, was one of Sammy's cows, quite dead with a bullet in the head. Although panicked, Miller had made the perfect shot; pure luck, but an instant kill.

Jimmy now realised that he would have to tell Sammy of the incident, or if no one had heard the shots, could he just ignore it? Sanity prevailed, and Jimmy made his way to Sammy's residence. It was nearly midnight.

Jimmy knocked on the door and a minute later a sleepy-looking Sammy opened the door.

'Why are you waking me at this time of the night, Corporal? There better be a good reason.'

'There has been a shooting incident at the magazine.'

Before Jimmy could explain, Sammy went ballistic. Shit, thought Jimmy, wait until he finds out it is one of his cows.

'What the fuck is going on? I'll get my weapon and sound the camp alarm.'

'No need, Sarmajor. It's under control. It's just one of your cows. Trooper Miller thought it was a terrorist and shot it.'

'That boy is an idiot! I will have his balls,' shouted Sammy, looking apoplectic.

Sammy turned around and headed inside, leaving Jimmy standing in front of the open door. He returned minutes later, fully dressed and looking far less aggravated. He tapped Jimmy on the shoulder and said, 'Let's go, son.'

On the walk up to the scene of the 'crime', Sammy rambled on about his cows (there were seven of them wandering around the camp), they were like his children; all prize beasts. Jimmy thought it better not to mention that in fact, there were now six cows.

It was after midnight when they approached Johnny Miller who was religiously standing guard over the dead cow. Sammy went nuts. This was his favourite cow, a prize among prizes; someone is going to pay for this. Johnny looked like he was ready to shit himself. The remaining five guards and the assistant guard commander had joined the crowd by this time. Mulling around and trying to look inconspicuous, all were waiting for the shit to hit the fan.

To everyone's surprise, Sammy calmly instructed Jimmy to get down to the motor pool and draw a Bedford truck and get his favourite cow transported to the mess. Wake up the cook and get the cow into the freezer. With those instructions, he turned and headed home. There was look of relief amongst the gathered crowd, especially Miller, who looked close to tears. You couldn't help but feel sorry for him.

Jimmy tended to Sammy's instructions and by two thirty, everything was back to normal.

Next morning at PT parade, Sammy inquired, 'If there were any of you farm boys knew anything about cutting up slaughtered cows, you should step forward.' Normally, in the army you never volunteered for anything, but the word had got around about the shooting. Phil Mina and Mark Schreiber were two Natal farm boys who stepped forward and were immediately assigned to the mess for the day. Anything to get out of PT for the day.

It turned out that Sammy claimed compensation from the army for the death of his prize 'bull'. He sold the cut-up meat to the army and the cowhide to a local shop. The camp, in turn, were treated to a full on 'braai'. Johnny Miller was a hero, at least for a few days so all turned out well.

Sammy's compensation process through the army took its normal slow process and his 'replacement' bull didn't arrive until after Jimmy and Gus departed. They heard that Sammy named him Miller.

The last three weeks at Zeerust passed without much incident. There was the dreaded fitness test still to do, with the threat if you didn't pass, you couldn't '*klaar uit*' (clear out)and would have to stay until you passed. The troops weren't to know that that was a load of crap, so a sense of nervousness was around.

September 23, 1968 (three days before their departure date) all were awoken at three twenty in the morning for their nine mile run in full kit. Loaded up on Bedford's they were driven out the nine miles, roll call taken and given two hours to get back to camp.

A group of corporals and *oumanne* had arranged to meet at the bottom of the road leading up to the camp and as a group, they would finish together just inside the two hours.

One hour and fifty-five minutes later roughly thirty soldiers ran up the last five hundred meters and crossed the finish line, all singing that well known Simon and Garfunkel number '*Homeward Bound*'. To say that it pissed off the PF's would be putting it mildly.

Normally there was a break after the nine miles before the next exercise. This day it was straight into the two hundred meter '*skaap draai*' (carrying someone of equal size and weight over your shoulders). Then directly into the swimming pool where you had to tread water for two minutes. Fortunately, the craziness stopped there as a couple of the Dutchmen, who were not much good at swimming, nearly drowned.

Breakfast was taken and then straight into the two-mile run from the camp up to the 'neck' and back in nineteen minutes. An absolute killer in any conditions.

September 25, 1968 eventually arrived much to their excitement. Final pay day, twenty-five days at R1.85 per day, less 50 cents for haircuts and R1 for mess fees leaving you with the grand total of R44.75.

A number of the troops had their own transport and the remaining sixty-five NMR and UMR boys were loaded up on Bedford's and headed for Zeerust station. There were a couple of RM boys included. The bulk of the remaining RM troops would be transported to Mafeking and dispersed from there.

The Zeerust train would arrive in Johannesburg at 8pm and the connecting train to Durban would leave at 10pm. This didn't leave much time in Johannesburg to find a pub for a few civilian beers, not that anyone had much money, especially Gus and Jimmy.

'Not to worry, I have a plan,' said Alan Kozinsky and left it at that.

Half past eight the train pulled into Johannesburg station, thirty minutes late. Typical South African Railways. Sixty-five excited troops poured onto platform five dragging their Army kit with them. The plan was for the Natal boys to head over to platform seven where the Durban train was waiting, grab a compartment, dump your kit and head out looking for a pub.

There, waiting on platform seven, was Alan Kozinsky's older brother Mark. Although Alan lived with his parents in Johannesburg, he had decided to continue on to Durban for a holiday with some relatives who lived there. He had arranged for his brother Mark to meet him with six cases of Lion Ale (the beer Natal made famous).

Alan, Gus, Jimmy and Phil Mina grabbed a four-berth cabin and began loading beer; a generous gift from Alan's father who just happened to own several liquor stores.

144 beers between four people who hadn't been allowed to drink for the best part of nine months was going to end badly. The consensus was that, apart from the four of them, the beers would be sold at 25 cents each to anyone who wanted one.

The train pulled out on time and the journey home began in a festive atmosphere. A brisk trade was done on the now lukewarm beers, and it was not long before troopers were passing out left, right and centre.

By morning, the train had crossed over into Natal and at each stop along the way goodbyes were being said to the NMR and UMR boys leaving. Watching them being greeted by loved ones, solicited rude and suggestive comments on how they would be spending the next couple of hours. It was mostly light-hearted and good fun. It was tough saying goodbye to buddies with whom you had spent nine months of your life.

Leaving Pietermaritzburg, the last major stop before Durban, conversation got around to what was next for Alan, Gus and Jimmy (Phil had left at Estcourt). Both Gus and Jimmy had nowhere to go and would have to find accommodation and jobs immediately, which was a bit worrying.

Alan would stay with his cousins for two weeks and then head back to his family in Johannesburg. Jimmy and Gus thought maybe they'd check in at the YMCA, find a job and then look for a better place to stay.

Alan Kozinsky had a plan as always. He had a cousin who owned an apartment in a newly built high rise, one block off the beach near the ice rink. He knew it was three bedroomed with a screened off balcony and was fully furnished. The cousin was loaded and owed Alan a favour, so he was sure he could make a deal for the two of them. Maybe they could find two more to share the rent.

Gus and Jimmy agreed that would be a good idea. Their thoughts turned to Chubby and Ian, maybe they could also move in. Rent divided by four is better than rent divided by two. They decided to contact their friends at the first opportunity, knowing that both were likely to return to their parent's home.

At three o'clock in the afternoon on September 26, 1968 the train pulled into platform one at Durban station. There was a huge crowd welcoming their sons home from the army. Neither Gus nor Jimmy were expecting anyone and both felt a bit out of sorts. They had decided to head for the YMCA and try and get a room while waiting to see how Alan's call to his cousin went.

Jimmy and Gus, in no rush to leave the train, waited until most of the others had disembarked before picking up their gear and leaving the compartment. Much to his surprise, Jimmy saw Kerry Vermeulen waiting for him. She walked slowly towards him, accompanied by some guy Jimmy didn't recognise.

'Hi Jimmy, welcome home,' she said and turning to the guy standing next to her, 'this is Dave Fagan, my boyfriend.'

So, this is the famous 'Invisible Dave', he does exist. This is a bit strange, Jimmy thought, I haven't had any letters from her since

Tempe and truth be told, I hadn't thought much about it. Seeing her here is quite a surprise and what's with the boyfriend? Not too sure what this is all about. I had planned to look her up at some point, but I don't get why she is here with boyfriend in tow.

'Hi, nice to see you Kerry and you too, Dave. Thanks for coming to meet me. You remember Gus.' Nodding towards Gus, who looked equally surprised.

'Hello Gus, good to see you as well. Jimmy, the reason I am here is that your mother left R100 for you when your folks left for England. She said not to give it to you until you got out of the army, as you would probably blow it.'

Kerry stepped forward, gave the money to Jimmy and with a quick peck on the cheek, said goodbye, turned and left with Dave hanging on to her hand.

'Shit, a hundred bucks we are made. Let's head for the YMCA and get sorted, Gus.'

The two friends picked up their gear and started the reasonably short walk to the YMCA. Alan promised to call as soon as he heard from his cousin.

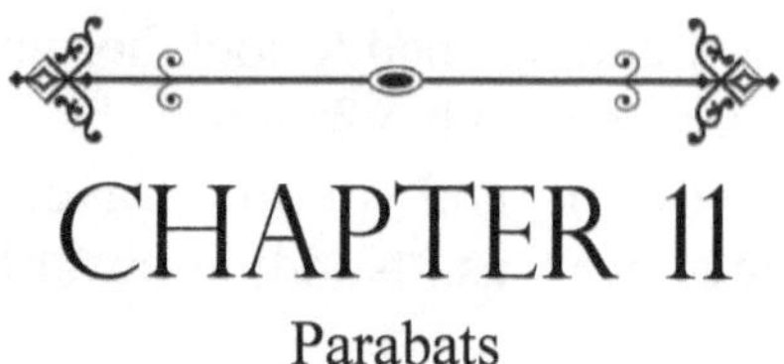

CHAPTER 11
Parabats

Ian

The last time Ian had any contact with Gus and Jimmy was the day before they were shipped off to Zeerust. The following day, Ian packed up his gear and made the short trip to 1st Parachute Battalion.

Ian would spend the next three months undergoing the most intensive training given to a soldier in the South African Army. Naturally fit, he would excel at all the drills and obstacles placed before him. From a sporting point of view, there were only two possibilities at 1st Para, rugby or cross country running. Ian chose to run.

Parrabat training at that time was geared towards quelling township riots, so house to house fighting was top of the list. Given his history, this suited Ian down to the ground; heaven help any Kaffir crossing his path.

The concept of a parachute regiment was to airdrop troops behind enemy lines and kill anything that moved. So, the prime focus was to qualify for your 'wings' and purple beret. To do this, you had to complete five jumps, one of which would be a night drop.

To qualify, a rigorous training schedule was needed. Situated next to the Armour camp was the contraption known as the '*Aapkas*' (monkey cage). This was a construction approximately one hundred feet high with a box-like platform at the top.

Before they could start training on this contraption, many hours were spent perfecting the correct method of landing. Hours of repetitive jumping from a ten-foot platform, landing feet together and then rolling. You didn't get to face the dreaded *Aapkas* until you had perfected the landings.

Troops had to climb up the ladder where they would be met by two instructors. They would be strapped into a parachute-like harness, step forward and when tapped on the shoulder, jump. The harness was attached to a static line allowing the person to free fall for about twenty feet. The static line would then engage with a cable, which then lowered the person down towards the ground, simulating a parachute drop. The static line would disengage during the last ten feet for the landing.

The first few jumps would be in standard overalls before graduating to full kit and rifle.

There were a number of ways troops could get the dreaded RTU (Return To Unit), meaning they had failed to make the grade and would be sent back to their original Infantry unit.

Firstly, any broken bones and you were out, no excuses. If you failed to climb to the top of the *Aapkas*, you were done. At the top you had two chances; if you didn't jump on the first shoulder tap, you got a second tap on the other shoulder. Failing to jump after that, you were immediately RTU'ed.

After two weeks of intense visits to the *Aapkas,* the survivors moved on. Endless hours of learning how to pack your chute. Parabats always packed their own chutes; failure to open, you had no one to blame but yourself.

Finally, the day arrived for their first real jump. South African paratroopers jumped from five hundred feet but in 'war time', depending on the circumstances, would jump from three hundred feet. The mode of air transport was a DC3 Dakota.

Chutes packed and checked, the remaining forty-nine troops were loaded on a Bedford and driven to Tempe Military Airport. A lot of nervous chatter but Ian remained calm as this was it, no turning back.

The two Dakotas were loaded up with three instructors on each flight and twenty-five and twenty-four troopers split over the two planes respectively. Ian ended up in the first plane and by chance in the first jump position.

The flight out to the training area would take around ten minutes, no time for nerves.

The troops would jump on a static line, meaning the parachute would open immediately on leaving the plane.

The command 'Ready' was called. Twenty-five soldiers rose to their feet, turned and faced the rear of the plane. On command, they attached their static line rip cord to the overhead cable. A red light came on and two of the instructors opened the rear side door. Ian, in first jump position, moved forward to the open door, halting one step back from the opening.

The green light flashed on and Ian stepped out of the plane on the command 'Go' Five seconds later he felt the tug of the open parachute. With no time to think, he braced himself for the landing. Feet together, he hit the ground, knees bent, rolled over, a perfect jump. 'A piece of cake, I want to do this again,' thought Ian.

The results of the first jump were three refusals, one broken leg and five sprained ankles. This meant four immediate RTU's. Those with sprained ankles had until the next jump to prove themselves fit to continue. Forty clean jumps constituted a success.

Over the next two jumps the number of troopers was reduced by a further three. No refusals but three injuries.

The fourth jump at three hundred feet, was a major disaster and resulted in a further eleven RTU's and an unwanted record. Five refusals and six with broken or dislocated bones. Based on the high number of RTU's, an investigation was launched, and it was found that the pilot had flown at two hundred and fifty feet and not at three hundred. Further investigation proved that the wind velocity was too high, and the jump should have been aborted. Those responsible were severely censured, unfortunately, for those who suffered it was too late.

Down to twenty-six, the troopers prepared for their final jump: the dreaded night drop.

The hardest part of the night jump wasn't leaving the plane, as you couldn't see a thing; it was the landing. When jumping with full kit, as you left the plane your kit, which you held at your stomach, was released and dropped to hang ten feet below your feet. The idea behind this was to give you an indication when you were about to hit the ground.

The reaction time when seeing (feeling at night) when your kit hit the ground was minimal. It was better to be braced in landing position the minute you left the plane, especially at night.

The results of the night jump were even worse than the previous jump. There were no refusals, but the injuries were bad. Two broken legs, a broken ankle, a fractured knee-cap, a dislocated shoulder and one death. The unfortunate who died had managed to find the only tree in a landing zone that should have had no trees. He smashed into the tree and broke his neck.

After any death there is always an investigation. A short but thorough investigation; it was found to be an unavoidable accident.

Down to twenty, the wings ceremony was a sombre event. Many had started the journey but only a few had made it. It was these kinds of numbers that made the Parabats an elite unit. One hundred and fifty had started the original fitness tests but only forty-nine had survived to even attempt the first jump. Twenty-nine of those made at least one jump yet never made it to the end.

Ian and his nineteen comrades were now proud Parabats, no longer seen as *blougats* but members of an elite unit; wearers of the purple beret with wings.

For their final three months, their options were open. Four men were needed for officer training and were selected by their outgoing officers.

The remaining sixteen could volunteer for several positions, all of which carried the rank of corporal. Ian chose the position of corporal in charge of the vehicle park, given his penchant for fixing vehicles. He had no desire to be an instructor.

To retain their wings, there was a requirement to make at least two jumps in your final quarter. Ian made four.

On September 25, 1968 Ian boarded the train at Bloemfontein station heading for Durban.

Elsewhere on that same train was Corporal Peter Murphy, unaware that his good buddy, Ian Williams, was also aboard.

CHAPTER 12
Tempe the last 6 months

Peter Murphy aka Chubby

After Gus and Jimmy's departure to Zeerust and Ian's departure to the Parabats, Chubby set about getting himself organised. The only way, from an Army point of procedure, to keep someone at their original base camp was to enrol them on an officer's or instructor's course.

The officer's course meant that the candidate would be removed from 1SSB but remain in Tempe under the command of the Officer in Charge of Officer Candidate School. This did not suit the Commanding Officer of 1SSB as he wanted Chubby at his disposal, so the only option was to put him up for the instructor's course. Chubby was originally mustered as a Driver and naturally he joined the course as one of the Driving instructors with the rank of private. On completion of the six-week course, he would become a lance corporal. At the end of the second semester they would be promoted to a full corporal.

The course started the day after his three friends departed. All trainee instructors formed up under the command of those corporals who had qualified from the previous intake.

Being late March, it was nearing the end of the cricket season. On the second day of the instructor's course, a runner arrived with a message for the corporal in charge. Chubby was required to report to the mess immediately. As the note was signed by a PF Major, Chubby was dismissed, and he headed for the mess.

On arrival he was informed he had been selected for the Tempe cricket team that would participate in the Defence Force Cricket week (thirteen days in effect). He was to pack his kit and report that afternoon for the trip to Cape Town. He would miss one third of the instructor's course but would not be penalised.

Chubby, doing reasonably well, managed to get selected for the Defence Force under twenty team which would partake in the university week immediately following.

By the time Chubby got back to Tempe, the instructor's course had been going for a little over a month. With no point in rejoining the course, he was seconded by the Sergeant Major to organise and play in the inter unit baseball tournament. He was promoted to lance-corporal, ensuring he had the rank and with it the authority, to order the troops around in the Sergeant Major's absence.

Meanwhile, the cricket and baseball season had given way to rugby. It had been Chubby's prowess at the two former sports that had guaranteed he would stay at Tempe and not be sent to Zeerust. It took only the first rugby practice to seal Chubby's status at Tempe. Tempe fielded twelve rugby teams in the Free State leagues, the pride of which was the under twenty side, which played in the first division along with teams of the same age group.

One of the benefits of being a talented sportsman in the Army is that you are given every chance to continue honing your skills during your National Service. The military, when assigning conscripts to various camps, made sure that those sportsmen who would best benefit their cause were assigned to the 'correct' camps. The bulk of this talent usually ended up at the headquarter camps in Pretoria. Talented sportsmen were targeted during their high school or university careers and snapped up by the high-profile camps.

Some like Chubby, who had not attended the well-known and highly visible educational institutes, slipped though those scouting networks. What would become one of the most meteoric rises through the South African rugby world started that cold June day in 1968.

The South African Defence Force had the first call on any sportsman in its ranks, surpassing even any national sports affiliation. The 'honour' of representing the SADF surpassed even that of representing your country, at least in the eyes of the SADF.

South African sport was very much at the crossroads in the international arena. The country's apartheid system was universally abhorred, and many countries had outright refused to participate in any sporting event where South Africans were partaking. All national sporting teams excluded anyone of colour, immaterial of their sporting prowess. Many a talented white South African sportsman would suffer as a result of their Government's racial policies.

All these issues were far removed from the day to day Army life experienced by those fortunate enough to be posted to Tempe Army base in Bloemfontein. Chubby was to spend his entire Army career playing sport for the SADF.

Ian, on the other hand, spent six months in the 'Parabats' where most of the time he was too exhausted to partake in any sporting activities. He did, however, reach a level of fitness seldom achieved by most. He honed his body into a lean, hard frame. It was around this time that the Springbok Rugby Union was looking forward to the upcoming tour to the British Isles. This was one of the few international events still open to South African sportsmen. Although there was an almost universal demand for an international boycott of all sports that included South Africans, the perceived economic benefits of a rugby tour meant the tour would proceed. After all, how many black nations played rugby? What effect could a boycott have?

At five feet nine inches, weighing in at 170 pounds, the nickname Chubby hardly described Peter Murphy accurately. Not the quickest person in the world, Chubby had a low centre of gravity and an exceptionally quick mind and these attributes made it very difficult for opponents to contain him on the rugby field.

The Tempe rugby sides played in various leagues in the Bloemfontein and surrounding areas. The first team contained mostly permanent force staff with a smattering of the more talented national servicemen.

The average age of the national servicemen was around 18 years and 6 months, an age where young men are still developing. For sheer size, these boys were unable to compete with the big Free Stater's playing senior rugby, and usually found themselves playing in the less physically demanding under 20 leagues.

The opposition here were the under 20 sides of the various clubs, and the equivalent university teams. Historically the SADF sides gave a good account of themselves in this league. Excel in these games and you could look forward to being selected for the Free State under 20 teams that played in the annual national SADF tournament. At the completion of this tournament, a national SADF team was selected and two games played against the South African national under 20 side.

In earlier days, post sporting boycotts, either or both of these select sides could expect a two to three week national or international tour. With this in mind, the competition was fierce. It was a great honour to the camp when a member was selected for one of these teams. The plan for 1968 was for the South African National under 21 selection to tour the United Kingdom with the full Springbok team.

In his second three months, Chubby's *'blougat' life* at Tempe was: Monday through Friday, consisted of learning all there was to know about the maintenance and driving requirements of the standard Army Land Rover. The only exception was sports parade on Wednesday afternoons. As a *'blougat,'* there was a certain amount of chasing from the *'oumanne'* but nothing like the situation at Zeerust. These *blougats* were destined to become corporals and instructors during their last trimester.

Chubby's first step on the road to immortality at Tempe in 1968 came at the first rugby practice of the season. It was common practice for the *blougats* to play the *oumanne* in a practice game. Both groups were fit from the day to day army training so little attention was paid to physical fitness exercises and more geared towards game skills.

The first practice saw boys split up into teams based on what position they played and what size they were. None of the players had played together before and none of the coaches had any idea of their ability. Chubby, never one to stand on ceremony, took a rugby ball and strolled over to about forty yards out from the goal posts and effortlessly dropped kicked the ball straight through the middle of the poles. Running after the ball, he retrieved it and did the same again but from a wider and more difficult angle. It was this that caught the eye of the first team coach.

'Hey you, come here. What's your name?'

'Murphy, Captain,' Chubby replied to the Infantry captain.

'What position do you play?'

'Fly-half Sir.'

'Right, get over there and don't go away. By the way, are you Infantry or Armor?'

'Armor, Sir, driving instructor,' offered Chubby.

Damn, thought the captain, this one's going to give us trouble in the inter unit matches.

The first 'traditional' match was between the *blougats* and the *oumanne*.

The two teams, consisting of only Armour personnel, lined up with Chubby playing at fly-half for the *blougats*. Traditionally, the *blougats*, from fear of repercussions after the game, never got too physical with the *oumanne*.

The first five or so minutes of the game went with tradition and the *oumanne* scored a soft try and conversion to go five nil up. At this stage, Chubby had seen very little of the ball and decided it was time to gee up his team.

'Come on, you pussies, let's get into these guys!' rallied Chubby, at the top of his voice, 'We're playing like girls, these guys are easy.'

There was a stunned silence, all eyes on Chubby. Mickey Lyons, playing at scrum half, sidled up to Chubby.

'What the fuck's wrong with you?' he whispered. 'We take it to these guys and we will shit off after the game.'

'Fuck that, just get the ball to me. They can't do anything to us if we beat them fair and square.'

'Jesus, what world are you living in? They can find any excuse to make life tough for us, don't give them any reasons, let's just play the way we are, it's only a game.'

'Ok, you are right. No point in causing crap.' Chubby replied. From the resulting scrum, Lyons fed the ball to Chubby about thirty yards out from the goal line. Feinting to pass right, Chubby sidestepped left and took a gap between the opposing forwards and fly-half and made for the goal line. Forced left he beat two oncoming opponents and headed for the corner flag. With an elaborate dive, he went over in the corner, five three with a difficult conversion to come.

Ignoring the growing mutterings from his own team as well as the opponents, Chubby went through his ritual of building a sand pile, placing the ball, three steps back and two to the side. This method of kicking a rugby ball was still foreign to most and was met with amusement by both sides.

Seconds later, he strode forward, caught the ball sweetly with his instep and it sailed through the uprights, five all. End of amusement.

Unsurprisingly, the *oumanne* did not take kindly to this display and spent the rest of the game threatening the *blougats* with dire consequences if they dared to win. Except for Chubby, the *blougats* complied and gave a lacklustre performance. Despite his team's lack of assistance, Chubby managed another try and conversion and two drop goals for a total of sixteen points. The *oumanne* won the game forty-five to sixteen.

Trooping off the field at the end of the game, Chubby, in an angry voice, was heard to say. 'If this is the way you arseholes want to play, then fuck it, I'm off to play hockey.'

'Hey, trooper, come here,' bellowed the loud voice of Captain Bakkies Malan, manager and chief selector for the Armour Regiment first rugby team.

Chubby turned and ran over at the double; it was an officer after all. 'Yes sir!' shouted Chubby, snapping to attention.

'That was some display you gave out there. Where did you go to school? Any provincial experience?'

'Grosvenor Boy's High in Durban, and no sir, no provincial experience. No one ever came to watch us.'

'Well, boytjie, I've seen you play, and I like it. Report to the mess tonight after supper for a team meeting. Anyone gives you trouble, let them come see me.'

Aug 18, 1968
The South African cricketer, Colin Bland, is refused entry to England because of his Rhodesian passport.

The first chinks in South African sporting teams competing internationally appeared with the British government refusing the Rhodesian born Colin Bland entry into England to partake in a cricket match. This was due to Rhodesia declaring unilateral Independence from Britain.

Aug 28, 1968
The M.C.C. cricket selectors cause a controversy by omitting Worcestershire's South African born Cape Coloured all-rounder, Basil D'Oliveria, from the team to tour South Africa.
This was the second incident which would eventually lead South Africa on a path to international isolation from world sport.

The end of the instructor's course coincided with the start of the full rugby season and Chubby was really in demand. To ensure Chubby remained at Tempe, it was decided to promote him to full corporal immediately. This was the first time in known history that a second trimester had been promoted to corporal. Chubby was untouchable.

There were many rugby matches open to players. There was inter 'mustering' competitions, namely crew commanders, gunners, drivers, support troop and admin (cooks and clerks). There was the 'inter unit' games, Tempe armour, Tempe infantry and School of Armour. There was the *roofs* versus the *oumanne*. There was the Tempe under 20's who played in the Orange Free State under twenty league. Finally, there was the Tempe first and second teams that played in the respective Free State leagues.

Added to these leagues, there was always the possibility of making the South African Defence Force under twenty or first fifteens. These teams were selected after the Defence Force Rugby 'Week' (in fact, just over two weeks in length).

Further to this, if allowed, there was the possibility of being selected for the Free State Curry Cup side, to play in that season long competition. This would become a point of contention regarding Chubby's availability.

Based on performance, there was also the possibility of being selected for the Springbok under twenties or for the full side who would tour Britain in the spring.

What with rugby practice, inter unit games, etcetera, Chubby had very little time for 'soldiering'. He was in demand for coaching the kickers and playing in every team he was eligible for. He was elected captain for every team he played for, called the shots and took all the kicks. He was a points machine and as such, a marked man by the opposition.

After losing only one game to the School of Armour team, due in no small part to some dubious referring calls, it was obvious that Chubby was the star attraction. The first controversy occurred when he was selected for both the Tempe under twenties and the first team. It was decided he would play for the under twenties as he might be too young for the first team and likely to be targeted.

The first game was against Welkom Rovers under twenty. Chubby almost single handedly destroyed the Rovers. It was embarrassing. Those watching could not remember seeing a performance of this calibre at under twenty level. Word soon spread.

It was decided that Chubby should be promoted to the first fifteen. It was not a unanimous decision as the under twenties were reluctant to lose him and the seniors were worried that he may get hurt. The seniors won out but decided that rather than play him at fly-half, he would play at fullback. The reasoning being that at fullback, the team could make use of his prodigious kicking ability with less risk of him being collared at fly-half.

Chubby's first game was against Bloemfontein Police, a big physical team. It made little difference playing from fullback; he scored with five penalty kicks, two from inside his own half, three conversions and a try. If they didn't know who he was before, they sure did now. Chubby, ever modest, milked the moment.

Free State provincial team came calling over the availability of one Peter Murphy. They were given short shrift; he was only going to play for Tempe or the SA Defence Force team.

Chubby played the next two games at fly-half and was on the winning side both times. Tempe rugby was in seventh heaven. Then came the shocker. On Monday morning, September 23, 1968, the first team met to discuss Saturday's result and what tactics they would employ for next weekend's game.

'Hey, Chubbs, what do you think? Maybe Frikkie on the wing to replace the injured Swannie?'

'Don't ask me, boys, I'm going home on Wednesday. Civvie street, here I come.'

Hard to believe but no one had given it a thought that Chubby's nine months was over. They had assumed that Chubby would stay on until the Defence Force week in the middle of October.

In Chubby's own words, 'What the fuck were they thinking? I'm outta here come Wednesday.'

Chubby was summoned to a meeting with the camp commandant and all the rugby chiefs. He was first requested to stay on for the Defence Force Week, he graciously refused. He was then promised he could go home but he would be flown up to Pretoria to compete in the tournament. Again, he refused. He was promised that all future camps would be cancelled if he partook. After giving it a moment's thought, he politely declined.

There were some disgruntled mumblings and a few evil stares, but Chubby held his ground. Short of jailing him, he would be leaving on the 25th for Durban.

So, it came to pass on Wednesday September 25, 1968 that Chubby and the best part of two hundred newly declared civilians boarded the train bound for Durban. Chubby's actual 'soldering days' amounted to less than thirty over his nine-month period.

The train docked in Durban station late-afternoon on the 26th. Peter, met by his mother and sister, no girlfriend present, which was not surprising since he hadn't answered any letters and had had no contact since he left home.

Hugs and kisses over, he looked up and, spotted Ian being greeted by his mother and three sisters, much tears flowing.

'Hey, Corporal Williams, get the fuck over here at the double!' shouted Chubby at the top of his voice. Oops, he had forgotten he was not in the Army anymore and the use of the word 'fuck' in every sentence was not the done thing.

Ian turned around and spotted the heavily blushing Chubby.

'Hey, Fatman, how the hell are you? Long time, no see. Did you spot those two retards, Wilson and Gus, on the train?'

'No, I think they would have come in from Jo'burg. Jesus, how are you? I must watch the language now. I see you have a ride home; give me a call when you get settled and we'll hook up with Gus and Jimmy and tie one on. I bet we all have lots of tales to tell.'

And with that, Army days over, they headed back to the Bluff, missing Gus and Jimmy by just three hours.

CHAPTER 13
Back in Civvie Street

Shouldering their kit bags, Gus and Jimmy headed out of Durban Station for the short walk to the YMCA. On arrival, they enquired on what accommodation was available and what the rates were. Rooms could be rented by the week or month. Daily rentals were only allowed as a one off, no consecutive days. The rooms available were: private single, private double or ten bed dormitory with lockers. Showers were communal.

They boys settled on a private double room at the weekly rate of R10 per person. They signed in and paid their first week's rent. The room had two single beds and two separate cupboards. After unpacking their kit bags they contemplated their next move.

'We need to find jobs pretty damn quick and also get some clobber. We can't go for interviews in Army gear.'

'No, that's where you are wrong. We should go in Army gear. Work on their conscience. We have just given up nine months of our lives to protect the country's borders. I reckon that way we have more chance. I think we should try the banks first,' replied Gus.

'Good idea but I don't think we should go together. Standard or Barclays? Pick one.'

'Okay, I'll take Barclays, you can have Standard. They are virtually next door to each other on West Street. '

Early next morning after a cup of coffee and a toasted cheese sandwich, they headed off to the two banks. South African banking was a very controlled institution monitored by SASBO, South African Society of Banking Officials. Opening hours were 9am to 3pm Monday through Friday but with an early closing of 1pm on Wednesdays. Saturday's opening hours were 9am to 11am.

At one-minute past 9 Gus entered Barclay's Bank Main Street and headed for the Enquiry counter. He was greeted by an attractive lady, 'How may I help you today, Sir?'

'I would like to see the person in charge of the hiring of staff please.'

'That would be the Chief Accountant, Mr. Williamson. Take a seat, I will see if he is available to see you.' She picked up the phone and Gus could hear the one side of the call, it sounded positive. 'Excuse me, sir, what is your name, he will see you in about five minutes?'

'Angus Stewart,' replied Gus and listened while she passed it on to the person on the end of the line.

A few minutes later, the lady on Enquiries motioned for Gus to follow her. She led him through the open plan office, up the stairs to the first floor and to the door marked 'Chief Accountant Mr. JJ Williamson'. She knocked, opened the door and ushered Gus in. He entered and found a cheerful looking middle-aged man, with a Friar Tuck hairstyle, dark blue suit, white shirt, plain tie and black horn-rimmed classes, your typical vision of a banker. He stood up, shook Gus' hand and motioned him to sit down.

'My name is Mr. Williamson and I am in charge of hiring new staff. I believe you are looking for employment with my Bank. Tell me about yourself and why you think I should hire you.'

'Well Sir, I have just finished my National Service and I am looking for a career in Banking. I completed my Matric at the end of last year. I have no parents so I am desperate to start working.'

'I see you attained the rank of corporal, that's impressive. Do you have your Matric certificate with you?'

'Thank you, Sir. Yes, I do have it.' Gus leaned over and passed him the certificate.

'Oh my goodness! Very impressive indeed. I am sure we could use someone of your potential. I will need to you to take a Bank-approved test and if successful, I am sure we will offer you a position. You can take the test today; my assistant will give you the necessary forms. Once done, hand it in at reception. Leave a contact number where we can reach you. We should have an answer for you by Wednesday next week. Oh, and we will also need a reference from your High School.'

Williamson stood up, shook Gus' hand and wished him good luck and passed him on to his assistant. The assistant guided Gus to an empty office, handing him a pile of forms to fill in and also the 'Test papers'. She told Gus to fill in his personal details, complete the test and when done, hand it all in at the Enquiry counter. He could take as long as needed.

Gus completed his personal information, leaving the 'next of kin' blank and gave the contact number for the YMCA. He opened the test pages and burst out laughing. The first section was one English comprehension, it was an absolute joke. He finished it in five minutes; a standard six pupil would have taken maybe twenty. The second section consisted of rows of numbers to be added up, also pretty basic. He found his way back to the Enquiry counter and handed in his forms, confident that come Wednesday, he would be offered a job.

Walking out of the Bank's front doors he spotted Jimmy sitting on a nearby bench. Jimmy was staring off into the distance and didn't notice Gus until he tapped him on the shoulder.

'Hey, China, I think I'm in like Flint. Good interview and I aced the test they gave me. I will hear on Wednesday if I have a job. Pretty sure they will offer me one. How did you do?'

'Shit, you took your time. I've been waiting here for ten minutes. Oh, I start at Standard Bank ABC Branch on the Tuesday, October 1. Ninety-one Rand per month. I just have to get a letter of reference from school and bring it in with me to work.'

'What? How come so quick?'

'I saw the Chief Accountant, a Bill Wright; he is an NMR guy, World War II veteran. He got all emotional and when I showed him my Matric results, he hired me on the spot. I reckon you should get in there and have a go.'

The two of them walked across the street and with Jimmy waiting outside, Gus went in to see Mr. Wright. Less than ten minutes later, Gus reappeared grinning from ear to ear. 'Same deal as you, ABC on Tuesday.'

'I reckon we should get hold of Chubby and Ian and see what's going on with them. We have to go to the Bluff to get our references anyway. Maybe Monday, but let's give them a call.'

'Okay, but we also need to get some clothes for work. I've got jeans, shorts, takkies and a fucking Army outfit, not quite up for banking. What about you, Gus? Anything left at your aunt's place?'

'No, nothing I could use. I'm going to phone Chubby and make a plan to get out to the Bluff.'

The two of them walked across the street to the Post Office and Gus called Chubby. Chubby's mother answered and called her son to the phone.

'Hey Chubbs, how the hell are you? Jimmy and I are in Durban; we are staying at the YMCA. We are organised with jobs starting Tuesday.

We need to get references from school and thought maybe you can get hold of Ian on Monday and we can have a few beers.'

'Great to hear from you. Hey, why wait until Monday? Come out tomorrow. They are playing Grosvenor first team against the old boys. Most of the teachers will be there so I am sure that you can get your reference letter. Bring your boots, maybe you can get a game; I know I'll be taking mine. What do you think?'

'Good idea. What time?'

'Get out here by nine, the game is at eleven. I'll call Ian. We can throw down a few pints later and catch up.'

Gus relayed the details to Jimmy, who agreed but said, 'We need to make a plan for some clobber. Let's check how much cash we have and see what we can do.'

Returning to the YMCA, they sat down and laid out their meagre finances. Fully aware of Gus' situation, Jimmy suggested they pool the money. After a short protestation, Gus gratefully agreed. Cash on hand: Jimmy – R100 from his mother and R16. 20 left of Army pay; Gus – a balance of Army pay R15: total 131.20. With YMCA rental until first pay day of R40 each, this left R51. 20 for food and clothing; not a good sign. Jimmy still had nearly R150 in his savings account if needed.

'Okay, I think for clothes we need to open an account somewhere, maybe Markham's or Greaterman's. We should also look for more reasonable accommodation; otherwise YMCA is going to claim half our salary each month. What do you think?'

'I may have a plan for clothes and maybe Koz will come through with his cousin's flat. I reckon we play that one by ear, just rent week by week.'

'Sounds like a plan. What's the deal with the clothes?'

Pulling a business card out of his wallet and waving it at Gus, 'Let's get changed into civvies and take a walk up to the top of Pine Street.'

The upper end of Pine Street was mainly Indian shops and the jewel among them was the House of Lords, maybe the best in the whole of Durban. Fighting their way through the crowds that thronged the pavements, they made it to the entrance of the shop. Jimmy had barely taken two steps inside when he heard his name being called from someone sitting on top of a ladder.

'Hey Jimmy, it's me Raj. How are you? Long time no see.'

'Hey Raj. Yeah I know, just got out of the Army, how you keeping? Still getting to see City I hope.'

'Up the City. Yes, still there every game, me and the old man. Bit shitty now that we have to pay! Just joking but we miss the good times. What are you doing here?' said Raj, scrambling down the ladder to shake Jimmy's hand.

'Me and my buddy Gus here need some clothes for work, so just checking it out.'

'Rajesh, what is all this noise you are making? Why did you stop stacking those shirts?' shouted an irate Mr. Moodley. Spotting the source of the commotion, he strode over and gave Jimmy a bear hug. 'Rajesh, why didn't you tell me Jimmy was here?'

'We have just arrived, sir. This is my good friend, Gus. The two of us have just finished with the army and looking to buy some clothes for our first job. My folks left for England while I was in the Army and Gus is an orphan.'

'Well, you have come to the right place. Raj, get these boys a coke I will take care of them personally,' he ordered and ushered the two of them to the back of the shop.

'Now, what sort of job? You must have the correct clothes.'

'We both got jobs at the Standard Bank Sir, starting Tuesday, so maybe long pants, a jacket and some shirts and a tie?'

'No no no, you want to get ahead, you must look the part, leave this to me. I'll get my tailor to take your measurements. You go over there and select the material you like.'

'Sir, we are on a limited budget and I wonder if we can maybe open an account until we get paid.'

'No accounts for you, my boy. I will make you a very good deal. You took care of Rajesh in his need, I'll take care of you. Now go pick your material, both of you. Mr. Naidoo, come measure these boys, you measure everything.'

Mr. Naidoo spent the next half an hour taking every measurement known to man and some beyond that. Completed, he called his boss over. Messer's Moodley and Naidoo retreated to the boss's office and spent the next few minutes in animated discussion. Finally they reappeared.

'Jimmy, you and Gus come back here Monday afternoon and I will have everything ready. You will have a really good look for work. Now go and don't worry we will make a deal.'

Jimmy thanked him, waved goodbye to Raj and left with a rather nervous Gus in tow.

'Gee, what was that all about? I hope there is no cock up as it won't leave much time to get organised if it is. How come he is your big buddy?'

'Remember I told you about the guy getting robbed and all that, and how I let his family in for free at Kingsmead?'

'Vaguely. So what?'

'Well, his Dad said if I ever needed clothes to come and see him. He gave me this business card, and here we are. We will see on Monday, I reckon he is okay. Let's go and have a dop.'

The next day they hitch-hiked out to the Bluff to meet Ian at Chubby's house. Not having seen each other for the best part of six months, there was much catching up to do.

Ian had decided to take up a trade and was signing up as an apprentice electrician. He figured with his mechanical background, adding another skill would put him in a good position for opening his own business someday. He was planning to sell his motorbike and buy a small car he could fix up. He was starting his apprenticeship on November 1 and would work at Steyn's until then and on Saturdays. He would soon have enough for a car.

Chubby was still undecided. His parents wanted him to go to University. His grades were just okay so the only way he could get a scholarship was with his sporting abilities. Unfortunately, his skills were virtually unknown outside of the Bluff. He was going to play some cricket with Durban Collegians and think about where to play rugby next season. University only started in mid- February so he had four and a half months free, maybe he would get a job.

Gus and Jimmy told them about their jobs at the Standard Bank and that they were living at the YMCA. They also told them about their friend, Kozinsky, who might be able to get them a furnished flat near the beach front. It had four bedrooms and they thought Ian and Chubby could join them, otherwise they would look for two flat mates to share the rent. Ian said he would stay at home because his job was at the oil refinery near the Bluff. Chubby declined as he had no job and no money.

Looking at his watch, Chubby said, 'Right, let's go. Gus, I reckon we'll get a game today. Time to sort out the boys from the men.'

By the time they arrived at the school, the preliminary matches were well under way and a fair size crowd were in attendance. Chubby's appearance caused quite a stir and it took some time to wade through the mob and reach the change rooms. The new first team coach, Tony Visser, spotted Chubby and came over to greet him.

'Hey Chubby, you are looking well. The Army life must have agreed with you. When did you get out?'

'Got home Thursday. Any chance of a game?' Gus brought his boots as well. Maybe we can show your boys how to play Rugby.'

'You remember Terry Niven? He's next door and picking the old boys team. Go and have a word with him, I think he needs help to avoid a good thrashing.'

Chubby and Gus, with Ian and Jimmy in tow, went next door to the 'visitors' change room.

Terry Niven spotted the group and rushed over to greet them. 'Wilson and Stewart, come here you wonderful bastards. Thanks to you I won my bet with the Boss, first time ever. How the hell are you?'

'Pretty good, Mr. Niven and how are you.'

'Fuck it with the "Mister" bullshit, it's Terry. Have a beer. I have already had a couple; I need them as this team is going to get royally screwed today. Visser has a pretty strong team.' Noticing Chubby for the first time, he bellowed out, 'Hey Chubby, do you fancy a game and help me out?'

'Ready and willing. Gus had also brought his boots. I reckon we could give the first team a good klap.' Looking around the change room he counted seventeen other players, most of whom he did not recognise. He spotted big Binkie Kapp, a first team lock from the year before last and one of the hard as nails Ribbink brothers, Alan. With the four extra players, they would be allowed replacements and would probably need them.

Never one to shy away, Chubby announced that he would play at fly-half and Gus as scrum-half. Although Chubby didn't know most of the others, it was apparent that all knew of him. He enlisted Alan Ribbink and between Gus, Alan and himself went about putting together his team.

Jimmy and Ian had taken up Terry's offer and helped themselves to a beer each. Jimmy took the opportunity to corner Terry. 'Hey Sir, Gus and I need a school reference; who is the best to organise one?'

'Enough with the "Sir" bullshit, it's Terry. I suggest you go up to the deputy head's office, he's there now. I am sure he will fix you up, if he doesn't then I'll give you one. Fucking mathematical geniuses, you both are. Do you know what your actual marks were?'

'No, they just give us the symbol. So anything from 80 to 100%, who knows?'

'Well I do. I contacted the Matriculation board. Good news is that you placed first in the whole of Natal with 97%, Gus was tied third on 94%. The bastards docked you fifteen points, you got the correct answer but took too few steps. I had a huge argument with them over that but they refused to budge. Their excuse was that if anyone got 100% then people would think the exam wasn't hard enough. So fuck 'em; as far as I am concerned you got a perfect score.'

Jimmy just shrugged his shoulders, thanked Terry and headed for the vice principals office. He knocked and was invited to enter. Mr. Valentine recognised him immediately. 'Ah, Mr. Wilson, welcome, what can I do for you?'

'Gus Stewart and I have just got out the Army and have found jobs but we both need a school reference. I hope you can help?'

'Absolutely, my boy. After the glory both of your Matric results brought this school, it will be a pleasure. When do you need them by?'

'We start work Tuesday, so any time before then, if possible. We are staying at the "Y" in Durban so would prefer to pick them up. You can't rely on the Post Office.'

'I am here the whole day, if you are here to watch the rugby, I will get them done by then. Just come around the office after the game and pick them up. Good luck, Son, and again well done.'

Jimmy returned to the rugby field and joined up with Ian just in time for the start of the game. The school team had had a pretty good year and a strong team. They were better organised and played to a plan. The old boys were bigger and stronger but not all of them fit. Although Chubby and few others kept the old boy's in the game, the school won by nine points.

After the game Jimmy returned to the vice principals office to pick up the two reference letters and then it was back to Chubby's place for a braai and a few beers. As the evening wore on Jimmy and Gus made plans to get back to the 'Y'. Chubby went over to his mother and inquired if his two friends could sleep over as it was late. She agreed.

'Hey guys, my mom says you should sleep over and go back to Durban tomorrow after breakfast. One of you can sleep in George's bed and the other can use Mary's room.'

'I'll sleep in George's bed and you can sleep in Mary's; after all, you spent a lot of effort in trying to get in her bed in the past,' said Gus in a half joking way.

'Hey, got you there, James. I'll drive you guys back to Durban tomorrow; I can use my mom's car,' offered Ian.

The next morning after a hearty breakfast, the four of them piled into the car and headed for Durban. On arriving back at the 'Y' they found a note under their door. It was from Alan Kozinsky, with a phone number to call.

Gus took the note and headed for the call box in reception. He returned a few minutes later with good news.

'Koz has spoken to his cousin and if we want to, the flat is available. I arranged to meet Koz at the flat in an hour from now. Ian, will you give us a lift, it's down near the snake park?'

Ian agreed at once. Both he and Chubby had no idea what this whole flat thing was about and during the drive questioned Gus and Jimmy, wanting details; they remained mute just shrugging their shoulders.

Arriving a bit early, the boys had some time to check out the surroundings. The building was called Mutual Beach Centre, a brand new twenty-six story apartment complex. It was situated one block away from the beach, directly next door was the ice rink and two movie houses. On the corner was the Cumberland Hotel with its infamous men's bar. A few minutes later, a grinning Koz pulled up in a racing red Alpha Romeo Spyder convertible, roof down.

'Hello boys. You can close your mouths; it's not mine but it looks fucking great though. Let's get the show on the road.'

On the way up to the twenty sixth floor, Koz explained that his cousin owned several properties. This one was fully furnished. It had three bedrooms and an enclosed balcony currently usable as a fourth bedroom. One full bathroom and one shower and toilet. Koz unlocked the door to 2605 and ushered the boys into the hallway.

There was a kitchen fitted with a stove and fridge. The small dining room had a table and four chairs. The lounge had a three seater sofa, two matching chairs and a coffee table in the centre of the floor. Two of the bedrooms each had a double bed, the third bedroom a single bed. Each bedroom had built-in cupboards. The enclosed balcony had a single bed and a stand-alone cupboard. All the beds had sheets, blankets and pillows.

'Jesus. How about this place? How much does he want for rent?' exclaimed Gus.

'He was going to advertise it for R100 per month but I knocked him down to R80. What do you think?'

'We will be paying that at the "Y" for a single room and shared ablutions. What about lights and water? I see there is also a phone.'

'Lights and water are for your account; he will just get the account posted here to you. The phone calls are also for your account but he will pay the rental as it's too much hassle to get it changed at the Post Office. What do you think?'

'I think we'll take it, when can we move in? Hey, you two changed your mind about joining us?' Ian and Chubby just shrugged their shoulders.

'It's available from the 1st. You can pay me the first month's rent in advance. I'll drop they keys off with you at the "Y" tomorrow afternoon sometime.'

All business concluded, Koz rode down with the four of them, bade farewell and streaked off in his red Alpha. Ian drove Gus and Jimmy back to the 'Y' and dropped them off.

Gus and Jimmy sat down to work out their 'new budget'. The initial cost of rent would be the same but to add lights, water, phone and possible daily bus fare, it was going to be tight.

'I don't mind walking to and from work, it's a bit of a schlep but it'll save about R6 or R7 a month,' offered Gus.

'I agree but what about sub-letting the other two rooms? I reckon we could easily cover our costs by getting in someone for the other rooms Maybe we just put an advert in the paper.'

'Yes, let's check that out tomorrow. We need to tell the office here we are leaving and maybe try and get a refund if possible. I am up for Wimpy and chips, what about you?' Jimmy agreed and they headed out.

First thing Monday morning they headed to the office to let them know they would be leaving the next day as they had found a flat down at the beach front. No, there was no refund as they had spent more than two consecutive days.

Leaving the office, they were approached by a guy about the same age. 'I couldn't help but overhear you in the Office. You've found a flat on the beach front? Could you tell me what you are paying as my brother and I are looking for a place? The "Y" is okay for a while but not the coolest place to stay.'

'Howzit. Maybe we can help you. What's your name?' asked Jimmy, shaking the boy's hand.

'Mickey Andersen and my older brother is known as Dog, real name Gustav, but don't call him that. Some name that, my folks are Swedes.'

'I'm Jimmy and this is Gus. We have a fully furnished place just off the beach. It's a bit on the expensive side and if you are interested we can make a plan. Are you and your brother working?'

'Yes, we are. I have a job at Barclays Bank and Dog works at Wetland's Surf shop. He is a board shaper.'

'Another banker? We are with Standard. Okay, here's the deal. We have two spare bedrooms each with a single bed. The bathrooms are shared. We pay the lights and water, we all pay for our own phone calls. If you are interested, it's R40 each per month. You take care of your own meals. Check with your brother and let me know what you think. Get back to me by this evening as we have a couple of others interested.'

Mickey thanked Jimmy and said he would check with brother but was sure they would take it. Shaking hands all round, Gus and Jimmy left for their appointment with the House of Lords.

'Shit, you really are schemer. If this works out we'll be in the pound seats, rent covered. I just hope they are not arseholes. Mickey seems okay and Dog as a board shaper, maybe we can get a good deal on another surfboard,' said Gus.

'Okay Gus, me old China, let's go and get ourselves some clobber. Things are really looking up.'

Feeling a bit more confident about their financial situation, they made the relatively short trip to Pine Street and the House of Lords. They had barely entered the shop when Raj noticed them. He called to his father that Jimmy and Gus had arrived. Mr. Moodley emerged from his office with a big grin on his face.

'Come boys, Mr. Naidoo has everything ready for you. Time for a fitting,' he said, guiding them to the back of the shop where a somber-looking Mr. Naidoo waited. 'I leave them with you, Naidoo, make sure you do a great job. Call me when you are ready. Raj, you get back to work, no time for slacking.'

Mr. Naidoo beckoned the boys towards the two fitting rooms. He directed Gus to the left and Jimmy to the right. Each room contained a shirt, tie, belt, full suit, socks and a pair of shoes. The boys were told to put on the complete set of clothes so he could check and adjust if necessary. A few minutes later both emerged, Gus in a navy blue suit, white shirt, red tie and black lace shoes. Jimmy decked out in a beige suit, pale yellow shirt, blue tie and brown lace shoes.

He walked over to Gus and checked out the fit, everything was perfect. He did the same with Jimmy finding the same result. He called over Mr. Moodley for his inspection.

'You boys look perfect. What did I tell you? Naidoo here is the best tailor in Durban, no, the whole damn country. Get changed and we will pack up the clothes. I have added five shirts as well. All except the shoes and belts are handmade, good quality. Okay, change back to your old clothes.'

'Sir, I don't know what to say,' said Jimmy.

'Nothing to say. Come let's go and talk business. Gus, you wait here we'll be back shortly,' leading Jimmy to his office in the back of the shop. Once in the office, Moodley shut the door and indicated Jimmy to take a seat.

Jimmy started to say something only to be interrupted by Moodley. 'Before you say anything, let me tell you a story. That day you let my boy Raj into the game for free and gave him bus fare to get home, made a huge impression on me. It told me that even in this country with its oppressive race laws, there are good people like you. I am a very rich man and your actions of refusing to take money from me and letting my family in for free was an unbelievable friendly gesture. Your friendship with Raj helped us all. I thought that was all but I found out something further about you and also Gus.' Moodley reached across to his intercom and pressed the button. 'Send my driver in please.' Turning to Jimmy he said, 'I have a surprise for you.'

A few moments later there was a knock on the door and in walked someone Jimmy recognised immediately. 'Cyril Pillay. Man, long time no see.' Jimmy got up and shook Cyril's hand. 'Do you work here now?'

Before he could answer, Mr. Moodley interrupted, 'Cyril is my wife's cousin's son and yes he works here. Growing up he used to tell my kids about his soccer games. He used to brag about playing with a bunch of white boys at Fynnlands on the Bluff. How he played with the famous Chubby Murphy. He also talked about you, Gus and a boy named Ian, not so fondly about Ian though. He told us that you always picked him first for your team.'

'I'm not stupid. I always picked the best for my side. I liked winning.'

'He also told us that one of the boys, you, would come back to his house and sample his mother's curry. This was confirmed by his mother. You even invited him back to your home, although he was too shy to go.'

'I think him refusing was a good move on his part; my mother was a terrible cook. Her food would probably have killed him.' Jimmy laughed.

'Yes, maybe. Right now, we have some business to deal with. Cyril go and see if Gus remembers you, you can all catch up later. Jimmy, let me tell you a few things. All of the clothes except the shoes and the belts are made up from our own cloth. The belts and shoes are from my stock so I sell them to you at cost. So I tell you what, for all of the clothes you pay me R10 each and we call it quits. You okay with that?'

'No, I'm not okay. I cannot accept your generous offer. All I did was save you and Raj a couple of Rand. This is way too much.'

'It's not the cost that is important, it was the gesture. Your friendship to us all and the way you treated us and not looked at the colour of our skin, you cannot put a cost on. This is not a gift; it's payment for making us part of your life. You are a good man and maybe one day in the future there will be more like you and together we can fix this country. Come, let Naidoo pack these clothes for you and we can rejoin Raj, Cyril and Gus.'

'Thank you, Sir. I am very pleased to know you and your family and to consider you my friends.'

They rejoined the others and waited while Naidoo packed the clothes. A few minutes later, he returned with two parcels and Jimmy and Gus warmly thanked him for his magnificent work.

'My friends, I regret that Raj and I have to get back to work, time is money you know. Cyril, you take my car and give these boys a lift back to wherever they need to go. You come back anytime and tell your friends about The House of Lords. They mention your name I give them a good discount,' said Mr. Moodley, shaking both boy's hands.

Saying goodbye to Raj, they followed Cyril to the parking garage and got into a large shiny Mercedes.

'Cyril, how the hell are you driving around in a Mercedes? Last time I saw you, you were five-foot tall and barefoot. What are they feeding you on? You must be at least five ten now!'

'Actually, five eleven. I have been with my uncle nearly two years but only been his personal driver since I got my license three months ago. Where to, Mates?'

Jimmy gave Cyril directions and off they went. During the trip they reminisced about the good old days and what had happened since. Cyril told them they were very lucky to be on Moodleys good side as he never forgot a favour. He dropped them off at the 'Y' and they all agreed to keep in touch if possible.

The minute they got back to their room, Gus raised the issue about the cost of the clothes, 'Jesus Jimmy, what's this stuff going to set us back?'

'It's going to be quite expensive but I think you'll be okay.'

'I have to save for Varsity next year. I have the bursary, thanks to my old man being a Doctor, but I still need a bit of ready cash. So, what are we in for?'

'R10 each.'

'What? Are you shitting me? R10?'

'No, the R10 was for the shoes and belt, which he sold us at cost. The suit, shirts, sock and ties he made for us free and for *gratis*.'

'Wow. I understand him doing it for you, but why me?'

'Well, you are my buddy, but you can also thank Cyril for part of it. He is Raj's cousin and he told the family about our football days and how we treated him and his friends like our friends. Good deeds were rewarded. Now, all we need is Koz and the keys and the Andersen boys to join us and we will be in business.'

At four thirty, Koz pitched up with the keys and stated they could move in tonight if they wanted. Both thought it was a good idea and Koz offered to give them a lift to their new accommodation. He would come around tomorrow evening for the first rent. Jimmy left a note for the Andersen brothers, giving them the address and to say if interested, to come around this evening. Packing up their meagre belongings, they headed for Mutual Beach Center.

One of the bedrooms was better than the other and Jimmy said they should flip for it. Gus said no, seeing as he would only be there until February next year, Jimmy should take it as he would be there longer than him. They settled in to unpack.

Shortly after 6 o'clock there was a knock on the door; Mickey and Dog Andersen arrived complete with luggage and R80 for the month's rent. Introductions over, the two newcomers checked out the accommodations. Dog took the third bedroom and Mickey got the screened-in balcony. It was time to set some rules. which Jimmy laid out.

'We split the light and water charges. We all pay for our own phone calls, just enter the date and time on a soon to be available log. Take care of your own food. Sort out your own laundry. Clean up after yourselves. No girlfriends to move in long term. An occasional 'sleep over' is allowed, provided it doesn't impact the rest of us. Rent is payable first of each month.' Jimmy handed Mickey a set of keys, 'If we need more, we'll get another set cut. Anything not covered yet, we will deal with if it arises.'

Everyone agreed and shook hands and Jimmy announced, 'Right Okes, welcome! We are in business. To celebrate, let's head for the Cumberland Hotel Bar; the first round is on me.'

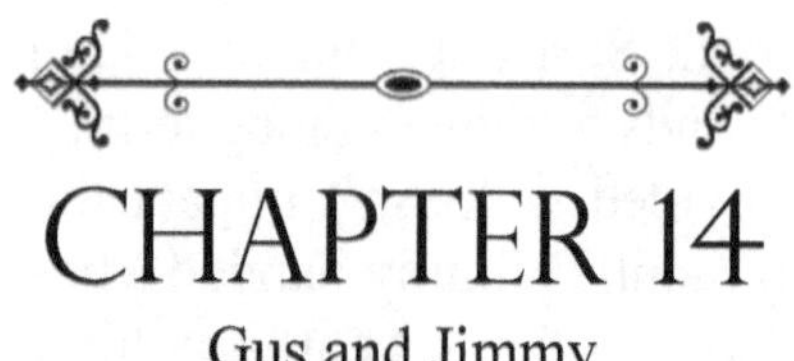

CHAPTER 14
Gus and Jimmy

October 1 Gus and Jimmy awoke early and readied themselves for their first day of work at Standard Bank. They decided that rather than walk to work, they would take the bus and get there fresh and early. A cup of coffee and a sticky bun at the Corner Cafe and they were ready for action.

Standard Bank ABC Branch was located on the corner of West and Gardener Streets. It differed from the traditional Banks as it was located on the first, second and third floors of the building and accessed by an escalator in West Street. Working hours were from 8.30am to 5.00pm but the bank only opened to the public from 9.00am to 3.30pm.

Arriving at 8.00am and finding the doors to the escalator locked, they looked around for help. Gus went around the corner onto Gardner Street and found a door manned by a white security guard. On inquiry he found out it was the staff entrance; he went back to the corner and called Jimmy.

When they attempted to enter the staff entrance, they were blocked by the security guard, 'Staff only allowed through here, you must wait for the Bank to open at 9.'

'We are staff; we begin work today,' said Gus.

'Where are your employee cards?'

'We don't have any, this is our first day.'

'No card, no entry.'

They both looked at the guard and shrugged their shoulders. You can't beat the system; they would just have to wait. They turned away and started to walk back to West Street. They had barely reached the corner when they heard a voice calling after them. 'Wait up. Are you two Wilson and Stewart?'

'Yes, we are,' replied Gus.

'Good. I am Les Sharpe, the chief accountant, glad to see you are here early. Come with me. I will take you up to personnel. You have a pile of forms to fill in. Did you bring a reference letter from your school?'

Gus replied in the affirmative and passed his and Jimmy's envelopes to Sharpe. They followed the man to the lift which took them up to the second floor. Sharpe unlocked the door and ushered them in. 'Come with me and I'll introduce you to our personnel manager, Mr. Don Jones, he will have a chat to you.'

Sharpe walked up to a closed door with the name Donald Jones, Personnel Manager, engraved on it, knocked and not waiting for an answer, opened it and walked in followed by Gus and Jimmy.

'Don, these are the two young men you have been expecting, James Wilson and Angus Stewart. Here are their reference letters. Do the necessary and when you are done, send them down to my office.'

Sharpe turned and left, Jones indicated that they should each take a seat. After properly introducing himself, he spent the next half an hour extolling the virtues of a career within the Standard Bank. He also went through the dress code, the working hours, the medical insurance and the various exams you could take to enhance your chances of promotion. Eventually he stood up and motioned to the boys to follow him.

Gus and Jimmy were ushered into a small interview room which held a table and two chairs. On the table were two piles of forms and two pens.

'Take a seat, men and complete all the forms. When you're done, come back to my office and bring the forms with you.'

The forms consisted of all personal information: full names, date of birth, family data, next of kin, schools attended, matric results, sports, hobbies etcetera. There were also copious pages of rules and regulations that required a signature of understanding. Next of kin proved a point of contention for Gus as he did not want to add his mother, so he just put down 'none'. For 'Name to contact in case of emergency' each boy wrote in the other's name. Forms completed, they returned to Jones' office where he guided them down to Sharpe.

'Follow me boys, and I will show where you will work and introduce you to your direct supervisor. Mr. Stewart, you will be working in our Bills Department and you, Mr. Wilson, will be in our Correspondence Department. Both workplaces are on the second floor.'

First stop was the Bill Department. Sharpe walked over to a small office and introduced Gus to a Mr. Sexton who was the Sub-accountant for Bills. Next stop was the Correspondence Department. Here Jimmy was introduced to a thirty-something female, Miss Martin, who was the check-clerk. The department was smaller than Bills and did not merit a Sub-accountant.

The Billing Department was comprised of three different sections. Local Bills was headed by a check-clerk, Mr. van Rooyen, a senior clerk Mrs. Bright and a junior, Gillian Reynolds. Foreign Bills had a check-clerk, Miss. Clark and a senior clerk, Greg Swales. The third section was 'Stop Orders' with a check clerk, Mr. de Villiers and a clerk, Meg Atkinson. Gus' function was to work in Foreign Bills and assist 'Stop Orders' if required.

The Correspondence Department only currently contained three people; Jimmy would be the fourth. The senior clerk was Miss. Janet Jameson and would be Jimmy's direct supervisor. She was a rather miserable woman in her late twenties who had left school after Standard eight. She had probably already reached her peak in the bank. The Bank's switchboard was located in this department and manned by Mrs. Smethurst, whose son Derrek Jimmy knew as a prominent Durban City football player. The small inquiry counter was attended by Coral Thompson, who was also back-up to Mrs. Smethurst. Coral was the same age as Jimmy and had been in the bank since the beginning of the year.

Gus and Jimmy hooked up in the lunch room for their hour's break at twelve thirty. Not having brought any prepared lunch, they decided to head for the OK Bazaars for a pie and chips. Sitting down to eat, they swapped notes on their first morning of work at the Standard Bank.

'The work is pretty boring, going through incoming mail and directing it to whatever department it needs to go. My 'boss' is Janet; she seems scared to show me anything, wants to do it all herself. She seems a bit slow but harmless. The 'inquiries girl' is Coral; she stays at the YWCA but lives in Scottburgh. She looks a bit of alright, maybe I will have to slip her one. The switchboard lady is Derrick Smethurst's mother. What about your lot?'

'There's a whole crowd of people there. I work in Foreign Bills and it is quite interesting. The guy I work for is Greg and his boss is Miss. Clark. A bit funny that, Clark the clerk. She seems quite cool. I also have to help with Stop Orders but haven't yet, the girl there, Meg, is nice.'

'I have to take the mail around to the various departments; Janet has shown me where everything is. I reckon she sees me as her gofer and now she can stay locked to her desk. I got the impression she isn't very popular with some of the other staff. I had to deliver stuff to the main Inquiry Counter. Shit, you must see that chick who works there. Her name is Heather Wallace, she wears the shortest skirt I have ever seen and has these long legs that go all the way up to her bum. We are going to have to find out more about her.'

'I reckon we should head back,' said Gus.

'Okay, I'll see you at the end of work. Are we bussing or walking?'

'Walking, it's cheaper.'

At four thirty, Janet, showing her authority, reluctantly let Jimmy leave for the day. He walked over to the Bill Department and collected Gus to begin the long walk home. Walking down West Street they passed the Lonsdale Hotel and noticed a sign in the window advertising Happy Hour Tuesdays and Thursdays at the Bullring. Entrance was 25 cents and the first beer was free; an opportunity too good to miss.

They paid the entrance fee and were handed a ticket for one free beer. Walking up to the bar they exchanged the tickets for two Lion Ales and sat down at the bar. The first thing they noticed were a number of small bowls of curry and rice scattered across the bar counter.

Calling to the barman, Jimmy asked, 'What's with the curry and rice?'

'They are free during Happy Hour, help yourself.' Needing no second invitation, they did. No sooner they had scoffed one lot, more appeared. The net result was for the price of 25 cents they had one beer and consumed half a dozen small bowls of curry and rice. They probably would have had a few more except for the frowning glances from the barman. On Tuesdays and Thursdays, the Bullring became a regular stop, but they took care to at least order a couple of half price beers so as not to piss off the barman.

Work days settled into a mundane process, the work was not difficult. Gus was kept relatively busy and Jimmy had to slow down to make the work stretch out and to not show up Janet. There were a few guys around the same age but apart from one in the Managers department, Clive Cairns, none that were likely to be buddies.

Jimmy was spending his time flirting with both Heather and Coral. Things here were going to get complicated. Heather fancied Jimmy and Coral fancied Clive. Jimmy preferred Coral but wouldn't kick Heather out of his bed; he had no idea whether Clive fancied either girl.

Jimmy made the first move and asked Coral out to movies on a Wednesday afternoon, she thanked him but refused saying she had a date with Clive. Never one to give up easily, he turned to Heather, who jumped at the chance. Fortunately, the two couples decided to go to different movie houses. With Heather there was some hand holding and a bit of kissing but nothing too intimate.

Oct 10, 1968
Enoch Powell warns that the immigrant may 'change the character of England.'

On the third Friday of every month the Bank had a social event. This usually meant that a number of the staff remained after work and relocated to the 'lunch room'. Snacks and drinks in the form of sodas, wine and beers were provided. Anything that fed them and provided free booze was a lock in for Gus and Jimmy.

A fair number of the male staff attended and a smattering of the females. Heather, Coral (if she was due to work on Saturday), Gillian, Meg and Mrs. Bright were among those working directly with Jimmy and Gus who were in attendance. By this time, Clive had hooked up with Heather leaving Jimmy to concentrate on Coral. Gus had made no attempt to get involved with any of the female staff as he was saving his money; he would need it next year while at university.

Jimmy took this opportunity to get to know Coral better. She was receptive to a certain extent but spent a lot of time asking all sorts of questions about Gus. Gus, on the other hand, was deep in conversation with Mrs. Bright. Mrs. Bright was difficult to read, she looked in her mid to late twenties, wore glasses, not much makeup and her hair tied in an unflattering bun. She did have a very good figure that not even the drab bank uniform could totally hide.

Jimmy felt he had made good progress with Coral and had arranged a movie date for the next day after work. Gus finally gave the sign it was time to go as the party was breaking up. Coral, Heather and Clive, Gillian and Meg had already departed; the food and beers depleted so time to go.

They started the long walk home a little worse for wear. 'It looks like you were making progress with Coral. Are you planning a move on her?'

'Well, I don't know about a move, but we are going to the movies tomorrow after work. We'll see how that goes. What's with you and

Mrs. Bright? You spent the whole time chatting to her. She looks pretty good for an old married women though.'

'Yes, I did spend a lot of time with her; she cornered me when we first got there. We had a really good chat. Her name is Cathy; she is twenty five, married with no kids. She's pretty cool; it's a pity I don't work in her section.'

It was almost eight o'clock by the time they got home. Mickey and Dog had just finished eating and were cleaning up the kitchen. 'Hey fellows, Mickey and me are heading up to the roof; we have a gallon bottle of Lieberstein wine and a couple of joints, do you want to join us?'

'Sure thing. We have already downed a good few beers so might not last too long. Come on Jimmy, let's go.'

For the next couple of hours the four of them mellowed out. Between passing around a joint and the jug of wine, they exchanged the stories of their lives. Dog was twenty three years old and looked eighteen. His school career ended in standard seven as he had a severe learning disability. He was an amazing surfboard designer and shaper and on top of that, one of the best surfers on the east coast. Mickey, eighteen months younger than his brother, had been exempt from army training and been working at Barclays Bank for nearly three years. They had been born and grew up in the small town of Stanger on the north coast.

Sometime after midnight, the four of them staggered down the stairs and hit the sack. All but Jimmy were working the following day. By the time Jimmy awoke, everyone else had left for work, so he decided to phone Ian.

Ian's mother answered the phone, 'Hello Mrs. Williams, it's Jimmy, is Ian home?'

'Why, hello Jimmy, we haven't seen you for some time, how are you keeping?'

'Keeping well, Mrs. Williams, work keeps Gus and me busy. We will have to make a trip out to the Bluff soon.'

'Ian is working at Steyn's this morning; he will be back at about one o'clock. I will tell him you called.'

Nonplussed, Jimmy called Chubby, 'Hello Mrs. Murphy, it's Jimmy, is Peter in?'

'Hello Jimmy, yes he is. I will call him for you.'

A few minutes later Chubby picked up the phone, 'Howzit China, long time no see. What's going on?'

'Same old shit, work and sleep. What's up at your end? You working yet, you lazy bastard?'

'Not a proper job, I've got a part time one at Stead's Clothing. My folks enrolled me at Natal University for next year; I'll be doing a B. Com. So I'll just play a bit of cricket and hockey until mid-February. When are you and Gus going to pay us a visit?'

'I tried calling Ian, he was at work. If you guys aren't busy, maybe we can get out there tomorrow and if the weather is okay, we can do a bit of surfing.'

'I have no plans, I'll get hold of Ian and we can meet at Anstey's. If the weather is crap, come around to my place instead.'

'Sounds like a plan, either way we can catch up. Cheers.'

Leaving to pick Coral up at the YWCA, Jimmy passed Gus on his way home from work. 'What's your plan for the day? If I get lucky with Coral, I may be late.'

'I'm just going to chill and maybe take a stroll down to the beach and take a swim.'

'I spoke to Chubbs and arranged to take a trip out to the Bluff tomorrow, you okay with that?'

'Yes, good idea. Well, have fun with Coral and try and behave.'

Jimmy made the long walk up the YWCA to pick Coral up. He arrived at reception and gave his name and said he was there to meet Coral Thompson. The receptionist checked him up and down, smiled and then reached over to her microphone and paged Coral. She came walking down the stairs, dressed in a short low cut miniskirt. She had freed her long dark hair from its usual pony tail and it now hung to just below her shoulders: Jimmy hardly recognised her, a huge improvement from her working persona.

Hand in hand, they made their way to the Playhouse Theatre, where Jimmy secured two tickets in the back row of the upper gallery. The movie was the Beatles in Yellow Submarine; if the movie was crap, at least the music would be good. They took their seats and sat through the trailers, the news reel and a short about travel in Europe.

After interval, Jimmy put his arm around Coral's shoulders and she snuggled up to him, a good start he thought. Sitting cheek to forehead, Jimmy turned towards her on the premise of asking if she was enjoying the movie. She looked up towards him and they made direct eye contact, the next thing he knew was that they were kissing. She was an enthusiastic kisser, not quite in the Kerry league but not too shabby at all.

That first kiss lasted about thirty seconds and as they broke it off and looked at each other, both went in for seconds. This kiss went on for some time, their tongues intertwining, wrestling and exploring. Jimmy, feeling her passion and intensity decided to try his luck, reasoning it would be bad manners to not at least make an attempt.

He moved his right hand up slowly, stopping just below her breast area. Leaving it so positioned, he waited to see if there was any resistance, sensing none he moved his hand up to her left breast on the outside of her dress. They continued to kiss, Jimmy gently massaged her breast, sensing she was okay with this, he decided to slip his hand down the front of her dress and into her bra. She immediately half sat up, pulled him closer and checked around to see if anyone was watching. Not seeing anybody looking at them, she slid back down in her seat, turned slightly inwards and started kissing again.

Jimmy began exploring her breasts. They were quite smallish but had really hard erect nipples. Not being an expert and only being able to compare to his previous experiences, he judged them smaller than Fiona's but bigger than Kerry's, somewhere around the size of Mary's. All in all, a nice pair of boobs.

They spent most of the movie kissing. Jimmy kept his hand firmly on her right breast, deciding not to explore anywhere below her waist. Coral kept her hands well away from any of his body parts. As the final credits rolled off the screen, they finally detached themselves. Coral managed to rearrange the front of her dress before the lights came on. She smiled sheepishly up at Jimmy who grinned back, 'Wow, I really enjoyed that movie. Do you have any idea what it was about?'

The two of them left the movie house hand in hand and made the short journey back to the YWCA. They took a very slow walk, dragging out their time together as long as possible. By the time they reached the entrance gate it was nearly six o'clock, suppertime at the 'Y'.

Coral stopped before entering the premises and turned to Jimmy, 'Thank you for asking me out, I really enjoyed it. The people at the "Y" don't approve of us girls having any physical contact with members of the opposite sex on the premises, so if you are going to kiss me, you better do it now.'

Never needing a second invitation, Jimmy obliged. 'I had a great time, a good movie; at least I think it was. Thanks for saying yes. I would like to do this again.'

'Yes of course. Well, I must go in and have supper. Sorry I can't invite you in. So I suppose I will see you at work on Monday? Bye.'

Giving her one last squeeze, he turned and started to walk away, looking back over his shoulder, 'By the way, you are a fabulous kisser. See you Monday.'

Full of the joys of life, he caught a bus back to the flat and took the lift up the twenty sixth floor. He entered that flat and the first thing he noticed was a note on the kitchen table. It read 'There is some cooked boerewors in the oven and bread rolls in the bread bin. We are all up on the roof, come up and join us.'

Grateful for the food, Jimmy wolfed it down and headed for the roof. He opened the exit door and was immediately struck by the pungent smell of *dagga*. Sitting in the corner were Mickey and Dog, well on the way. 'Hey guys, where's Gus?'

A very stoned Mickey replied, 'Hey China, welcome home. Gus was in his room when we came up here. He didn't feel like a *zol*. What about you, fancy a pull?'

'No thanks, I need to speak to Gus. See you Okes later, hey, thanks for the chow it went down well.'

Jimmy walked back down to the flat and knocked on Gus' bedroom door. 'Howzit, I have just seen Mickey and Dog. Fuck it, those two sure smoke a lot of *boom*, I reckon I need to stay far away from that stuff. What have you been up to?'

'I took a walk down towards the beach and on the way I bumped into Dog. I told him I was going to do a bit of body surfing. He suggested I borrow one of his boards and do some real surfing. He took me to the back of Wheatland's and we picked up a couple of boards and headed for Dairy Beach. He may look like a bit of a fuck nut but man, he can surf. He is actually quite a good guy, we caught some pretty good waves. Afterwards we came back here and Mickey made supper. I don't want too much *dagga* as you are right, I reckon it fucks up your brain. How was your date with Coral?'

'It went okay. She looks very different outside of work. What time are we heading for the Bluff tomorrow? I reckon we catch the bus from Durban by eight. Hopefully Ian gives us a ride home. Fancy a pint at the Cumberland?'

'No, I have some reading to do. I need to get ahead of things before I go down to University. I can't fuck it up, the bursary doesn't allow for me failing any subjects.'

'They say there are two certainties in life, "Death and Taxes", I reckon there is a third one "Gus Stewart never failing an exam". You are the most intelligent person I have ever met.'

'Right, then how come you do as well as or better than me with no apparent effort?'

'I don't know, my brain must be kind of fucked up. If I hear or read something that interests me, then it seems to get filed away for future use. If something doesn't interest me, then no amount of studying it will be of any use. Take Afrikaans, for instance, no fucking hope with that. I'm heading out for that pint, see you in the morning.'

Leaving bright and early the two of them headed to the central bus depot and caught the first bus to the Bluff. They alighted at the stop opposite Anstey's and headed for Benny's house to pick up Jimmy's surfboard.

By the time they got to the beach, there were half a dozen or so of the regulars sitting around shooting the breeze. The surf was pretty crappy so they joined the group and spent the next half an hour catching up on the news. No sign of Chubby or Ian.

Benny caught Jimmy's attention and motioned him to one side, 'I am looking for a favour. It's my Matric Dance coming up and I need a date. You are big buddies with Kerry, what's the chance of fixing me up there?'

'Sure, I will have a word with her. I just hope "Invisible Dave" has eventually fucked off into the distance.'

'Invisible Dave? What are you talking about?'

'You'll find out one way or another if she agrees to go with you. I'll let you know what she says.'

Chubby and Ian arrived and joined the group. The surf never got going and by the middle of the afternoon the crowd started drifting away. Jimmy suggested that they make a turn at the Vermeulen's house and see if they could get a cup of coffee. They thought it a good idea and after storing Jimmy's surfboard, Ian drove them up Marine Drive to see Kerry and family.

Kerry was home with her friend, Dee Davis, and invited them in. She left them on the veranda and with Jimmy following, went to make coffee. When she reached the coffee, she turned around and flung her arms around his neck, 'I have missed you terribly, why haven't you called? You have been back for over a month and not so much as a phone call. Why?'

Jimmy was taken aback. 'If you remember, the last time I saw you was at the station with "no longer Invisible Dave" in tow. You were pretty blunt. So, having broken up with me before I went to the army, I got the message.'

'Who is "Invisible Dave"? Do you mean Dave Fagan? Why do you call him that?'

'Yes, Dave Fagan. You went out with him once and then dumped Gus, as you were in love. Anyone who made any move on you was given the treatment; "I'm in love with Dave so I don't want to get involved". So, as he was nowhere to be seen, we called him "Invisible Dave". He got in the way of a number of us, and then you dumped me for him. I took it pretty hard as I always thought the two of us would be together.'

'Dave is no longer part of my life; we broke up the same day you got back from the army. When I saw you I realised that I still have all these feelings for you. Can we please get back together?'

'Kerry, you will always be a friend and I will always love you, but I am not sure I can be in love with you right now. I am seeing someone at the moment but I am not sure where that's going,' said Jimmy. Realising never say never, he added with a forlorn look on his face, 'Maybe one day I will get over the hurt you caused me and then who knows.'

'Oh my gosh, I am so sorry, please forgive me.'

'I do forgive you and I have a favour to ask of you. Benny Holmes wants to ask you to his Matric Dance but is too shy. He is a good guy; it would be nice if you went with him.'

'Oh. That is a bit of a surprise but tell him to ask me directly, I won't say no. A pity we never went to one of the dances together.'

Kerry and Jimmy returned to the verandah with coffee for all. They spent the next couple of hours chatting and catching up with all the news. Ian was saving up to buy a car; he figured that he would buy one of the cars at Steyn's Garage. He had worked on all of them and knew the good from the bad; Steyn had told him he would give him a good deal. Chubby and Ian had their driver's licenses and access to their mother's cars, making it an option to see more of each other.

As it was getting late, they decided to break up the party. Ian offered Gus and Jimmy a lift home but both agreed it would be easier to catch a bus home as the nearest bus stop was virtually outside the Vermeulen house. Ian and Chubby left, giving Dee a lift home. Kerry decided to wait with Jimmy and Gus at the bus stop.

'Hey Gus, was it my imagination that Ian was eyeballing Dee?'

'No, I saw it too.'

'Do you think Ian likes Dee? She will be so excited, I can't wait to phone her and let her know,' said Kerry. 'Here comes the bus. I will come and see you guys at the bank. Bye.'

Oct 27, 1968

US athletes. Tommie Smith and John Carlos. give a black power salute on the podium after finishing first and second in the 200 meters at the Mexico Olympics.

The end of the month and their first payday. Both cleared the exact same amount of R86.25 after deductions. After rent, lights and water and minimal phone calls both pocketed nearly R70. Gus reckoned he could save at least R40 per month towards next year's University expenses. Jimmy, on the other hand, thought he could get out and about a bit more and maybe be able to take things further with Coral.

The next few weeks settled into a routine of work, eat and sleep. Wednesday afternoons, weather permitting, Gus would borrow a board from Dog and go surfing. Jimmy would take Coral to the movies and spend most of that time getting as intimate as she would allow him.

Up to this time there had been no females visiting the flat, at least to Gus and Jimmy's knowledge. Things were about to change. Getting home after a happy hour session at the Bullring, they found Dog had hooked up with some girl he had met at the beach. She was maybe nineteen or twenty, a pretty blond named Sandy. After introductions the two of them, accompanied by Mickey, headed for the rooftop.

By the time Gus and Jimmy headed for bed, the trio had not re-emerged. The next morning while Gus was making coffee before leaving for work, Sandy appeared out of Dog's room. With a half-hearted greeting, Sandy grabbed two cups, filled them with coffee and headed back to the bedroom. Gus and Jimmy left for work.

Being the third Friday of the month, both boys stayed for the social event. Almost all the same crowd was in attendance except for Clive. When Gus inquired as to Clive's non- attendance, Heather explained that they had ended their short romance and she was now footloose and fancy free, no more jealous Clive. As the evening wore on and the crowd started leaving, Gus, Jimmy, Coral, Heather, Meg, Gillian and Mrs. Bright were all who remained.

215

The dynamics of the group who remained took a definite shape. It appeared to Coral that Heather was flirting with Jimmy, who seemed to be enjoying it more than he should. Coral, not normally showing Jimmy any affection in public, moved closer to him as if marking out her territory. Meg and Gillian appeared to hang on Gus' every word, both obviously interested in taking it further. Mrs. Bright, strangely still in attendance just looked on with an amused smile.

Finally, Jimmy broke up the gathering. 'Hey Gus, can I have a word with you?'

The two of them made for the men's restroom. 'I'm going to walk Coral back to the "Y" and hopefully get in a bit of loving. Are you okay to head home alone or are you going to make a plan with Meg or Gillian? Both seem hot to trot with you.'

'Nah, I'm going to head home. Mrs. Bright offered me a lift home; she says she passes by our place on the way to Durban North. So, see you later.'

Jimmy and Coral bade their farewells and left leaving Gus and the four females to tidy up. Friday night curfew at the 'Y' was eleven o'clock, plenty of time for a bit of loving. Up to this stage, the romance had not got any further than kissing and breast feeling. Coral had firmly stopped anything more intimate but Jimmy still tried, knowing there would be a firm 'No'.

Finding a nice secluded bench near the 'Y' they sat down, and Coral looked up at Jimmy. 'Heather seemed to be making eyes at you all night. What's going on there? You looked like you were enjoying it.'

'I have no interest in Heather. I just didn't want to be rude. You are the girl for me.'

Coral pulled him towards her and locked lips. Always a passionate kisser. this one seemed more intense than usual. Jimmy loosened the top two buttons of her blouse and moved her bra up freeing both her breasts. To his utter surprise. Coral reached over and placed her hand over the bulge in his trousers and started rubbing back and forth. Jimmy, recovering from the surprise, thought 'great' and attempted to slide his hand up her skirt, only to have it firmly removed.

Sensing it would be useless to try again, he decided on a different tactic. He removed Coral's hand, reached down and unzipped his trousers. He pulled aside his underpants and exposed his fully erect penis. He took hold of Coral's hand and placed on his penis. Coral looked at him and smiled, taking a firm grip gave a couple of tugs before pulling up his underpants and zipping up his trousers. Once zipped up, she replaced her hand on the outside of his trousers and gave his penis one final squeeze. She sat back, rearranged her bra and buttoned up her blouse and looking Jimmy in the eye. 'I think it's time for me to go inside before we get into trouble. This is not the place to take any chances.'

Confused, Jimmy walked Coral up to the front door of the 'Y,' kissed her on the cheek and left. On the walk home he contemplated what had occurred that evening. Heather had been coming onto him; Coral had seen that and was maybe a bit jealous. She had been more adventurous in their love-making, probably something to do with Heather. Either way, it was to his benefit and he was sure there was more to come. By the time he got home the place was in darkness, so he went straight to bed.

Jimmy woke up the next morning to an empty flat, he knew Gus was working and he assumed so were the other two. He decided to phone Coral at work to see if she wanted to come over to the flat and maybe spend some time on the beach. She agreed and said she would catch the bus with Gus, as she knew he was coming straight home.

Gus and Coral pitched up armed with bread rolls, sliced ham, cheese, a large bottle of red wine and a six pack of Lion Ale. Jimmy took Coral on a tour of the flat while Gus prepared six rolls of ham and cheese. Armed with food and drink, they headed up to the roof to enjoy the sunshine.

By the time the food and much of the drink was consumed, Coral had related the story of her life. She was born in Scottburgh and grew up living on a sugar plantation. Her father worked for Hulettes Sugar as a manager and they lived in a company house on the plantation. She went to junior school in Scottburgh and high school as a boarder in Port Shepstone. She had two younger sisters, Jennifer, seventeen, and Kate, fourteen, both at boarding school in Port Shepstone. Every time she was off on a Saturday, she would catch the Friday evening train for Scottburgh returning late Sunday afternoon.

As it started to get dark, they returned to the flat to finish off the remaining wine and beer. Coral started to make signs that it was time for her to leave. Before she could get the message across, Dog and Mickey arrived with Sandy and another girl. Introductions were made; Mickey's girl was Magda who was visiting Durban from the Free State; he had picked her up on the beach that afternoon.

The four newcomers dropped their gear off in Dog's room and headed for the roof.

Coral got up and looked for her handbag, which she found behind the couch, 'It's time I got going, will you walk me to the bus stop and wait with me? There is no need to come all the way to the "Y" with me, I will be okay.'

'Why don't you stay over tonight, we have plenty of room?' suggested Jimmy.

'I can't; if I stay out overnight then I have to make arrangements with the "Y" beforehand. If I don't, they write me up as missing. I can't phone it in; it must be in person and not at the last minute.'

Giving Gus a peck on the cheek, Coral headed for the door followed by a frustrated Jimmy. He has really hoped she would sleep over. Twenty minutes later he returned to find Gus laughing and shaking his head, 'You lucked out there, Buddy and you tried so hard. Better luck next time.'

'Shit, I don't think I'm ever going to get my leg over there. That fanny is more secure than Fort Knox. I hate to admit this; eighteen years old and still a virgin.'

'I know how you feel; maybe one day soon we will both come right,' said Gus.

'Hey, what do I owe you for the food and booze?' asked Jimmy.

'Nothing, your girlfriend paid.'

'She paid? Shit, that's a first, there is hope yet. Let's pop up to the roof and maybe have a quick *zol* with the boys.'

'Nah, I have some reading to do; you go ahead.'

Jimmy made his way up the fire escape stairs and opened the door. His eyes nearly popped out of his head. All four of them were naked. Mickey was fucking Magda doggy style and was being cheered on by Dog and Sandy. Oblivious to their surroundings, they did not see Jimmy who took one prolonged look and headed back to the flat posthaste.

Knocking on Gus' door, he walked in without waiting, 'Jesus Gus, the four of them are on the roof fucking their brains out, all completely *kaalgat*.'

'Well, good luck to them. I just hope they don't get caught by the superintendent otherwise we will all be in the shit. Maybe we have a chat with them in the morning once the women have left.'

Early the next morning Gus was awoken by a loud agonising noise coming from somewhere in the flat. He leapt out of bed and rushed into the lounge, where he was met by both Jimmy and Mickey. The noise was coming from Dog's room. It was a woman's voice calling out for God and doing a lot of agreeing with someone. As it was reaching a crescendo, you could hear Dog's voice joining in, he was also doing a lot of agreeing and then Sandy telling him to' fuck me harder.'

The three of them burst out laughing as the pitch of the sound got higher and higher and eventually ended in a series of 'yes's.' 'Jesus Mickey, have a word with your boet about the volume, it'll wake the fucking neighbours. While we are on the subject about last night. I happened to go up to the roof and saw you boys performing, I don't have a problem with it but if the superintendent finds out, we are all in the shit. I don't want to get kicked out the building so if you want to fuck, do it in your rooms, okay?'

'Sure Jimmy, we just got a bit stoned and the next thing we were all naked and one thing led to another and you saw the result. I will speak to Dog.'

Nov 5, 1968
Shirley Chisholm becomes the first black women to be elected to the House of Representatives.

Nov 6, 1968
Richard Nixon is elected as the next USA president.

The next few weeks saw life settle into a steady routine. Happy hour after work on Tuesdays and Thursdays, Wednesday afternoons Jimmy and Coral went to the movies and Gus to the City Library to study. If Coral was off on Saturday, she headed off to Scottburgh on Fridays giving Jimmy a free weekend.

Things took a dramatic turn. Wednesday November 20, 1968; a day that will live in infamy. Gus had left work and as usual headed for the library, Jimmy and Coral went off to the movies. Shortly after interval, Coral informed Jimmy she was feeling unwell, it was that time of the month and she needed to get back to the 'Y'. He didn't need to come with her as it was just a short walk, so he headed home.

He let himself into the flat and saw no one was home, so he went into his room to change out of his work clothes into shorts and a t-shirt. As he left his room, he noticed Gus' bedroom door slightly ajar; he could have sworn it was closed when he arrived. Thinking nothing of it he headed for the kitchen and there he got the surprise of his life.

Bent over with her head in the fridge was a completely naked woman. Surviving the initial shock, he stepped back to avoid startling her, but it was too late; she turned around.

His eyes nearly fell out of his head, 'Mrs. Bright, what are you doing here?' he stuttered. She was magnificent, a stunning body not encumbered by that godawful bank uniform, almost unrecognisable.

She stood there blushing; an empty glass in one hand and a bottle of Sprite in the other, unable to cover up any part of her naked body. 'Jimmy, we weren't expecting you home so early. I'll let Gus know you are home.' With that she walked past Jimmy and headed for the bedroom.

A few seconds later Gus emerged, dressed only in a pair of shorts, 'We have to talk.' Closing his bedroom door, he headed for the lounge.

'Fuck Gus, what the hell is going on? Mrs. Bright? She's married, for fuck's sake. Is this the first time?'

'Okay, calm down. Do you remember the last social event Mrs. Bright, I mean Cathy, gave me a lift home? When she dropped me off, I turned to thank her and the next thing I knew we were kissing. It went on a bit longer than just a thank you kiss. I invited her up for "coffee", she declined saying she had to get home, but maybe we could have "coffee" on the following Wednesday afternoon. So, for the last few Wednesdays we have spent it here, she is unbelievable.'

'Yes, but she is married. What happens if her husband finds out?'

'She tells me they never have sex anymore and he pays her no attention. She wants to have a bit of fun, nothing serious, no commitments, just sex. I am going to keep this up as long as she lets me.'

The conversation was interrupted by Mrs. Bright reappearing, all dressed and acting as though nothing untoward had happened. Jimmy, instead of going with the flow, blurted out, 'I'm sorry Mrs. Bright, I did not mean to barge in on you like that.'

'Call me Cathy. Jimmy, it wasn't your fault, we weren't expecting you. Gus, I better leave now. I will see you tomorrow at the Bank; don't let this stop our fun. Jimmy, please keep this confidential and I will try not to walk about your flat naked in future.'

'Don't get dressed just for me,' replied Jimmy regaining his composure. 'Your secret is safe with me. You are absolutely gorgeous. Gus sure is one lucky bastard.'

Jimmy spent the rest of the afternoon grilling Gus for details. Gus, to his credit, kept most of the details to himself; the only question he answered was about wearing a condom. He told his friend that he didn't need to use a condom as Cathy was taking birth control pills. He said he was crazy about her but knew it was probably just a fling for her, but he was going to enjoy it until it either ended, or he left for Cape Town.

The next day at work both boys were called into the chief accountant's office. Fearing the worst, they were surprised to find out the bank had made a mistake in their starting salary. They had been given the salary of someone starting directly from high school. What they should have got was one grade higher, due to completing their Army training. The increase was an extra R12 per month taking their salary to R103 per month. It would be backdated to their starting date, giving them each an extra R24.

They thanked Mr. Sharpe and turned to leave, 'Wilson, can you remain? I would like to talk to you. Stewart, please close the door as you leave.' Gus left and closed the door behind him.

'Wilson, I have had reports that your current job appears to be too easy for you. I have decided to move you to the Foreign Exchange Department up on the third floor. I have informed Miss. Jameson so you can report to Mrs. Goosen immediately. I predict good things for you in the Bank young man, well done.'

Jimmy made his way up to the third floor and asked for Mrs. Goosen, 'Ah Mr. Wilson, we have been expecting you, come on. I'll show you to your desk and let you settle in.'

Mrs. Goosen was probably somewhere in her late forties with very friendly disposition. She was responsible for the buying and selling of foreign currencies and travellers cheques. Jimmy's job was to convert Rands to whichever currency the client wished to purchase and vice versa if the client was selling. He would calculate any commissions and once the transaction was complete, he filled in the necessary documents for processing through the bank's systems. Not rocket science but more challenging than working in the Correspondence Department.

Gus, unaware of the change in duties, was surprised to see Miss. Jameson doing the mail rounds. He asked after Jimmy but was ignored, so he decided to pay a visit to the Correspondence Department. Not finding Jimmy, he walked over to Coral's desk to ask if she knew where he was.

'I don't know what happened, he was here for a few minutes this morning, and then I saw the two of you leave, you came back but he didn't. Janet is really pissed off. I asked her what happened, but she ignored me. Do you think he has been fired?'

'I don't know but I am going to find out.' Gus turned and left. I wonder if Cathy had anything to do with this because of what happened yesterday he thought. That would be so unfair.

He headed back to the Billing Department to talk to Cathy. Before he could confront her, he heard a cheery voice behind him, 'Guess what? Sharpe moved me up to the third floor to Foreign Exchange Department. Beats the crap out of Correspondence.'

'Jesus, you scared the crap out of me, I thought you had been fired or something. You better go and tell Coral, she looked near to tears.'

'On my way old chap. So, she was a bit emotional, was she? Maybe I will get lucky one of these days. I better not tell her about our increase otherwise she'll never pay for anything in future.'

At 4.30 Jimmy finished up his work for the day and went down to the second floor to say hello to Coral and pick up Gus for the trip home. Coral had got over the shock of that morning and was happy that he had got a better job.

Gus packed up for the day, gave Cathy a sly smile and walked over to the waiting Jimmy.

'Why don't we skip happy hour and go and tie one on at the Cumberland? Celebrate our new-found wealth,' suggested Jimmy.

'The increase is great, just what I needed, but it's staying in the bank. I'm going to need every cent I can lay my hands on for Varsity next year.'

'Come on, this one's on me, double celebration; increase and a new position.'

'Thanks, but I can't let you pay for me, you've already helped me a great deal.'

'Listen Mate. In a couple of years, you are going to be a rich doctor, I will still be a poor bank clerk, you can pay me back then.'

'Okay then, but if you are still working in the bank by the time I'm a doctor, I will personally kick your arse. On the other hand, if you own the bank that's a different discussion.'

With a change of job came a change of the Saturday off rotation. Jimmy now had the same day off as Coral. As they were both off this weekend Coral asked Jimmy if he wanted to come down to Scottburgh for the weekend, he could sleep in her sister's room. He said that he would, so she phoned her mother to check if it was okay and got a positive response. It did mean Jimmy had to rush home at lunch time to pack a change of clothes and toiletries.

With Jimmy away in Scottburgh and the Andersen brothers away in Stanger for the whole week, Gus had the flat to himself. As it wasn't a social event Friday, Cathy was unable to get away but she arranged to visit Gus the next day and would be able to spend the afternoon and evening with him.

Coral and Jimmy caught the 5.30 train from Durban Station for the ninety-minute ride to Scottburgh, where they were met by Coral's mother. This was the first time Coral had brought a friend to stay so Jimmy was quizzed in great detail. By the time they reached the Thompson house, Jimmy was still answering questions much to Coral's chagrin.

Jimmy was shown to Jennifer's room to drop off his bag and then it was into the dining room for supper. Mr. Thompson was one of the plant managers for this branch of Hulettes Refineries and as such qualified for a house and a company car. Jimmy judged him as being a serious person, very much in charge and not too sure of this stranger's intentions with his daughter. He would have to be on his best behaviour.

After supper the four of them sat around chatting. Jimmy saw an opportunity to score some brownie points with Mr. Thompson. 'Sir, you must have a very interesting job unlike us two in the bank. I would love to see the plant in action, major industry fascinates me.'

'We run a shift on Saturdays so I can show you around. Having only females in the house it will be a nice change to have at least one other male around. None of the girls have shown any interest to see what I do.'

'Thank you Sir, I look forward to it.'

Mrs. Thompson stood up and turned to her husband. 'Come on Gary, it's time for bed, let's leave these kids alone. I'm sure they are tired of listening to us old folks.'

'Mom, I'm also tired. I reckon we will also head for bed,' Coral said. 'Come on Jimmy, let's get an early night, you have a big day tomorrow.'

Did I detect a note of sarcasm there? thought Jimmy. Maybe I was bit obvious but what the hell, it's best to get on the parents' good side. Following Coral, he headed for the bedroom. Coral's bedroom was adjacent her parents, Jennifer's room was at the far end of the passage.

Coral pecked Jimmy on the cheek and said goodnight. He went into the room and closed the door. Stripping down to his underpants he switched off the light and got into bed.

Jimmy was just dozing off when he heard a slight noise at the bedroom door. He sat up just in time to see it open slightly; it was Coral. She entered quickly and quietly closed the door behind her. She motioned to Jimmy to be quiet, he needed no second invitation, not with her folks close by. She was wearing a short see-through nightie with panties of the same material.

She walked over and sat on the bed next to Jimmy, leaned down and kissed him. He responded. She pulled back the bed covers and slid in next to him. She lifted the front of her nightie and snuggled up against his bare chest, the effect on him was immediate. Aware of the effect she was having on him, she slid her hand down inside his under shorts and took a firm grip on his erect penis.

Jimmy, taking her lead, slipped his hand down into her panties. He felt her legs part slightly, so he moved his fingers between the lips of her vagina, it was soaking wet. This is it, he thought, we are eventually going to do it. Basing his next move on his only previous experience with Fiona and Kerry he tried to slip his finger into her vagina.

She grabbed his wrist and stopped further penetration, 'No, not inside. I am a virgin and want to stay that way until I meet the man I'm going to marry. Just rub me on the outside please as that feels good.'

Jimmy spent the next few minutes doing as she requested. She seemed to be enjoying it but not as much as Kerry and Fiona had. Through it all she maintained a firm grip on his cock, not doing anything, just holding it. Jimmy rubbing away suddenly felt her shudder slightly. She sat up smiled at him then leaned down and kissed him lightly on the lips.

To his surprise, she reached in and pulled down his shorts freeing up his cock. Facing him she spread her legs giving him the full view of her vagina. She then reached down she began to massage his cock slowly at first and then more vigorously until he came. She wiped the semen from her hands on his chest, stood up, kissed him and said, 'Sleep well, I'll see you in the morning.'

Jimmy didn't know what to make of the situation. They had had plenty of previous opportunity to do what they had just done but never came close. Yet, here with her parents just down the passage, she decides it was time. If you finger a girl, is she no longer a virgin? he mused, I'll have to do some research.

After breakfast the next morning, Mr. Thompson loaded Jimmy in the company car, and they headed out to the sugar processing factory. Coral and her mother took the other car and drove into Scottburgh for a day's shopping.

Back in Durban, Gus finished work for the day and headed home. Cathy had the day off so Gus hoped she would visit him as promised. Shortly after one, there was a knock on the door, Gus, full of anticipation, rushed to answer the door expecting Cathy. Standing there was a postal delivery man with two registered letters; one for him and one of Jimmy. He signed for both letters and went back into the flat.

He opened the one addressed to him to find a letter from Natal Mounted Rifles. The letter instructed him to report on Saturday December 14 at 7am for a monthly parade. Summer dress code was required and to bring your rifle. Attendance was compulsory; if there was a work conflict then present this letter to your employers who are required by law to release you. Also in the letter was the schedule of all monthly parades for 1969, every third Saturday. Based on him moving to Cape Town at the end of January, it would mean only two parades before he was done. He had a quiet chuckle thinking of what Jimmy's reaction was going to be.

His thoughts were interrupted by a second knock on the door. Opening the door, he found Cathy standing there armed with food and drink, beer and wine. She looked amazing dressed in a short skirt and a multi button blouse. Dumping the food and drink on the kitchen table, she threw her arms around Gus' neck and kissed him.

'I thought you might be hungry, so I brought some home cooked spaghetti and meatballs. It should be good with a couple of beers and some red wine. Are you sure we have the place to ourselves?'

Gus confirmed and started to open the wine. Cathy unbuttoned her blouse and threw it onto one of the lounge chairs, she unhooked her skirt and dropped it to the floor, 'Come on Mr. Stewart, join the party.' Gus turned around just in time to see bra and panties follow her skirt. Grabbing the opened wine and two glasses, he joined her sitting at the coffee table on the lounge floor.

Cathy proceeded to remove him from his clothes, playfully kissing as she removed each garment. By the time he was naked he was fully aroused. She leant back to admire his hard, young body, she reached in and looking at his cock gave it a quick squeeze and said to it, 'I'll get to you soon. In the meantime, darling, cheers; here's to a lustful afternoon.'

Gus couldn't believe his luck. Here is a beautiful woman with an unbelievable body and incredible sex drive and at least for the moment, all his. They had hardly had the first sip of wine when Cathy reached over and took his glass and placed it next hers on the coffee table.

She pulled Gus towards her; she kissed him, her tongue working hard against his. She leaned back until she was lying flat on her back, she opened her legs wide and pushed Gus' head down across her flat belly until he was positioned firmly between her legs. Using both hands she spread her lips exposing her swollen clit. Gus started to slowly move his tongue around and over her clit; he inserted two fingers inside her vagina. Cathy held his head firmly in place and began grinding her hips. It didn't take long before she was in the throes of an orgasm. The more she moaned, the more Gus licked and fingered; she seemed to go on forever.

Finally, she pulled Gus' head away and pulled him up onto her, raising her hips she manoeuvred his penis into her. Clasping her legs around his waist, she thrust him into her, her orgasm continued to explode. Gus came quickly and rolled off her gasping for air, wondering what the fuck happened.

'Where have been all my life?' panted Cathy, sitting up, 'I have never experienced anything like that, ever.'

'Cathy, you are the first woman I have ever had sex with. I will never forget this for as long as I live. I cannot believe you are here with me.'

'Oh Gus, I want to do this as long as you want me to. I know it is a short term thing because of our age difference and me being married, but I love our time together.'

She raised her glass and toasted, 'Long may it last, you are a beautiful young man.' She took a sip of wine and glanced down at Gus and noticed his cock starting to harden again. 'Ah the stamina of youth, come here.'

She pushed him onto his back and kneeling over him took his cock in her mouth. It became instantly hard, using her tongue and lips she proceeded to drive him to a mind-blowing orgasm. Never having had a blow job before, Gus was unsure whether he should pull out his cock or not. He needn't have worried. Cathy held him tightly and swallowed the complete load.

Sitting up, Cathy smiled, 'I think we should have some food with our wine after all that exertion.' Not bothering to dress she walked over to the kitchen and proceeded to warm up the spaghetti and meatballs.

They spent the afternoon eating, drinking and making love. Cathy was insatiable and Gus willing and able. Just around seven, Cathy stood up and said to Gus, 'Come on, let's get dressed and go to the Cuban Hat for milkshakes.'

This was the first time the two of them went out in public together; it was a bit of a risk that they might be spotted, but they went anyway. On their return, Cathy parked the car and turned to Gus, 'I am not going to come up; if I did, I may never leave. As much as I want to come up there and have my way with you once more, I have to go home. You are a gorgeous young man and this afternoon you took me places I have never ever been before. I feel like a young girl again. See you at work on Monday.' She kissed him on the cheek and moments later she was gone.

Back in Scottburgh, Mr. Thompson, having given Jimmy the grand tour, suggested that they return to his house and pick up the girls. 'Every Saturday night there is a braai held at the social club. I think we should attend. There is free food and drinks and usually a local band playing. I am sure you youngsters would enjoy the music and dancing.'

The evening turned out to be good fun. The meat from the braai was top quality and abundant, nothing too good for the sugar workers. Beer, wine and spirits flowed freely. Jimmy was careful not to have too much to drink as he didn't want the Thompson's to get the wrong impression. Coral, on the other hand, didn't have the same concerns and helped herself to a good few glasses of white wine. By the time they got back to the house everyone was ready for bed.

Like the previous night, no sooner had Jimmy got into bed Coral paid a visit. This time though, as soon as she reached the bed, she removed her nightie and panties. Stark naked, she crawled into bed and immediately started kissing. Her hand wandered down to his penis, she made a move to remove his under shorts, he assisted, and they were both naked.

Coral rolled Jimmy onto his back and climbed onto his upper thighs. She grasped his penis and pushed it flat against his body and then slid upwards. She parted the lips of her vagina and straddling him, moving backwards and forwards up and down the length of his cock. At no point could he enter her but the movement up and down his shaft obviously stimulated her clit. Jimmy could feel himself coming but unable to move he just let it happen. Coral continued to grind away until with a barely detectable shudder, she stopped and rolled off.

She leaned over and kissed him then sat up and reached for her nightie and panties. Not bothering to get dressed, she wished him good night and left. Jimmy was left to contemplate what had just happened. He was sure he hadn't penetrated her, but it felt like they were fucking, did this count or was he still a virgin?

The next morning, Coral made no reference to the previous night's activities. After breakfast the Thompson family and Jimmy went off to church. Jimmy hadn't been in a church of any sort since before Granny Bridget had died and definitely had never been in an Anglican church. The rest of the morning was spent just hanging around until Mrs. Thompson drove them to the station for the trip back to Durban.

Arriving at Durban station, Jimmy caught the bus home and Coral took the short walk back to the 'Y'. No mention was made of what had happened the previous night. Jimmy felt awkward but Coral seemed nonplussed, maybe they would discuss it at some other time.

Jimmy got home to find the flat unoccupied; he dropped his bag off in his room and headed for the refrigerator. Opening the fridge door, he noticed two bottles of Lion Ale, a bit strange he thought, Gus doesn't normally buy beer. He checked the garbage bin and found an empty wine bottle and four empty beer bottles. Before he spent any more time wondering what had happened over the weekend, Gus arrived home. Wearing baggies and carrying a towel, it was obvious he had been to the beach.

'Hey, welcome back. How was Scottburgh?'

'Howzit. It was okay.' Pointing to the garbage bin. 'Looks like you had a couple of *dops* this weekend. You must have been lonely; I'll have to fix you up with a bird. We can't have you drowning your sorrows.'

'Don't you worry about me. How did it go with Coral?'

Jimmy explained in great detail about the goings on with Coral and ended with, 'I don't know what the fuck is going on in her head. She pulls these stunts two rooms down from her folk's bedroom but when we are alone here, nothing. I can do everything but put my dick or fingers inside her.'

'Don't worry Mate, at least you are making some progress. By the way, there is a letter for you from NMR; we have a parade next Saturday. I am off but you will have to get time off, the bank has to let you go, no excuses. I wonder if Chubby got a letter.'

Friday December 13; the night before their first parade. Army kit had to be unpacked and gotten ready for the following morning. Boots, putties, long socks, khaki shirt and shorts, web belt, beret and rifle. The rifles had to be cleaned as they were sure to have an inspection.

Staring at his kit laid out on his bed, Jimmy concluded that this parade was going to be a pain in the arse. 'Hey Gus, I've just had a great idea. How about we swap shorts and shirts? Yours will be too small for me and mine too big for you. We go in civvies but take our kit with us. We tell them that our kit doesn't fit, and we need to exchange them for ones that do fit. I bet they have no stores or even if they do, we waste half the time doing an exchange. It beats marching around all day. What do you think?'

'I think you are fucking crazy; it'll never work.'

'It's the fucking army. I bet they fall for it. They don't know we live together. Come on, it's a great idea. What's the worst that can happen? The letters were addressed to "Trooper", we have no rank any more.'

'You know, you have a really weird mind. Okay, I'll go along with it.'

The next morning the two of them reported to NMR headquarters dressed in civvies and carrying their army kit. They noticed another half dozen guys also in civvies and decided to join them. They were the only two who had brought any kit with them. There was no sign of Chubby.

A staff sergeant approached the group, 'What the fuck is going on here; why are you not in kit?'

Jimmy answered first, getting his story in before the rest, 'Sir, I have my kit with me, I've put on a lot of weight since the army. I brought it with me so I can exchange it.'

'Okay, straight after roll call go and wait for the quartermaster and see what he can do. Anyone else need to change kit?'

Gus raised his hand and was told the same as Jimmy. The other six had varying excuses and were told to see the sergeant major after roll call and he would deal them.

Roll call over, Gus and Jimmy headed for the quartermaster's store. On arrival, they found the store locked and no one about. They decided to take a seat and wait. About an hour later the quartermaster arrived and unlocking the store said, 'What do you two reprobates want?'

Jimmy explained that they needed to change kit, only to be told that there was no kit available and none was expected until sometime next year.

'What should we do, Sir?' inquired Jimmy.

'Bring your kit to the next parade, maybe we will be able to exchange it then. In the meantime, make yourselves useful, go and help tidy up the Officers' Mess.'

Jimmy and Gus spent twenty minutes cleaning up empty beer bottles, washing dirty glasses and the rest of the day playing snooker. Meanwhile the rest of the regiment was drilled in preparation for the 'Freedom of the City Parade' scheduled for January 11, 1969. They would go to that parade as they had done today and hoped no new kit would be available. The only gain on the day was that they were issued with their new NMR beret badges replacing the SSB ones.

Mrs. Murphy had invited Gus and Jimmy to spend Christmas Eve and Christmas Day at her house. George had moved to Johannesburg and Mary was still in England, having given up on the idea of being a teacher. There was plenty of room at the house so they could stay over. Chubby borrowed his mother's car and picked the boys up straight after work.

Gus and Jimmy stumped up for a pot plant for Mrs. Murphy and a bottle of Bells Whiskey for Mr Murphy. All had agreed that due to lack of funds, an exchange of Christmas presents was not on the schedule.

The Murphy's had arranged a braai for Christmas Eve. Ian and his girlfriend, Dee, were invited to join the festivities. Most of the chatter was about catching up. Ian was still doing double shifts; weekdays at the oil refinery working on his apprenticeship and Saturdays at Steyn's. He almost had enough saved to buy a car. Chubby was passing time working at Stead's in the sports section. He was still single but not necessarily celibate, no further details forthcoming.

Gus suddenly remembered Chubby's absence from the NMR parade, 'Hey Chubbs, how come we didn't see you at the NMR parade a few weeks back? Didn't you get a letter?'

'Ja, I got a letter, but I also got a call from Major Hearn who asked me if I would play cricket for NMR against UMR. It was a tough choice; marching around all day or playing cricket and a few beers. Big decision, but I chose the cricket match. What was the parade like?'

Gus told the story about Jimmy's plan with the kit and how they ended up playing pool all day. Both Ian and Chubby broke down laughing, 'Jesus Wilson, you are a chancer, where do you come up with this stuff?' asked Ian. 'An evil genius I reckon.'

By the end of the evening the four of them, and to a lesser extent Dee, were well on the way. Plans were made for Christmas Day, Ian and Dee bade their farewell and left on the short walk home. The three remaining had one last beer together and thereafter hit the sack, a little worse for wear.

On Christmas morning Gus and Jimmy were awakened by the smell of breakfast cooking. After a quick shower and changing into clean clothes, they joined the Murphy family. Presents were being exchanged. Much to their embarrassment Mrs. Murphy had a gift for each of them. Each received a gold Parker pen with their name engraved on it.

'I'm sure this will be useful in your daily banking jobs,' she said. They both thanked her for her kind thoughts.

After breakfast Chubby borrowed his mother's car and they headed for Anstey's, picking up Ian on the way. The weather was perfect. And being Christmas day, hopefully not crowded. While the rest headed for the beach, Jimmy headed for Benny's house to see if he could retrieve his board.

On arrival Jimmy found the garage door open and Benny inside, 'Benjamin, my mate, how the hell are you? I haven't seen you in ages.'

'Jesus, Jimmy, where did you spring from? Your board is still safe; no one has used it since you were last here.'

'Hey, I forgot to ask you how it went with Kerry and the Matric dance.'

'It went great, we are going steady now. I must thank you for setting me up with her. Anytime you need a favour let me know.'

'Letting me store my board is payment enough. Aren't you off to the Army soon?'

'Yes, on January 6 to Bloemfontein with Durban Light Infantry. I am not looking forward to going; I reckon I am going to miss Kerry.'

'Well, I hope you have better luck with her than me, she dumped me the week before I left. Say hello to her for me as I haven't seen her in yonks.'

They spent the morning with Jimmy and Gus taking turns with the surfboard and the other three swimming. Lunch was hamburgers and chips washed down with cokes at the Wimpy. Just after lunch several locals started arriving, among them Benny with Kerry in tow.

On spotting Jimmy, Kerry rushed over and flung her arms around his neck, 'Gosh Jimmy, I haven't seen in you forever. Why don't you ever come and visit? My Mom was asking after you. Oh, hi Gus, Ian and Dee. Sorry, I didn't mean to ignore you I was just so surprised to see Jimmy.'

'It's difficult to get out to the Bluff. We work all week and most Saturdays. If we do want to come out on a Sunday, the buses don't run as often. Say hello to your Mom, I hope she is keeping well. I'm going to hit the surf one last time.' Grabbing his board, he headed for the surf, keen to avoid any further drama with Kerry.

On the drive back to Chubby's house after dropping off Ian and Dee, Gus turned to Chubby and asked, 'Hey Chubbs, I don't know if you noticed but Kerry greeted everyone except you. She also seemed to ignore you the whole afternoon. What's going on there, did you piss her off somehow?'

'I don't want to talk about it.'

'Come on, you are not getting off that lightly, there is something going on. Confess,' persisted Gus.

'Okay. I have taken her out a couple of times. Benny doesn't know about it and he seems totally in love with her. We don't want to rock the boat, so she ignores me in mixed company.'

'Benny is a really good guy and also an amateur boxing champion so watch out. Jimmy and I thought we might have a New Year's Eve party at our place. It's bring your own booze and some music and we will provide breakfast for those that make it through the night. Dog always has a few birds around, so we should have plenty of female companions but bring someone if you want. I will give Ian a call as well,' said Gus.

Dec 25, 1968
In her Christmas message to the nation, Britain's Queen Elizabeth II calls for racial tolerance.

With only a few days to organise the party, Gus and Jimmy got to work. Unfortunately, Coral had decided to take off on the 31st and would head for Scottburgh, only returning on Monday January 6. Due to some old tradition, most companies closed on the 1st and 2nd of January; the banks were not one of those organisations. Ian confirmed he would attend the party and bring Dee with him. To avoid drinking and driving they would, together with Chubby, bus into the city. Dog and Mickey would both attend and bring a few of their girls along. Gus contacted Koz to find out if he would be in town, he confirmed he would attend plus his girlfriend, Rebecca.

With Gus, Jimmy and Chubby having no female attachments, it was hoped that Dog and Mickey would provide enough females to go around.

On December 31 the Bank closed early and after Jimmy said goodbye to Coral, the boys headed home to get ready for the party. Although it was a 'bring your own bottle' party, they had organised a case of Lion Ale and a case of Castle Lager, a bottle each of vodka and cane, plus mixers. A gallon of Kellerprince Red and a gallon of Lieberstein white wine. A mixed dozen large bags of crisps would be all the 'snacks' available, unless someone brought something else.

Dog and Mickey arrived home around six. They dropped off their booze and added some samosas and more crisps, before heading out saying they would be back around nine with some female friends.

Ian and Dee arrived with a pile of records, more booze and some cheese scones that Dee had made. Ian said Chubby had contacted him and would be along a little later as he had some things to take care of.

Chubby arrived with Kerry in tow, they added their contributions. Koz and his girlfriend, Rebecca, pitched up and added to the growing pile of food and booze. Koz brought everyone up to date; he was working in the family business, mainly in Johannesburg but was spending a few days in Durban with Rebecca.

At first opportunity, Jimmy took Chubby to one side. 'What the fuck are you doing bringing Kerry? Jesus, if this gets out to Benny the shit will hit the fan. Aren't Dee and Kerry big buddies?'

'Calm down. Kerry and Benny have broken up. He is off to the Army in a few days and Kerry thought it unfair to keep him hanging on for the next nine months. Anyway, she and I are just friends.'

'Shit, I have heard this story before; I wonder if she used "Invisible Dave" again. You better take care of her tonight. I don't want any drama,' said Jimmy.

'Dee told her about the party, she phoned me and begged me to take her along. I agreed but the whole way here all she did was quiz me about you. Would your girlfriend be there, do you think he still likes me, etcetera? Sorry Mate, but I think she may be after you tonight,' replied Chubby.

'Gee, thanks a lot. I could really have gone for Kerry but there has been too much drama with her over the years. I will play it cool, make sure you dance with her tonight, tell her I am the host and have to circulate.'

Although there was music playing, no one was dancing, folks were just standing around chatting and drinking. Kerry had sensed Jimmy was uncomfortable, so she walked over, 'Hey, are you okay? You seem a little off, is it because of me? I asked Chubby to bring me as I was feeling miserable because Benny and I broke up. I hope you don't mind.'

'No, I don't mind, I was just surprised to see you with Chubby as I thought you and Benny were going strong. Sorry to hear about the breakup, just have fun tonight. I am sure the party will get going soon.'

Jimmy was saved with the arrival of Dog, Sandy, Mickey and three blond surfer-looking girls. Mickey made the introductions. The new arrivals got the party going, Dog and Sandy hit the dance floor, quickly joined by Mickey and one of the blonds. They were then joined by Chubby, Kerry, Dee and Ian. The two remaining girls decided to dance together, leaving Gus and Jimmy to observe.

'I reckon I'm going to make a move on the one in the shorts. Hopefully it will send a message to Kerry. What about you, Gus, reckon you can handle the other one?' said Jimmy.

'Nah, I'm going to cool it for a while. Maybe later after a few drinks.'

Before Jimmy could ask the girl for a dance, there was a knock on the door. He went to answer it. To his great surprise it was Cathy and another lady. 'Hi Jimmy, I hope you don't mind. I brought my friend, Lynne, along. I didn't check with Gus, but I assumed it would be okay. We are both footloose and fancy-free tonight.'

Gus, seeing the gathering at the door, rushed over. 'Cathy, so glad you could make it, who's your friend?'

'Let me make proper introductions, Gus, Jimmy this is my good friend, Lynne. Lynne, these are the two guys I was telling you about.'

Lynne was stunning, light blond hair, blue eyes and a body that made Fiona look positively plain. Gus and Jimmy shook hands with her and invited them both in. 'What can I get you to drink?' Jimmy asked. Both decided a glass of red wine would be good.

Gus introduced Cathy and Lynne to the rest of the crowd. Ian, Chubby, Dee and Kerry all looked surprised as these two older women had joined the party. Jimmy pulled Gus aside. 'What's the deal, Gus? Aren't you worried that Cathy will get into trouble? Shit, that Lynne broad is so hot! What do you know about her?'

'Cathy had mentioned that she might make it but wasn't sure. I have never met Lynne, but Cathy has mentioned her before. They are old school mates, Lynne is unattached, and I'm not sure what that means exactly. Why don't you go and have a chat to her? I'm going to ask Cathy for a dance.'

The two of them walked over and Gus took Cathy by the hand and led her onto the dance floor. Jimmy turned to Lynne but before he could engage in conversation, she took him by the hand and headed out to dance. Kerry, who was dancing with Chubby, glared daggers at them.

A lot of drinking, eating and dancing ensued. As the night wore on, the music slowed down and the dancing got a bit more intimate. Lynne had hung onto Jimmy since that first dance and as the music slowed, she moved in real close and placed her arms around his neck. Jimmy held her close, they were joined at the hips, but he made no attempt to kiss her. Tired of waiting, Lynne turned her face up towards him and moved her lips up to his. Opening her mouth slightly, she kissed him softly, lingered for a few seconds and then moved away. Jimmy got the message and responded.

Dog, Mickey and the girls had retreated to the roof, armed with beer, wine and weed. The remaining five couples continued dancing to the slow mellow music. Around eleven, Koz and Rebecca made a move to leave. 'We are taking off now. I told my family we would see in the New Year at their place. Thanks a lot, we had a great time. See you in the New Year some time.'

As soon as Koz and Rebecca left, Cathy declared, 'Come Gus, let's take some wine and go up to the roof and see what's going on around Durban.'

Before he could object, she was out the door dragging Lynne with her, 'Jesus Jimmy, I hope those fuckers are behaving themselves up there. Cathy will have a heart attack; we better catch up.'

They caught up with the girls just as they opened the door leading onto the roof. Gus stepped out first, hoping to hold back Cathy but too late. The sight that greeted them made them stop in their tracks. Dog,

Mickey and the four girls were all stark naked, sitting in a circle passing round a flagon of wine and a joint. They were oblivious of the newcomers until Lynne cried out, 'They are all naked, we should join them, it looks like fun!' She moved towards the group and started to remove her top, Jimmy managed to hold her back, and Cathy being restrained by Gus was speechless.

'They are all likely to start screwing each other at any time so unless you want be screwed as well, it's not a good idea,' said Jimmy firmly.

'Well, not by one of them for sure, but I really would like to be screwed sometime tonight. I have heard all about Cathy and Gus and I would like some of that,' she whispered into his ear. 'Why don't we join them for a while and any screwing that goes on, we can leave to them? I'm getting naked, please join me.'

Lynne stripped off and reluctantly so did Jimmy. Cathy and Gus retreated and went back downstairs. Lynne and Jimmy joined the circle. With all these naked people, especially Lynne, Jimmy was conscious of the fact that he needed to keep control of his penis, desperate not to have an erection. Sitting down next to Lynne, Jimmy turned towards her taking in her nakedness. She had a great body, smallish breasts but long hard nipples, a flat stomach, long shapely legs and neatly trimmed pubic area.

Cathy and Gus returned to the party to find the last two couples just sitting around chatting.

'Where is Jimmy?' asked Kerry.

'They are up on the roof with Dog and Mickey, probably having a *zol*. There's not much going on up there,' replied Gus, hoping that his answer would stop the need for any others to venture up to the roof.

He was wrong. 'Come on Chubby, let's go and take a look.' Kerry pulled Chubby up and taking him by the hand, dragged him off to the fire escape. Gus looked across at Ian and shook his head, with a 'don't go' expression on his face. Ian took the hint.

Two minutes later an angry Kerry returned. 'They are all fucking naked up there, drinking wine and smoking *dagga*. That bastard Chubby went and joined them.'

'Why didn't you join them?' asked Gus sarcastically. 'I think they are just having a bit of fun, nothing serious.'

'Fun? Are you crazy? They are probably all going to be screwing any minute. How can Chubby stay up there with them? He's supposed to be with me but I'm not going sit up there with no clothes on. Ian, can I leave with you when you go? I don't want anything to do with Chubby.'

'Okay, we are going to leave after we see the New Year in. Should I go and tell Chubby of our plans?' offered Ian, eager to get an eye full of the goings on up on the roof.

'No, you bloody well won't!' snapped Dee. 'I'm not having you disappear up there. If he is not back just after twelve, he will find out on his own.'

As the clock struck twelve, the five downstairs all wished each other 'Happy New Year'. Ian and Dee exchanged kisses as did Gus and Cathy. Kerry, eager to get away before Chubby's potential return, hustled Ian and Dee along and the three of them departed minutes later. Gus and Cathy headed for the bedroom where they ushered in the New Year with hot steamy sex.

Meanwhile up on the roof, a fairly drunk and stoned group only realised the New Year had arrived when the fireworks around Durban started. First, they all stood up for a group hug and led by Dog sang Auld Lang Syne. The song ending was the key to each person wishing each other 'Happy New Year' followed by a kiss that was not just a peck on the cheek.

Lynne kissed Jimmy with her mouth open and tongue searching the inside of his mouth. She broke off and turned to Chubby and to Jimmy's surprise did the same to him. Looking around, he noticed everyone doing much the same, boys kissing girls and girls kissing girls. Going with the flow, Chubby and Jimmy joined in.

Having done the rounds, including the four other girls, Lynne walked up to Jimmy and detached him from one of the surfer girls, grabbing him by his semi erect cock, 'Come on lover boy, pick up your clothes and show me what your bedroom looks like.'

Leaving Chubby to his own devices, they headed downstairs. They found the place deserted and Gus' bedroom door closed. 'I wonder what they are doing,' said Lynne with a chuckle. 'Let's see if we can give them some competition.'

They entered the bedroom and closed the door behind them. Lynne backed Jimmy towards the bed, both still naked, she pushed him onto the bed and bent over and took his cock in the mouth. After drawing her tongue down the length of his cock, she pushed herself up and on top of him. Spreading her legs, she manipulated his cock into her soaking wet vagina and slid down its length.

As she began to grind up and down, Jimmy could feel himself coming and with the utmost concentration he lasted all of thirty seconds. Lynne could feel his orgasm and fully aware of how nervous he had seemed, didn't miss a beat. She lifted herself off his still semi hard cock, looked him straight in the eye and said, 'Well, that one's out of the way, now we can both have some fun. You lie back and let me show you what fucking is all about.'

She took hold of his cock and began slowly licking all the juices off it. Jimmy instantly hardened. 'Ah the stamina of youth, ready for seconds instantly.' She smiled.

Over the next few hours, Jimmy was introduced to the various ways a skilled lover can take one to great heights of sexual pleasure. He had two more orgasms and Lynne seemed in a perpetual orgasmic state. Eventually completely sated, both fell asleep at about 2am. A little over an hour later Jimmy felt Lynne moving away from him. He awoke and turned towards her with an inquiring look. Lynne with skill, coaxed one last orgasm out of Jimmy and joined him in collapsing in a heap.

The two of them dropped into a deep sleep. Sometime later they were awakened to loud wailing and moaning. Checking his watch, the only piece of 'clothing' he was wearing, he saw the time 5.20am. Jumping out of bed, Lynne headed for the source of the commotion, 'What the hell is going on? Is someone dying or something?' she shouted, deeply irritated at being woken up in such a manner.

She traced the noise to Dog's bedroom and angrily threw the door open. There she found Dog and Sandy engaged in intercourse. Sandy was on top of Dog, both were wailing about God, interspersed with many yesses. Totally oblivious to Lynne's presence, they continued unabated. 'Hey! What the hell is wrong with you two? For fuck's sake, there are folks trying to sleep; keep the noise down!' With that, she turned and slammed the door.

Jimmy, now fully awake, pulled on a pair of shorts and headed for the kitchen, time for some coffee. Passing through he found Chubby and the other blond surfer girl, her name turned out to be Mandy, both naked and fast asleep on the couch.

Jimmy walked over to the couch and slapped Chubby's naked bum. 'Wake up Murphy, find some clothes, you are scaring our guests.'

Reacting to the noise, Gus appeared dressed in shorts, followed by Cathy with a towel wrapped around her body. Seeing all the other girls naked, she decided to dispense with the towel. Gus, though somewhat startled, tried to act all nonchalant.

Startled, Chubby sat up trying to work out where he was, Mandy stirred next to him. He looked at her naked body and for a moment he was confused. He looked over towards Jimmy who was standing next to Lynne both still naked. He started to remember the sequence of events. He had come down from the roof with Mandy and Tina and remembered having sex with both of them, singly and together.

Now fully aware of what happened and with everyone staring at him, he looked around for his clothes. Finding nothing, he realised that they must have been left on the roof. He looked helplessly at Jimmy, 'Jimmy, help me out man. I think I left my clobber on the roof. Lend me a pair of shorts or something.'

'No chance Mate. By the way, happy birthday. I see you are appropriately dressed in your "Birthday Suit".'

Realising it was his birthday, Lynne and Tina rushed over and pulled him to his feet. Each gave him a kiss, and both gave him a quick teasing tug of his cock. Unable to stop himself, his cock started to rise. 'I think you better run upstairs and get some clothes on before you embarrass yourself, unless you want to give Mandy a quickie while we watch.'

Reacting to Lynne's taunt, Chubby, covering his genitals with a cushion, ran for the stairs with a rendition of Happy Birthday ringing in his ears. He returned a few minutes later fully clothed and carrying the pile of clothing that had been left on the roof by others.

With Dog, Sandy, Mickey and the girl named Denise, all having emerged from their various rooms, Lynne declared, 'Okay, boys and girls, let's have an early breakfast. Tina, if you are any good in the kitchen, come and help Cathy and me.'

With only Chubby, Jimmy and Mickey having any form of clothing on, it was quite a surreal situation. With Dog and Sandy sitting on the couch absently feeling each other up and Denise sitting on Mickey's lap, Mandy decided to join the girls in the kitchen.

Chubby took Jimmy aside. 'Jesus, what happened here last night? I went up to the roof; Kerry got pissed off and went back downstairs, what happened to her?'

'She was seriously pissed off. She conned Ian and Dee into accompanying her home. What the fuck were you thinking?'

'I wasn't thinking clearly. I saw all you naked people and I had to join you. I thought Kerry would as well. I remember drinking a lot of wine and maybe a few pulls of the *zol*. I remember kissing your lady at one point. You must have left, then I remember Dog fucking Mandy and then all hell broke loose. Mickey and one of the girls got at it and then I think Dog's girlfriend started playing with my cock, a bit weird that, then I was rescued by Tina or Denise and the three of us went down to the lounge. I know there was a lot of fucking going on I don't know where the hell Mandy came from. Next thing I remember is you rudely waking me. Jesus, no one is going to believe this.'

'Tell me about it, what a way to lose your virginity. Look at those women in the kitchen, not a stitch of clothing.' Turning to Gus,' I'm going to have some difficulty in seeing Mrs. Bright at work. All I will see is the gorgeous naked body, you are one lucky bastard; she is magnificent,' said Jimmy.

'Yes, I know. What about you? Lynne is stunning. I reckon she was good in bed. How did that go for you?' replied Gus.

'It was amazing. With no benchmark to judge, I reckon I had my brain well and truly fucked. Unlike your arrangement, this was probably a one-off for her. Man, I've got to try and get her alone again.'

Their conversation was interrupted by the call. 'Breakfast is ready, come and help yourselves,' shouted a voice from the kitchen.

Anyone stumbling into the apartment would have been stunned by the scene in front of them. There were there six totally naked females, one naked male and four semi-dressed men seated at various spots in the kitchen and lounge feasting on bacon, eggs, mushrooms and toast, drinking beer and wine at six o'clock in the morning on New Year's Day.

Breakfast over, Gus and Jimmy had the task of cleaning up the kitchen; Chubby cornered Mandy and was in deep conversation. The two of them disappeared, Mandy still unclothed. Dog, Mickey, Sandy and Denise retired to their respective bedrooms. With the kitchen all tidied up, Gus and Jimmy went in search of Cathy and Lynne.

Gus found Cathy in the shower and he joined her. 'I have to leave soon. I told my husband I was spending the night at Lynne's place, it's unlikely that he will check but we should get going soon.'

Jimmy found Lynne still naked, sitting on the bed; she motioned Jimmy to join her. 'I need to tell you a few things about myself. I am nearly the same age as Cathy, and I hope that is not a problem for you. I am recently divorced, no kids. I have a house in Hillcrest and work in Pinetown. I have had the most amazing time ever last night. I cannot believe how liberated I felt, and I have you to thank for that, I have never experienced such uninhibited sex and I want to do it again. I know you have a girlfriend and would reluctantly understand if you don't want to see me again, but it was so good for me I hope we can continue.'

'Of course, I want to see you again and as often as I can. You are beautiful and sexy, a stunning lady that I consider myself lucky to have met you. I have never ever had anything like this before and like you, I want more. I don't think there is much of a future for me and my girlfriend,' said Jimmy.

'That's great but just one thing. Don't make any rash decisions over your girlfriend; you may regret them later. I hope our age difference doesn't become an issue. I am going to enjoy you as long as you want me.'

Jimmy stood up and pulled her to her feet. He dropped his shorts and pulled her naked body tightly towards him. He knelt and gently spread her legs, he parted her lips and drew his tongue slowly up from the bottom of her vagina right up and settled on her clit. She moaned slightly and moving his head away, pulled him to his feet. 'I love it when you do that but right now, I want you inside me please.'

She turned and knelt on the bed exposing her buttocks and vagina; she took his cock and guided it between her sopping wet lips. She leant back and gripping his backside, pulled him hard against her. 'Fuck me really hard. I want to feel you inside me,' she moaned.

Despite his overworked and almost raw cock, Jimmy obliged. In no time at all she came and shortly thereafter, so did he. They uncoupled and turned to face each other; she kissed him and said, 'You are a beautiful young man and an amazing lover. I need to go and shower as I have to get Cathy back to my place before her husband starts looking for her,' said Lynne.

While Lynne showered and got ready, Jimmy went looking for Chubby. He found him on the roof with his head buried between the thighs of the still naked Mandy. Mandy tapped him on the head and pointed to Jimmy.

'Sorry to disturb your fun old man, but I reckon you should phone home. Your folks might be worried; after all it is your birthday. You don't have to leave but just tell them where you are.'

'Sure thing, you are right. I did tell them I was staying over at your place, but I'll give them a call. Mandy, don't go anywhere; we have some unfinished business. I'll be right back.'

Mandy, nonplussed, just nodded and sat down in the shade, spread her legs and slowly began masturbating. Jesus, thought Jimmy, this is like some porn movie, what have I been missing? I'm not sure I can deal with Coral after this.

All washed and dressed, Cathy and Lynne said their goodbyes and left Jimmy and Gus to contemplate the evening's shenanigans. Chubby returned to the roof and Mandy, promising to be back shortly. Shortly turned out to be just over half an hour. Chubby returned with the still naked Mandy in tow. 'We are going to have a shower and I promised Mandy a lift home.'

Gus and Jimmy just shook their heads. With the sounds emanating from the bathroom, there was more than just showering going on. 'I reckon they are at it again. Chubby just can't seem to get enough. Just as well Kerry went home, he was never going to get this much action if she had stayed,' laughed Gus.

Chubby and Mandy reappeared all clean and dressed. He thanked his buddies for a fantastic time and suggested they do it again soon. Mandy, being a girl of few words, muttered her thanks and the two of them left.

They had no sooner closed the door and Dog and Sandy started up. Their voices started the normal flow and would soon reach an annoying crescendo. 'Come on Gus, let's hit the beach for a swim before those two start calling for God. Fuck it, we must do something about that noise. The fuckers woke Lynne and me up this morning. Luckily, we had been shagging all night otherwise I am sure she would have been put off by that noise. We need to make a plan as they don't think they are making any noise at all.'

The two of them grabbed their gear and headed for North Beach.

So ended 1968, a year that started with a whimper and ended with a bang, literally. 1969 would be a year of change in the lives of the four friends.

To be continued in Book Two

# ABOUT THE AUTHOR

James spent his professional life designing and writing software for business solutions. He retired and relocated to Conway SC where he lives with his wife Pippa with whom he shares 5 children. *The Day the Rainbow Died* is his 5th novel to be published but the first one he wrote. The other books are "*Wildfire,*" "*Wildfire the Revenge*" and "*Be afraid.*"